Angela Thirkell

Angela Thirkell, granddaughter of Edward Burne-Jones, was born in London in 1890. At the age of twenty-eight she moved to Melbourne, Australia where she became involved in broadcasting and was a frequent contributor to the British periodicals. Mrs. Thirkell did not begin writing novels until her return to Britain in 1930; then, for the rest of her life, she produced a new book almost every year. Her stylish prose and deft portrayal of the human comedy in the imaginary county of Barsetshire have amused readers for decades. She died in 1961, just before her seventy-first birthday.

"This book's greatest delight is in its wise or amusing observations on life tucked in as thick as raisins in a rich cake."
—*Chicago Sunday Tribune*

"[Angela Thirkell's] sense of the ludicrous is enchanting. Perhaps, above all, it is her basic human kindness and her remarkable insight into the delicate relationship between parents and adolescent and grown children that endear her books to so many people."
—*The New York Times*

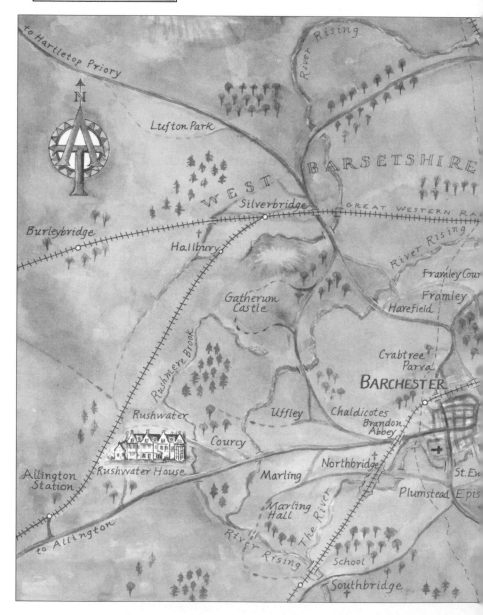

Table of Explanation

Roads...............	═══════
Railways............	┼┼┼┼┼┼┼┼┼┼
Rivers...............	∼∼∼∼
Towns...............	HOGGLESTOCK
Parish Villages...	Puddingdale
Small Villages....	Little Misfit
Mansions...........	*Pomfret Towers*

0 1 2 3 4 5
Scale of Miles

A Map of the County of
BARSETSHIRE
Showing the Situations of the various great Estates and Seats

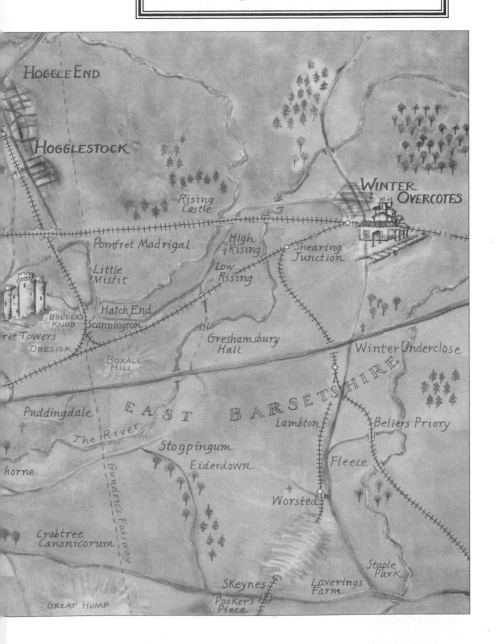

Other books by Angela Thirkell

— Three Houses (1931)

— Ankle Deep (1933)

1 High Rising (1933)

2 Demon in the House, The (1934)

3 Wild Strawberries (1934)

— O, These Men, These Men (1935)

4 August Folly (1936)

— Coronation Summer (1937)

5 Summer Half (1937)

6 Pomfret Towers (1938)

7 Before Lunch (1939)

8 The Brandons (1939))

9 Cheerfulness Breaks In (1940)

10 Northbridge Rectory (1941)

11 Marling Hall (1942)

12 Growing Up (1943)

13 Headmistress, The (1944)

14 Miss Bunting (1945)

15 Peace Breaks Out (1946)

16 Private Enterprise (1947)

17 Love Among the Ruins (1948)

18 Old Bank House, The (1949)

19 County Chronicle (1950)

20 Duke's Daughter, The (1951)

21 Happy Return (1952)

22 Jutland Cottage (1953)

23 What Did It Mean? (1954)

24 Enter Sir Robert (1955)

25 Never Too Late (1956)

26 Double Affair, A (1957)

27 Close Quarters (1958)

28 Love At All Ages

A Novel by

Angela Thirkell

▲ MOYER BELL
Wickford, Rhode Island & London

Published by Moyer Bell
This Edition 2001

Copyright © 1959 by Angela Thirkell
Published by arrangement with Hamish Hamilton, Ltd.

LIBRARY OF CONGRESS
CATALOGING-IN-PUBLICATION DATA

Thirkell, Angela Mackail, 1890–1961.
    Love At All Ages : a novel by
  Angela Thirkell. — 1st ed.
      p.   cm.
  ISBN 1-55921-297-7
  1. Barsetshire (England: Imaginary place) — Fiction.
  I. Title.
  PR6039.H43L69   2001
  823'.912 — dc21   00-052546
                                        CIP

Cover illustration: *The Letter* by Pierre Bonnard

Printed in the United States of America
Distributed in North America by Publishers Group West, 1700 Fourth
Street, Berkeley, CA 94710, 800-788-3123 (in California 510-658-3453).

LOVE AT ALL AGES

CHAPTER I

There are, it appears to us, though living in London as we do we really know very little about it, far more ponies in the world than there used to be. Wherever one goes in the school holidays one is apt to find coveys, or gaggles, or troops of boys and girls on pony-back. As they all ride astride and dress alike it isn't always easy to say which is which; but doubtless their parents know, and if their parents aren't with them at the meet there is always Nanny in the background; omnipotent, omniscient. Those who deal with ponies in the country are usually pretty tough characters and in Barsetshire they were mostly gipsies, the Romany chief or king in those parts being Jasper Margett, keeper on Sir Cecil Waring's estate Beliers Priory. He was also a licensed poacher, trapper, gin-setter, rogue, and vagabond, cherished by his nominal employer and various other landed proprietors because he still had all the country lore of field, wood, and river. Partridges and pheasants would come to his magic gipsy call. Fish in the stream would crowd to be tickled, lifted out of their element, and gutted. It was rumoured that a vixen always came to him for some extra bedding when she was expecting cubs and we would not be in the least surprised if this were true. He lived alone in an extremely picturesque, decaying, insanitary cottage whose ground floor was flooded at least twice a year; he was commonly reported to swallow frogs and toads whole and had no opinion of women at all.

On this day of an inclement May which as we now know was to be followed by an inclement June, July, and August, and a very poor September and October and will probably so go on for ever, Mrs. Morland the well-known novelist was having a small party of the George Knoxes, her publisher Adrian Coates and his wife who was George Knox's daughter, and the Goulds from the Vicarage. The reason for the party was, first, to have a party and, second, to discuss the founding of a pony club in High Rising. As we do not know anything about how pony clubs are started or run, we shall not go into details. Very little else had been discussed at High Rising for the last few months so we suppose something will be done. But as so often happens, even at serious Board Meetings (if we are to believe Mr. Dickens— which we do—and the Anglo-Bengalee Disinterested Loan and Life Assurance Company), what is said really means very little and what is done is done by a few people who know what they are doing. All we do know is that George Knox and his son-in-law Adrian Coates, who knew very little about ponies, were among its backers, but as both of them were very comfortably off and had a good many friends in the neighbourhood there were vague hopes that the club would be started on a sound footing and gradually increase its numbers.

The Vicarage party had not yet arrived. Mrs. George Knox said did they know that The Towers was now open to the public on certain days.

Mrs. Morland said she didn't, and it must be so horrid for Lord Pomfret to have strangers all over his house.

"Oh, not *Pomfret* Towers," said Mrs. George Knox. "I mean the Duke of Towers's place—it's just The Towers and it certainly is rather confusing."

George Knox said it would certainly be annoying if one told one's chauffeur one wanted to go to The Towers and he drove one to Pomfret Towers.

"But George, you would notice that you were going the wrong way," said his wife

"Who? I?" said George Knox. "I, to whom a car is a mystery; I who can never follow the convolutions—shall I say—of a map? Nor is a map of any great use if you do not know where the place is whither you are bound."

Mrs. Morland said What was the Automobile Association for. If you didn't know how to get where you wanted to go you wrote to them and they sent you a typed description of how to get there.

"To you, Laura, whose mind is clear—lucid—pellucid shall I say—" George Knox began.

"No, George, you shan't," said Mrs. Morland indignantly. "My mind *isn't* clear. And to say pellucid as well as clear is tautologous. There!"

Mrs. Morland's statement, though quite plain to us, made Mrs. Knox look up with a rather worried expression, for she could not always quite catch up with her gifted friend. Not that she grudged Mrs. Morland her conversational exchanges with her husband. She was indeed grateful to her for being as it were a shock-absorber of some of his ponderous divagations, but sometimes the snip-snap of their conversation was too much for her.

George Knox might have tolerated his old friend's attack except for her parting shot of "There."

"Bear with me, Laura," Mr. Knox began, "If I say that 'There' is no argument."

"But George, nobody said there *was* an argument," said his wife.

"Nay!" said George Knox. "You do not take me."

"Oh, don't be so Shakespearian, George," said Mrs. Morland. "What you mean is, Anne didn't understand you."

"But I *did*," said Mrs. Knox. "When you said 'There' Laura, George meant it wasn't a real argument. I mean he meant that to say 'There' didn't really explain."

Mr. Knox groaned.

"Very well, we will leave it at that," said Mrs. Morland, with the air of an examiner who thinks but poorly of his examinees. "What I said was that if you get a thing that tells you exactly what road to take and where you branch off and how many times you have to go round the roundabout, and if you do as it says—well, you usually get there. Of course in America they have clover-leaves."

At this point George Knox nearly burst. Partly because his old friend had out-talked him, partly because he had only imperfectly followed her train of thought. And we may say that most of her friends were in much the same state of addlement over some of her more Sibylline pronouncements and rather looked forward to them.

"Not *lucky* clover-leaves," said Mrs. Morland, who saw that George Knox was in difficulties and wished in the kindness of her heart to help him. "I mean ones that go over and under: rather like darning."

If she had stopped at over and under we think George Knox might have picked up the thread of what she was saying, but the darning was beyond him. Fortunately the door was flung open by Stoker, Mrs. Morland's faithful and despotic elderly cook-housekeeper, who said: "It's Mrs. Gould and the Reverend and Mr. and Mrs. Coates and I'll bring tea in now," all in one breath and went away leaving the door open, so that the guests could come in.

Mr. Gould said laughingly that he had seen from his study window the Coateses having trouble with their car and had wondered if he ought to offer his help. This gave Mrs. Morland a chance to enquire from Mrs. Gould after the Vicar's family and to be delighted to know that all their daughters were well and enjoying their jobs. As Mrs. Morland could never remember what their jobs were and we cannot at the moment trouble to invent them, we shall probably never know. All we can say is that some years ago Sylvia, the eldest, had once been engaged to Dr.

Ford and by mutual consent and to the relief of both parties they had both got unengaged, which was so dull that no one had paid much attention, and that Rose and Dora had jobs somewhere and we are sure did whatever they did very competently.

Stoker then opened the door again and blocking it with her massive form said tea was ready and they'd better come in. The party heard and obeyed.

"I *am* so glad we are having tea indoors," said Mrs. Gould. "The older I get the more I don't like picnics, or even tea on the verandah."

Mrs. Morland, pushing her hair back in a very unbecoming way, said how delightful it used to be to have tea on the Terrace when one was young.

Mr. Gould said so few of the newer houses had a terrace now. He supposed the cost of making a terrace was now prohibitive. Also there were wasps.

"But I mean THE Terrace, Mr. Gould," said Mrs. Morland. "I mean The House."

Mrs. Knox looked despairingly at her husband. Touched by her appeal he glared everyone into silence.

"As," he began, "the seat of the Mother of Parliaments is The House, par excellence, so is its terrace The Terrace. Ah! how those buildings take one back; the Mother of Parliaments, its pavements trodden by how many feet, its hall retaining the echoes of so many great voices. Chatham, Burke, the younger Pitt—"

"No, George," said Mrs. Morland. "You are going too far. The Houses of Parliament were burnt in 1839. I don't know why I know it—and then they were built again, only quite differently of course, all Gothic—if that is what I mean."

Mrs. Gould said she supposed that was the Gordon Riots.

George Knox, ever eager to know better than other people and let them know it, said the Gordon Riots were Newgate, not the Houses of Parliament.

"I had a nice book from the library once," said Mrs. Gould,

"about Queen Victoria's Coronation, by someone with a name like Turtle, and there were some very interesting illustrations. I don't mean illustrations exactly but reproductions of real pictures, done at the time, of places like the Houses of Parliament, and they looked quite different from now. Of course there weren't any photographs then. I daresay they would have looked quite different if anyone had a camera in those days."

"Indeed they would," said George Knox, who had been apparently holding his breath the better to burst in as soon as—or even sooner than—politeness allowed. "What is the camera—I ask myself."

"You needn't, George," said Mrs. Morland, nipping in before George Knox's myself could answer his question. "It's a thing you take photographs with and send them to the chemist to be developed. My uncle who was a doctor used to develop all his own films, which must have been very bad for his patients."

Mrs. Knox asked why.

"Well, one had to have a dark room to do the developing then," said Mrs. Morland, "and lots of chemicals, and his hands were always getting dirty with the chemicals and he had to scrub them with a hard brush and Pears' soap before he went to see his patients. It took him *hours* to develop his films and mostly they were spoilt because of the sun getting into the camera or something. Now you send your snapshots to be developed."

"And in fact things are not what they were when you were what you were, Laura," said George Knox, who thought his old friend was taking too much of the limelight and wished to lower her pride, because his own pride was hurt because no one recognized his apt quotation.

"Of course they aren't," said Mrs. Morland indignantly. "That is the great advantage of getting older," and she looked round her with a pleased expression. "'Grow old along with me. The best is yet to be.' Browning, I think. Perhaps he exaggerated a little. If one could make a mixture of his poem and the bit in the Harrow School song about 'Shorter in wind and in memory longer, What shall it help us that once we were strong?' it would be very fair comment."

Her hearers made no comment fair or unfair on this statement. Partly because they were enjoying her excellent tea, partly because they felt that nothing they could say would be relevant to anything Mrs. Morland had been saying and again partly because they couldn't think of any criticism, relevant or irrelevant, that would help anyone.

"There!" said Stoker, who had come in—rather with an eye to seeing what Master Alfred was doing and telling him not to—also to listening to the conversation and if necessary taking a part in it. "That's what my auntie—the one that died of a dropsy—always said. Talk of short in the wind—she couldn't hardly fetch a breath without choking. Dreadful it was to see her. The doctor did give her a bottle, but she coughed it all up. She did ought to have taken ten drops every two hours the way the doctor said, but she was always a one to save herself trouble and she said ten drops every two hours was just the same as one tablespoon at morning and one at night, and if she had to take that she might as well take the two tablespoons together first thing."

"So did she?" said Mrs. Knox, fascinated by this new way to take doses.

"You didn't know my auntie," said Stoker, with a sort of kindly contempt. "If she meant to do a thing, she *did* it. That's how she come to marry my uncle Tucker. *He* didn't want it, but she did; so she married him and when he died she gave him a lovely funeral. I went to it in me best blacks and I couldn't have done no more for a Sputnik or whatever them Russians call themselves," a remark with which everyone sympathized, for Sputnik is a silly word, look at it how you will, and useless for an anagram unless you could call a sheep's fleece a tup-skin. She then went away leaving the door open.

"Well," said Mrs. Morland, "it is about a Pony Club."

George Knox said What Pony Club.

His wife said not to be deliberately dense and obstructive and he knew perfectly well that a number of the High Rising residents felt that a Pony Club would be a good thing.

"Ponies!" said George. "Ah! those days on Margate Sands when I was young—ere my prep school had set its mark—those gallops on sturdy ponies over the hard glistening sands."

"George, you *cannot* say 'ere,'" said his wife. "No one will understand—and they won't believe you either. And you know your prep school didn't set its mark anywhere because you wouldn't work. How you got into Marlborough I shall never know. Besides it wasn't ponies at Margate, it was donkeys, and you didn't even ride them—you sat in a sort of little chair strapped to its back. Your mother told me all about it and showed me a photograph of you in your donkey-saddle with Nanny in a straw boater holding you on."

"I have always wanted to get you to write your Memoirs for me, George," said Adrian Coates. "What is the use of having a publisher for a son-in-law if you don't make use of him? I know old Johns handles your heavy stuff, but if you did something about your childhood I should like to see it."

"Ah! childhood!" said George Knox. "Emotion remembered in tranquillity and transferred, by the magic of words, to the printed page."

"Tranquillity remembered in emotion, you mean, George," said his wife. "Your mother has often told me what a treasure your nurse was, and what a quiet happy child you were."

On hearing this George Knox felt he was missing an excellent opportunity for self-pity.

"Ah! the little child in that great house in Rutland Gate," he said, addressing his old friends as if they were a Literary Society and he a visiting lecturer. "The heavy front door—my perambulator in the hall and the footman who took it up and down the steps—that great staircase with its thick piled Brussels carpet—the more friendly back stairs—my nursery with bars to the windows to keep the child that I was from flying away, the—"

"No, George, you were *not* Peter Pan," said his wife.

"—the walks in Kensington Gardens with my nurse and the Black Day when I began going to a day school; the blacker day—" George Knox went on when Mrs. Morland interrupted him.

"That is enough, George," she said. "What is really important is the Pony Club."

The Vicar and his wife, who had almost given up any hope of talking while George Knox continued his divagations, smiled at one another and caught a flicker of a smile from Mrs. Coates.

"May I suggest," said Mrs. Knox, who had been quietly observing her husband, "that we go into the garden for our talk? It is such a lovely evening."

As everyone had finished tea—though they would willingly have prolonged it had their stomachs been larger—they all went into the garden. But not, we are glad to say, to sit in deck chairs, which are always uncomfortable unless you have a mattress and several cushions and an extension for your legs; for Mrs. Morland had discovered a new brand of chair which adapted itself ingeniously and kindly to the human frame at whatever angle the human frame wished, including the human legs.

"Well, Laura," said George Knox. "Here we are. What next?"

"Well, George," said Mrs. Morland, we regret to say faintly parodying her old friend, "it is about having a Pony Club. If my boys were all here and about twenty years younger they would know at once. I don't know anything. I did have riding lessons when I was a girl but I was always frightened, so Mother let me stop because it was just waste of money. If only it had had a pole through its neck I might have managed."

Her publisher asked her what on earth she meant. His wife, who had not taken much part in the conversation up till now, said she did so agree with Mrs. Morland, because then one couldn't fall off; like the horses on Packer's Royal Universal Derby Roundabout. By the way, she said, did Mrs. Morland know if Packer had been booked for this year's Flower Show and

Fête. Mrs. Morland said Mrs. Gould was arranging all that and the Vicar looked proudly at his wife and said she had indeed put her hand to the plough.

"But first things first, my dear Laura," said George Knox. "We are met here today to discuss a Pony club, I gather. Do I also gather that we are also to discuss a Derby Roundabout? Correct me, if I am wrong."

The Vicar said that so often one thing led to another.

"There's something like that in the Bible," said Mrs. Morland. "You must know, Mr. Gould."

Thus appealed to, the Vicar, with great presence of mind, said there was in Hebrews, chapter three he thought, a recommendation to exhort one another.

"Oh, *thank* you, Mr. Gould," said Mrs. Morland. "But there must be something else, isn't there? I have a Cruden's Concordance. We could look it up."

"My dear Laura," said George Knox, "even you must realize that you cannot look a thing up if you do not know what it is. Gould has done his best. Now comes the question, the object of our so pleasant meeting: the Pony Club."

There was then a good deal of confused talk from which there emerged two facts. The first was that no one knew how a pony club should be started; the second that even if a pony club had been started no one present had the faintest idea how it should be run. At this point everyone lost interest and the talk wandered to really important subjects such as the discovery—when Professor Lancelot came to visit the church to look for non-existent mural paintings—of a bundle of very old, ragged surplices shoved into a corner of the shed where the coke for the heating of the church was stored; which discovery was of far more interest to the village—or little town we must almost call it now, so much has it grown—than the one or two blotches on the arch above the chancel steps which might or might not be the Seventh Day of Creation, or alternatively the Day of Judgement.

Stoker, who had washed up the tea-things, now came in to say there was only one bottle of sherry left and it wasn't opening-time yet but she would run down on her bike and get a couple more at the back door, and so went away.

"Good woman, Stoker," said Adrian Coates.

"It's always like that," said his wife. "When I was at home, Daddy was always running out of something—"

"Nay, my child," said George Knox. "I must protest—" but what he was going to protest we shall never know, because everyone began to laugh.

"Oh, I know what I wanted to say," said Mrs. Morland. "The Towers—I mean the Duke of Towers's place and *not* Pomfret Towers—is open to the public now, tickets half a crown and teas in the old servants' hall. Does anybody know it?"

Several people spoke at once. The facts emerged that the Towers was perhaps the most hideous house in West Barsetshire, leaving Pomfret Towers absolutely nowhere, and would be well worth the half a crown admittance.

Mrs. Coates asked who lived there now.

No one, said Mrs. Morland. That was, she added, because the present Duke of Towers, owing to heavy death duties, had to lease it to a syndicate of Barchester magnates who wanted it as a kind of country club.

"I haven't seen it," she said, "but Stoker went and brought me back some picture postcards. It looks awful."

"I'd love to go," said Mrs. George Knox, "but I *do* feel sorry for the Duke being turned out of his house."

"I was talking to Lady Pomfret about that," said Mrs. Morland, "because they had to let most of their house too. But she says she is much happier in the servants' wing where they live now than she ever was in the house itself, because the business people who have it—Mr. Adams and Mr. Pilward and their friends—have cleaned the house and put in central heating and they keep the garden tidy and the drive, and they've got the fountain working again. That's the advantage of having a big house you can't afford."

Even Mrs. Knox, used as she was to her former employer's gnomic sayings, could not grapple with this, and said so.

"Well, Anne, it is quite simple," said Mrs. Morland. "The Pomfrets get c.h.w. and c.h. free."

"Laura, pray be intelligible," said George Knox. "What see-achedoubleyou means passes my poor comprehension."

His wife, who had never yet been baffled by her husband and always knew what he meant to say even if he could not express it intelligibly, said "Constant Hot Water, George; and Central Heating." Her hearers all added "You Fool" in their minds, but of course did not say it aloud, and Mrs. Morland thought of George Sampson and Lavinia Wilfer.

"I am too old for this Brave New World," said George Knox, suddenly becoming a doddering greybeard. "So be it. I do not understand."

"That," said his wife, "is simply because you don't trouble to think. Anyway it doesn't matter. Let's all go over and pay our shillings, Laura, or our half-crowns, or whatever it is. We ought to support dispossessed landowners. We may all be dispossessed persons ourselves. When we are I shall let people see George pretending he is working at sixpence a head and sell the vegetables we don't want at the back gate."

Everyone agreed to this and it was decided unanimously that the present party should, on a day to be fixed, go over to the Towers.

"But," said Mrs. Morland in her most imposing voice, "we have not yet settled the question of the Pony Club."

"*Need* we?" said Mrs. Coates. "Daddy, what do you think?"

If George Knox had spoken the truth, he would have said that he knew nothing about ponies and cared less. But if an opportunity to speak offered itself to him, he was not the man to let opportunity slip.

"What I may think, my child," said George Knox—by these

words bringing his wife and his old friend Mrs. Morland to the verge of giggles—"is doubtless irrelevant, of no value, a feather in the wind. What do I know of ponies? Are they horses that have never grown up—the Peter Pans of the equine race; or are they a race—a genus—a tribe set apart? You should know, Gould."

The Vicar, suddenly appealed to, had not been listening (which trait was common to many of George Knox's friends, much as they loved him) and said Indeed, indeed, he must apologize and beg to know on what subject his views were required.

"George wants to know," said Mrs. Morland, espousing as it were the side of the boy who was always lowest in the class, "if ponies are a small sort of horse—I mean a quadruped—or are they just ponies."

Mrs. Coates said what about mules. She only asked, she said, because mules were rather like oxes, weren't they, and then wondered if she knew what she meant, or ought to have said it.

The Vicar said that the earliest record of mules that came to his mind was in Genesis. Someone called Anah, who had a brother called Ajah, found some mules in the wilderness as he fed the asses of Zibeon his father; and he had two children called Dishon and Aholibamah and their descendents were dukes.

"But they didn't have dukes then, Mr. Gould," said Mrs. Coates. "I mean not *real* dukes, did they?"

Mr. Gould said any warlike nation would have dukes; that way to say, leaders. In English schools the head boy used to be the dux of his class.

"When I was last in London, I had to go to the London Library," Mrs. Morland began, to which George Knox replied that when Mr. F.'s Aunt lived at Hendon, Barnes's gander was stole by tinkers. His wife said No need to show off and would Mrs. Morland go on with what she was saying.

"Oh, I know!" said the gifted novelist. "I thought I would look at the *Almanach de Gotha* because one had always heard about it and how you couldn't get into it unless you had lots of quarterings, whatever they were. Anyway I don't see how one could have more than four because that would make a whole."

"How do you mean a hole, Mrs. Morland?" said Mrs. Coates. "I mean what would it make a hole in?"

Mr. Gould said there was a play by Browning in blank verse called *The Blot in the 'Scutcheon* and perhaps that was like a Hole.

"I *loved* that play when I was a schoolgirl," said Mrs. Coates. "Especially the bit near the end when Thorold, at least he is sometimes called Tresham because he was an earl, poisons himself, and his cousin or someone says:

> A froth is oozing through his clenchéd teeth;
> Both lips, where they're not bitten through, are black.

Kate Carter—at least she was Kate Keith then—and I used to recite it to each other in the cloak room at school. I haven't seen her for ages."

"To return to the point from which this talk has so far divagated," said George Knox, rather coldly, "—by the way, what *was* it?"

A variety of voices said The Pony Club, The Towers, The Bible, the *Almanach de Gotha*, Browning.

"Nay!" said George Knox.

"No, George; *not* nay," said his wife in a kind of parenthesis and then in a louder voice she said What about their all going to see the Duke of Towers's mansion for half a crown a head, because if it was really uglier than Pomfret Towers it would be well worth seeing.

Mrs. Morland warmly approved this suggestion and said perhaps someone there would know about Pony Clubs. And did they remember Edith Graham, Sir Robert Graham's youngest daughter, because she married the Duke's brother, Lord William Harcourt.

"And he is a clergyman," she said, "which seems peculiar."

Mr. Gould, eager to uphold his cloth, said why peculiar.

"I don't know," said Mrs. Morland, which to some of her hearers seemed like a kind of rather touching childlike innocence, and to others like almost deliberate idiocy. "At least I mean if one talked about The Lord in church—"

"My dear Mrs. Morland, forgive me if I make a protest," said the Vicar, "but—"

"Well, anyway you know what I mean," said Mrs. Morland. "There ought to be different spellings, or different voices anyway, for saying The Lord when it is church and The Lord when it's a person."

"But, Laura," said George Knox, who had been champing his bit and pulling at the reins during this conversation, "if you talked about Lord William in church—which seems to me improbable—you would say Lord William and everyone would know what you meant, so there could not be the slightest confusion."

"But I *wouldn't* talk about him in church, George," said Mrs. Morland. "I *never* talk in church. Do I, Mr. Gould?" she added earnestly.

"Well, to be perfectly candid," said the Vicar, "I have never thought about it. People don't as a rule. That poor half-witted nephew of Mrs. Mallow's down in the village does commune aloud with himself sometimes, but if it is too loud his aunt always takes him out and sits him on a tombstone till he's fit to go home. Otherwise he is no trouble at all."

There was a kind of hum of approval of the Vicar's words and also of a way of life in which village people still had idiot children and were tolerant of their deficiencies.

So long had they been gossiping and discussing in the warm sun that Stoker appeared, pushing a small trolley laden with sherry and glasses and some orange juice if needed.

"It's just gone six," said Stoker, "and I'm going down to the village to see Mrs. Mallow about the hat she's trimming for me and I dessay I'll have another cuppa with her so don't you worry.

There's some biscuits I made today in the red tin with the picture of Balmoral on the lid if you want any with the sherry, so don't say I didn't tell you. And if the man comes about the gas ring, you tell him I gave it a good boil with plenty of soda and it's going fine. And do you want them letters posted?"

"Oh yes, please, Stoker," said Mrs. Morland. "That is if you can catch the half past six post. If not, it doesn't matter."

"I'll catch it all right," said Stoker. "And if that Sid Brown has cleared it too early the way he sometimes does, I'll go round to his mother's. *She'll* sort him. Well, good-bye all."

The party then began to say it must go home, but was not above accepting some more sherry. When the bottle was empty the Goulds went back to the Vicarage and the George Knoxes to their house which was a little away from the village (though houses were creeping along the lane and the road had been resurfaced) and still safe with its own large garden and the water-meadows behind.

"*What* a nice party," said Mrs. Knox to her husband later in the evening. "I *do* like Laura. I always did. She is the only woman I ever met who has you taped."

"Taped?" said George Knox. "Taped? Am I a bundle of documents tied up with red tape—or a babe in swaddling bands?"

"No, darling, you aren't," said his wife. "You are just what you always have been and always will be."

"And what is that?" said her husband. "Suddenly there come to my mind—in that strange way that thoughts, idle thoughts, float like gossamer athwart one's consciousness—there come, I say, moments of doubt. Words fail me. What was I going to say?"

"Rubbish, George," said his wife. "Words never have failed you yet and they never will. What a bore this pony club would be. Half the village are too old and the other half too young. Even those Vicarage girls are getting on. If only we had two or three families with teen-age children, I could manage the small fry myself at a pinch. I had a pony of my own, years ago, when father was alive. When he died mother and I were pretty badly off and I sold my pony. I don't think I've ever cried so much in my life."

"Why wasn't I there?" said George Knox. "Or to quote from older days Why were I and my Franks not there?" but his wife did not know that historical episode and her husband did not know that she did not know it and they talked of other things.

The suggestion of a visit to the seat of the Duke of Towers was not dropped though it had to be postponed for various reasons. But little was lost by this postponement as the building would be just as hideous and overpowering at any time. Sad as it is to see a house—mansion—any kind of home—turned into business premises and the chief rooms shown for lucre, at least the building is kept in good repair. The Towers was not a historic monument, being of about the same period as Pomfret Towers, but as an example of mixed architecture it was a remarkable survival. If we say that it was a massive pile, a cross between a French seventeenth-century *château*, a mid-Victorian railway station, and the Natural History Museum, we shall have sufficiently described it and will only add that it was of purple-red brick and yellow stone, with more peaked roofs and pepper-pot turrets than anyone would have thought possible, while a kind of iron frill along its peaked roof lent enchantment to the view. And what was more, a select Club had been formed under the name of the Harcourt Alpine Group, the members of which took a perilous joy in roping themselves together, climbing out of one of those attic windows which give onto a steeply sloping roof and infinity, finding *arêtes*, cols and glissades as exciting as those in the Alps, with the added spice of being on the whole more dangerous, as a slip from any part of the roof onto the stone terrace below would have been even more damaging to the human body than falling into a snow-filled crevasse—though easier for the rescue party to deal with.

It was also a matter of immense pride to West Barsetshire that for sheer glory of unadulterated hideosity, including storied windows richly dight, not casting any kind of light, which could not be opened and let in neither sun nor air, it had no rival. Pomfret Towers was its wash pot and over Lord Aberfordbury's (formerly and equally unpleasantly Sir Ogilvy Hibberd) own hideous modern mansion it cast out its shoe. Mr. Middleton, the well-known architect at Laverings, had, after many circumlocutions, described it as Battlemented, Castellated, Bluebeard Bosh: and this was generally considered to be very fair comment.

Its grounds—not so extensive as they were, for a fringe of bungaloid growth was rapidly spreading from the Barchester side over land which the previous duke had had to sell—were well looked after by the Shareholders' Committee, who had laid out a full-size golf course. The West Barsetshire Hunt had taken a long lease of the stabling and altogether it was a solid, flourishing concern, and as none of the Towers family had been able to live there since the last war, there was little sentiment about it. The Managing Directors, including Mr. Samuel Adams of the big Hogglestock ironworks and his co-father-in-law, Councillor Pilward of Pilward's Entire, were on the whole a capable and intelligent lot, and such farmers as still had land on the estate were well content.

When the Managing Directors were discussing the terms for members' subscriptions, Mr. Adams had suggested that the Duke of Towers should be made an Honorary Member and we think that His Grace, though he did not feel sentimental about the hideous, unmanageable pile, was genuinely touched, as was his American wife. We may add that many other members were extremely grateful to the committee who were, for the present, more than willing to accept the stuffed and mounted heads of large game shot by the aforesaid members in Africa, Asia, Canada, South America, and other sporting places as their life's work. The only valuable mammal missing from the collection was the duck-billed platypus, that strange prehistoric survival being heavily protected in its native land: though that did not stop people shooting or trapping it, but as they dared not let their deed be known for fear of just retribution, it was rare for a specimen to reach England.

The large hall—now horribly known as the Lounge—of rather ugly stone, had been painted cream. The Barsetshire Archeological Society had tried to raise a protest against this, as Vandalism, but Mr. Adams had got hold of a Senior Council Member of the B.A.S., shown him the Towers, taken him to dinner at the White Hart in a private room, plied him with the rare port and brandy that the old waiter Burden reserved for favoured customers, and so extracted from him a verbal statement that it would immensely diminish the cultural value of the building if the stone were not painted; as (*a*) it probably had been painted in earlier days and (*b*) if it hadn't been it ought to be, as it was well known that the fumes from Hogglestock, where Mr. Adams and his co-father-in-law Mr. Pilward the brewer had their large works, were guaranteed to corrode, erode, and generally destroy any stonework they met within a radius of several miles. This verbal statement he then, at Mr. Adams's request, repeated into a dictaphone. Mr. Adams had it typed in the office and circulated to the members, who really could not have cared less and said O.K., Adams; or Leave it to you, Adams; or Oh, anything for peace, Adams.

As for the present Duke of Towers, he had never liked his ancestral home and took very little interest in what was being done and enjoyed the very handsome rent paid to him as ground landlord. His delightful American wife was enchanted to see a real English Mansion, but made no bones about saying that she wouldn't change their present commodious house at the end of the village for all the castles in the world. Into this house the Duke had moved some of the best furniture from the Towers, mostly French, or Regency period, and also such of the best pictures as had not been sold to help with death duties and were not too large to house. But there was no cause to repine, for the

celebrated Guido Guidone, the depressing Primitive by Pictor
Ignotus (1409–1451?), and the really dreadful late Etruscan
statue of the Many-Breasted Mater Feconditatis—as also the
Très Jolies Heures de St. Panurge, from which all the best
illuminations (i.e. the most scabrous) had been cut long ago by
art lovers, were sold at auction in New York for enormous sums
to the multi-millionaire Woolcot van Dryven who had married
one of Mr. and Mrs. Dean's daughters from Winter Overcotes.

We are quite ignorant about the taxes on such sales, but we
can state that unless the British Empire and the Treasury
became insolvent there would be, even with rising imposts,
enough to keep the estate as a good going concern for the
present. And further we cannot look.

The Towers family was a pleasantly united one. The Dowager Duchess with her two unmarried daughters, Lady Gwendolen and Lady Elaine, lived in a commodious red brick house
at the lower end of the village rent free. The present Duke and
Duchess with some young children lived in a large commodious
house at the upper end of the village street. The Dowager's
youngest son, Lord William Harcourt, had a cure of souls not
far away and there was a perpetual coming and going between
the various houses.

As for the Dowager Duchess's unmarried daughters, although
she was very fond of them she always felt a slight mortification
that they were still unmarried and apparently likely to remain so.
Lady Gwendolen had very early shown a marked preference for
the celibate clergy—by which on the whole we mean those that
feel they ought not to marry unless they want to, which quite
often they do. Her younger daughter Lady Elaine had got so far
as being informally engaged to one Dobby Fitzgorman of good
minor county stock. Of this engagement the family could not
wholly approve, for Mr. Fitzgorman was a Liberal and was
suspected of having once shot a fox. Luckily he had broken his
neck in a steeplechase, so the two sisters remained at home with

their mother and were quite happy in an uninteresting kind of way. It must however be said that after Mr. Fitzgorman's demise Lady Elaine did wear a locket of black enamel with a piece of hair in it. Only she knew that she had bought it at a Charity Bazaar some years earlier, but as all lockets with hair in them look much alike and no one wants particularly to look at them, Lady Elaine's passed muster and her friends said Poor girl— only really girl was not quite the word now, was it.

The two sisters got on very well together and often talked about how nice it would be if they could have a cottage to themselves in the village and a woman to come in from the village who would cook and clean, and how they would go to Barchester in the bus and not go to London when the rest of the family went; but their mother's Dowager-Duchess apron strings were tied tightly round them. Their sister-in-law, the present Duchess, was fond of them and did what she could, but her chief interest apart from her flourishing young nursery was racing, of which they knew nothing and had no wish to learn. She had, with mistaken though well-meaning kindness, taken them once or twice to the local point-to-point; but they had the wrong shoes and the wrong clothes and didn't know one horse from another (unless it had a very large number stuck on it, in which case they could if they wished look it up in the race-card) and really didn't much want to. A few people who had known the late Dobby Fitzgorman would sometimes say a kind word to Lady Elaine, but as she never knew how to answer them no one knew if she liked to discuss her brief romance or not. We think not; for though she had conserved a Precious Memory of the occasion when he had danced with her at the Hunt Ball and trodden on her new golden shoes and dropped her mother-of-pearl fan and broken one of the sticks (or whatever their proper name is) she never alluded to him, nor did she show any interest if his name was mentioned.

Her sister, Lady Gwendolen, had for some time been express-ing devotion for Mr. Oriel, the vicar at Harefield, a scholar with mild High Church leanings, and as he was of very good county blood no one objected; unless it were the Adored One himself who had in his time had what in lighter mood he would call a fair sickener of female devotion; but we think that he and Lady Gwendolen understood each other. The distance from The Towers to Harefield, though not very great, was pretty well insurmountable except by car. As there was no connecting railway line, it meant taking the motor bus, which ran at its own times, to Barchester and then a local train which seldom if ever ran to time, so missing the little bus that passed at rare intervals within walking distance of Harefield, except on Thursdays when, for no ascertainable reason, it stood in the little market place for two hours before making the return journey. So when Lady Gwendolen wished to visit her chosen pastor she drove herself over, much to his admiration as he had never understood machinery: nor had he wished to.

When their younger brother, Lord William Harcourt, in Holy Orders, had married Edith Graham, there had been talk of the young couple living with the Duke and his wife in patriarchal fashion—as used to be done in the ducal and noble houses in earlier days. But the bride's mother, Lady Graham, wisely we think, discussed the situation with the Dowager Duchess, and both ladies agreed that if you wanted trouble, that was the way to find it. The question of Lord William's duties at the Cathedral also had to be considered when, by a special intervention of Providence, the family living in the High Street of the little town on the edge of the estate fell vacant and His Grace in whose gift it was said, Simony or not, William had better have it. Lord William wondered at first how his country-bred wife would like this very small-town life, but she was ready to do whatever pleased him; and we may say that she was also as ready to love her mother-in-law and to like, love, and argue with her ducal brother-in-law and his American wife and her two un-married sisters-in-law as they all were to like and love her and argue back. The families were within easy reach of each other but not in each other's pockets, nor on each other's nerves.

Another advantage of living in the Parsonage—a pleasant house with a good garden—was that service of a kindly if rather sketchy nature was always available, and the Dowager Duchess, irreverently known as Dow to most of her family, was delighted to rope in as soon as they left school young women whose mothers had been notable housewives and hand them over to her Duchess daughter-in-law for her growing nursery; and for Edith she was prepared to do the same.

As soon as Edith—whom we must sometimes remember to call Lady William—knew that she was to be, in the words of the County Paris, a happy mother made, all the passion for arranging of her grandmother Lady Emily Leslie, all the business capacity of her father General Sir Robert Graham, rose in her, almost to the alarm of her husband, who had heard or read that a future mother should take things easily and have her feet up as much as possible. Edith had rather wanted to have Dr. Ford, now an elderly man but much loved all through West Barsetshire, from High Rising where he lived, to the uttermost parts where the Omniums and the de Courcys lived in ducal or earlish discomfort in such parts of their mansions as were not let to schools or big business. When Edith told Dr. Ford about her husband's anxiety, he said with an unfeeling laugh that they were all like that the first time and she was in admirable health and care killed the cat. But, he said, much as he would have liked to attend her, he was not doing babies now, so he would see Dr. Perry at Harefield, one of whose sons was excellent with babies and didn't mind what time of day or night he was called on. So Edith very sensibly went on doing what she wanted to do, and when dining with her husband at the Deanery, asked Octavia Needham, eighth daughter of the Crawleys with a delightful clerical husband and a large family of her own, what her advice about a monthly nurse was.

To arrange other people's lives was meat and drink to Octavia. So she summoned Sister Chiffinch from Northbridge, where she now lived with an old friend, to go and see a potential future patient.

It is many years now since we made the acquaintance of that excellent woman, who first came into our life—we think—as monthly nurse to Adrian and Sibyl Coates's first baby. For some years past Sister Chiffinch had said Now she really must retire. But although she did not now need to work, she had a soft spot for her ex-patients, of whom Octavia Needham was a prolific and shining example. So when Octavia mentioned an expected baby—and one who would also be the grand-daughter and niece of Dukes—she said she would be glad to do what she could for Lady William.

Accordingly she drove herself over to Harcourt and had tea with Edith who had invited her mother- and sisters-in-law to be of the company, and it was a great success. The Dowager and both her daughters, inheriting from the past a tradition of getting on with people about the place, were so agreeable to Sister Chiffinch that she compared them in her mind with other titled ladies of her large acquaintance, including Lady Cora Waring, daughter of the Duke of Omnium, and was pleased with what she found. So dates were settled (contingent on the future Harcourt knowing its own mind) and Sister Chiffinch, having given Edith a list of what she would need, was about to take her leave when the Duke and Duchess walked in, whom the Dowager with consummate tact introduced to Sister Chiffinch. Whether that worthy creature realized that by this she was being given, as it were, a social position superior to the new arrivals, we are not sure. But we are very sure that the meeting lost nothing in the telling when she got back to her home.

It was at once obvious to Sister Chiffinch that the Duchess was American, so she said she had nursed an ever so nice American once and he sent her a wonderful box of sweets— candies she ought to say—every Christmas.

The Duchess asked his name.

"Well, it doesn't sound a bit English," said Sister Chiffinch.
"It was Lee Sumter."

"For the land's sake!" said the Duchess. "It's my cousin. And
he was one of Edith's beaux when she was over in the States.
Well, for crying out loud!"

Of course after this Sister Chiffinch was taken to the Duchess's heart and Edith, in spite of her interesting condition,
became as nought. A few years ago the Edith of those days
would have had a fit of the sulks and considered herself very
badly treated, but this Edith, safe in the kind firmness and the
deep love of her husband, not to speak of the real affection shown
to her by her brother-in-law and his wife and the Dowager and
her unmarried daughters, was quite happy to listen to them as
they exclaimed and found other friends in common.

Before Sister Chiffinch left she wished to know who was the
doctor. For, she said, it was so much more pleasant to work with
someone you did know. Not but, she said, some of the young
doctors were coming on nicely—apparently regarding them as a
kind of flower to be planted, watered, re-potted, mulched,
unpotted, and planted out, under her experienced eye.

"I did rather wish I could have Dr. Ford," said Edith, "but he
doesn't do babies now. But Franklin says she thinks Dr. Perry
is very nice. Franklin's my sister-in-law, the Duchess, Sister
Chiffinch."

Sister Chiffinch pursed her lips (a phrase we have always
liked) and she said she didn't think he took maternity cases now.

"Oh, I don't mean *old* Dr. Perry," said Edith. "I mean the one
they call Gus."

Sister Chiffinch unpursed her lips. "Oh, Dr. Augustus Perry,"
she said. "He started with Leprosy and Skin diseases, but his
father was getting older and Dr. Gus gave up his idea of being a
specialist and went into partnership with him. He is first-rate,
Lady William."

"I'm awfully glad you think so," said Edith, "because

William—I mean my husband—and I like him and he isn't married so he doesn't mind doing babies."

The Dowager said she did not quite understand.

"Well, I mean," said Edith, "it doesn't matter if he has to go out suddenly in the middle of the night, because no one worries if he does. If William were called out suddenly in the middle of the night I would wonder where he was and if he had remembered to put some more petrol in the car."

Sister Chiffinch, pursing her lips in an "I could an if I would" kind of way, said it was really quite a moot question. As it was obvious, even to her, that her audience did not understand, she explained that in some ways a wife was a wonderful help to a doctor and in other ways she might almost be a hindrance. Of course Dr. Perry's—she meant old Dr. Perry—eldest son Bob had married the daughter of a very wealthy London consultant with a title who had pushed her husband so well that he was now himself one of the highest paid consultants in Harley Street. And Dr. Perry's second son Jim was now head surgeon at Knight's and doing very well.

"But this I must say," said Sister Chiffinch, apparently addressing a hostile or not altogether convinced audience, "that Dr. Gus—I should say Dr. Augustus—is one of the best G.P.'s in West Barsetshire and I would sooner work for him in a maternity case than anyone. And I may say, though it is an open secret, that people want Dr. Gus now, as his father isn't as young as he was, and I know Dr. Gus tries to persuade them to stick to the old doctor. But a little bird told me that Dr. Perry thinks of giving up the practice soon and letting Dr. Gus take it over. In a way, it is Experience of course that counts and Dr. Gus will get Experience as his father did."

The Dowager, who had been not listening with a specious air of attention, said she was so glad Edith had decided to have her baby at home and that Sister Chiffinch would be looking after her.

"Would you care to see our little house, Sister?" said the

Dowager. "It's only at the other end of the village, up the hill, if you don't mind walking. It's quite good late Georgian."

Sister Chiffinch said she would love to, as she had quite a Thing about old houses and she had her car and would drive them up. So everyone said good-bye and Sister Chiffinch drove the Dowager and her daughters to their house and was properly impressed by the pictures and the furniture and other portable property that they had brought from the Towers.

Edith tidied the drawing-room and wondered when her husband would be back. But with the cunning of the male when too many females are about, he had come round the side of the house and so in by the garden door and gone very quietly to his study. Edith heard his voice calling her and went in.

"Oh, William, why didn't you come in?" she said. "Dow was asking about you, and Sister Chiffinch was simply longing to see you. She seems very nice, William, only—"

Her husband said Only what?

"I was wondering if she would be a bit overpowering—I mean a kind of boringness, if one was shut up with her," said Edith.

"My precious, puffle-headed pet," said Lord William (which words appeared to Edith the most beautiful and touching she had ever heard) "to judge by what Franklin has told me, she always felt exactly the same about each of her Gamps, but when the baby was born the Gampish conversation suited her down to the ground," which cheered Edith a good deal.

"And you will find," he went on, "that when you and Marmaduke or Clytemnestra, whichever it is, and Chiffinch are alone together, you will enjoy her babblings. You needn't listen and it passes the time. Besides, I shall be at hand to rescue you. So just forget. And you look more beautiful every day, even if you do look like a roasted Manningtree ox with a pudding in his belly," which fine Shakespearian words made Edith laugh till her husband was almost alarmed. But it was not hysterics—it was Shakespeare; and doubtless Shakespeare, from some Olympian green-room or back-stage, heard it and was pleased.

So the stage was set and Edith waited tranquilly for the curtain to rise. The weather was as warm as it could manage—not that it was much. Life went on. The Dowager looked in nearly every day, but never outstayed her welcome. The Duke and Duchess were away for ten days or so. Lady Gwendolen and Lady Elaine, a little shy of their sister-in-law, so much younger than they, but experienced now in a life of which they knew nothing, looked in daily and told her any local gossip and knitted various garments of a small size and also made for their young sister-in-law some nightgowns and bedjackets which she felt she could never use, so exquisitely sewn and ruffled and be-laced they were. Time seemed to her to stand still. Even her mother's visits hardly ruffled the calm in which she was living; for Lady Graham understood her youngest daughter more than she had ever understood the two elder girls. And more than once she had said aloud to herself, deliberately misquoting—". . . now this wild thing is wedded. Just as much love I have but much more care."

But most mothers must feel that about a daughter—and the care is hardly less dear to them than the love.

CHAPTER 2

W e do not wish for a moment to harrow our readers. To everyone's gratification Edith, nobly seconded by Sister Chiffinch—and as it were thirded by Dr. Gus Perry who, as he afterwards told his father, nearly missed being in at the death— had an extremely nice baby and everyone was delighted. It was a girl—not that it mattered which sex as it had no particular inheritance to come into—weighed six and a half pounds, had a bright red face, some lanky dark hair and—which most pleased and aroused the admiration of its parents—the most elegant hands and feet with little delicate nails. Edith's only comment had been to ask Sister Chiffinch if it had the right number of fingers and toes; hearing that all was well she at once went to sleep again and Sister Chiffinch took the baby into what was now The Nursery and laid her asleep in her cot. Of course the Dowager was the first to see the baby, as she lived near by, but Lady Graham was not far behind, having driven over from Little Misfit as soon as she got the news. We wish we had the brush of an early Italian painter to show the meeting between the co-grandmothers—a kind of Salutation. Each had considerable liking and respect for the other and both were quite incoherent with excitement; each lady, while secretly knowing that the baby was exactly like her own family, pointing out with admiration its likeness to the other granny's family.

The reigning Duchess was the next arrival, and was of course enchanted by the baby—quite the nicest she had ever seen, she said to Sister Chiffinch, except her own. She then completed her conquest of Sister Chiffinch by producing six blankets of the softest wool, pink, and bound with pink satin, of a suitable size for Miss Harcourt's cot.

Sister Chiffinch said However did she know it was to be a girl.

The Duchess said she didn't know; but she had bought six of each colour to be on the safe side and she would keep the blue ones for the next baby if it was a boy; a piece of extravagance which shocked and delighted Sister Chiffinch. And, said the Duchess, the baby's aunts were downstairs and longing to see her and so went away. Sister Chiffinch went down to the drawing room where Lady Gwendolen and Lady Elaine were waiting and with her most gracious condescension invited them to come upstairs.

We do not think either of the ladies was really interested in babies, except in so far as they were part of the family; but they did their best. Lady Gwendolen said she looked exactly like her father. Lady Elaine said she thought more like her mother and a bit of old Aunt Fredegond. Sister Chiffinch said Well, that wasn't the Lady Fredegond who bred Arab ponies, was it, because she saw her once at a pony show driving the *sweetest* pair in a small basket-work pony carriage and smoking a kind of thin cigar.

"Cheroots, she called them," said Lady Elaine. "She let me try one and it nearly put me off smoking for ever."

Sister Chiffinch said she rather liked a cigarette, but of course *never* when she was with babies and which kind did Lady Elaine like.

Lady Elaine said Turks, in what her sister felt to be a rather showing-off kind of way, and she said *she* never smoked at all.

"Well, Lady Gwendolen," said Sister Chiffinch. "I'm not sure that you're not right. With some people you find the smell of the tobacco quite overpowering, though not with Lady Elaine I'm sure. I rather like a gasper occasionally myself but there's no accounting for tastes and now my lady, we must have a nice shut-eye," which words took Lady Elaine aback till she realized, almost at once, that it was Miss Harcourt who was being addressed. So the visitors went downstairs and Miss Harcourt continued her slumbers with a violence that only very young babies can show.

The ladies then all talked at once. And though there were three aunts and a grandmother on the Harcourt side Lady Graham was quite equal to them all.

At this moment Lord William came in. On seeing so many women he nearly backed out again.

"Come in, William," said the Dowager Duchess. Her son, who was coming in in any case, hugged her warmly and said he couldn't believe he was a father.

"If you aren't, William, who is?" said his mother with a piercing glance.

Not to be outdone, Lord William said it might be anyone, as the baby didn't look like anybody he knew.

"*You* were the most hideous baby I ever saw," said the Dowager. "Only five pounds, all eyes and nose. Gwendolen and Elaine were such lovely babies. So was Towers except that he had some rather long black hair but it all came off and then he had the most delicious golden fluff," a remark which Lord William treasured, to be worked off on his elder brother as occasion offered.

"I think she is going to be just like Mamma," said Lady Graham, who had not yet joined this conversation. "She looked at me just as Mamma used to—darling Mamma, how she would have loved to see Edith's baby—and *how* she would have interfered!"

Lady Gwendolen, feeling that a change of subject was indicated, said where was the christening to be and who was going to do it.

"I hadn't got as far as that yet," said Lord William. "One couldn't *possibly* ask the Bishop."

"One not only couldn't, one wouldn't," said the Dowager with a vehemence that surprised her family. "It would mean that I would have to call at the Palace and that I will *never* do."

Lady Graham said she knew Mr. Choyce, the very nice vicar at Little Misfit, would be delighted, but perhaps that wouldn't quite do and the Duchess—the baby's grandmother she meant— might know the right person.

Of course said the Dowager, it would be much simpler if William christened the baby himself, considering that it was his baby, but she didn't know if clergymen could christen their own children.

Lord William, basely avoiding any discussion as to the rights of clerical fathers, said perhaps Mr. Oriel might be asked. And though he did not actually look at his sister Gwendolen, he felt a kind of surge of gratitude coming from her.

"Oh, I know he would love to," said Lady Gwendolen. "He holds them so beautifully. I was at the christening of one of Dr. Perry's grandchildren at Harefield and Mr. Oriel was wonderful. It was like the Bible."

Lord William said How, exactly.

Lady Gwendolen said people in the Old Testament made a heave-offering and Mr. Oriel at Harefield had preached a beautiful sermon about it when she was godmother to one of Mrs. Belton's grandchildren there. The way he took the baby up to the altar and lifted it was something she would never forget.

Lord William said that was a good idea and if everyone agreed he would write to Mr. Oriel, which made his elder sister go almost red in the face with gratification. Of course, he added, he would ask Edith first, a sentiment applauded by all present.

"Well, here I stand like the Turk with my doxies around when I ought to be working," said Lord William. "All right, mamma, it's only a quotation from the *Beggar's Opera*. I've got to go over to Barchester, but I'll be back for tea. I'll just go up and say good-bye to Edith," and away he went.

"What he *means* is that he wants to look at the baby," said

Lady Graham. "I expect Sister won't let him. Nurses always seem to think fathers are full of tobacco-smoke and brandy-fumes. I know when I had Emmy at Rushwater because darling Mamma felt I wouldn't be safe anywhere else, Robert was terrified of Nurse. Of course he was only Colonel Graham then. If he had been a General and a Sir, nurse would have let him come in at once."

"But after all William is his baby's father," said the Dowager.

"Dear Dow," said Lady Graham, who had adopted the family name, "you know fathers simply don't count, when it's a baby. But I would love to see whatever her name is once more before I go. Suppose we both go up."

So they did and found Lord William on the landing.

"She says we can't *see* Edith because she's asleep," he said. "But you can *look* at the baby because she's fast asleep. It sounds rather muddled, but that's what Sister says "

But men have no status whatever where Lucina presides and the two grandmothers simply walked over and through Lord William to Sister Chiffinch who most condescendingly let them silently admire Miss Harcourt.

When they got down Lord William was in the hall.

"I thought you had gone, darling," said the Dowager.

"Well, I had," said Lord William. "At least I was going, but I had a thought. Why not the Cathedral? Dr. Crawley would love it—and after all I was working under him there for a time. And it would be one in the eye for the Bishop."

The Dowager and Lady Graham were overcome by the suggestion. Charming as a small family christening would be, there was something about the cathedral which was very attractive, and to do the Bishop in the eye was a work of piety and necessity.

"There is only one thing," said the Duchess. "Isn't the organist away on holiday? The sub-organist, a pupil-teacher or whatever you call him, is hopeless."

Black despair descended on all present till Lady Gwendolen

said Canon Fewling played the organ beautifully and was great friends with the organist. Her sister-in-law asked her how on earth she knew. Lady Gwendolen said Mr. Oriel, when she was last over at Harfield, had told her, and he said Canon Fewling was a very fine musician.

"Good girl!" said her brother admiringly. "I'll see Fewling some time today. I'm sure he will say yes and I'll square the Dean. Good-bye, mamma," and off he went.

But before the ladies had even begun to have the happy talk we have when free of the sterner sex, he was back again.

"Oh, mamma," he said, "if you want me, ring up the Deanery. They'll know where I am and I'll come back at once."

The Dowager had not dealt with a husband of her own for nothing and told her son nobody would want him and a man about the house was a perfect nuisance and if he liked to dine at the Club no one would mind in the least, and not to make a noise when he came in.

"Well, I *was* going to dine with the Arabin Club," he said, this being a select dining club which met once a month or so to enjoy itself, "but I thought I'd put them off."

"On *no* account, William," said the Dowager. "Husbands are less than useless, especially in a small house. When your brother was born your father and I were still living at the Towers with a proper staff and he had men's dinner parties, quite small ones of course, nearly every night and nurse wouldn't let him come and see me till next day which was *most* restful. Men are less than no help at all unless it's carrying coals up or getting under the car to see what's wrong and neither of those things did your father ever do."

"Of course he didn't, mamma dear," said Lord William, who was very fond of his mother and quite unperturbed by her. "The servants and the chauffeur would never have allowed it. What do you say, Franklin?"

His ducal sister-in-law said he had said it and his mother had said it too and of course he must keep his appointment for dinner and come in very quietly.

Lord William, rather overpowered by all the petticoat government that had suddenly taken possession of his house, said Oh, very well. He then repented those harsh words, kissed his mother and sisters and his sister-in-law, and went away.

It was now nearly eleven o'clock. Everyone felt that the day had been going on for ever and the party dispersed. As the Dowager and her daughters walked back to their house Lady Gwendolen said she would ring up Mr. Oriel and tell him what the plans were and that her brother was going to write and ask him if he would come to the christening. If the Dowager thought her elder daughter was getting a little above herself she did not allow it to appear, but she said they had better wait till William came back and see what he said.

Our reader may feel that while all this turmoil had been going on, the Duke was rather out of it. For this there were three good reasons: the first that he felt his brother was perfectly competent to manage his own affairs, the second that his wife Franklin would bring him all the news, the third that Sir Edmund Pridham was coming over to give his opinion on some trees which might or might not need felling as they were becoming a menace not only to visitors but—far worse—to other trees in the vicinity.

Sir Edmund, whom we have known now for some twenty years, was the doyen of the county as ex-armyman, landowner, forester, general arbiter in local disputes, a great admirer of The Sex, still able to flirt with them, and a determined enemy of Lord Aberfordbury. He could not ride now as he used, but he had made himself learn to drive a car and imperilled his own life and a great many other people's by insisting on driving himself about in a vintage Ford which had at least the advantage of being much higher than the modern models, so enabling the driver to see what was coming in a sunk lane with hedges on each side much better than he could from a long low car which was also far too wide for the side roads.

With him the Duke had an assignation at The Towers itself and when he drove up to his former home he found Sir Edmund's disgraceful shabby old car on the gravel sweep. Sir Edmund himself was not visible, so the Duke parked his car in the official parking place and went in search of him. With a sure instinct he went round to the servants' quarters where he found Sir Edmund sitting on an upturned tub in the yard talking to the old head gardener.

"Mornin' Duke," said Sir Edmund, who dropped his "g's" when he remembered, as a kind of delicate archaism. "You're late."

"So would you be, Pridham, if you were me," said the Duke, regardless of grammar. "You know my younger brother, William—"

"That's the parson," said Sir Edmund. "Good thing to have a living or two in the family. What's he up to? I wish they wouldn't alter the prayer book. That man at Harefield, Balliol that's his name—no it isn't, it's Oriel—knew it was one of the Colleges—I was at the House myself and got rusticated after a Bump Supper—I was a bit wild then—what was I saying? Oh, yes that man Oriel. He's too high for my liking—still it's better than being too low. Well what about your brother?"

The Duke said his brother had just had his first child—a girl—and was of course very proud of it.

"Well, better luck next time," said Sir Edmund, dismissing the subject. "Now Duke, about those trees of yours. Where are they? I brought my man with me. He's one of that half-gipsy lot and I've seen him mark the place where he was felling a tree and where he put his mark there the tree fell. When he and a few others are dead no one will know about timber. Well, well it's time I was dead too. Where are your trees?"

This sudden attack somehow made the Duke think of Mr. Lammle's "Give me your nose" to Fascination Fledgeby and he began to laugh, but luckily Sir Edmund as well as being deaf took little or no interest in other people's comments. The Duke said about a quarter of a mile away and he had told one of the men to bring the estate Ford lorry up as it was rather rough going. The lorry duly appeared and the driver touched his cap.

"Can I give you a leg up?" said the Duke.

"Now, don't be in a hurry," said Sir Edmund. "Who's that with the lorry?"

"He's one of the men about the place," said the Duke. "A useful sort of fellow."

"Well, I must have a word with him," said Sir Edmund. "Here, you, what's your name?"

"Lee, Sir Edmund," said the driver, a dark man with keen eyes.

"Now wait a minute," said Sir Edmund. "You're one of those Lees up in the woods beyond Grumper's end."

"That's right, Sir Edmund," said the man. "My mother was a Margett, Sir Edmund."

"Oh well, you're all right," said Sir Edmund, who knew his county inside out from the Duke of Omnium to the half-gipsy people that lived up in the woods. "Now, what about those trees?"

The Duke, realizing that apart from owning the trees, and paying the men who looked after them and in due time cut them down when they had to be thinned out, he did not exist at all, remained silent, but listened as intently as Dido's court did to that cad Aeneas.

A long and to the principals an exceedingly interesting conversation then began. We can hardly say that it took place, for there appeared to be no limit of time or subject. Beginning with Lee's parentage it wandered to the various merits of deciduous and evergreen trees regarded as wood; the way some of those trees a man did ought to work them *with* the grain and some of the others, well he'd do better to work *across* it; that if you were felling a tree, well, it stood to reason you'd lop off all the big lower branches and then you'd look and see which way there'd be the most room for her to fall and then you'd get a man up her to hitch a rope round her and then you could begin with your axe, but careful-like, because you mustn't cut too deep nor too shallow. And if there was some boys about, which there mostly was, you did ought to see they had some good thick sticks the way that if the rabbits began to scuttle about as they usually did, the boys could knock them on the head and take them home and no questions asked. But if a grass-snake or so came out of the ferns and briars below you'd better catch him if you could, because, let anyone say what they liked, snake's grease was the best thing for the rheumatics and the sky-atticker, and a live snake was better than a dead one. And his, Lee's, uncle Jasper over at Sir Cecil Waring's place did know the snakes that had a charm in them, but you had to know where, because with some it was in the head and with others in the tail and his, Lee's, father always used to bite off the tip of the tail when he'd killed a snake because it was good for the innards, but you mustn't let a woman touch it or everything would go contrary.

To this the Duke listened with great interest and wished he could make a few notes for an article he had rashly promised to write for the Barsetshire Folk Lore Society: but his instinct told him that if Lee saw a pencil or a pen he would dry up at once—or quite possibly vanish silently into the undergrowth, not to be seen till he chose to turn up again; or, more probably than either, at once invent even more folklore on the spot.

The Duke, having given Lee his head, mounted the lorry with Sir Edmund and they drove onwards and upwards.

"Nice rides you've got here, Towers," said Sir Edmund. "Well kept too."

The Duke said his head forester—only that sounded rather a high-faluting name—had once spent a year in Denmark on some of the big estates and had learnt a lot about trees, both evergreen and deciduous and the method seemed to answer very well here. Then they came to the top of some rising ground.

Here there was an open space and beyond it a wide avenue in the woods and beyond that again a pure Constable landscape with green meadows and the River and beyond it Barchester and the cathedral. There was a dark thunderous cloud over the city and suddenly it was split by a ladder of light which caught the white spire of the cathedral.

"*That's* all right," said Sir Edmund. "Best view in West Barsetshire. Like a picture."

"You know we've got a Constable, painted from pretty well where we are now," said the Duke. "Probably we shall have to sell it."

"Good God! you can't do that!" said Sir Edmund, shocked.

The Duke said unfortunately he could, but now that the Towers had become a limited company as it were, he had hopes that they would buy the pick of the pictures, with the Towers as a permanent home; but it depended if they could raise the money; to which Sir Edmund made no reply. The Duke, thinking he might have shocked Sir Edmund by such mercenary thoughts, said unless they could be bought by the Company and kept together he would probably have to sell them separately to rich Americans.

"You can't do that, Towers!" said Sir Edmund, again.

The Duke said Needs must when the devil drives and his children would be lucky if they had a saucepan and a toasting fork as their share, which led Sir Edmund to so fine and varied objurgations as caused the lorry driver to commit as much as he could to memory, the better to edify his friends at The Harcourt Arms public bar.

"My old father," said the Duke, "used to say he'd like to be buried here, but it couldn't be managed."

"Well, *de mortuis*, you know," said Sir Edmund, "and I daresay he's just as well where he is. Where is he?"

The Duke nearly said In heaven I hope, but pulling himself together he said he was buried in the village churchyard where most of the family were.

"That is, the old lot," he said. "You know my people are more or less parvenus. Rum thing life. But one rubs along. And I've got Franklin, and our children aren't bad and now we've got that awful Towers off our hands we don't do badly. Franklin has money of her own from America, thank goodness. And my mother and my sisters have a very nice house in the village near us, and so have my brother William and his wife."

"Your brother William?" said Sir Edmund. "Oh, I know, he's a padre—does his collar up at the back instead of the front. Who's his wife?"

The Duke said Sir Robert Graham's youngest daughter.

"Well, that's all right," said Sir Edmund. "Good Barsetshire stock. Any children?"

The Duke said one child, a girl, who was not yet a day old. He hadn't seen her because all babies looked alike to him—even his own when they were small—but he would soon, and his wife had told him the baby was a very nice one.

By this time they had reached the trees, which were in the long avenue and some of them a sad sight. Sir Edmund lumbered out of the lorry, took a few steps forward and then came back.

"Have to limber up my legs," he explained. "I ought to be in a Bath chair. Daresay I shall soon. Now, where's this timber?"

The trees that the Duke, helped by the old woodman who still lived on the estate, had thought suitable for felling were closely examined by Sir Edmund in a silence which rather depressed their owner, who stayed near the lorry so that Sir Edmund could freely talk with the woodman as expert to expert. Presently they came back, still deep in argument. The Duke was of course anxious to have the expert's verdict but didn't want to press him or seem too eager. The woodman remounted the lorry.

"Interesting trees you've got there, Towers," said Sir Edmund. "Whoever planted them must have bought a mixed lot in a sale. But they're not bad. Your man understands his job. He has marked all the trees we think ought to come down. If I were you I'd get onto the people at Grumper's End. Do you know Wickham, the Mertons's agent?"

The Duke said he didn't know him, but he had heard about him from Lord Pomfret who thought highly of him.

Sir Edmund said Pomfret wasn't a fool. His host was tempted to say that no one said he was, but thought better of it.

"You get onto Wickham," said Sir Edmund, "and another man you might ask is Welk, the undertaker. He gets all the wood for his coffins up there above Grumper's End where your lorry driver's people live. I don't say they won't all cheat you, but it will be much cheaper and more comfortable if you let them. It won't be much, but worth it."

The Duke thanked Sir Edmund for the advice and they got into the lorry and were rattled back to the Towers.

"Remarkable place, yours," said Sir Edmund. "I'm glad it isn't mine."

"That's what I felt when it was taken over," said the Duke. "It was ruining us. Now we are actually in pocket from it. The people who have it—mostly big business in one way or another—seem to like it. I can't tell you what a relief it was to get into the house where we are now. We're luckier than the Pomfrets. They live in a wing of their own house, but we have our own small house to ourselves. Do come in and see Franklin and the children and stop to lunch."

But Sir Edmund said he had to get back to Pomfret Madrigal, where there was a Parish Council meeting and Mrs. Brandon had asked him to lunch. So the Duke thanked him warmly and Sir Edmund went on his way.

By this time it was nearing the lunch hour, so the Duke went home, rather tired, for a lorry is not the easiest form of transit especially over grass rides with an uneven surface—though luckily the ground was dry and they did not have to stop and put logs over squelchy places. A pleasant babble of voices greeted him as he went into his house and he found his mother and both his sisters there, with his wife, all talking nineteen to the dozen.

"I suppose," said the Duke, "you are all talking about the baby," but he said it very kindly.

"What else, darling?" said his wife. "It's so restful when there aren't any men. Oh, and William rang up from the Deanery and said the Dean was delighted at the idea of a Cathedral christening and would like to do it himself and they are settling a date. And Mrs. Crawley is going to ask Canon Fewling if he will play the organ, but she said she would have to tell a lie and say he was a distant relation or the sub-organist would take offense."

The Duke said he could blow the organ instead.

"Darling, you *are* out of date!" said his wife. "The cathedral organ has been electric or whatever it is for ages now. If the electricity goes wrong they can pump by hand I believe, but we needn't look for trouble. There's only one snag."

The Duke asked what it was and he hoped lunch was nearly ready.

"It's just coming up, darling," said the Duchess. "It's your sister Gwendolen. She wants Mr. Oriel to take part."

"Well, she can go on wanting," said the Duke, "as far as I'm concerned. It's William's business. It's his baby, not mine. Oriel is a good fellow but we don't want a whole gaggle of clergy for one baby. And if there is any more trouble I shall ask the Bishop to do it," which threat made the company laugh, though we believe the Duke almost meant what he said. Lady Gwendolen deliberately looked sad, but as no one paid any attention she cheered up again. Then the Dowager removed her daughters and peace descended.

"My poor lamb," said the Duchess to her husband. "What a life."

"Well, darling, it is my life," said the Duke, "and that's that. And you wouldn't like me to be nobody. When you married me you took me for better for worse."

"Much for the better," said the Duchess, almost violently.

"You know the Towers is open to the public this afternoon,"

said the Duke. "I think I shall go into Barchester and hide behind the *Financial Times* in the Reading Room at the Club. "

"If you *really* must," said the Duchess.

The Duke was silent. Then, "You are right as usual, Franklin," he said.

The Duchess looked at him with compassion.

"I wish you were me and I was you," she said.

The Duke asked what good that would be.

"Because I could stand the racket," said the Duchess.

"And I suppose I don't," said the Duke rather sadly.

"Oh, you *know* I don't mean that," said his wife. "But you are too kind. I could be *beastly* to people if I liked."

The Duke said Rubbish and need he go to the fête or whatever it was and looked so tired that his wife was almost alarmed.

"No, darling, you needn't," she said. "I shall go anyway and if I see anyone really nice I'll send them over to you here. I mean people like Lady Graham and Sally Pomfret who can be trusted."

"I like Sally," said the Duke. "I think it's because she's like you."

"What nonsense," said his wife. "She looks just like English county and I look like an American."

"You can both look like anything you like," said the Duke, "but what I mean is that Sally keeps Pomfret alive and you keep me. I wish to goodness my people had never come into the title. I would much rather be a landscape painter like the lord in Tennyson's poem. You know, The Lord of Burleigh. In the poem he was a lord disguised as a painter and got some fun. But I can't even paint and I don't know that I particularly want to. Well, there it is."

"No, it isn't," said his duchess. "If you don't feel up to it, you shan't go. You shall stay at home and I'll bring some nice people across to you. Is there anyone you'd specially like?"

"Mrs. Crawley of course if she is there," said the Duke, "and Cora Waring if you see her. But don't bother."

"I'll see to it," said the Duchess. "Anyone else. What about Mrs. Morland, who writes nice novels about ordinary people? Edith knows her quite well—she stayed with her once and enjoyed it frightfully."

"That does sound rather appetizing," said the Duke, looking distinctly more alive. "And the Pomfrets if they come."

So his wife promised to collect and bring them if possible and her husband quietly thanked heaven, as he did every day, for a wife who was a guardian angel.

The Duchess, as always, was as good as her word. Not without a slightly envious thought of Edith safely and comfortably in bed, with Sister Chiffinch to talk to—if she wanted to talk—and a divine baby on tap. But her heart was strong, her blood was New England, and soothing as the monthly nurse's conversation is, she wanted something more stirring. So very soon after the hour of opening she went over to the Towers, leaving her husband with the latest novels by Mrs. Morland and Lady Silverbridge who still wrote a fresh thriller every year as Lisa Bedale, an anagram of her maiden name, Isabel Dale.

At the gate she found Lee, the half-gipsy useful man, sitting at the receipt of custom. It was still early for visitors, but a small regular flow of them was passing through the barrier which had been put up on visiting days ever since the day when some louts from Hogglestock had burst through the gate and trampled over a flower bed. But we are glad to say that Lee, who had been keeping an eye open for gate-crashers, had knocked one of them down and thrown another with a bit of Romany trickery; and before the others had summoned enough courage (being only three to one now) to attack him, the head keeper had come up with his gun. It was a 1914 model and not loaded—for he was not going to waste his up-to-date official gun on Barchester scum—but the louts had fled at the sight of it, jeered at by the women who had come up to see what it was all about and if necessary drag their husbands away by the scruff of their necks.

And we are pleased to be able to state that in their haste three of the louts fell into the ha-ha which was damp and muddy at the bottom and when they scrambled out were chased by what they called, when boasting to their friends, a herd of wild bulls, who were simply cows outraged by the intrusion. They managed to get across the field in safety, but vengeance was waiting for them in the shape of another deep muddy ditch and two policemen, summoned by telephone from the lodge, by which time they were thankful to be shoved into a police car and driven away.

"Everything going well, Lee?" asked the Duchess.

"Main well, your grace," said Lee, who spoke to ladies of the Higher Orders with a deliberate affectation that pleased him and amused him. "There was some bad 'uns, your grace, more of those young fellows from Barchester out on a spree, but I told them they could go back where they came from."

The Duchess laughed and said rather untruthfully if that sort of thing had happened on her brother's ranch in Arizona he would have shot them at once. Then she congratulated him and passed on, leaving him full of romantic longings for a country where to shoot a bad man was meritorious, whereas if he had used a gun here or even his fists it would probably have been a fine or jail for him and sympathy for the intruders.

As it was early in the afternoon the grounds were still fairly empty, so the Duchess went into the great hall to see if any friends were there, and as she entered it felt—as she always did—a deep satisfaction that this great unmanageable monstrosity was off her husband's hands; and also a real gratitude to the queer mixture of people who now ran it and paid a good rent and kept it so well. A large man in tweeds was talking to a middle-aged woman with a middle-aged hat and middle-aged clothes. As she looked at them, they were invisibly drawn—as one often is against one's wish or knowledge—to look at her.

"Aren't you Mrs. Morland?" she said. "I was at the talk you gave to the Mothers' Union at Hogglestock last year and did enjoy it so much. Mrs. Adams was in the chair."

It was obvious that the well-known novelist was completely nonplussed, but the Duchess was not for nothing a good American, brought up to recognize people and address them by their correct name and—which we so rarely do—to mention her own.

"Isn't the Towers *awful*," the Duchess went on. "If my husband—that's the Duke—had wanted to live in it I should have gone right back to Lumberville—that's my home town. But I love this country. It's just as English as it can be."

"I'm so glad you think so," said Mrs. Morland, "because things do keep changing. I'm not a real Barsetshire person but I've lived here for a great many years and I hope to die here. Not in front of the Towers of course, but at High Rising where I live. I came with an old friend, George Knox. He writes lives of people."

"My sister-in-law Edith said she knew you," said the Duchess. "She has just had her first baby—a girl—and I know she would love to see you, if nurse will allow it."

"And I would like to see her—and of course the baby," said Mrs. Morland. "Will the nurse mind? Who has she got?"

The Duchess said a very nice Sister Chiffinch.

"Oh, but of *course* I know her," said Mrs. Morland. "Ever since I can't remember when, but quite ages ago when she was with George Knox's daughter for her first baby. I remember so well, because Tony—that is my youngest son but he is almost a middle-aged man now with a large family—nearly pushed the baby's perambulator into the river."

The Duchess said how dreadful.

"But the baby wasn't in it, so it didn't matter," said Mrs. Morland.

The Duchess said what a good thing and felt she wasn't doing herself justice and would soon go mad: an effect which Mrs. Morland's conversation not infrequently had on people who didn't know her well.

As George Knox was hovering about them, Mrs. Morland asked the Duchess if she knew Mr. Knox.

The Duchess said she would say she did—at least she had all the American editons of his books in the library as well as the English ones, but she found them rather heavy and liked Mrs. Morland's books ever so much better.

"I *am* so glad," said the distinguished novelist. "I don't mean that exactly but after all George Knox writes *real* books. Mine are only invention."

"But that's what I *like*," said the Duchess. "And my husband likes them too. Now, do introduce me and then I hope you will come over to our house when you have done the tour here and have some tea. My husband would be so pleased to meet you. It's only the family and perhaps my mother and sisters-in-law."

Mrs. Morland said she would love to come and had her car with her if she might bring it down to the Duchess's house, which seemed to her Grace a very modest request. Her Grace then spoke most charmingly to George Knox, did not let him get in a single word even edgeways and so extricated herself with her usual efficiency and self-possession. Then the ladies separated; the Duchess to do her duty as she always did, and Mrs. Morland to observe humanity.

This was not difficult, as a fine day had brought a considerable number of people; some in coaches—for the Towers was now included in most of the local sight-seeing tours—some in their own cars, varying from the bubble cars which had lately reached Barsetshire to great monsters that looked as long as a railway coach and were often only two seaters and always a nuisance in the narrow country roads. Report said—and we believe correctly—that in the river valley, where there were apt to be tributary streams with rather high humpy bridges, several of the outsize cars had been brought to a standstill; the framework on the hump and all four wheels spinning in a vacuum while the passengers vainly shifted their negligible weight to one end or the other, thus rousing much interest in small boys and passers-by. And this may well have been true, for we have seen it ourself elsewhere.

Presently Mrs. Morland joined forces with the Knoxes and they went to see the inside of the mansion which none of them had seen before.

It was indeed revolting, far past their highest hopes. No amount of paint or curtains could conceal its horror. Compared with it Pomfret Towers was a *bijou* residence, a *cottage orné*. Its windows were unrivalled for the hideousness of their greenish glass and all the furniture which had been newly installed by the business people who had taken over the place was uncomfortably comfortable (if we make ourselves clear) being more suited to an outsize hippopotamus than to the human frame. But as the various Company Directors and High Executives liked it, we suppose it was all right—for them at any rate. There were by now quite a large number of visitors, mostly ordinary, quiet, dull people. Some of them had bought the Guide to Harcourt Towers (price 1/ - on sale in the hall), some had been there before and talked rather loudly about it but usually incorrectly; while others just walked about or sat in the huge and uncomfortably comfortable chairs and eased their aching feet.

The Knoxes and Mrs. Morland also wandered rather aimlessly about and felt with Touchstone that when they were at home they were in a better place. Mrs. Knox said What about having some tea at half-a-crown a head, but when they looked into the great dining room with its heavy red damask curtains and enormous carpet and saw lots of little tables with clean but ironmouldy white cloths on them and an array of urns, obviously all overstewing tea and taking the taste out of coffee, their gorges rose.

"Let's go home," said Mrs. Morland, "Oh, good gracious me, I can't. The Duchess asked me to tea."

Of course when she had said this she at once felt snobbish— which she was not in the least. But the Knoxes appeared to find it quite natural that she should accept a tea invitation from what were, in name, the hosts of the present gathering. So they said good-bye and Mrs. Morland got into her car and drove herself down to the Duke's house which was so near the Towers that it was easily found.

It was a pleasant red brick house, perhaps a hundred and fifty years old, with spacious rooms; not that they were so very large in measurement, but their proportions and the placing of their fireplaces with elegant carving round them and the large handsome sash windows were extremely satisfactory. The Duchess and her American dollars had done all that was needed for them with new curtains (but not looking too new), some fine Aubusson carpets from a sale in London and chairs combining, on the whole, ease with elegance. Also in the dining room a very good round table which could seat eight comfortably and had four quite elegant legs with brass lions' feet to stand on.

The Duchess was in her sitting room with Lord William and Mr. Wickham, the Noel Mertons' estate agent. And if our readers wonder what Mr. Wickham was doing in her Grace's room, he and she had met a few years earlier out cubbing and each greatly admired the other; the Duchess envying Mr. Wickham's knowledge of the county and its ramifications, Mr. Wickham admiring her looks, her manner of speech, and the way she rode her horse.

Mrs. Morland greeted Mr. Wickham as an old friend and made most searching and friendly enquiries from Lord William about his wife Edith's health.

"Oh, she is *marvellous*," said Lord William. "She looks so well and happy. It's too wonderful."

Mrs. Morland said one always was happy when the baby was born, because it was such a bore while it wasn't, adding that she had had four and ought to know.

"Well what do you think of the Towers?" said Lord William.

"Really? or something polite?" said Mrs. Morland, looking round cautiously.

Lord William said Really, only he must get Franklin to come

and listen. Mrs. Morland said Certainly to get Franklin whoever he was.

"Not *he*," said Lord William. "My sister-in-law. Towers's wife. Like Frankie and Johnny."

For a moment Mrs. Morland's brain reeled. Then it stopped reeling, and she said: "Oh! Frankie and Johnny you mean."

"That's right," said Lord William, torn between admiration of the gifted novelist's childlike innocence—or idiocy—and a keen desire to know what she would say next. "She was christened Franklin, because it's a good old family name, but they always called her Frankie."

"Now I understand," said Mrs. Morland. "Root-i-ti-toot, three times she did shoot, Right through the hardwood door."

"Frankie knows it *all*," said Lord William, who had for his American ducal sister-in-law an affectionate admiration. "She can sing it to a guitar. Frankie! Here is Mrs. Morland whose novels you like so much."

At this point Mrs. Morland wished to kill Lord William, get into the nearest car (if it was one she could drive) and go home, but the Duchess came up, full of outspoken admiration for Mrs. Morland's Madame Koska books.

"I've read every one of them, in the American edition, again and again," said the Duchess. "When will there be another? I shall buy ten copies of the English one to send to all my people at home and all their friends will be wild, because they had it first. Our American edition is always a bit later. I've never known a real author before. When I was in college I had some of your books in the American edition and hid them under my mattress."

Mrs. Morland, who though often absent-minded was also practical, said she must tell that to her American publisher: but quickly added that she wouldn't, because if he put it in a blurb, which she didn't think he would, it might put people off because people in America were democrats.

The Duchess made a serious protest. Her people, she said,

were all Republicans and always had been. Mrs. Morland said But wasn't that all exactly the same thing? The Duchess said indeed it wasn't and her cousin Lee Sumter from South Carolina would bear her out if he were here.

Mr. Wickham, who as was his custom had been laying low and saying nothing like Brer Fox, suddenly remarked:

> "Many a bullet, many a dozen
> He fired upon Fort Sumter,
> And he thought upon his cousin
> As he thought each bullet bumped her."

"Why, Mr. Wickham, for the land's sake," said the Duchess, "I didn't know you knew that."

"Well, Duchess, now you do," said Mr. Wickham. "But that's all I do know. Is there any more?"

This did not seem to the Duchess the moment to begin discussing or singing the songs of the Civil War, but when Mr. Wickham added that he knew a verse of All Quiet along the Potomac and would swap it with her for Fort Sumter, she at once said he must come to dinner when she and Towers were alone and they would have a concert and Towers would sing them some of the gipsy bodgers' songs from up beyond Grumper's End.

"Not 'The Broom and the Besom'?" said Mr. Wickham. "I've been after that song for years. I believe Welk the undertaker knows it, he deals with the bodgers for his coffin wood. He won't sing it to me. He said it was main rude."

The Duchess said, not without some pride, that Towers knew quite a lot of unprintable local songs and would be delighted to swap any main rude ones with Mr. Wickham.

"Kamerad!" said Mr. Wickham, and so departed.

"If that man asked me to elope with him, I'd be off at once," said the Duchess, but as it was well known that Mr. Wickham had sedulously avoided matrimony all his life and was likely to do so till his death, no one felt the least anxiety.

The Duchess then asked Mrs. Morland if she would care to look at the other rooms, which of course she did, because it is always interesting to know how other people live.

"There isn't much to show," said the Duchess. "When Towers's father died there were your dreadful death duties to pay. That's why we had to get rid of the big house, not that we could possibly have lived in it. Come and see what we have. We put the best things in the long drawing-room. We use it in summer, but we have to shut it up in the winter and just keep the heat going because of the furniture and pictures."

She led Mrs. Morland across the hall and opened a door. Mrs. Morland nearly gasped aloud at the beauty of the long room. It was panelled in white wood framed with delicate carvings of gilded fruit and flowers. A bay window at the far end looked out over the park to the wooded heights. At the front a French window gave onto stone steps to the lawn with a pedestal on each side at the bottom, and on each pedestal a shallow stone urn with cheap, brilliant flowers growing in it, overflowing in coloured cascades.

"My *goodness!*" said Mrs. Morland, as if she were praying.

"I know," said the Duchess. "That's what I felt when Towers brought me here for the first time, and I've never quite got used to it. I only wish I could do more for the place. Dollars don't do everything. Do you like the Millais? The one over the sofa."

Mrs. Morland looked and saw a young woman in full evening dress of perhaps a hundred years ago, more or less, extremely handsome, looking straight out of the canvas, and asked who it was.

"Isn't she a real beauty," said the Duchess. "She was a Duchess of Towers—a mixture of Irish and Hungarian—and everyone raved about her. The Duke at that time seems to have been a very nasty piece of work and they were separated—of course one didn't divorce then. They had one boy who was a bit queer and luckily he died. That's how my husband's people came into the title. I believe she did good works and that sort of thing afterwards. But Towers's grandfather used to say that this little photograph was a better likeness," and she took from a table a rather faded photograph in profile of what one can only call a Beauty, with the rider that Beauty lives with Kindness. "It was done in Warsaw when her husband was *en poste* there—before he came into the title. The photographer's name is on the back but as it has ten consonants and only two vowels I've never tried to pronounce it."

"She *is* a beauty," said Mrs. Morland. "And what a good thing that your husband's family came in."

"Yes, I suppose it is," said the Duchess. "Well, we all have our burden and mine is to try to carry some of his. Now shall we go back to the others?"

So they went back, Mrs. Morland pondering upon the trials of well-born, not-too-well-off conscientious people in this Brave New World, and feeling very grateful to Providence for having placed her in the Middle Classes, where he that was middle need fear no fall, nor be proud about anything in particular. Then the Dowager with Lady Elaine and Lady Gwendolen joined them, and though Mrs. Morland felt a little out of the family gathering, she was quite happy to listen and possibly to carry away, quite unconsciously, some crumbs that could be used in the novel she was trying to write—or if not in that one, in the next one. But she was not long left to her private reflections, for the Dowager came and sat beside her and asked if she had ever read the novel called "A Step too Far" by the sixth Earl of Pomfret's wife, which had shocked Mr. Gladstone.

"I've heard about it," said Mrs. Morland, "but I've never been able to find a copy."

"You would like it," said the Dowager. "I have two copies, one for myself, one for lending. Never lend a book unless you have another."

"I don't," said Mrs. Morland. "I will give a book to anyone

who can't get a copy or really can't afford it, but lend I will not. I did lend a book to George Knox once and he lost it for a long time and I was furious but it was all the housemaid's fault."

The Dowager asked if the housemaid had stolen—or borrowed would perhaps be a better word—the book.

"Oh, no!" said Mrs. Morland. "What happened was that George has a rather large, heavy bed right up against two walls. I mean the head of it is against the wall up in a corner and then one of the sides of the bed is against the wall that comes down from that wall—you know the way they do."

The Dowager said she knew exactly what Mrs. Morland meant.

"Well then," Mrs. Morland went on, "George was reading the book I had lent him in bed with the light on—though I don't know why I said that, because of course he couldn't possibly have read with the light off—and he went to sleep and then he woke up about three in the morning and didn't know where he was—you know how one sometimes doesn't."

The Dowager said it had happened to her more than once and some years ago when she was staying with George Rivers— Mrs. Morland must know Mrs. Rivers who wrote those novels about middle-aged women having love affairs only nothing ever really happened and as far as she knew Mrs. Rivers—though rather a trial to poor George Rivers—was a perfectly faithful wife and hardly ever at home because she found she wrote better in the flat in London—she had woken up at three o'clock in the morning, a thing she never did as a rule, and couldn't think where she was and there wasn't even a box with some stale biscuits by the bed which most people did have in their spare bedrooms and she felt as if she had gone quite mad.

"So then," Mrs. Morland continued, having abstracted her mind from the Dowager's sympathetic words, "when I asked George Knox if he were enjoying the book he said he couldn't account for it but the book had vanished in the night."

The Dowager asked what happened.

"Well, it was all rather a muddle," said Mrs. Morland, "because the housemaid was a bad one—I don't mean personally because it really wasn't her fault that she had an illegitimate baby, right away in the country with no cinemas or anything."

The Dowager said it was part of English life and one couldn't do anything about it and the father nearly always married the girl.

"I know," said Mrs. Morland sympathetically. "Borough English or something—I know we learnt it at school in history but I never quite understood it. But the housemaid hadn't pushed the bed right up against the wall when she had finished making it, so the book slipped down onto the floor and no one thought of looking for it there till one of his studs fell onto the floor and rolled under the bed, and that *had* to be found, so they found the book too. And then he went back to London."

"Must one be in London to be literary?" said the Dowager, who, in common with many intelligent well-bred people, felt that anyone who wrote books should be approached with caution, as Man Friday might have approached Robinson Crusoe.

"I don't think so," said Mrs. Morland. "At least I don't live in London. I did have a flat there but I gave it up because life is so much more interesting in the country."

"That is exactly what my mother-in-law always said," said the Dowager. "So many interesting people to talk to. I only go up to London once a year now and stay with my brother the Archdeacon and I am absolutely *devastated*. Last time I was there, who do you think came to dinner?"

Mrs. Morland tried to think of all the people in London that the Dowager would not enjoy meeting and said, weakly, the Red Dean.

The Dowager said not *quite* so bad, but why she should go all the way to London to sit next to the Hibberd man, she did not know.

"Do you mean Lord whatever-his-name-is-now-one-never-can-remember-it?" said Mrs. Morland. "Lord Aberfordbury isn't it?"

"Yes. THAT man," said the Dowager. "I have avoided that person successfully ever since he began making himself a nuisance in Barsetshire when he was Sir Ogilvy Hibberd and then I have to meet him in London. I told my brother it simply *must* not occur again. Really, Simon, I said, there are limits and I am glad to meet any friends of yours, but if that man is your friend, you don't know what you are doing."

Mrs. Morland asked what the Archdeacon said.

"Oh, he sat on a fence like all the clergy," said the Dowager, "and Hummed and Hawed," which statement deeply impressed Mrs. Morland, for though she had often met the expression in books she had never heard anyone say the words aloud and had a vision of a gaitered ecclesiastic, perched on a five barred gate, humming and hawing. Humming one could understand, but how did one haw? Luckily she only said this aloud to herself inside herself, for if she had said it aloud the Dowager would have been entirely at a loss to understand her.

So then Mrs. Morland said good-bye and drove down to the village to enquire after Edith and the baby.

The door was opened by Sister Chiffinch, who looked at Mrs. Morland and said: "Well! if it isn't you, Mrs. Morland. I was thinking only the other day about you. I was reading your last Madame Koska book and when I got to the bit where she's going up in the lift and the villain jams the machinery and she can't make anyone hear because it's one of those nasty, newfangled lifts where the door shuts of itself and it's all wood and you can't see where you're going—they always give me the creeps—I really felt I was *there*. When I was training, one of the big lifts did stick one day and we had three patients in it in wheel chairs and one of them was an epileptic which we didn't know and he threw a fit. I expect you've come to see the New Arrival. Come up. Lady William *will* be pleased."

So Mrs. Morland followed Sister Chiffinch upstairs and

there was Edith in bed, looking extremely well, with a divine
baby, looking as if it were made of gossamer jelly.

"Oh! Mrs. Morland! How lovely!" said Edith. "Look at her!"
and indeed Miss Harcourt was well worth looking at, in her
quiet slumber, beyond the depth of plummet, her lovely starfish
hands outspread.

Mrs. Morland was profuse in admiration, and Sister Chiffinch
said Now Lady William must have a little shut-eye; and though
Mrs. Morland was—as we all are—revolted by the expression,
she realized its importance, kissed the baby's elegant hand and
Edith's cheek, shook hands warmly with Sister Chiffinch, and
drove home. When she got home she remembered that she had
forgotten to make any enquiries from anybody about pony clubs
and how to start to run one. So, very wisely, she went on
forgetting.

CHAPTER 3

We have made a brief comparison between the hideousness of the Duke of Towers's ancestral home and the not quite so revolting ugliness of Pomfret Towers. The two families frequently compared horrors, though the Pomfrets had to admit that they were only Alpha while the Towers family were Alpha Plus with three stars. Since Lord Pomfret's cousin Edith Graham had married the Duke's younger brother Lord William Harcourt there had been a good deal of very friendly intercourse on the older level, for as the years gain on us, our ages all begin to approximate and Aunt Mabel whom one used to look upon as an elderly witch is now almost our contemporary—or we hers. And we believe that the Duchess of Towers's children, who were still only of schoolroom age, got on very well with young Lord Mellings, the Pomfrets' heir, who was now beginning to follow the army tradition of the family.

If any one had questioned him on his feelings about a military life he would probably have put the question aside, but very politely, having inherited from his father a natural courtesy made up partly from a kind heart and a wish to please, partly from a feeling that to be discourteous would somehow let the whole family down; in which he was probably right. Sandhurst now occupied most of his time and a considerable amount of his intelligence, but unlike his parents he had almost a second home in London, being in spite of his youth a great friend of the well-known theatrical couple Aubrey Clover and Jessica Dean of the Cockspur Theatre, whose united efforts in dragging him onto the stage a few years earlier for the Northbridge Coronation Pageant in a one act play (actress, roué, young lover) had suddenly broken down his crippling shyness and given him confidence in himself. The army was to be his career, as it had been of the Lord Mellings who was killed in a frontier skirmish so many years ago. He liked his profession and wished to do well in it, which did him a great deal of good in every way. He had stopped growing and put on weight, and his hands and feet were now entirely under his control. As for the tender passion he had already broken his heart several times and it had been mended with speed and neatness, under that excellent theatrical leech Jessica Dean.

The Pomfrets had invited the Towers—by which we mean the Duke and Duchess—to dine with them to meet the Noel Mertons. Both sides had met on various public occasions and both were desirous to pursue the acquaintance. Lord Mellings was at home for a couple of nights and his parents asked the Mertons if they would bring their daughter Lavinia as the party was otherwise rather grown up; and of course they asked Mr. Choyce the clergyman from Little Misfit with his delightful wife, who as Miss Merriman had been secretary and true friend to old Lady Pomfret and after her death to Lady Emily Leslie, when that delightful, difficult, loving creature was living, during the last years of her life, with her daughter Lady Graham, now mother-in-law to Lord William Harcourt.

The round table took ten nicely. No one made a last minute excuse and all the guests were punctual. Being an English summer evening Lady Pomfret had a fire in her sitting-room which was really one of the former bedrooms. The dining-room was the old Upper Housemaids' room, and the dinner, cooked in the new kitchen made from the former still-room, was just as good as when it came on trolleys from the huge kitchen along miles of stone corridor and, we may add, much hotter.

It was a very comfortable kind of party, for hosts and guests, connected in a way most confusing to outsiders and perfectly clear to all those closely concerned, were interested in much the same part of Barsetshire and largely occupied with the welfare of their property and their tenants. The Duke of Towers and the Earl of Pomfret, though by no means really poor, were saddled not only by taxation, but also by the heavy—and increasingly heavier—responsibilities that come with land and the people who live on it, from the farmers who till it and graze it and keep or do not keep their live-stock in good condition to the cottagers who deeply resented being rehoused in modern cottages and sighed for comfortable warm dirt and slovenliness, many of them—aided by their wives—refusing stolidly to mend their ways from a kind of atavistic feeling that in their own cottage and bit of garden they were absolute and didn't want no one coming interfering. On the Pomfret estate we think there was no real poverty and on the whole the children of the various tenants were well fed and clothed. Even down at Grumper's End near Pomfret Madrigal, celebrated in the memory of the oldest inhabitants for inefficient and defective drainage (which can be much worse than none at all), where the delightful, good-looking, and quite intelligent Thatcher family grew and throve whether legitimate or illegitimate, and were also very kind to animals, frequently combing their mongrel dogs with the family comb, or drying them on a wet day with a sock they had only worn for a fortnight, or sweeping the rubbish—when they did sweep—into the yard to rot; even here there was plenty of good health, good temper (varied with a good smack when needed) and plenty of the wrong food at the wrong hours on which the children throve—even there, to return to the beginning of this sentence which has got quite out of hand, there was no real poverty. Most of the families were earning well and also spending perhaps not so well, as it was mostly on hire-purchase—better known as the Never-never. Further they did not look and under the Welfare State got on quite nicely, with pensions ahead.

Lady Pomfret had the Duke on one side of her—not because of his rank in this case but because there were family links, highly complicated to outsiders but perfectly simple to those within, for families are like mathematics, or indeed any exact science. If you know them everything is simple. If you don't, you probably try very hard, study Burke or Debrett, and go gently mad. And it is necessary to bear in mind such matters as that Lord Stoke, still going strong in his old age, had once been deeply in love with Edith Thorne of a very good old Barsetshire family. He had not told his love and she had married the seventh earl of Pomfret. Edith Graham, now Lady William Harcourt, had been named after her, but the old love story was hardly known to anyone now, unless we except Mrs. Morland for whom Lord Stoke had a great liking and to whom he explained all the relationships of the old families. We are glad to say that Mrs. Morland put all he said upon paper for her son Tony and had left a copy of it in her will to the Barsetshire Archaeological Society where it will be safely put away unless anyone particularly wants to see it and is willing to badger the secretary long and persistently enough. Another copy she had given to the eighth and present earl of Pomfret who had come into the title sideways as it were on the death of his distant and much older cousin and had a kind of ancestor worship about his remote kin; or perhaps connection-worship would be a more correct term, as he was not in the direct line. All that was an old story now: but the old stories are worth remembering for they become part of history, whether of the cottage or the mansion.

Lady Pomfret's own family were of no particular birth, but good yeoman stock from which all aristocracies do well to renew themselves, and on her strength her husband in many ways depended. She did all a wife with health, energy, and good sense can do; but he was often tired and also too apt to drive himself as he would never have driven anyone else. Luckily his wife's perfect health and good business mind had descended to the two younger children, Lady Emily Foster and the Honourable Giles Foster. The elder boy, Viscount Mellings, had outgrown his strength too early and given them considerable anxiety, but now all seemed to be going well and he was settling to his soldier's life.

We have already reminded ourself of the dinner party given by Sir Noel and Lady Merton in the year of the Coronation when the Aubrey Clovers had first met young Lord Mellings and ever since then had helped him to shed his shy awkwardness. His gratitude to Aubrey Clover had overflowed into gratitude to the Mertons of whom he had seen a good deal off and on and he was a kind of unofficial uncle to their younger children. To Lavinia the eldest, now a good-looking bouncing girl of fifteen or so, he was very much of an elder brother; fond of her, criticising her very freely, keeping up a kind of correspondence with her. The young friendship had been good for them both. Ludo did not make friends with girls very easily, and found in Lavinia a good listener. Lavinia had a poor opinion of Ludo's being a soldier when he might be an actor or an airman; her heroes of the moment, though only by proxy as it were, by picture postcards as she did not know any of them in the flesh except the Aubrey Clovers who were to her just people—though very, very nice. And it is always so. The mere fact of a person being a near relation or close friend somehow makes one feel that they are not as real as the actors, soldiers, writers, singers, politicians one doesn't know. And this view of Ludo had made her slightly condescending to him. It had not passed un-noted in her family and her mother had spoken to her in no uncertain words about being polite to her friends.

"But mother, I don't *need* to be polite to Ludo," Lavinia had said, to which her mother had replied that she needed to be polite to *everyone* and as Ludo couldn't answer back it was also unfair not to be polite; for she had more than once observed her daughter's behaviour with an impartial eye and thought but poorly of it.

Lavinia, we regret to say, had said rather sulkily and defiantly that it was Ludo's own fault for not answering back. Her father who had heard the talk then came down upon her with his best Q.C. manner and had really frightened her a little; a proceeding which had somehow made Lavinia reflect on what he said. After his scolding, or warning, she had sought comfort from Mrs. Joram, the wife of Canon Joram in the Close, who as Mrs. Brandon had known Noel Merton very well and done all she could to encourage his attachment to Lydia Keith as she then was, and Mrs. Joram had said exactly what Lavinia's father and mother had said, so that when she went to bed that night she cried for hours—or such was her impression; but as nurse had looked into her room about a quarter of an hour after she had said good-night and had found her fast asleep we cannot feel that her grief was very long or deep. And if our reader wonders why a nurse when Lavinia was sixteen, it was because of the younger children; and even when they are out of nursery life we think Nurse will stay on as a kind of ambulating help in almost every department and will, if she is spared, keep the nursery as a nursery till the Mertons have grandchildren, which is perhaps just as well, for there are already far too many people in Barsetshire. Some of the elders have died as time went on and their places are being filled by what we used to consider the young people and as such Lord and Lady Pomfret will always appear to us, because we met them first more than twenty years ago. Time is most confusing, as Orlando felt when Rosalind delivered her rather prosy dissertation on the varieties of his pace. But in one point Orlando was at fault. Time may gallop with a thief en route for the gallows, but as we get older he gallops faster and faster with ourselves as we watch friend after friend, enemy after enemy and even bore after bore, being borne along on what is less an ever-rolling stream than an endless, passionless convectorbelt (if that is the word we mean)—and we also are on it.

Lady Pomfret, talking with the Duke of Towers, managed to cast a hostess's eye round the table and was pleased to see that all the guests were talking on the proper side (a comment which will be quite clear if our reader stops to think), so she was able with a clear conscience to exchange views with the Duke on really important and interesting topics, such as how difficult it was to get proper dung for the kitchen-garden. The Duke said there were several polo players who kept their ponies at the Towers and he had arranged for all the straw from the stables to be his perquisite. Like Borough-English, or Tare and Tret, said Lady Pomfret sympathetically, and though neither speaker nor listener knew what either of these terms meant they quite knew what they meant them to convey. Neither do we know, except for a vague impression that the first is something to do with the ten to one chance that your first child will (if you are a man) not be yours, while Tare is a word sometimes painted on railway trucks and *not* something out of the Bible (and why Matthew was the only one to use the plural of the word we cannot say; nor perhaps could Mark, Luke or John) and Tret a word that one looked up in the dictionary and then forgot at once what it meant. And if the above passage seems a little confused, that is because it is.

The Duke tentatively put forward a suggestion that Borough English was what we have described it as. Lady Pomfret said of *course* it was, because there was a saying, still used among the real old cottage people, "If a boy's born in *August*, He won't be yours but father him you must," which enchanted the Duke. Lady Pomfret asked him if there were any witches in his part of the county and he had to admit that he had never heard of one, though he believed one of his ancestors in the seventeenth century, when they were plain county squires, had stuck pins into a witch to see if she was one and the witch had died (though not till some twelve years later) and on her death all the pins flew in at the window of the wicked ancestor's house and stuck themselves points upwards in the cushion of his chair, and when he sat down they all stuck to him and could never be got out of him or out of the cushion.

Lady Pomfret said she had read the same story in the Ingolds- by Legends so it must be true, only then it was the beard of a murdered unwanted husband which was put into a cushion and his wife sat on it and all the hairs came through and clawed themselves like a bustle into her and she couldn't get rid of them for the rest of her life.

The Duke said Those were the days. For a moment Lady Pomfret did not understand—and we think this was because she spent herself so selflessly for her husband and what was left of the estate and the people on it, not to speak of her growing-up children, that sometimes she could not even laugh at herself as Sally Wicklow would have done. Then she looked across the table at her hard-working, unselfish, tired husband and took courage, for she must always go in order to help him to go on.

By this time both speakers had wandered so far from what- ever they had been talking about that it was high time to change partners. Lady Pomfret's eyes met her husband's and she turned to Noel Merton. Lord Pomfret resigned the Duchess to Mr. Choyce and turned to Miss Lavinia Merton who had been enjoying a talk with Lord Mellings but was always ready for a new experience.

"I remember when you and Lady Pomfret and Ludo came to dinner with my people," said Lavinia, with so grown-up an air that Lord Pomfret couldn't help laughing. His wife looked across the table and was pleased, vowing to herself to be particu- larly nice to the Mertons if that girl of theirs—a handsome creature—could pull her hard-worked husband out of himself for a few moments.

"And I remember the dinner-party," said Lord Pomfret. "It was one of the nicest we had ever been to. Everybody was so kind and so amusing and we did enjoy it so much. So did Ludo."

"He has got more grown-up now, hasn't he?" said Lavinia, looking to her other side. But Lord Mellings was safely in talk with Mrs. Choyce, the vicar's wife, so she returned to her present partner. "I expect it's partly the Stage," she added.

Lord Pomfret said he didn't quite understand—Ludo wasn't on the stage and had quite enough to do, learning to be a soldier.

"Oh, I mean the Clovers," said Lavinia. "Of course they are divine actors, and so nice, and that was what I meant. I think they made him be more grown-up. Anyway he looks more grown-up and I'm so glad we helped a bit."

Lord Pomfret said the Clovers had been a great help to Ludo, but most of it was really all his wife's doing, and he looked across at his countess, whence came his help.

"Well, mothers do mostly do all the doings, don't they?" said Lavinia.

Lord Pomfret said he had never really thought about that, and she was probably right.

"Well, I know mother does," said Lavinia. "I mean father goes to London a lot because that's where he works, but he doesn't have to oil the wheels. Mother arranges *everything*, down here or in the London flat. Luckily lawyers get a very long holidays and then father *does* work. Would you like to have been a lawyer?"

Lord Pomfret, with his usual tired courteous manner, said he would never have been clever enough. He had been a good deal in Italy when he was a young man, he said, with his father who mostly lived out there, and he hadn't been to a university.

"I'd love to go to Italy," said Lavinia, "only it would be a bother to learn Italian."

Lord Pomfret asked if it would be more of a bother than learning French.

"Well, there's some sense in French," said Lavinia. "I mean there are lots of books to read and Mademoiselle Hamonet, that was the head French teacher at school, always said read as much as you can while you are young."

"I wish I had," said Lord Pomfret. "But my father had me in

Italy for nearly all the holidays and I had to talk Italian and as far
as I can make out there aren't any books in Italy. At least my
father never had any—only French ones. I suppose your father
and mother vet your French books a little."

"Oh no!" said Lavinia. "They say read whatever you like
because there's nothing in the house we don't want you to read.
At least there was a book by someone called Hardy, called *A
Group of Noble Dames* and I began reading it because I thought
they would be interesting, but father said not to, because the
dames might have been noble but they weren't at all suitable
company for me."

"So I suppose you went on reading it," said Lord Pomfret.

"Of course I didn't," said Lavinia, her eyes—so like her
mother's—flashing righteous indignation on him. "He said
NOT. But I read it afterwards and it was awfully dull."

Lord Pomfret said he had a great respect for anyone who
could say Not.

"Sally can say it," he added, looking across the table to his
countess. "She has just been saying it to Lord Aberfordbury. I
daresay your people know him."

Lavinia said she didn't know if they knew him, but her father
had said he wouldn't have him in the house. "Nor would
mother," she added, which remark gave Lord Pomfret great
satisfaction.

A certain amount of noise now drew the attention of the party
to Mrs. Choyce the vicar's wife from Little Misfit and Lavinia's
father Sir Noel Merton who were having a conversation which
made them both laugh a good deal. Taking advantage of a brief
lull in their talk, Lord Pomfret said: "Do tell us what it is all
about, Merry."

Lavinia looked up.

"Please," she said in a low voice to Lord Pomfret, "who is
Merry?"

He said she was Mrs. Choyce, the vicar's wife, formerly Miss
Merriman, who had been secretary to his aunt, old Lady Pom-

fret, and to several other old friends and had been a very good friend to him; and then he felt Lavinia had had enough attention and turned again to the Duchess.

"Wait one moment, Gillie," said the Duchess to Lord Pomfret. "I want to know what all that laughing is about."

"As everyone is looking at me," said Noel Merton, "I suppose I had better explain. It is only that Lord Aberfordbury—if that is his name but it always strikes me as being a highly improbable one—brought a very expensive Cascara-Sagrada 100 h.p. car and ran it into the Sewage Works outside Hogglestock."

"Glory, Hallelujah," said the Duchess of Towers. "It sounds as good as a verse from Frankie and Johnny."

"You must excuse my wife," said the Duke in a gentle voice. "When the American eagle begins a-raring and a-busting and a-biling, you can't stop Franklin."

Several people then spoke at once. Noel Merton, bringing a lawyer's trained educated mind to bear upon the subject, asked whether the Duchess had been named after Sir John Franklin the explorer who was lost while in search of the North-West passage, or Benjamin Franklin from Boston who was deputy postmaster for the colonies and had honorary degrees from Oxford and Edinburgh, not to speak of being made a Fellow of the Royal Society and conducting the deliberations which resulted in the War of Independence.

When the tumult had died down the Duchess said she was named for her mother's mother who was a Franklin from Franklinsville in Georgia.

Lord Mellings, of whose heart the Duchess had made a considerable impression, said Everyone was peaches down in Georgia and then went bright red in the face in a way most disconcerting to his family; and even more to himself, for though he could not see his face, being behind it, he knew exactly what he felt like and must look like, which was an animated beetroot or tomato.

Luckily crêpes suzette and/or ice cream were handed at this

stage by one of the many helpers from the village who were always available for parties. The grown-ups partook of one or the other, and the younger members partook largely of both. While they were enjoying themselves there was a scuffle at the door and in came Lady Emily Foster and the Honourable Giles Foster, looking very well and rather untidy, both in jerseys and breeches.

"I say, mother," said Emily, "is there any ice cream left? Oh, goody, goody! Giles and I went over to see the gipsies. They're camping—"

"They are not camping *here*," said their father's quiet voice. "Go and change and then you can come back for the ice cream. And don't forget to wash your hands—and faces."

Both the young people smiled tolerantly, as at the slightly trying whims of grown-ups, and went away. In a very short time they were back, clean and polite. As dinner was over except for the ice and the coffee, they put themselves at a small service table and began eating as an appetizer anything that had not yet been taken away, with a view to topping up their meal—their expression, not ours—with all the ice cream that was left. This did not take long and Lady Pomfret was collecting her ladies with a hostess's look when Giles said he had something awfully important to tell them.

"Well, not just now, Giles," said his mother, "or the table will never be cleared. You and Emily can come into my sitting room and tell me there, only don't talk *too* much."

Her husband looked at her gratefully. She led her ladies back to her own room, where there was the wood fire so necessary for an English summer. The coffee was waiting and Lady Pomfret noticed, with rather weary amusement, that two coffee cups had been added to the equipage without her orders. This she pointed out to Mrs. Choyce who at once realised the Monstrous Regiment of the Teen-Agers (a dreadful expression, but it does express a good deal that one couldn't explain without a great expense of words) and felt—as so many of the elder generation do—that never had the gulf between parent age and child age been so wide and yet so narrow. Not even when children lived entirely in the nursery or schoolroom and had their hair brushed and their faces and hands examined before they were allowed to go downstairs. Not even when the mother's dressing-room (now called sitting-room—or in some remote and old-fashioned quarters boudoir) was the hub round which the household moved, as Miss Yonge has immortalized it in *The Heir of Redclyffe*. Then at least they were under the motherly wing, with nurse not far distant. Now, with great politeness and firmness, they slipped away from it in every direction, without saying what they were doing or with whom.

Ludovic, Lord Mellings, who was the first child—the child on whom all parents have to learn how to be parents—had not always been easy, but he had mellowed, if we may say that of one so young. Sometimes his parents had wondered if he was going to have the physical strength and the mental energy that would get him through the adolescent stages, but he loved his home, and liked his life as a soldier-to-be and if the old Earl of Pomfret who had died in the dark summer of Dunkirk could have seen his young kinsman, he would not have been displeased.

Lady Emily Foster and the Honourable Giles Foster would bang and crash through life, making many friends and some un-friends and enjoying everything. Lord Mellings would—like his father—do his duty at whatever expense of body and mind. But would he stand up to it physically? His parents could only stand by and do their best.

Meanwhile he was safely at the dinner-table being a man among the other men and looking handsome in the fading light, for it amused Lord Pomfret to sit and watch his guests drinking their port by candlelight in winter, or by the level sunset light in summer.

Noel Merton had beckoned Ludo to come and sit by him. Lord Pomfret and the Duke of Towers had co-opted Mr. Choyce to talk about Lord Aberfordbury who, to the great delight of all men of ill-will, had involved himself in a very doubtful financial deal or loan (we know nothing of these things) with the Mixo-Lydian government and no one yet knew who had cheated whom; the general feeling on the Stock Exchange being that it was a neck and neck thing and no one could spot the winner, but the latest odds were seven to four against his lordship and all men of good will hoped the odds would increase.

Noel Merton, not unversed in the ways of the young, had taken an interest in Lord Mellings ever since his parents had brought him to dinner during the summer of the Coronation and—so far as a Q.C. who is in London for most of the week can do—he had followed his career of public school and Sandhurst, with the Brigade of Guards in prospect, and thought well of him. He had also noticed his good manners at dinner. A young man of his age and surroundings might be rather bored at sitting next to a girl of seventeen or so, with the clergyman's wife on his other side, but if he had been bored he had shown no sign of it. With all his love for his own eldest-born, Noel Merton sometimes wished she would be less self-assured and less of an "I'll-tell-you-whatter," which phrase, though affectionately spoken, had become common usage among the many true friends of Mrs. Samuel Adams, wife of the wealthy industrialist, formerly Lucy Marling, who was apt to preface her lightest word by "I'll tell you what." Not that his Lavinia exactly told people what, but she was—in the nursery phrase—not backward in coming forward. A self-conscious, gauche daughter would not have pleased Sir Noel Merton, Q.C., but he would have wished his daughter to have a little more retenue and was sometimes tempted when he saw her showing off to use Touchstone's fine words to Audrey and tell her to bear her body more seemly. His wife, though more tolerant than her husband, felt rather the same and they had decided to send Lavinia next year to a family in Paris where good manners would be expected. Noel had more than one French legal friend especially Maître Pierre Boulle, whose English was as good as any well-educated Englishman's and who had a charming wife and a family of round about Lavinia's age. As a young man M. Boulle had spent a summer at Rushwater, where his parents had taken the Vicarage for the holidays and had been completely captivated—as who was not—by the unpredictable wayward charm of Lady Emily Leslie, and her daughter Agnes Graham. So Maître Boulle was more than willing to receive an English girl, known to the family of Lady Emily, whom he remembered as *toute pétrie d'esprit et de grâce*—and how true his words were only Miss Merriman, now Mrs. Choyce, really knew now.

Lady Pomfret and her ladies had retired to her sitting room, once a best bedroom and having the double advantage of a small room off it where she could be quite alone and a view of the stable yard on one side and the gardens on the other. As it was summer (so-called) the curtains were not yet drawn, but a good fire was burning with logs from the estate and coal by courtesy of the various business men who had taken a long lease of the main building and were sorry for the owners—exiles in their own patrimony.

The Honourable Giles Foster and Lady Emily Foster, now washed and properly dressed, joined themselves to the ladies, with an almost alarming politeness from Giles who had been described by the old groom—his devoted adherent—as a rare one for showing-off. But—as his mother realized with considerable relief—the fact of Mrs. Choyce being there would keep him in order. Not for nothing had Mrs. Choyce, during her many years as companion and secretary and friend to the Pomfret and Leslie families and their ramifications, been the quiet ruler and arbiter of large houses, of all the staff and also of her employers. Then a late and very happy marriage had given her a home of her own and she was as good a clergy-wife as West Barsetshire could produce, though sometimes she missed—a very little—the power behind the throne that had been hers

while she was only the secretary-friend. But to her great satisfaction the young were apt to come to her, either to get good
advice as to how to get out of a silly scrape or to ask her to be on
their side when they wanted to go to the Barchester Odeon to
see Glamora Tudor in *Hearts Aflame* (in Glorious Technicolour) or—mostly in Giles's case—how best to break to his
father that he had, against Lord Pomfret's strict orders, ridden
that new colt bareback and been thrown off at the cross-roads
and nearly been run over by a motor coach. If the colt had been
hurt the whole of the stable staff (now one old groom and a
young gipsy boy who had the gipsy magic that George Borrow
knew) would have concealed it from their employer, but luckily
it was only Giles, whose hands and knees were a fine sight with
gravel and dirt off the newly-tarred road.

Giles, for once rather alarmed as to how his father would take
it, had gone to see Mrs. Choyce who said it always paid to tell
the truth, which was a kindness to Giles who was far too honest
to be a good liar. His father had forbidden him to ride for the rest
of the holidays and Giles had bowed the head to this decree, but
as his father had not specified exactly *where* he must not ride, we
regret to say that he had been among the queer half-gipsy people
who lived up in the woods, especially Jasper the gipsy horse-
coper over at Beliers, and had ridden their half-broken ponies
with great pleasure, not a jot of fear, and complete success. It is
but fair to Jasper to say that he privately sought out Lady
Pomfret and told her what had happened. She had been a
fearless rider herself before she married, but since she had taken
on the cares of her husband's position and public duties she
hardly ever rode. She was delighted to find in Giles a real
horseman and did not mention the affair to her husband. We
must say in justice to Giles that after a decent interval he did
confess, but as Lord Pomfret was just going up to Town—for
he took his duties in the House of Lords as seriously as his duties
in the county—and didn't listen attentively, it all blew over.
Giles, seeing that Providence was on his side, did not allude to it

again and made a resolution, which he kept, that he would not in future do anything that his father had expressly forbidden. And as hardly any father can think of all the silly things he would not like his child to do, the whole subject had lapsed.

"Come and talk to me, Giles," said the Duchess of Towers. "I want to ask your advice."

Giles at once came over to her, pulled a large hassock or pouffe to her feet and sat down on it.

"It's about pony clubs," said the Duchess. "Do you know Mrs. Morland over at High Rising?"

Giles said he had read some of her books but he thought they were a bit childish.

"So are you," said the Duchess, deliberately exaggerating her pretty Southern intonation. "I simply love them. Especially the one where the detective can't find the clue to the Noseless Horror and Madame Koska knows the Horror must be hiding in the coal-cellar with his face blacked so that no one can see him—"

"—and then Madame Koska finds footprints at the top of the cellar stairs, and they are bloody too," said Giles, warming to this great literature. "It's just Hectic."

"I suppose that is the latest word in your school," said the Duchess. "But it's overworked now, not to speak of being nonsense."

Giles said Everybody said hectic.

The Duchess said a lot of them said contróversy and despíckable, but that didn't make it any better and he had better ask the classics master at school what hectic really meant. Giles listened with the politeness a gentleman should show to a lady, but was obviously not convinced.

"But there is something really important I want to ask you," said the Duchess. "You ride a bit, don't you?"

Giles, who had been a horseman ever since he was put on a Shetland pony at a very young age and had moreover been given a pony from the breed that the gipsies had and could now ride any horse that he could get his young legs across, said he knew a bit, but Jasper was the man to ask if she wanted one.

"For a friend," said the Duchess. "I don't ride much now," though she omitted to say that she rode whenever she could, for she did not want to talk of her excellent hands and seat. "It's some people over at High Rising who want to start a pony club but they don't know how. Could you help them?"

To be asked by a Duchess, who is very pretty and friendly and has a charmingly exotic touch of American in her voice, if one will help her is enough to make a thousand swords flash from their sheaths. But Giles was not puffed up.

"If it's friends of *yours*, Duchess—" he said, using her title reverently.

"Oh, not Duchess, Giles," said the holder of the title. "My name's Franklin."

Giles went bright red in the face.

"It's a splendid name," he said, "but I couldn't say that. It would feel a bit uppish."

The Duchess was touched by his obvious reverence and wondered if she had gone too far. But the blood of Virginia stirred in her and the courtesy of her Southern forbears.

"Why not just call me Frankie?" said the Duchess.

Giles went—if possible—even redder in the face and hesitated. Then he said, "I'd like to; if you will call me Johnnie," at which piece of combined impudence and gallantry the Duchess laughed till she nearly cried and Lady Pomfret said What was it all about?

The Duchess nobly threw herself into the breach and said it was all about a Pony Club that Mrs. Morland wanted to start at High Rising, which statement took everyone's attention away from Giles, because everyone knew that Mrs. Morland had no interest in horses beyond nervously offering them a lump of sugar or a carrot and was never known to be willingly near a horse except when her old friend Lord Stoke took her for a drive in his brougham—for to his fury his doctor had forbidden him to climb up onto the dog cart. His old cob he occasionally rode, always with a groom in attendance—just as old Lord Pomfret had in his latter days after his countess's death. Lord Stoke had outlived old Lord Pomfret and most of his contemporaries, was likely to outlive a good many more, was neck and neck with Sir Edmund Pridham as doyen of West Barsetshire and boasted quite openly about it.

When everyone had spoken at once and at considerable length, the Duchess said she did really want to know about pony clubs, because Mrs. Morland had asked her; at which moment the gentlemen came in and the Duke said What was that about pony clubs?

So the whole question was re-opened, rather boringly most of the grown-ups felt, till Lord Pomfret said Giles and Emily must go to bed now; and to bed they went and the wrangling of their voices died away and the grown-ups could breathe.

> "Is not on cheeks like these lovely the flush?
> Ah! so the silence was, so was the hush,"

said Mr. Choyce.

Lydia Merton said she quite agreed and who had said that.

"I think it was Matthew Arnold," said Mr. Choyce. "A poem called 'The New Age'—but again I only think—I cannot say for certain. It is very mortifying how one's memory fails one just as one needs it. If you have a Matthew Arnold I could easily find it," but the Pomfrets had not a Matthew Arnold and Mr. Choyce was slightly depressed, for Running the Quotation to Earth is a favourite pastime among well-read people and keeps them quiet for hours. It used to be *Bartlett's Familiar Quotations* in our youth and a very good book too. Now it is also the large *Oxford Book of Quotations* of eight hundred and seventy-nine double-columned pages with everything included except the one thing we want—and of course including a great deal of poetry which we do not call poetry at all; for as there are books

which are really not books—*biblia abiblia*—there are poems
that we do not consider good enough for anthologies. Everyone
must choose according to his or her own liking, and there could
be as much heated argument over the editor's choice as over rival
Parliamentary candidates, or—most heated of all—religious
beliefs.

"But," said Lord Mellings, "if they really want a pony club at
High Rising they could write to the Head Pony Club, couldn't
they? There must be one."

The Duchess said the pony club at her home had five hundred
members and a lovely club house, formerly the home of a fine
old Virginia family, which glimpse of wealthy freedom slightly
depressed some of the party. Both the Mertons were very much
in favour of the club and Lavinia had to raise her voice and say
she loved ponies and would like always to wear jodhpurs, but no
one paid any attention to her owing to the irruption of Giles in
his pyjamas, looking extremely clean and rather damp, carrying
a large book.

His father and mother said with consentient voice What *was*
he doing and why wasn't he in bed?

"Well, I *was*, mother," said he in an aggrieved voice, "but I
couldn't go to sleep, so I was reading this book about horses out
of father's office and I thought Jasper would like to see it. Could
I take it to him when I go to his cottage next time?"

"Certainly not," said his father. "Put the book down on the
table and go back to bed."

"Jasper has a pony he says I ought to have, father," said Giles.
"He says he sold you the first pony I ever had. Is that true?"

His father said it was—and possibly the only true word Jasper
had ever spoken and now Giles could go straight back to bed and
not to read any longer.

"Can I read it when I wake up in the morning?" said Giles,
with the smile of an angel.

"Go to BED," said his father, "or I shall get Nanny Peters," for
the children's ex-nurse lived on at the Towers, as old servants

still could do, and from her very comfortable bed-sitting room ruled over what had been her nurslings, listened to their tales of adventure or disgrace, insisted on good manners, saw that Lady Emily brushed her hair properly and turned her bed back when she got up, and still had complete mastery of the otherwise irrepressible Giles who tried to hide his hands whenever Nanny Peters appeared.

"I'll leave it here, then," said Giles, "in case you'd like to read it," and he laid the book on a table, made as courtly a bow as one can make in pyjamas and left the room, shutting the door with meticulous care.

"Hurry *up!*" said his father, as it came open again.

"I only wanted not to bang the door," said Giles reproachfully and shut it again with such care that it gently swung open for a second time, while he padded swiftly upstairs. The grown-ups began to laugh, though Lord Mellings was not too pleased with his younger brother, for whom he had always felt a certain responsibility—part of his inheritance from his father.

"Was that impudence, or a mistake?" said Lord Pomfret, appealing to the party in general.

No one quite liked to give the obvious answer, but the ladies flung themselves gallantly into the breach and soon the party were happily discussing the Close and the Palace, always fruitful topics of conversation, while Ludo and Lavinia went off to the old school-room, now a kind of sitting-room for the young, and talked about the evening when Ludo and his parents had dined with the Mertons and the Clovers had been so nice and so to a description of the Clovers' last play, which Lavinia had not seen.

"I say, Ludo, can you still sing?" said Lavinia. "You did sing at the Coronation in that little play of Aubrey Clover's."

Lord Mellings said he thought he could. There had been a ghastly time, he said, when his voice broke and he never knew if it would come out from his forehead or his boots.

"I say, do let's sing," said Lavinia. "This piano isn't bad. Our old one got pretty awful and we only played Chopsticks and silly things. Let's play Chopsticks now."

But Lord Mellings didn't know what Chopsticks were. So Lavinia showed him that delightful musical improvisation of our childhood when one of us played the same chords again and again in three-time while the other improvised tunes—of a very limited variety and range—in the upper register and it could go on as long as Nanny's patience lasted, or mother didn't come up to say we MUST shut the nursery door while we are amusing ourselves. And so well did Chopsticks go that they tried some songs from a Victorian collection and Ludo played Cherry Ripe for Lavinia to sing and then she played The Bay of Biscay-O for him to sing and they both tried to sing the Death of Nelson and found to their common surprise and even shame that they were near tears.

"I can't help it," said Lavinia, blowing her nose violently. "Whenever I think of Nelson I have to cry."

Ludo said he couldn't quite cry, which was the worst of not being a girl, but he felt *ghastly* when it came to the bit about "At length the dreadful Wound. That spread Dismay around. The Hero's Breast received." So then they tried again and gave it up and returned to Chopsticks.

"I say, come over to Northbridge soon and we'll go on the river," said Lavinia. "And Giles too. We've got an old donkey who bucks everyone off, and throws his hind legs right up into the air."

Ludo said that would suit Giles down to the ground and he would bet sixpence that he would hang on, which sounded so dashing to Lavinia that she said she would bet sixpence he wouldn't. But all pleasant evenings come to an end and the Mertons were ready to go home.

"I can't tell you what a pleasure this has been, Lady Pomfret," said Noel Merton to his hostess. "I am not at home as much as I should like to be, but when the courts rise I hope we shall get you to dinner and Ludo too, and Lydia will try to get the

Luftons from Framley. Lufton is doing extremely well in the county now and has once or twice put Aberfordbury right in his place at the County Council meetings."

Lady Pomfret said they would like it of all things and how very nice his Lavinia was and got on so easily with people.

"I hope our Ludo will," she said, as the rest of the party were saying good-byes and she would not be heard. "He has come out so much since he met the Clovers—and we have to thank you and your wife for that evening."

"And we have to thank you for this evening," said Noel, and then made his farewells to the Duchess.

Lydia also was saying good-byes and thanked Lady Pomfret for a happy evening and the pleasure of meeting the Duchess quietly, as they were both busy and only met at committees. Then she turned to her host and as she gave him her hand at parting she suddenly was back in the evening—some years ago now—when he and his wife had dined with them and Aubrey Clover had made Lord Mellings sing. So much time had passed and yet time seemed now for a moment to stand still. For a moment her hand remained in his and his hand held hers with the same gentle pressure that she remembered. Their eyes met, Lydia withdrew her hand and the guests all departed.

"Ouf!" said Lord Pomfret, as he sat down.

"Was it too much for you, Gillie?" said his countess, always on the watch.

"Not a bit," he said. "It's only my long back and my long legs that are tired—not me. I wish I were short and stocky and strong. Only then I suppose you would have turned me down."

"Certainly not," said his wife. "You could never have done anything to make me turn you down."

"I have always felt that myself and I'm glad you feel it too," said Lord Pomfret, with whom humour did break in from time to time.

"Not even when you were a bit sloppy about Lydia Merton,"

said Lady Pomfret cheerfully, as she began to plump up the cushions and put the room tidy.

Lord Pomfret said, rather in the voice of an aggrieved child, that he hadn't the faintest idea what she meant.

"You know perfectly well, Gillie, that you know what I mean," said Lady Pomfret. "The night we dined with the Mertons—in the Coronation summer—and Aubrey Clover made Ludo sing with him. When you said good-night to Lydia—'The husband listens and sings. But the wife remembers.'"

"What *do* you mean?" said her husband.

"I was just quoting," said Lady Pomfret, "from a charming, nostalgic poem which was charmingly set to music, only I parodied it. Forget it."

"And very kind of Clover it was and gave Ludo just the push he needed," said her husband. "But there was nothing of what you choose to call sloppy. Lydia isn't sloppy."

"Of course she isn't," said his wife, up in arms for her own sex (as most of us are). "She is as straight as—" and she paused for a word.

"'Steel blue, blade straight. The Great Artificer made my mate,'" said Lord Pomfret rather affectedly. "I can quote too."

"That," said his wife, "is a very silly poem of Stevenson's and does him no credit at all. In fact quite a lot he wrote doesn't do him much credit now. And anyway Lydia wasn't your mate and I'm not either, any more than I'm the Cook and the Captain bold."

Lord Pomfret said what on *earth* was his wife talking about. She said Gilbert—*not* Gilbert and Sullivan though—which made him, very reasonably, wonder again what she meant. Suddenly light burst upon him.

"Oh, you mean the *Bab Ballads,*" he said. "If I ever get a bit above myself I think of 'The Periwinkle Girl.'"

His wife, in her turn slightly puzzled, asked why. Because, said Lord Pomfret, of Duke Bailey and Duke Humphy. Duke

Bailey, she might remember, had golden boots and silver under-clothing, while as for Duke Humphy—though mentally acuter—his boots were only silver and his underclothing pewter.

"But when we come to the Earl, I mention him with loath-ing," Lord Pomfret went on with gusto. "*He* wore a pair of leather shoes And cambric underclothing."

"I remember now," said Lady Pomfret, "and the Dukes only offered Mary guilty splendour, but the Earl married her at St. George's, Hanover Square."

"And don't forget the end, Sally," said her husband.

"Come, Virtue in an earldom's cot!
Go, Vice in ducal mansion!

but unfortunately all our local dukes are very respectable. Cer-tainly Towers is and so is Omnium. I suppose they can't afford to be heartless gambling roués now, even if they wanted to," which made his countess laugh.

And this pleased him immensely, for he had gradually real-ized that though she was perfect as wife, mother, friend, grande dame without pretensions, she did not always laugh where he would have laughed. But she was his rock, his fortress, and his might, and still rode like Diane Chasseresse—though she hardly ever hunted now. And he didn't either, he thought ruefully, because he never had and didn't want to. No, Giles would carry on the family horsemanship and given a chance would run the estate and hunt as his elder brother never could. And as they were very good friends this would probably be what would happen. Ludo would sit in the Lords though he didn't like London and would do all that he should do in the county however dull or difficult, but never would it be glad confident morning with him. Giles would be a kind of super Mr. Wick-ham and be on intimate terms with everyone from the Duke to the lowest poacher.

"'Never glad confident morning again,' if we must quote," said Lord Pomfret in his kind tired voice, looking with melancholy eyes at the past and the future. "Let's go to bed."

He switched off the lights. When he opened the door the passage lights were not on and while he felt for the switch with one hand, his wife took the other, laid her cheek against it and restored it to him. So they both went to bed.

But just as Lady Pomfret was almost lost in the drowsy gates of sleep her husband called to her.

"What *is* it?" said the countess, gently annoyed by the interruption of a nice sinking into nothingness.

"Only that you saved my life when I was on approval at the Towers and just young Mr. Foster, terrified of old Uncle Giles," said the eighth Earl of Pomfret. "I don't seem to have repaid you very well. You do so much for me—you mean so much to me."

"Well, if I do," said his countess, "I do it because I *want* to do it and I always have and I always shall. Go to *sleep*."

And the eighth Earl of Pomfret did as he was told.

We think that the evening had been a success with everyone. Noel Merton had much enjoyed talking with Lady Pomfret at dinner, and had got on well with Mrs. Choyce whom old Lady Pomfret had valued when she was Miss Merriman. The Duke of Towers liked his hostess and was agreeably impressed by Lady Merton. She found the Duke pleasant company and then was quite glad to talk to Mr. Choyce on her other side. A good deal of cathedral gossip came to Mr. Choyce. Partly, we think, because he dearly loved it, though most discreet, and partly because there were stirrings in cathedral circles where he had a good many friends.

A highly agreeable rumour was going about that the Bishop, who, it was said, had for some time contemplated resigning, might take the sinecure of St. Aella's Home for Stiff-Necked Clergy, a very well-paid post with a good house and garden and merely nominal duties. The chief drawback, in the minds of all men of good will, was that if the Bishop were at St. Aella's he would not be in Barchester, and though he was almost universally unpopular, his loss would be felt and, as M. La Fontaine puts it (whether you believe it or not) *Voici Comme.*

Those who were present at the Deanery some seven years or so ago, may remember that the Bishop had been forced by the Bishopess to take a round trip in the motor cruiser *Anubis.* The weather had been bad and newspapers had reported that she (if one can say that of a motor cruiser) had run into bad weather, which report had raised the secret hopes of all present to fever-point, though outwardly all was smooth. A further wireless report later in the evening had sent out the news that the *Anubis* had arrived safely at Madeira, among the passengers being the Bishop of Barchester and Mrs.—at which point the Dean had turned it off.

It was then that the ci-devant Mrs. Brandon, now the wife of Canon Joram, had made the remark which had never been forgotten by right-thinking men and women.

"I must say," she had said, looking pensively at the diamond ring, a bequest from her first husband's old aunt, on her still lovely hand, "that after all these years it would be quite uncomfortable not to have someone at the Palace that one can really dislike," which words had been treasured by all who were present.

There was, naturally, a great deal of ill-informed talk about this rumour. There were those—as there always have been since Hamlet's days and probably as early as Genesis—who could and if they would; but they usually won't, for the simple reason that they can't, having nothing to impart.

We ourselves (or ourself) know nothing of the making of a bishop, except from The Warden by the deceased Mr. Anthony Trollope, who combined hard work as a high official in the Post Office with hunting several days a week and writing at least fifty novels of varying degrees of merit, the best of which—and there are many in that class—have given us pleasure ever since we could read and will go on giving us pleasure till we read no longer and the silver cord is loosed, the pitcher is broken at the fountain, and the wheel broken at the cistern.

This is not the moment to divagate, but in parenthesis we may say that if the Great Anarch lets the curtain fall and Universal Dullness buries all—which we sometimes feel it is doing its best to accomplish—we shall beg to salvage our books.

With such rumours going about, a considerable part of the County was naturally in ferment. Not that the Bishop was actually disliked, for his personality was not strong enough, but dislike of the bishop of the moment, whoever he might be, was now a kind of tradition in Barchester. And added to this was the almost universal dislike for his wife, for various reasons, among which perhaps the most cogent was the way she used the beautiful mahogany wine cooler with its silver handles as a receptacle for ferns. It was also devoutly believed in anti-palace circles that the Bishopess had caused the silver handles and hinges to be treated with something that made it unnecessary to polish them once a week, as had always been done—even in Mrs. Proudie's time—so that they never looked quite themselves again.

The mere possibility of a change at the Palace had of course led to an enormous amount of discussion, sometimes academic, sometimes nearly as bad as the House of Commons when it loses its grip, and mostly founded upon prejudice and ignorance. We do not use the words unkindly, especially as they describe pretty nearly our own attitude to all those subjects of which we know very little. Statements were made which seemed like acts of faith but appeared, on consideration, to have no grounds at all. The Close Upper Servants' Club, led by Simnet, the Jorams' butler, kept a strict eye on all that was happening, and it was even said that the second housemaid at the Palace—for a slight consideration—removed the contents of his Lordship's waste-paper basket every day for the later edification of the Club. It was a very close body in every sense of the word and though it would willingly piece together any letters that might be of interest, it would certainly keep the contents to itself and no one under a certain rank might read them on pain of social ostracism.

Canon Fewling's faithful housekeeper, Mrs. Hicks, who had accommodated herself extremely well to Mrs. Fewling (the Admiral's daughter whose first husband was Mr. Macfadyen the big market gardener) had been made an honorary member of the Upper Servants' Club, but had not spoken of the matter, though her employers were apt to discuss it in season and out of season—that is to say at meal-times when she was present, or, most thoughtlessly, at meal-times just when she was out of the room. For Canon Fewling liked to eat in peace and ring when he was ready for the next course and it was his wife's pleasure to conform with his likings.

So the whole Close was boiling over and we think it will almost serve them right if the rumour proves to be what our formerly lively neighbours the Gauls call a duck: but, in Mrs. Gamp's great words about Rooshans and Prooshans, they were born so and must please themselves. The Towerses also boiled over slightly, but as they were pretty sure that they could get reliable news from the Reverend Lord William Harcourt, the Duke's younger brother, they bided their time. As for his sister Lady Gwendolen Harcourt she will need another chapter.

CHAPTER 4

The Honourable Giles Foster, as our reader may have noticed and his parents rather wished they could refrain from noticing, was one of the lucky people who are born knowing exactly what they want to do and at once doing it. His parents saw in him much of his old cousin several times removed, the former Lord Pomfret, but they hoped that some of that nobleman's qualities would have softened in the change. We think their hopes will be justified. Like so many of the young in his generation horses were his chief joy and the old groom had said that Master Giles could get a job at Newmarket any day. Luckily Giles had not heard these words, for he would have been quite capable of looking up Newmarket in the map and setting out on his pony with a small bundle of clothes and last month's pocket money, Richard Whittington-ing his way there and by a mixture of cheek, charm, and really knowing how to handle most horses got a good job and risen in time to an upper groom or stableman with others under him.

Still, there was metal more attractive nearer to hand for his half-term holiday. At breakfast he announced to his parents that as Mrs. Morland said the people at High Rising wanted to start a pony club, he thought he had better go over or they would do it all wrong. Lord and Lady Pomfret looked at each other, with the slightest shrug of the shoulders and lifting of the eyebrows, but said nothing. There was no real reason to forbid it. Giles would at once have a round dozen of specious and highly unconvincing reasons (to his parents' mind at any rate) for what he wanted to do and they would be beaten in the end by his pertinacity and—one must confess—the charm that he turned on so easily: too easily they sometimes thought.

After a slight morning refection of porridge, eggs and bacon and sausages, several large slices of toast thickly buttered and marmaladed, and two cups of coffee almost stiff with sugar, Giles rode away. His parents had feared that his sister Emily might have wanted to go too. She was a quite good rider though nowhere near her younger brother, but always wanting to keep up with him and the less she did this the better pleased—and the less anxious—her parents would be. It is possible that Emily might have made a protest and even let loose some of the famous Pomfret temper, but the keeper was going out with a ferret or two which to her spelt bliss and she let Giles go without any argument. We may say that she was rewarded, for the head ferret had a kind of Famous Battle of the World with another ferret, property of the old man, and they were fighting it out underground, in the rabbit's burrow, emerging bloody but satisfied. At this point the gipsy Jasper—who could smell a hunt miles away—lounged onto the scene with his own special ferret looking out of his pocket. At the sight of their rival riding in glory as it were, in a well-heated coach, both combatants began to shriek Fire, Murder, and Revenge and were collected by their respective owners.

"Jasper's brought the finest ferret in the countryside," said the old gipsy who—doubtless with some dim notion of propitiating unknown deities by remaining more or less anonymous—always alluded to himself in the third person.

"You haven't, Jasper," said Lady Emily. "That's only your second-best one. You *are* mean."

"The Lord's little lady is too clever for a poor old gipsy-man," said Jasper. "If the Lord's little lady crosses the poor old gipsy-man's hand with silver, he might find a better one."

"Oh, father, can I have sixpence, please?" said Emily.

Lord Pomfret who had been looking on with amusement, asked why.

"Oh, you know, father," said Emily rather impatiently. "It's only to cross Jasper's hand with."

Lord Pomfret laughed and found a sixpence which he gave to Emily who gave it to Jasper. He bit it, spat on it, smiled his mysterious gipsy smile, and put it in his pocket. Lord Pomfret went away.

"At your old tricks as usual, Jasper," said a voice of authority, and there was Nanny in her everlasting grey coat and skirt and her uncompromising felt hat, much as she had been for the last dozen years and more.

"If it isn't Miss Peters again," said Jasper. "As large as life and twice as natural. You do look younger every day."

"More than your poor mother, my aunt by marriage did," said Nanny. "It's a good thing she died when she did. What she'd have done with you going on the way you do, Jasper, the good Lord knows."

"And he's not telling," said Jasper. "I say my prayers proper every night."

"And a long way *they* go," said Nanny contemptuously. "A lot of Romany rubbish."

"Well, if the Lord don't want them, there's others as do," said Jasper. "There's Ones as the Romany people know, and they aren't particular."

What might have happened next we hardly like to think, but Lady Pomfret's brother Roddy Wicklow, who was also the estate agent, came up with his wife and children, and Jasper silently withdrew. Lady Pomfret joined them and there was some family conversation. Lady Pomfret told her brother that Giles had gone over to High Rising, apparently to explain to anyone who would listen how to start and run a pony club. Roddy Wicklow said Just like Giles and as he was fairly free he would go over to High Rising and give a hand.

"Pony clubs don't grow in a day," he said. "And as far as I know High Rising, it's all elderly married people whose children are out in the world. Still, I've nothing particular to do. I say, Sally, have you heard any talk about the bishop?"

Lady Pomfret said nothing particular except that there was a rumour about his retiring.

"Exactly what I heard," said her brother, "but I don't much believe it. Wishful thinking probably. Any names mentioned?"

His sister said she didn't quite understand—it wasn't divorce was it?

"Bless your heart, my girl, who said it was?" said Roddy Wicklow. "I mean, who's the lucky man? Who will smoke his meerschaum pipe when he is far away?"

But his sister, though as good as gold and as hard-working as if she were one of the Royal Family, did not know that nostalgic song.

"Well, in words of one syllable, Sally," said her brother, "is it true that old Puss-in-gaiters is going and if he is, who is the next on the roster?"

"I don't know," said Lady Pomfret. "It's only a kind of hearsay. I wish I'd asked Mr. Choyce last night," but her husband said he didn't think Mr. Choyce was up in Close gossip.

"But I do know who might know," said Lord Pomfret. "Towers's sister Gwendolen—the one that loves the clergy. She's a great friend of Mr. Oriel over at Harefield and he always knows what's up. I daresay I'll hear something at the Club. Anyway it's probably not true. I sometimes think that I've never heard any local news that *was* true."

"You're right, broadly speaking," said Roddy Wicklow. "But we have had our moments here. There was that splendid affair just before the war, with the bodies in the well."

As Lady Pomfret didn't know what he meant, she said so.

"No you couldn't," said her brother. "Nor could Gillie, because he wasn't at the Towers then. He was in Italy with his awful father. It was Horace Tidden."

Lord Pomfret said as far as he knew the Tiddens were always in trouble and distinctly wanting in intellect, and which one was Horace.

"He was old Ned Tidden's son," said Roddy Wicklow. "He killed his old uncle and aunt that he lodged with—battered their heads in with a huge billet of wood—and then he told the neighbours what he'd done and threw himself down the well. His mother has been in the County Asylum for years and years and ever since she nearly killed one of the nurses she has been quite happy and quiet."

If any of those present were readers of Crabbe, they would have felt that here was a subject fit to his hand: but we doubt if they were. The short and simple annals of the poor—in the words of the poet Gray—are sometimes far from being either, as the police concerned in this case had found when confronted with two very unpleasant looking corpses in the cottage and what Mr. Mantalini so feelingly described as a demd moist unpleasant body in the well.

"Well, I'll go after young Giles," said his Uncle Roddy. "I've nothing special to do this morning," and after a few words with Jasper about a tree that ought to come down he trotted away.

It was a pleasant ride from Pomfret Towers to High Rising, leaving Bolder's Knob on the left, under the railway arch which always gave a pleasant hollow echo, and so through Hatch End and Low Rising to where the village—or almost a little town now, so had urbanization spread its horrid tentacles—of High Rising lay on the higher ground beyond the water-meadows. As is often done in the country, he chose to ride into the back yard where one can always get the lay of the land before attacking the householder him—or in this case her—self.

In the back yard, pleasantly paved with rather uneven red bricks of the proper red—none of your purply-red affairs—he found, as he had hoped, Mrs. Morland's cook and general factotum throwing a pail of dirty water down an outside drain.

"Good-morning, Stoker," he said, touching his hat. "How's the leg?"

Stoker clanked her pail onto the bricks upside down the better to drain, wiped her hands in her apron, and said she wasn't one to complain.

Well knowing that she was, and that the Complaint Barrier had to be crashed before one got any further, Roddy said we all had to pack up our troubles in the old kit-bag.

"You can hook him up on the wall if you like," said Stoker, such being her simple way of asking the visitor to put the bridle of his very good mare over an iron hook. "There was one of them ones that was quartered here in the war and he came back the worse for drink and the other boys hung him up on the hook by his British Warm."

Roddy very kindly said what happened.

"Happened?" said Stoker. "Our fine gentleman was hung up there by his coat tails and of course they tore right off and down he come. It gave me quite a turn."

Roddy asked if he was hurt.

"Well, if he was he didn't know he was," said Stoker. "Same like Stoker, once he'd had a drink or two" at which Roddy laughed. Not unkindly, for he had a good heart and good manners, but it was generally known that Stoker was officially Mrs. by her own wish and had bought a silver gilt ring which she always wore on the third finger of her left hand. Whether there had ever been a Mr. Stoker no one knew, nor did anyone trouble about it, but his possible relict kept his ghost or simulacrum in reserve against the pressing attentions of the butcher, the station-master, and Mr. Brown of the garage.

Roddy Wicklow asked if anyone had seen his nephew Giles.

"Seed him and heared him," said Stoker. "There was I in the kitchen stuffing a chicken and my young gentleman comes in as bold as brass. Kissed me he did, the imperence."

"Well, it shows his good taste," said Roddy. "I'd kiss you for twopence myself, but I couldn't get my arms round you," which light badinage was very much in Stoker's line and she laughed till Roddy feared she might choke.

"He's gone down to Mr. Knox's," she said when she could speak. "You'll find him somewhere down the lane. He said could he have some elevenses because he was hungry. So I gave my lord a good slice of bread and dripping—not butcher's dripping, some I'd got off the Sunday joint—and off he went. Mrs. Morland's gone to the shops. You'll find her somewhere down the street," and back she went to her kitchen.

Roddy rode slowly on down the village street—though when we say village we should, alas! say almost town now—and presently saw Mrs. Morland coming out of the fish. When we say this, we do not mean that she was like Jonah, for nothing bigger than a grayling had ever been found in the upper reaches of the Rising—but any intelligent reader will have understood that The Fish was so to speak the purveyor of the same. Rather like depressed Irish plays by Fermanagh O'Donobhain (pronounced O'Donovan) where everyone is Mickeen the Meat, or Pegeen the Wash, and Father O'Flynn—may the blessed angels make his bed for him—the finest lepper in the Four Provinces bless his sowl; not of course to be confused with lepers.

Mrs. Morland saw Roddy and came across the street.

"I suppose you are looking for Giles," she said. "He came here about an hour ago to tell us how to run a Pony Club."

"I'm not surprised," said Roddy. "He always has to do things at once. As far as I know—and I taught him how to ride and groom his pony—he knows nothing at all about Pony Clubs."

"Nor does anyone here," said Mrs. Morland, "but it's a nice subject for conversation. If you want him, I think he is over at George Knox's. I'm going that way if you can make your horse walk."

Roddy said he would like to make it walk, for the pleasure of Mrs. Morland's company—unless, he added, she would like to ride pillion behind him.

"Like 'A farmer went trotting upon his grey mare,'" said Mrs.

Morland. "Did you have those Caldecott books when you were small?"

Roddy said indeed they did and he had very nobly given all his share to his sister Sally for her nursery and now as the Reward of Virtue he had got them back for his own family. He had particularly missed, he said, "The Frog he would a-wooing go," and the picture of Mr. Frog jumping out of the window with his opera hat to escape the cat and her kittens who came tumbling in.

"And the *lovely* one of As Froggie was crossing a silvery brook, A lily white duck came and gobbled him up," said Mrs. Morland. "Bless Randolph Caldecott for his pictures. I've got pretty well all the books, I'm glad to say, except Mrs. Mary Blaize."

"Well, look here, Mrs. Morland," said Roddy. "We've got two Mrs. Blaizes. I'll ask Alice about it. I'm sure she would like you to have one. I'm not much of a reader myself—when you're out all day you're glad to do nothing in the evening—in winter I mean—because I go out again as long as the light lasts if the weather is good."

"And what, pray, does Your Wife do?" said Mrs. Morland, suddenly turning on Man—the Common Enemy.

"If it's nice weather she comes out with me," said Roddy. "If it isn't she doesn't. The children are allowed to stay up for supper with us on Sundays now, for a treat."

Mrs. Morland said That was the thin end of the wedge and once they began that, they were grown up; and then you had grandchildren and had to start all over again.

Roddy said cheerfully that he would wait and see.

By now they had reached Low Rising Manor House. It still looked like the farmer's home which it had been for a couple of hundred years or more, but had been very comfortable inside with all mod: con:, electric power and light off the mains which had by now come right up the lane, and a large room made from the old farm kitchen and the room above it, knocked into one.

For a long time George Knox had insisted on oil lamps, but when he married for the second time his wife had insisted on electricity. George had sighed as a *laudator temporis acti* and obeyed as a husband, and rather to his annoyance found himself much more comfortable.

"We'll go in by the back way," said Roddy, who had dismounted and was holding his horse. "Knox has a sort of stable in the yard and that—probably—is where we shall find Giles."

So they went round the house, Roddy leading his horse, and there—to witness if he lied—in the old stable yard was Giles, holding forth to the cook, the housemaid, the chauffeur-gardener, and various children belonging to them. The other maid—who was more or less parlourmaid but helped in the house—was leaning out of a ground floor window with a duster in her hand.

"Hullo, Uncle Roddy," said Giles. "Oh! hullo Mrs. Morland. I say, I got over in half an hour. Pretty good, wasn't it?"

"And what about the pony?" said his uncle.

"The pony, Uncle Roddy? Oh, the *pony*," said Giles, looking more like a young saint in an Italian picture than his uncle could quite bear. "I found a nice place for him in Mr. Knox's cart-shed, and I gave him a bit of a rub-down and then Mr. Knox's gardener said he would look after him and get him some water, but not just at once," said Giles with a kind of earnest and priggish virtuousness that made his Uncle Roddy wish for a reasonable excuse to smack him.

But this was not the place to do it and the ladies would probably misunderstand it, so Roddy said nothing—which, we may say, frightened Giles far more than a scolding or a blustering would have done, and like Christian he felt inclined to flee from the wrath to come. But probably the Slough of Despond was still in front of him.

"I gather," said Roddy to Mrs. Morland, "that my nephew Giles has come over here to see if he can help with a pony club. He is a pretty good rider, but it takes more than that to organize a club and he isn't old enough. I don't want to interfere, but if you are seriously thinking of it, do let me know. It's not exactly my line, but probably I could help."

"If you ask *me*," said Mrs. Morland, "*no one* can help. I don't know where the idea started, but nearly everyone here is rather old or quite young. I don't know one end of a horse from another, broadly speaking, except that my father told me *never* to stand anywhere near the back end of a horse in case it kicked."

Roddy said, in a serious voice, That was perfectly correct.

"There are the two Vicarage girls of course," said Mrs. Morland, "but they don't ride—and when I say Girls, one goes on saying that for ever about people who used to be girls but haven't got married. My sons do ride sometimes but they don't live here and are all married men with families. I never did ride, because I didn't like it when I tried as a child. But I do know that if you give a horse a carrot or some sugar you must *always* put whatever you are giving it on the palm of your hand and hold your hand very flat, if you see what I mean, in case they bite your fingers off by mistake, like a circular saw."

Roddy Wicklow was a very sensible, hard-headed man, with years of experience in country ways, but Mrs. Morland's divagations were too much for him.

"I think" he said, "that we had better call the whole thing off, Giles!"

"Yes, Uncle Roddy," said his nephew.

"You have bitten off more than you can chew," said his uncle.

"Well, one does, you know, Uncle Roddy," said Giles with a cheerful smile. "But I've had a wizard time here. They were opening the sluices down on the river and a lot of stuff came through and there was a bit of the sheep that fell into the river higher up last month. It was absolutely *stinking*."

"My nephew seems to have made more of a fool of himself than usual, Mrs. Morland," said Roddy dispassionately. "And about this idea of a pony club—has anyone any *real* suggestions?"

"Well, probably not," said Mrs. Morland. "I don't know where it started except that there are a lot of people one doesn't know in the new part of the town."

Roddy said in a comfortable voice that the best thing she could do in that case was to forget about it.

"I practically have," said Mrs. Morland. "I wonder if you and Giles would like some lunch. I haven't had mine yet and my cook loves company."

But before Roddy could answer, George Knox himself walked into the yard, a stout but knobbly stick in one hand, the lower half of his respected legs sheathed in homespun knickerbockers and those gaiters that look as if they were made of canvas. His shoes were apparently part of an Alpine outfit, their soles studded with nails as big as those one sees on church doors. He was hatless, his now rather scanty locks ruffled by his walk.

"Well, George?" said Mrs. Morland.

"So might this courtyard have appeared when my home, my beloved house was building," said George Knox.

"I say, sir," said Giles, much attracted by George Knox's appearance and manner, "how could it build?"

"I am an old man, Laura," said George Knox. "Youth is to me a far-off enigma. What *does* that boy mean?"

"I mean, sir," said Giles, whose composure was very rarely ruffled, "you said the house was building. How did it build sir? Houses can't build themselves, not even those pre-fabs."

George Knox groaned.

"Soda-bicarb for you, George," said his wife, who had just come into the yard, and she exchanged a look with Mrs. Morland expressive of the Monstrous Idiocy of men.

"If it's hiccups, sir," said Giles, eager to help, "you drink some water out of the other side of a glass, sir. I mean you put your face right over it to the other side and have a drink only it mostly slops over."

"It is NOT the hiccups," said George Knox indignantly. "I repel the idea. I repeat: I repel it."

"Tautology, George," said Mrs. Morland. "What Mr. Knox meant," she added, addressing Giles, "is that he wasn't having the hiccups; he was only groaning."

Mrs. Knox, basely deserting her husband, said she couldn't think what he had to groan about.

"Look here, Mr. Wicklow," said Mrs. Morland, "you and Giles had better come and have some lunch with me. My cook always has plenty of food and she likes feeding men. You can put your horse up at the Rising Arms, good accommodation for man and beast. At least that's what they say and I don't think they would butter your horse's teeth or whatever it is people do to make horses not eat so much."

Roddy knew that he would lose what wits he had in a few moments and rapidly deciding that Mrs. Morland was a better bargain than George Knox (in which we think he was right) he said it was very kind of her and he was afraid he and Giles were an awful niusance.

"You aren't, Mr. Wicklow," said Mrs. Morland. "Giles is. But I have four of my own. Boys are an open book to me."

"And each page you turn pretty much the same as the last, Laura," said Mrs. Knox, who was on excellent terms with her husband's old friend.

"If you mean all my boys are alike, they are—broadly speaking," said Mrs. Morland. "I mean I send them all presents for their birthdays and Christmas and they write and thank me when their wives—who are all very nice indeed—tell them to. Otherwise I don't suppose I would ever know anything about them. I think birds do it so much better."

Roddy, who had a very straightforward mind, asked what it was that birds did better. They couldn't even walk, he added. At least one or two could and very silly they looked, but mostly they hopped.

Gile said they flew, too, but no one laughed or was in the least impressed and he rather wished he had held his tongue.

Mrs. Morland said to come along now, or the lunch will be

cold, on hearing which words Giles at once went to the shed and led the pony out.

"If you don't mind, Anne," said Mrs. Morland, "may we leave the pony here, because I haven't got a stable," but before Mrs. Knox could answer, Roddy said in his quiet authoritative way that if Mrs. Morland had no objection he could leave the pony with Mr. Brown at the garage who had a kind of stable where visitors could hire horses or ponies, only it was mostly used as a store-house for mangel-wurzels and bales of compressed hay.

"Of course that is *much* better," said Mrs. Morland, "because if we take the pony back with us it will be nearer," which piece of accurate reasoning silenced all her hearers.

"I know what, Uncle Roddy," said Giles. "If you walk with Mrs. Morland, I can ride back and take your horse with me."

"And I know what too," said Roddy, which is that you will not do either. You will walk with us and so will your pony; and my horse will walk with me. And you will go in front so that I can see if you do anything silly."

Giles's face, still with a childish roundness in it, assumed a non-co-operative expression.

"Or I will take the pony and we will leave you at the station to go back by train, if you like that better."

"Oh, all right, Uncle Roddy," said Giles, who knew when he was beaten, bore no malice, and meekly led his pony back up the lane, limping from time to time in a hopeful way, that his uncle might be the more convinced that he should be on the pony's back. But Roddy, though he observed the limp, was entirely unconvinced by it and conversed cheerfully with Mrs. Morland about her last book.

"I liked it *awfully*," he said, "and so did Alice. Her mother gave us her last book at Christmas, all about some of her old Italians she writes about. They're a bit high-brow for me," which last words he spoke with a kind of apologetic modesty.

"So they are for me," said Mrs. Morland. "They all seem to have been Cardinals who had illegitimate children. I suppose that was because they weren't married. I think it is much better if clergymen are married, only they needn't be *quite* as dull as Mr. Gould and his wife. They are *such* good people and their girls are doing very well."

By this time Roddy thought he might possibly be mad and hoped it didn't show. But as his manners were good and Mrs. Morland was not suspicious, we think it all passed muster; the more so as that worthy creature was, like Hamlet, in the habit of unpacking her heart with words, though never did she curse like a drab or a scullion, for her swearing vocabulary was very limited: not unlike the crew of the Hot Cross Bun whose strongest oath was a mild "Dear Me!"

The pony was duly left with Mr. Brown at the garage, which was a kind of gathering place for all the village, especially after school hours for the village children, as it included a black-smith's forge where horses were re-shod and small repairs could be done while you waited, or the day after tomorrow for certain, as that was a job as needed a power of thinking of. Mr. Brown, who was used to putting up horses for the few who still rode, said Giles's pony was a nice little piece and he would keep an eye on him till the little gentleman came back. Giles's soft face became sulky under the words "nice" and "little" whether ap-plied to himself or his pony, but as no one noticed his sulks he stopped almost at once.

At the garden gate Stoker was waiting for the Milk.

"It's that young Sid Brown," she said. "Carrying on with Mrs. Gould's girl, that's what makes him late," at which moment Sid Brown came up, pushing his milk cart.

"Late as usual, Sid," said Stoker. "Four pints. We've got company and the soup for tonight *and* tomorrow's breakfast as you can't get here till after nine now-a-days. Fine doings!"

"That's not my fault, Mrs. Stoker," said Sid. "Dad's gone to Blackpool for his holiday and mother lays in a bit in the morning while he's away, so I tidy the house up a bit for her; sweep round like and put the kettle on."

"I know your sweeping round," said Stoker darkly. "A lick and a promise and sweep the dirt into the corner. You couldn't eat your dinner off the floor in *your* kitchen."

"I dunno, Mrs. Stoker," said Sid, to whom this idea appeared new and worthy of consideration. "If I was to sit on the floor cross-legged-like, I could manage all right, I dessay, but mother wouldn't like it."

"Bone lazy, that's what she is," said Stoker. "I had an auntie— my father's auntie she was—never got up till it was time to get the dinner. She had a bone in her leg, she said."

Sid said Ar, he'd heard of that and the doctors couldn't do nothing for it and they did say it all went green like cooked spinach and flew to the stomach, to which Stoker replied that there was a cure for that.

Mrs. Morland, always interested in country remedies, though she had no belief in them, preferring Dr. Ford's prescriptions to Root of hemlock digg'd i' the dark or Eye of newt and toe of frog, asked Stoker what it was.

"Old Doc. Pep-U-Up's Elixir," she said. "It's only half-a-crown a bottle and it fair shakes you up. You try it, Mr. Wicklow. A tablespoon in a nice strong cup of tea and you'll not know yourself. You'd better have your lunch—it's all ready," so they all went into the dining room where Stoker had prepared a kind of meal suitable for men coming back from a morning's shooting.

"Have you read Nicholas Nickleby?" said Giles to the company in general, "and the Awful medicine Mr. Squeers gives the boys."

"Of course I have," said Mrs. Morland. "More than half a century ago, long before you were born."

"Do you mean like the Middle Ages?" said Giles, not meaning to be rude but, like Miss Rosa Dartle, wanting to know.

"I suppose so," said Mrs. Morland. "Only everything is going backwards now and we shall be in the Dark Ages soon."

"Do you mean Knights in armour and castles and jousting?" said Giles. "like Ivanhoe?"

Mrs. Morland, please to find Giles reading his Scott, said Yes rather like that, but she didn't think people would be in armour.

"It wouldn't be any use if they did," said Giles, "because their enemies would have Death Rays that could get through the Tower of London. I saw a wizard film about it. It was called The Hand of the Atom and whenever the Goodland people fought the Badland people they simply stayed at home and turned on the Ray and all the Badland people were killed in heaps."

"'A loathsome mass of liquid putrescence,'" said Mrs. Morland thoughtfully.

Roddy said How extremely unpleasant.

"Well, *I* didn't invent it," said Mrs. Morland. "It's an Edgar Allan Poe story about a man who is kept alive by mesmerism or something and when he dies he is still kept alive if you see what I mean."

Roddy said he didn't, but Giles's eyes glistened.

"Oh, *please* go on, Mrs. Morland," he said, "what happened next?"

"Well, they kept on keeping him mesmerised for ever so long," said Mrs. Morland, "and he didn't go bad like a real corpse."

Giles said he would love to see a Real corpse going bad.

"Horrid boy," said Mrs. Morland, without animus. "You wait. When they stopped mesmerising him, he stopped going on being alive and went bad at once and all melted away in a loathsome mass of liquid putrescence."

"Golly! I wish I'd been there!" said Giles. "I'd have made some notes for the Science Class. Mr. Hopper takes the Science Class and we call him Grasshopper," at which example of brilliant schoolboy wit he fell into giggles.

"Or Sandhopper, or Hipper Hopper," said Mrs. Morland.

"Oh, I say, Mrs. Morland, that's *wizard*," said Giles. "I'll tell all the boys. Do you mind if I pretend I invented it?"

"Not a bit," said Mrs. Morland. "In fact I'd like it. I give you Sandhopper and Hipper Hopper now; for ever. And there was

Old Mother Slipper Slopper too," at which Giles had the giggles till he nearly fell off his chair.

"Who was she?" he asked, when he could stop laughing.

"She lived in a cottage with her husband and kept geese," said Mrs. Morland, "and one night the fox came and stole her grey goose and the other geese made a frightful cackling—"

Giles interrupted to say the geese did that in Rome and saved the Capitol.

"Quite correct and fairly irrelevant," said Mrs. Morland judicially, and as Giles did not quite understand her he was quiet for a moment.

"Old Mother Slipper Slopper jumped out of bed,
She opened the window and popped out her head,
Oh husband, oh husband, the grey goose is dead
And the fox is away to his den, ee-oh!"

chanted Mrs. Morland.

"Is that all?" said Giles.

"Not quite," said Mrs. Morland, "but I can't remember it all, except that the fox took the goose home to his baby foxes and The little ones picked the bones, ee-oh."

"Oh, goody! goody!!" said Giles, rocking himself in an ecstasy on the hind legs of his chair. One of them gave way and he fell over backwards.

"Oh, I say, Mrs. Morland," he said, cheerfully picking himself up, "what a wizard chair. I'd like to see Mr. Hopper sitting on it and falling over. I bet he'd swear. He was in the navy in the war and learned some awfully good swears, but he put us on our honour not to use them."

"Breaking up the Happy Home, I s'pose," said Stoker, who had heard the noise. "I always knew that chair wasn't safe, not since Mr. Knox sat on it at Christmas."

"Well, you might have told me, Stoker," said Mrs. Morland.

"I expect Stoker wanted it to be a surprise for you," said Giles.

His uncle Roddy gave him an avuncular look and he subsided. "And now we will go home," said Roddy. "Thank you so much for giving us lunch Mrs. Morland. If you really begin to consider a pony club, let me know if I can help."

"That is *most* kind of you," said Mrs. Morland, "but I don't think we shall hear much more of it. It was just an Idea and when people get ideas into their heads you can't do much about it except give them their head."

Giles looked rather puzzled and began to giggle. His uncle Roddy, who had had quite enough of his nephew, gave him a look. Evidently it was as full of meaning as Lord Burleigh's nod, and Giles was silent. The horses—or rather the horse and the pony—were collected. They said good-bye and rode away. Mrs. Morland went back to the drawing-room and settled herself to work, with a rug round her respected legs and the gas fire on, because it was an English summer late afternoon and could not be treated lightly.

The ride home was pleasant. A train went over the railway bridge with a loud shriek and Giles's pony began to dance, but he explained to it with his knees and his hands that no one ever paid any attention to trains and they were stupid things that had to run along lines and never wandered into the country to see the lanes and the woods and fields, or to climb the downs; rather, in fact, burrowing under the downs, going through a dark smoky tunnel and coming out onto the viaduct over the Woolram valley. The pony thought poorly of such behaviour and settled down to a brisk trot with its comfortable bed-sitting-room in view and a well-earned supper and bed. Roddy did not talk. Not that he was annoyed with his nephew for breaking his hostess's chair, for that might happen to anyone who leaned over backwards and goodness knew one was always leaning backwards for something; but he was wondering—as he sometimes did—why Giles, an extremely nice boy who would do well and make friends wherever he went, should also have the gift of being far too pleased with himself even when he broke other people's chairs. Not deliberately—he must admit that—but by what Roddy called Silly-assing: and what was even more annoying had not even bumped an elbow or bruised himself. Where he got it from one couldn't say. Not from his tired, conscientious father; nor from his mother, Roddy's sister, who was the support of the whole family and Pomfret Towers itself. If only Ludo could have a thimbleful of that vitality sometimes. The boy needed more fun in his life. The Aubrey Clovers had helped him enormously it is true—thanks to those nice Mertons. And he began making plans for getting them over to Pomfret Towers again. His sister liked Lady Merton very much. Something must and should be done before Ludo next got leave; something that would take him among younger people. Then he laughed at himself, because after all Ludo was entirely among his own generation at Sandhurst—but that wasn't the same as being among one's own personal generation among the children of one's parents' friends.

By now they were on the Pomfret land and took the bridle path over the hill past the Obelisk, erected in 1760 by the third earl of Pomfret, who had caused to be inscribed on its base that the Goddess of Fortune had reft this Egyptian stone from *Dux Omnium* to bestow it upon *Comes Pontefractus* whose victories, not by the sword of Mars but by the peaceful dice, were here commemorated; ending with the appropriate tag *Alea jacta est*. After pausing to look over the landscape they went round the obelisk and so down into Golden Valley, a view of which Roddy never tired.

"I say, Uncle Roddy, when I was at Rushwater with the Leslies I climbed all over the roof and I climbed a bit of the way up the Temple. Can I climb up the Obelisk?" said Giles.

"No," said Roddy.

"I thought you'd say that, Uncle Roddy," said Giles. "Did you ever climb it?"

"I did not," said his uncle. "I am much too busy to climb up things and in any case I expect it is all rather crumbling now and

I'm not going to have you break your neck or even your arms and legs on it."

"But Uncle Roddy, I did get out of the attic window on the top floor—one of those rooms no one uses—and I got right over the roof," said Giles.

"I know you did," said Roddy quietly.

Giles, feeling more guilty than he liked, said How did Uncle Roddy know.

"For two reasons," said Roddy. "One was that Nurse happened to be upstairs in the attics looking to see if everything was in order, and she saw you. Some women would have called out or even screamed and then you would probably have fallen off and broken your neck—or been a cripple for life. The other was that I was up on the hill bird-watching and happened to look at the Towers through my binoculars. If I had had my gun with me I would have picked you off with the greatest pleasure, you young idiot. You'd have been a nasty mess if you had rolled down and dropped off the edge."

"But I *didn't*, Uncle Roddy," said Giles, with an angelic candour.

"No. Because Nurse hauled you in by the seat of your pants. And if you ever do it again I shall get you sent to the Hackney Road Reformatory School," said Roddy, quoting again as he was apt to do. He had said it half jokingly, but Giles took it seriously enough.

"Where is it?" he asked.

"If you ever opened a book except books about horses, Giles, you would know the *Bab Ballads*," said Roddy, rather sententiously, but he was determined to down his nephew, for his nephew's own good.

Giles asked what that was.

"Ignorant boy!" said Roddy, assuming very well the attitude of an unsympathetic form master. "The *Bab Ballads* are a lot of poems by a gentleman called Gilbert, who wrote all the words for The Pirates and H.M.S. Pinafore, to which your kind Uncle

Roddy took you last winter. You will find the book in your father's study. Read them—or some of them—they are part of a gentleman's education. The poem is called 'The Two Ogres.' And now let's think about your supper. I'm going home and I know your Aunt Alice has an extremely nice meal waiting for me. You can tell your dear parents that the pony club is OFF. It's a washout, a fizzle, a dud shell, and a good riddance. Listen Giles. It's no good trying to do *anything* with horses if you don't know them. Your father, who is one of the nicest and best people I know, never learnt horses when he was a boy, so he never knew them. Your mother who is a remarkable woman and I sometimes wonder how she came to be my sister, knows horses very well, but she doesn't ride much now, for two reasons. One, that your father doesn't enjoy it enough to ride with her. Two, that she is a busy woman and she works very, very hard for her family and the place and to make your father and all of you happy. Also horses cost rather a lot and need looking after. When you are a bit older and bigger I'll see if I can find a good horse for you— but not till you've stopped growing—and give it to you for a birthday present, but you'll have to look after it yourself in the holidays; food, water, grooming, exercise. Your pony's all right and you ride him well, but you'll soon be too heavy for him. Then we'll see. I'll come as far as the stables with you. I want to see Jasper if he is about."

Giles suddenly felt rather older and rather anxious about the responsibilities his uncle Roddy had spoken of and he let his pony go at its own pace, which was a good trot, for the pony knew its comfortable bachelor establishment was waiting for it.

The stable yard was empty, except for one of two of the house servants taking the air outside the kitchen. Among them Giles saw Jasper.

"Hullo, Jasper," he said, "are you still here?"

"Old Jasper knew Master Giles was a-coming back," said the gipsy. "The Romany chal knows when Master Giles is coming.

And I'll lay you sixpence that that there pony club you talked abut was just moonshine."

"Well it was in a way," said Giles who had dismounted and let the old gipsy take his pony. "I mean I think it would be rather fun, but I don't think the people at High Rising have much sense."

"I'll lay they haven't," said Jasper. "There's not one of them can handle a young colt, nor take the eggs out of the nest without so much as disturbing the hen."

"Can *you*, Jasper?" said Giles, almost awestruck.

"Can I, Master Giles?" said Jasper. "*You* ask a Romany chal if he can take a hen's eggs? You as I've taught what the Romanys know? Oh dear, oh dear, what's the world coming to? You come with me one night when there's no moon, Master Giles, and old Jasper'll show you what the gipsy can do."

It was obvious that for sixpence — or for pure schoolboy wish for adventure — Giles would do anything Jasper suggested. Not that the old gipsy would have led him into any serious mess and, even if he had he would have lied them both out of it. But Roddy had been listening.

"Not this year, Jasper," he said. "Giles isn't old enough for your jobs, you old sinner."

Jasper's otherwise immovable expression, looking into the unseen with the eyes of a Pharaoh (though his eye seen in profile was *not* a full-face eye as the makers of the Pyramids apparently conceived it) was shadowed for a moment—hardly more than the faint ripple made by a passing breeze on waters stilled at even. It flowed swiftly away and we doubt whether any eye less skilled in country lore than Roddy's would have noticed it. There was in it no grudge against Roddy, no wish to contravene his orders, but a withdrawing of himself into ancestral fastnesses. These were his own private property and into them Roddy had no wish to enquire; nor, we think, in spite of his long knowledge of the country, would he have got very far.

"I say, Jasper, do you drab baulo?" said Giles.

The gipsy looked at him and made a quick motion with one hand, but did not answer.

"Or can you tell my dukkerin?" said Giles.

Jasper's dark face, though he said nothing, was turned toward Giles as if listening to a strange tongue.

"Off you go," said Roddy to his nephew. Giles sighed as a horseman and obeyed as a nephew and disappeared into the house.

"You can take the pony to the stable," said Roddy to the old poacher. "And not so much nonsense to Giles. He's getting too old for Romany lils. He is a Gorgio. You can talk about horses to him, and when he is older and the pony isn't up to his weight perhaps you will sell him a horse."

Jasper knew when he was beaten.

"O.K., Mr. Wicklow," he said, suddenly altering his way of speech and almost his appearance. "Jasper will find a fine horse for Master Giles."

"Good," said Roddy. "And Lord Pomfret's estate agent will see that Jasper gets a fair price for it, and maybe a penny for luck."

"Old Jasper will find a horse," said the gipsy again, and with a kind of masonic salute he went away across the field and was lost in the trees on the far side. Then Roddy rode quietly home to Nutfield, thinking as he went how lucky he was to live in Barsetshire and to know some of the gipsies and the bodgers and horse-copers and be as well up to their ways and their tricks as he was, though he would have been the first to admit that there was still a good deal that he did not know and probably never would. Giles would know the gipsies all in good time. He didn't want his nephew to see too much of them at present, but when he was older he would find it not unhelpful to spend a few days with them now and again in the woods up above Gundric's Fossway and see the bodgers at work and learn a bit of practical forestry and even—but he must talk to his sister about that—the less sinister side of horse-coping; or in more attractive words, to be up to some people's tricks.

So he rode quietly home, in the chill late-afternoon light of an average English late-summer day, letting his horse canter over the grassland of the park, and so at a trot onto the road and over the bridge. Although he had ridden and walked that way for all his life, he hardly ever approached Nutfield from the south without being moved by the beauty of the stone bridge and the generous curve of the road up to the steep high street. On the right, just beyond the bridge, was the handsome red brick mid-Georgian house where his wife's parents the Bartons lived, on ground known for some two hundred years or so as Mellings, from which property the second title in the Pomfret family was taken. Then the road, taking a sharp turn, ran uphill into the town and on the left of the steep High Street were several good mid-Georgian red brick houses, one of which had belonged to Roddy's parents and now housed him and his wife who was Alice Barton and several nice children. The work of his wife's father, Mr. Barton the architect, is known in all the county and beyond. The writings of her mother, who had cornered, as it were, the more obscure bastards of various Popes and Cardinals, most of whom appeared to have lived on murdering or poisoning or, if they were too busy, imprisoning and starving all the relations they did not like, were very good sellers. The Bartons were generous to their son Guy, also an architect, now in partnership with his father, and their daughter Alice Wicklow, and altogether there was a good deal of very pleasant inter-family life.

We need hardly say that when Giles got indoors he at once sought out someone to whom he could boast of his outing to High Rising. His mother was not yet back from Barchester and the meeting of the Friends of Barchester Cathedral, so he decided very dashingly to have a bath, as a man ought to after a day's hunting—at least not exactly hunting, but riding over quite a lot of country and seeing the stinking remains of the sheep. So he went up to his bedroom, undressed, took his bath towel, and went to the bath-room. The door was open and out came Nurse who had been washing the family stockings and socks.

"Well, *that's* a nice way to behave," she said. "Go back to your room, Giles, and get your dressing-gown on at once."

"But I've got my bath towel round me," said Giles, who had hastily wrapped it about him in toga fashion when he heard Nurse coming.

"Never you mind about that," said Nurse. "Go and get your dressing-gown. I never did!"

Had it been his father, or even his mother, he could have borne it. Even from Ludo he could have stood it. But to think that after a day of freedom and being treated almost like a grown-up person by Mrs. Morland who wrote books and talking as an equal with Mr. Knox who wrote books and Mrs. Knox and all the servants at the Knoxes' and Mr. Brown at the garage—then to be bullied by Nurse was intolerable.

An inner Giles with whom he often silently communed and who represented his Ideal, said anyone of any spirit would tell Nurse to snap out of it; push her out of the way, lock the bathroom door (this being strictly forbidden by Nurse) on the inside, turn on both taps, let them run till the bath was full, and then get in and see how much water sloshed over. And if anyone thought that was bad behaviour, it wasn't; because Mr. Hopper the science master at school had told them all about how Archimedes or someone filled the bath right up to the top and then got in to see how much water would slosh over and found out about Specific Gravity. Though what Specific Gravity was neither he, nor any of the other boys, ever understood. And if our reader thinks this is improbable, we should like to state that it is founded on fact and an episode in our own far-off youth, when we had to do an essay on Specific Gravity and as we could never understand in the least what it was, we copied out a paragraph in our parents' *Encyclopaedia Britannica* of about 1890 and got full marks. Nor—as far as we know—did the science teacher spot the cribbing and for the first and only time in our scholastic life we got full marks for physics. How extremely agreeable it is to think that never can we be compelled to do physics again. And while we are on the subject of mathematics, may we say how much we preferred the Euclid of our younger days to the Geometry which took his place. Such phrases as "Let it be granted" and, even better, "Which is absurd," are part of our cultural background (as the slang of today runs) and will ever remain so.

But the fact remained that Nurse was still able to command and Giles had to obey, so he went back to his bedroom, put on his dressing-gown and went back again to the bath-room where he found Nurse.

"That's better," she said. "I've turned on your bath and that's enough water and you are not to run any more. Slopping all over the floor and who do you think is going to clear up the mess! Hurry up now. I'm going to get your suppers. Emily's waiting for you. She wants to tell you about the ferrets, nasty little things," with which unsympathetic words she went away.

At the word supper Giles cheered up, got into the bath carefully, soaped his hands and feet and neck, even going so far as to soap behind ears, after which he turned the hot tap on, wrapped a small towel round it and let the water trickle down into the bath so gently that Nurse would not hear it. Oh, heavenly bath, with boiling water coming gently in. How good was life, how full of pleasures, of promise, even of performance. Then he was a whale and wallowed like anything slopping the water all over the floor again. Of course Nurse had to come interfering at that moment with his pyjamas which he had of course forgotten.

"Giles, you *are* naughty," said Nurse. "Who do you think's going to clear up this mess?"

Giles meekly said he would, but Nurse obviously did not trust him and said to get out at *once* and dry himself properly and put his pyjamas on and she would come back in a few minutes. Luckily there was a small drain at the far end of the bath-room, specially put in for emergencies like this, and the water mostly ran away. Giles then wiped the floor partially dry with his towel, dried himself in a sketchy way on the bath mat, which luckily he had not put down on the floor, re-dressed in his clean pyjamas and went to the nursery. Then he and Emily had their supper and as Giles was nearly falling off his chair with sleepiness Nurse packed him off to bed. When his parents came home they went to look at their sleeping offspring.

"*Lucky* Giles," said his mother. Her husband made no answer, and we believe the thought in the mind of each was of their first-born and how difficult life—through no one's fault—was to him and how easy and plain for Giles. Ludo would be back for the holidays soon and they must think of what best to do for him. If only he wanted to go abroad with other young men—but he didn't. Perhaps something would turn up. Those nice Mertons were good friends for him. Oh, well!

CHAPTER 5

Giles now being safely back at school his parents were able to breathe again. Emily was at the Barchester High School as a weekly boarder, going in on Monday mornings with her father or Uncle Roddy if business took them there, or if not by the local bus and returning in the same way or ways. To her parents' combined relief and horror she was the perfect schoolgirl, quite good enough at her lessons, keen on games, in love (though in a most remote and Geoffroy Rudel-ish way) with a fresh mistress every term and next year would probably be a prefect with lower form girls struggling in their turn for her friendship. What would happen next her parents had not decided. Perhaps a year in a good finishing-school in Paris and then for the summer holidays they might all go to Italy, for they had among their other inheritances a villa just outside Florence. None of them liked it and they could not well afford to use it, so they let it every year to rich Americans and went themselves to the less known seaside places where they had Italian cousins and Lord Pomfret could be encouraged to be perfectly lazy and the children could be in and out of the sea all day with their Strelsa cousins who—with the exception of Count Guido who had been turned out of every gambling hell in Europe and was now very shaky, hairless, and toothless and in the charge of calm, competent nuns who did their duty by him, and otherwise, much to his impotent fury, ignored him completely—were almost more English than the English. As for Lord Mellings he appeared to be giving satisfaction at Sandhurst and would probably be making his own plans for part of the summer. If he could spare some time for his home, his mother meant to have a few parties for him.

Edith, whom we still find it difficult to remember to call Lady William Harcourt, had put off the baby's christening till the warmer weather. Being a very kind creature who liked to give pleasure, she asked her husband if he thought it would be all right to ask Mr. Oriel to perform the ceremony, in their own village church, because he was such a friend of his elder sister Gwendolen.

"Have we really settled the god-parents?" said Lord William, for owing to an epidemic of influenza a good many plans had to be changed and both Edith and the two grandmothers felt that though the idea of the Cathedral was attractive, East or West the village church was best.

"I think so," said Edith. "Gwendolen for your family and Sally Pomfret for mine—" and she stopped.

Her husband said So far so good, and what about a godfather. He would, he said, like to be a godfather himself and also conduct the service, but was afraid it wouldn't do.

"Well, I don't know what you'll think," said his wife, "but I thought it would be very nice to have one of my brothers. I am sure *one* of them could get leave."

This Lord William thought an excellent plan and asked which she would recommend.

"Well, James has his Majority now," said Edith, "and he thinks he will get promotion. A Colonel godfather would be rather impressive."

Lord William agreed, but said he must fix a date for the ceremony and couldn't very well make it depend on a contingent Colonelcy.

"I do love you when you talk like that," said his wife. "Shall I ask John? He's a Captain now. Or there's Robert—he's a full

Lieutenant now and simply *adores* Glamora Tudor that's on the movies. It's rather difficult."

Lord William agreed.

"I think perhaps Robert," said Edith, "because he is the youngest and can play with her," and as Lord William really didn't much mind which, he agreed. And in any case, he said, it depended on who could get leave. So they left it at that and Edith wrote to her brothers to ask their views.

As the baby of the family she had always been rather their pet, alternately spoilt or neglected according to what their interests of the moment were, and as they were all in England at the present time and rather proud of their sister, they all wanted to be godfathers, but this was not possible, nor would their commanding officer have accepted their point of view. It was finally settled, by dealing a pack of cards with one joker in it, which fell to Robert's share. His commanding officer was quite agreeable to his having a couple of nights' leave for so interesting an occasion and that was that.

There was of course a good deal of excitement about the ceremony. Lady Pomfret wrote very nicely to say how delighted she would be to stand godmother, but did not mention that it would mean the re-arranging on that day of her very full list of engagements in county work. As for Lady Gwendolen she was in a seventh heaven of delight; partly because her brother William was her favourite—as the youngest of a family often is—partly because her much-loved friend Mr. Oriel was going to perform the ceremony.

We cannot say that the village church was beautiful, or historic, because it wasn't. It was patronized by Saint John, designed by a pupil of Pugin, and had some very poor stained glass, so poor in fact as to be almost inoffensive. The Towers family had always been generous benefactors and had at various times bestowed on the church some good oil heating, a new carpet for the altar steps, and a special anti-burglar and sneak-thief alms-box for contributions from visitors. This had been made necessary by the disgraceful number of petty thefts from the old wooden box, attributed variously to The Boys and Trippers, but eventually found to be the last Village Idiot whose want of wits was only equalled by the skill of his untaught fingers. Given a hairpin, or a bit of copper wire he could open almost anything and enjoyed doing so very much and as he always related his deeds to anyone who would listen there was nothing underhand about them. Unfortunately he had successfully tried his hand on the little wall safe in the grocer's shop and had been quite kindly sentenced to a Home where he was encouraged to help with all repairs and adjustments to the electric washer, the electric cooker, the electric lawn-mower, and the electric light and was as happy as he could be except when the kitchen cat had kittens and some were drowned. But the cook took pity on him and next time there were kittens she said Pussy had only the one dear little kitten this time and wasn't it sweet and he could take care of it. And as it was by this time what is known in polite circles as Pussy-who's-been-to-the-doctor, there was no more trouble.

As is so often the case, the congregation would be mostly female. Lord William of course would be there, and the Duke. Lord Pomfret could not come, but his wife would be there and the Dean and Mrs. Crawley who were old friends.

We need hardly say that the Duchess of Towers had ordered from New York by air the most lovely, elegant, coquettish christening robe that money could buy, and by so doing made things easier for Edith, for the Dowager had offered her own old christening gowns which had indeed once been lovely but now had spots of ironmould and a number of exquisite darns. She had had it washed, very carefully, in the finest soap and rain-water, but it had come to the term of its natural life and gently disintegrated. So Edith said How dreadful and *how* sorry she was and the Dowager, most generously, took the American nylon gown to her heart and said it would be an heirloom.

Of course the heroine of the day was not Edith and not even

the baby, but Lady Graham who, as she always unconsciously did, became the hostess and did it extremely well. It was Edith's house and her party, but Edith was too dazedly happy to do much about it, and was quite content for her mother to take command.

Lady Gwendolen had gone over to Harefield to fetch Mr. Oriel, for which he was very grateful, for not only did he enjoy her company but her car was more comfortable than his and she was an excellent driver, which he wasn't, being well-known for taking wrong turnings or going round in a circle and being vastly surprised to find himself back at his starting-point. But always a very careful driver, which drove other motorists nearly mad, as he did a steady ten miles an hour on the crown of the road in narrow lanes where there was not even room to pull into the hedge or the ditch. And if anywhere in the district cows or sheep were being driven to or from the farm or market, Mr. Oriel was fatally certain to block the way, whether they were going or coming.

Then Lieutenant Robert Graham roared up in a small uncomfortable racing car that was the joy of his life and had several times almost caused him to be drummed out of the army by its horrible noise. He was received with joy by his mother and sister, and went straight upstairs to see the baby, by whose smallness and softness and peacefulness he was considerably impressed and when Sister Chiffinch graciously invited him to kiss her tiny star-fish hand he was almost moved to tears and Sister Chiffinch sent him downstairs again.

There was a moment of anxiety for the godmothers, but Lady Pomfret had never yet failed to keep an engagement and came in with her usual calm efficient air, accompanied by Mrs. Crawley who had been lunching with her, and said the Dean hoped to get over later.

The telephone rang. Lord William—feeling certain that it was the Bishop trying to interfere or forbid the banns, so to speak—answered it. But it was a long-distance call from the

Duchess's cousin Lee Sumter to wish them all good luck for the christening and say he had been over in San Francisco and had only just got the news and was sending a little present for the baby by air. He then rang off, much to the relief of everyone present, including his cousin, and everyone said how charming of him.

Next Lady Gwendolen arrived with Mr. Oriel who brought for the baby a very delicate gold chain with a small pearl heart hanging from it and everyone felt sentimental with no particular reason. Mr. Oriel was absorbed as it were by Lord William and they went away to the church.

Then Sister Chiffinch came down, resplendent in her flowered voile and her halo hat, carrying Miss Harcourt, who very sensibly was fast asleep and determined to remain so. The company hushed their voices, but such is the sleep of babies that this was hardly necessary. Lady Graham of course became Chef de Protocol, marshalled the party, and took them away to the church, leaving the principals to follow, which they shortly did.

It is not everyone who can really handle babies. The Dean was perhaps the best baby-handler in West Barsetshire, having had plenty of practice on his own family, let alone his grandchildren and the descendants of many of his friends, and enjoyed explaining to young parents, with the aid of a sofa cushion, exactly how you should hold them to the best advantage. It was recognised all over the county that he was past master in the art; and after he had carried the twin girls of Mrs. Robin Dale, she who was Anne Fielding the Chancellor's daughter, one on each arm and both had at first slept peacefully and then woken to explain to him with a few melodious flutings how much they had enjoyed and appreciated the experience of being christened, his supremacy was unquestioned. But Mr. Oriel was almost his equal and everyone was pleased, especially Lady Gwendolen.

Lord William, while living in the Close, had also studied the art and it was generally agreed by such authorities as Dr. Ford, Sister Chiffinch, and old Nanny Allen at Philip Winter's school in Harefield, that he was still young, but he knew more about babies than most.

Mr. Oriel was waiting for them at the church, in charge of the Duke. The arrival of the christening party interrupted their interesting discussion of the cathedral sub-organist's holiday at Monte Carlo about which no one knew anything and everyone had something to say. But as he had stayed at the Pensione Smith kept by the widow of an English retired bank clerk, and had outstayed his leave by thirty-six hours, for which he blamed the Italian trains and his friends said "Oh, yes," we cannot believe that there was any substance for the rumours in the Close, and next year he went to Holland, to the great disappointment of the gossips, who then discarded him as useless.

The short and beautiful order of baptism was well spoken by Mr. Oriel while Miss Harcourt, duly presented by her godmothers and godfather, slept soundly. Then he took her quietly up the chancel steps in the cradle of his arm and held her before the altar, where she opened her eyes and uttered a few melodious noises which evidently meant that she was delighted and edified by the ceremony and most grateful to Mr. Oriel; after which she sank again into that deep peaceful sleep, past the plunge of plummet, which never again shall we know till we come to our final sleeping. Several of the ladies present were wiping their eyes and one or two of the men coughed.

Then they all came out from God's blessing into the warm sun, and walked back, with Sister Chiffinch as the centre of attraction holding the soft, peaceful form of Miss Gwendolen Sally Harcourt, her young godfather walking proudly, not to say conceitedly, beside her.

"I think, Lady William," said Sister Chiffinch when they got to the house, "the Baby had better go upstairs for a little rest. She has had quite an exciting afternoon."

This statement seemed slightly exaggerated to Edith, as her daughter had slept solidly through most of the ceremony, woken for a few seconds to salute the altar and at once fallen into sleep again. But this was no time to bandy words and she smiled a Yes to Sister Chiffinch and went back to her party.

As may be imagined, so many quiet, well-bred people in Edith's little drawing-room made a quite unconscionable amount of noise; Lieutenant Robert Graham, rather puffed up by his new godfathership, not being the least noisy. By great good luck the Duchess descended on him and what with her charm and her pretty soft Southern voice he was completely overcome by adoration. It was not the first time he had fallen in love but this—as it had been every time—was the Real Thing. The Duchess, who in her own land had taken adoration for granted as the attitude of young men, was delighted by her new conquest and informed Robert that he was her latest beau and she thought him just too cute for words.

Robert, who had a strong suspicion that the Duchess was putting over an American act for his benefit, said Everyone was peaches down in Georgia, but she was the peach Melba, which echo of a charming popular song combined with his unblushing flattery made her laugh so much that he laughed too.

"I say, Duchess," he said. "If you come to London sometimes, will you do a theatre with me? I'm at St. James's Palace just now," which not unnaturally impressed her.

The Duchess said he was too kind for words and she would just love to go to a theatre.

"What would you like to see?" said Lieutenant Robert Graham very dashingly.

The Duchess said she did just frightfully want to see *I Gonna Make You Love Me* with Chat Huckaback and Eliodora Hands because she had missed it in New York, but she believed it was terribly booked up ahead.

"You leave it to the Guards, Duchess," said Robert, feeling more dashing every moment. "Tell me what days you'll be up and I'll get the tickets. A fellow always can, you know, if he knows the ropes."

The Duchess said she would be at the Savoy Hotel for a week

or ten days next month and the simplest thing would be for her to call the Savoy and tell them to get tickets.

"Oh, it's most awfully kind of you," said Robert, going rather pink, "but I meant it to be *my* treat to *you*."

The Duchess said it was so sweet of him, but it would save a lot of trouble if she got the tickets because she knew he must be very busy, and she hoped Lee Sumter would be over by then and they would make him give them supper somewhere after the show. All which was so kindly and charmingly put that Robert could not but thank her and say yes. His good English breeding told him that if a gentleman suggests a treat to a lady of course he pays: on the other hand it would be almost rude to argue with so kind and delightful a woman. But he would send her some very expensive flowers.

"I say, Duchess," he said, "if a fellow gives a girl—I mean a lady—some flowers to wear, would that be all right?"

"*Well*, Robert Graham," said the Duchess amused, "I should say it would."

"It would be right to say a corsage, wouldn't it?" said Robert, accentuating the last syllable heavily.

"Absolutely right," said the Duchess. "I'm just longing for you to meet Lee—you will be such friends," and the extraordinary thing was—at least to Robert—that instead of feeling at once that this Lee Sumter—a mere cousin forsooth—must be a stuck-up bore, he felt he would be a very good sort of fellow. In which, we may say, he was perfectly right.

At this moment the Dean came in with apologies for being late. It was, he said, entirely the fault of the Palace.

The Duchess, who was well up in Close politics, asked what the Bishop's wife had done *this* time.

Dr. Crawley said it was not the Bishop's wife, but the Bishop himself. His Lordship, said the Dean, making the word sound as if it were not a word one liked to mention before ladies, had taken upon himself—doubtless at the instigation of higher powers—(by which most of his hearers knew that they were the

Bishopess, while the Duchess said to Lady Pomfret that she just loves these old English ways)—to tell Canon Fewling that he ought to lop the large acacia tree in his front garden because it was becoming a public danger. Which, said the Dean, was entirely untrue, for he had been to see Canon Fewling that morning, who told him that he had had it examined by the Barsetshire Society of Tree-Lovers when he moved in, and they had found it in perfect condition except for a few pieces of dead wood which Canon Fewling had caused to be taken off during the winter, and that had unfortunately detained him; at which point he had to pause to take breath.

"I cannot but think," said Mr. Oriel, "that his Lordship's intromissions are perhaps ill-placed."

"There was that *dreadful* time," said Edith, "when the Bishop took the bell away. You remember, mother."

"Do I?" said Lady Graham, who obviously didn't.

"Oh, you *must*, mother," said Edith. "It was the Palace garden party the year Lord Silverbridge got engaged to Isabel Dale and there used to be a bell hooked into the side of the pond in the Palace garden and the fish used to push it and make it ring when they wanted crumbs and the Bishopess had it taken away because she said it was waste of bread and Tomkins—that was the old gardener—rescued it from the rubbish heap and James gave it a polish and the boys hung it up again and we threw crumbs in and the fish rang the bell. And then I made a poem about it."

"I am sure it was a lovely poem," said her mother. "Could you say it to us?"

"Well, I don't think I quite could," said Edith, "because it was very satirical. But I'll tell it to William and he can tell you if he likes it. The last verse was about how James hung the bell up again and the end was '—So that the fishes quickly flew, To ring their old beloved bell, And now the bishop is in—' but at this point her mother, suddenly remembering what was coming, gave her daughter such a motherly look that she was silenced. So was the audience, though deeply appreciative.

"But that was when I was young," said Edith, which made everyone including her husband laugh.

Sister Chiffinch, back in her uniform which was so much more becoming than her civilian clothes, now joined the party. Lady Graham took her to a sofa near the window that they might the better discuss the baby and her future.

"I don't know if you have found a Nanny yet, Lady Graham," said Sister Chiffinch, "but if you haven't I think I know just what you want. Ellen Humble her name is; she's niece to Mrs. Belton's housekeeper Wheeler over at Harefield and she took Mrs. Robin Dale's twin girls after the first month, that is Miss Anne Fielding that was, and she has been in one other place and given great satisfaction, but she wants to be with a new baby again. She is at Harefield just now."

Lady Graham said it sounded exactly what they needed, and could she see the girl. Sister Chiffinch, delighted to help, said should she write to Ellen and tell her to come over by the bus and see Lady Graham.

"Yes, do," said Lady Graham. "If she comes to Barchester I will meet her at the bus station and bring her out here so that she can see the baby and I can easily run her back to Harefield, or else Lady Gwendolen will, as she often goes over to see Mr. Oriel and knows the road better than I do. Perhaps Mr. Oriel knows her. I will ask him and I am most grateful to you, Sister What a day it has been."

Sister Chiffinch said it was indeed quite an occasion.

Robert Graham had been hanging about, waiting for a favourable moment to speak.

"What is it, darling?" said his mother.

"What are we going to call her?" he said. "Gwendolen's awfully long, besides one would get mixed up with Lady Gwendolen. And you couldn't say Gwen. It's not lovely enough for her."

His mother suggested Sally, as that was her second name, but he frowned and said it would be too confusing with Lady Pomfret.

"Well, why not ask Mr. Oriel?" said Lady Graham, rather basely laying her burden on someone else.

Robert thanked her politely and went across the room to where Mr. Oriel was being talked to by some of the guests.

Forcing his way to the front, Robert said: "Sir!" with a fairly accurate imitation of his sergeant-major.

Mr. Oriel, with his usual courtesy, asked who he was.

"Well, sir, you do really know me, because I'm Robert Graham, sir. My father's Sir Robert Graham," said Robert.

"And your grandmother was that delightful Lady Emily Leslie," said Mr. Oriel who, partly by virtue of his Barsetshire blood and partly by a passion for genealogies and families, knew pretty well the cousinships and other relationships of most of the county. "She was one of the loveliest and kindest people I have ever known. I hope the baby may be like her. You are the baby's uncle of course."

"Yes, sir," said Robert. "That's why I wanted to ask you what would be a good name to call her."

Mr. Oriel, slightly perplexed, said she had been given two baptismal names.

"Yes—but, *sir*," said Robert, "she couldn't be Gwendolen because it's much too long for her yet. And if she is called Sally it might be confused with Lady Pomfret."

Mr. Oriel, feeling slightly confused himself, said he quite saw what Robert meant.

"And I don't think Gwen is very good," said Robert.

Mr. Oriel, in spite of his long experience as a pastor, was rather nonplussed by Robert's attitude. But feeling that attack is the best defence, he suggested that Robert should ask Lady Gwendolen herself. Robert thanked him and gently wormed his way into a group near the window.

"Hullo, here is the uncle!" said the Duke kindly. "What does it feel like?"

Robert, who had seen the duke several times but never spoken with him, was suddenly overcome by shyness—a feeling to which he was as much a stranger as was possible to him.

"Oh, it's all right, sir, I mean Your Grace," he said. "I mean it makes you feel a bit old to be a godfather. I've been an uncle for a long time because of Clarissa and Emmy—my elder sisters. But I've never been a godfather before."

"You did it very well," said the Duke. "And Sir is quite adequate. Or you could say just Duke."

"Thank you, sir," said Robert. "When you know the drill it's all right."

"You did your part *very* well," said Lady Gwendolen. "Mr. Oriel was asking who you were. He said you moved and spoke just in the right way."

Robert, not without a small feeling of elation, said very simply that once a fellow knew the drill everything should be all right and he had got the padre at the barracks to run through it with him.

"I rather wondered what we shall call the baby," he said. "I mean Gwendolen and Sally are awfully nice names, but Gwendolen's a bit long. I don't mean for you, but for her," which made Lady Gwendolen laugh.

"One could say Gwen of course," she said. "I never much cared for my name, but one has to be called something. Do you think Sally would be better?"

Robert, the cares of avuncular godfatherhood weighing heavily on him, said it might seem a bit unkind to Lady Gwendolen.

"I wouldn't mind a bit, whatever you choose," she said. "I never liked my own name much. But I expect as soon as Miss Harcourt can talk at all she will invent a name for herself. When I was a little girl I called myself Glubby and no one ever knew why and I don't either. Sally isn't a bad name, either. We could do with a Sally in the family."

"She is the darling of my heart and lives in our family," said, or rather chanted Robert in a soft voice, which caused Lady Gwendolen to have what, at even her age, might be called the giggles and say: "I'm so glad to know you, Robert."

"I say, Lady Gwendolen," said Robert, "do you ever come to London?"

Lady Gwendolen said not often, because there was so much to do at home, but sometimes she went up to her club, the Octopus, for a few nights to see her dentist and go to a play.

"Well, if you do come up, could you let me know?" said Robert. "We might do a show."

We think it was a good many years since Lady Gwendolen had been invited to any such treat, and certainly not by so young a cavalier. But breeding tells and with the swiftness of that strange unexplored machine, our mind, she decided that to refuse might look like a snub. Also the idea of such an excursion was exciting. So she said it sounded great fun. And at that same moment a Great Idea was born in Robert. If the Duchess and her American Cousin were going to a play, as his guests, why not ask Lady Gwendolen and make it four. There might be a spot of bother with the Duchess who was going to get the tickets, but—dash it all—a man had his pay and a generous allowance from his father, so why not give Lady Gwendolen a treat as well and tell the Duchess he was jolly well going to pay for the tickets himself. Four was always better than three. The old bank balance would just run to it, especially if Bobby Skipper repaid him the ten pounds he had borrowed. Anyway she was awfully nice and deserved a treat.

Whether the champagne which had been drunk to Miss Harcourt's health had made him bold, rather like Lady Macbeth, we cannot say. The die had been cast. But as we do not go to London, preferring the milder air of Barsetshire, we shall not be able to give any particular description of this party and can only assure our reader that it will take place in due time and be a great success. But not in these pages.

"This is indeed a pleasure, Harcourt," said the Dean, who had not been able to attend the service but had come over to show goodwill and had hardly had a chance to speak to Lord William. "We miss you in the Close, but you are doing good work here."

"That is kind of you, Dr. Crawley," said Lord William. "I was very happy in Barchester and I hope I gave satisfaction."

"If the disapproval of the Palace is any criterion, you have Alpha plus," said the Dean. "The Power behind the Throne thought very poorly of your taking this living. But I must not trouble you with such petty affairs," which was of course a frightful lie, for the Dean wanted nothing more than to unburden himself of some good anti-Palace gossip. Nor was Lord William averse to listening.

"Do go on, Dean," he said.

"She—or rather I should say the *Éminence grise*," the Dean began, rather pleased with his own wit—

"What a *perfect* description," said Lord William. "I apologize for interrupting you, but I didn't get it at first. I did hear gossip about it, but I never knew she really looked on the wine when it was red. All she gave us at their dinners was a glass of cheap sherry and some vegetarian cider with our meal. For vegetarian, read nonalcoholic."

The Dean was for a second a little puzzled by the apparent irrelevance of Lord William's remark, but suddenly saw light and began to laugh, and both gentlemen made such a noise that several people looked round. But it was only two clergymen talking, so the other people returned to their own noises.

Then Lady Pomfret said she must go as she had a Committee in Barchester and could she give anyone a lift. Two dull elderly cousins of Lord William said they would be most grateful and the party gradually dispersed, till only the family remained and Mr. Oriel who was quietly waiting for Lady Gwendolen's orders.

"I do *hope* you aren't tired," she said and he assured her that to have the privilege of taking her niece to the altar was on the contrary most uplifting and then wondered if he had said what he didn't mean, but Lady Gwendolen did not notice the possible ambiguity and said it had been the loveliest christening she had ever seen and would he like to go now.

Mr. Oriel said if it was convenient to her he would, as he got rather tired when there were a lot of people; which caused Lady Gwendolen to have some splendid heart-searchings in that she had not given more attention to her chosen pastor, and she said the car was outside if he was ready. So after saying good-bye to the Harcourts he took his leave together with Lady Gwendolen. Gradually the room emptied. Edith had gone upstairs to see if her precious baby was surviving the excitement and found her—her normal state—fast asleep in her cot, in a warm nest of peace. Edith leaned over her and very gently kissed her cheek.

"Gossamer jelly," she remarked aloud to herself with the satisfaction of one who has found the *mot juste*, and being rather tired she lay down on Sister Chiffinch's bed, just for a few moments. But nature demanded more and she was asleep almost at once.

Meanwhile the party had gently melted away and only a few relations were left. The Duchess and Lady Graham were having a delightful talk about Victoria Lady Norton and how dreadful she was and what chance there was of dropping her from the Women's Institute committee. The Dowager and Lady Elaine had gone back with the Duke. The Crawleys also had gone and the few remaining guests were saying good-bye. Then a blissful silence fell, only broken by Lady Graham who heard a clock strike and exclaimed aloud at the lateness of the hour.

"I *must* get home," she said. "My husband will want to hear *all* about it when he comes back. He was so terribly sorry he couldn't be here today but he is abroad on one of those missions. He thinks very highly of dear William," which was a Noble Lie, for though Sir Robert Graham liked Lord William and thought Edith had done well for herself, his mind was now otherwise occupied with his politico-military duties.

The Duchess said she was all for men having plenty to do, but they must be able to give some time to the home and her husband seemed to have a fresh committee at least twelve times in the year.

"They like it, you know," said Lady Graham. "It is so much easier for them at their club because the water is always really hot and though the food might be better at The Club, they can be as boring as they like. Do you know Rushwater where my people lived? My nephew Martin is there now and runs the estate splendidly in spite of his foot."

The Duchess asked sympathetically what was wrong with the foot.

"Oh nothing *wrong*," said Lady Graham. "In fact one is perfectly all right, but he lost the other one in Italy, and he tried several artificial feet but they were so uncomfortable that he only puts his foot on for church, or a funeral, and then takes it off again. He is quite *wonderful* with a kind of special crutch, and rides, and drives a car but of course he can't climb any longer, poor darling."

The Duchess said—quite truthfully—that she was very sorry for him.

"How *very* understanding of you," said Lady Graham. "I should love to bring him to see The Towers and perhaps you would let him have tea with you. He can manage a tea-cup perfectly," which words, spoken with aunty love, made the Duchess nearly have the giggles.

"I know," said Lady Graham, pursuing her own train of thought, "that one does not need an extra leg to manage a tea-cup, but he tells me that it does alter one's balance when one leg is real and the other has to be strapped on, and frightfully expensive because you have to have two—one to wash the other as our old nurse used to say about our bathing towels when we went to the sea. I mean two *artificial* legs."

The Duchess, though her brain was reeling, kept her sang-froid and said Of course she would simply love to have Lady

Graham's nephew over for lunch or tea, or whenever he liked; and perhaps he would like to go round the estate. If so, she said, her husband would take him in the estate lorry if he didn't mind it being rather uncomfortable, but the driver would give him a leg up into it over the back.

"At least, I don't mean that," said the Duchess, for the first time in anyone's knowledge showing slight confusion, "I mean—" and she stopped.

"I know *exactly* what you mean," said Lady Graham. "But Martin can get into *anything* if there is an old box he could stand on first, to make a step, and then someone *in* the lorry who could take his hand very firmly and then Martin could put his other hand on the edge of the lorry and get his good leg over and then perhaps your man could help him to get his other leg over."

"Of course," said the Duchess. "But, I was thinking, would it be easier if we let the tailboard down and ran your nephew up it in the old invalid chair. We did that when one of the pigs would *not* go up."

This Lady Graham felt to be an excellent plan provided Martin's pride did not suddenly revolt.

"He can revolt as much as he likes," said the Duchess, her Confederate blood rising, "but if he wants to see the place it's the only way. Unless of course he could ride. We've got a horse or two."

Lady Graham said Martin did ride, but it was tiring for him and the remains of his leg nearly always hurt him afterwards and the lorry would be just the right thing.

As both ladies had now said practically everything they could say, Lady Graham went upstairs once more. Sister Chiffinch was sitting in her own room with the door open like a benevolent spider and got up when she saw Lady Graham.

"I expect you would like a peep at Our Baby," said Sister Chiffinch. "She is having her supper," and she took Lady Graham into what would now be the nursery, where Edith was sitting in a low chair, her baby in her arms, while the said baby imbibed from nature's fount with quite horrible greed. Her face became bright red, her few dark hairs were dank with perspiration, one starfish hand was clenched on a bit of her nightgown—which was just for the present her *robe de chambre* and *robe de ceremonie* as well—while the other was warmly tucked away between her and her mother.

"That's enough for a moment, Sally," said Sister Chiffinch, gently detaching Miss Harcourt. "Let's get the wind up, shall we?" And she patted Miss Harcourt on the back. When she was satisfied she put the baby back on her mother's lap again, where she at once began to appease the pangs of starvation.

"She *is* greedy," said her adoring grandmother.

"Little pig!" said her even more adoring mother. "And then she'll sick half of it up. Won't you my sweet idiot angel?" but Miss Harcourt, even had she understood, could not possibly have answered for she was victualling herself as far as her adoring grandmother could make out for a six weeks' siege at least.

"That's enough now," said Sister Chiffinch, gently and firmly removing the baby. "Would you like to take her for a minute, Lady Graham, while I just tidy Lady William?"

So Lady Graham took Miss Sally in her arms and thought how much nicer all her grandchildren were than anyone else's grandchildren. Then Sister Chiffinch put the baby back in her cot and covered her lightly, for the day in spite of being summer was almost warm and the evening sun was shining outside.

Lady Graham thanked Sister Chiffinch for the treat and went downstairs. In the hall was her son-in-law.

"How beautifully it all went, dear William," she said. "I have just been upstairs with Edith and Sally."

"Oh!—baby, you mean," said her father. "Is she all right?"

"Of course she is," said his mother-in-law, "and so is Edith. She will be down in a moment. And Sister Chiffinch says she must go to bed *early*."

"'The Monstrous Regiment of Women,'" said the happy

father aloud to himself, but his mother-in-law paid no attention to him, nor would she have taken his allusion.

We think that the christening of Miss Gwendolen Sally will long be remembered in the village. There was not exactly a roasted Manningtree ox with a pudding in his belly, but the Dowager and her daughters had organized a tea for the village children on the following day to celebrate the occasion, to take place in the little church hall at five o'clock so that the children wouldn't need any supper that evening and the mothers could have one evening's freedom. The Dowager with Lady Graham and the ladies Gwendolen and Elaine and Mr. Oriel went across to visit the feast. The W.V.S. had volunteered to look after the tables, and when possible suppress greed and cheating. The Harcourt Arms had contributed a large tea-urn and the Duchess an enormous cake covered with white icing and pink sugar roses and a little gilded wooden angel standing on the top of it.

The scene was—as all who had organized treats for the dear little kiddies will know—rather like the morning after the night before, or the storming of Badajoz, or the sack of Troy. The dear little ones had arrived punctually and, owing to the efforts of their mothers, clean. Within a quarter of an hour they were yelling, pushing, snatching, chocolate-bedaubed, tea-spilling, and in general Nature red in tooth and claw.

The ladies were used to these scenes of violence. Mr. Oriel in whose cure of souls there were not many children—for Harefield was rather a middle-aged town and the young marrieds tended to leave it for brighter scenes—was not only grieved by their lack of manners but literally frightened. One of the young scholars pointing a sticky finger at him asked in a loud voice where the body was. On being pounded on and cross-questioned he said It was the man as took Auntie Mabel away in the box, his innocent mind evidently confusing him with the undertaker. Those who knew better then displayed extreme and unctuous snobbishness, announcing in loud voices that a proper clergyman had a proper collar as did up behind, thus putting Mr. Oriel's neat collar with a little stiff white bow tie to shame. Lady Gwendolen could not bear it.

"That's enough, children," she said. "One more word and there won't be any chocolates after Sunday School. Mr. Oriel wears a very nice collar and it's no business of yours. Sammy Rogers, it's no use pretending. I saw you put a slice of cake in your pocket. Take it out at once and give it to Gary Bunce. And if Gloria Panter can't stop giggling she can go home *now*. Have any of you girls and boys got a baby at home?"

A Babel of voices said there was Winston and Odeena and Glamora and several more whose names could not be heard.

"Very well, then," said Lady Gwendolen. "What would you think if *your* baby grew up as silly as Gary or Gloria? They will if you can't behave nicely."

To anyone who tries to analyse this philippic it will be obvious that it had, broadly speaking, no meaning at all, but somehow it impressed the children. Partly because there was still a faintly feudal feeling about the Towers, partly because the names of well-known film stars were so sacred that to hear the word silly used in conjunction with them was almost shocking. The children applied themselves to eating again and were temporarily silent.

"We cannot thank you enough, Lady Gwendolen, for your well-timed words," said Mr. Oriel. "It has done the trick, if I may so express myself. I have enjoyed this occasion deeply— most deeply. It is indeed a privilege to be allowed to welcome a baby into its heavenly heritage."

"That is exactly what I felt while you were saying those beautiful words," said Lady Gwendolen. "And—to turn to other matters for a moment—will you let me know when you wish to go home? My car is waiting outside our house—I mean my mother's house."

"I cannot think," said Mr. Oriel, "that the word 'our' is misused. You have a wonderful gift for sharing the good things that come to you, and to share with a beloved parent is indeed a privilege. My parents, alas, have been gone from me for many years, but I think of them often. They would have taken such pleasure in knowing you, Lady Gwendolen."

"And I know I should have liked them so much," said Lady Gwendolen. "It must be sad to lose both parents. I am lucky to have my mother. Though sometimes," she added rather nervously, "I would like to do some things on my own. I mean little things like paying visits, or doing the flowers in the drawing-room. Elaine always does them. She has such a gift for arranging them. They are so lovely. I should love to do it myself sometimes."

"I agree with you," said Mr. Oriel. "My dear mother always called arranging the flowers Doing Her Homework. We both used to laugh about it. One day when you are free and can drive over to Harefield as you sometimes so kindly do, would you give me a little advice on decorating our church? As you know, it is a not unpleasing edifice."

Lady Gwendolen said it was quite the loveliest church in West Barsetshire and she believed it was part of the Harefield Abbey which had been built when the wool trade was at the height of its prosperity.

Mr. Oriel said that unfortunately all its records had been destroyed by the Puritans during the Civil War, as was the glass; and that was why they only had those eighteenth-century painted windows—doubtless of great merit, but he could not feel that King George II dressed as Mars in a wig and attended by Commerce, Prosperity, Lord Chatham, and Britannia were quite suitable in a sacred building.

"But, dear Mr. Oriel, we have to be all things to all men, don't we?" said Lady Gwendolen. "But perhaps not in *art*, of course."

Even Mr. Oriel's trained scholarly mind could not quite grapple with this, though he felt that Lady Gwendolen somehow had the root of the matter in her. She said good-bye to Lady Graham, told her Dowager Mother that she was just going to run Mr. Oriel home and went out to her car, where Mr. Oriel was waiting.

The drive back to Harefield was pleasant. As it was rather a bad time of the day with cars coming out from Barchester to their various places of residence, Lady Gwendolen took various lanes and turnings ignored by the ordinary motorist, went over the downs where the juniper bushes on the short grass looked like battalions of little fighting men, and so into Harefield from the far end, away from the church. The High Street was pleasantly full of people but not crowded, and as they drove up the street a good many friends recognized them and waved, or saluted. Lady Gwendolen pulled up neatly in front of the Vicarage and Mr. Oriel got himself out of the car. We use this expression because he was tall and had long legs and though motor cars are useful beyond words they have never discovered that the human leg only bends at the knee. If it bent into two places it would so be much easier to get in and out. Either one gets out with one's head and feet, leaving one's behind in the car to follow one, while one clutches any available bit of the chassis; or one puts one's legs out first and then slides the rest of one out after them, hoping that one will not fall, a disgraceful heap, into the gutter. And the more up-to-date and New Look cars get, the sillier a woman looks as she tries to step or glide elegantly to the ground. But these things are sent to try us.

"Shall we just look at the garden?" said Mr. Oriel. "And then perhaps you will let me offer you a little refreshment before you go back."

Lady Gwendolen said she would love to see his border and how the *Fibrositis Vomitaria* cutting he got from Mrs. Macfadyen—she ought to say Mrs. Fewling—was doing. So they went round the Vicarage to the long flower bed along the north wall and there was *Fibrositis*. It was a robust-looking plant with a thick hairy stem and large serrated leaves—also hairy. From it rose a bare stem on the top of which five or six flowers rather like outsize campanulas hung, each with a sticky white stamen hanging over its lower lip as it were.

Lady Gwendolen said it was indeed a peculiar plant. The Vicar said he gathered that she did not altogether admire it.

"Dear Mr. Oriel, I think it is quite AWFUL," said Lady Gwendolen, "but I must speak the truth."

"How thankful I am that you do," said her host. "I also think it is an abomination. Mrs. Macfadyen—dear me, I *must* remember to say Fewling—says it is very valuable and Kew would willingly buy some of the seeds. You see my difficulty."

Lady Gwendolen was not of noble blood for nothing.

"One must face facts, Mr. Oriel," she said. "It is *dreadful*, but I believe my mother wants one badly—she is interested in exotic plants you know—I mean rare, not exactly tropical—and can't hear of one. Would you consider parting with it?"

"There is nothing I should like more," said Mr. Oriel fervently.

"We had better wait till the seed-pops are ripe," said Lady Gwendolen. "Then we can get it moved. And I think the West Barsetshire Horticultural would buy some seeds."

"I do like your 'we,'" said Mr. Oriel.

"A kind of mutual benefit society, I think," said Lady Gwendolen.

"I am so glad you say 'mutual,'" said Mr. Oriel, "in its proper connotation—as our beloved Charles Dickens didn't with Our Mutual Friend. A common friend would be correct—that is a friend common to each of two—or of several people."

"But we are friends even without being mutual, aren't we?" said Lady Gwendolen. "I mean just friends."

Mr. Oriel was silent.

"What is it?" said Lady Gwendolen.

"Nothing," said Mr. Oriel. "Only Browning."

Lady Gwendolen, feeling it rather strange, asked him why.

"Oh, only one of his poems—'The Lost Mistress,'" said Mr.

Oriel. "'Mere friends we are—well, friends the merest Keep much that I resign.'"

There was silence.

"I don't understand," said Lady Gwendolen, looking away. "What have you resigned?"

"A hope that you might care for me—'Your voice when you wish the snowdrops back Though it stay in my soul for ever.' That's all."

"But *do* I understand?" said Lady Gwendolen.

"That," he said, "is for you to say."

"*May* I understand?" she said. "Oh, let me understand."

Mr. Oriel took her hand and drew her to him. They stood side by side in the stillness.

"'The silence grows To that degree, you half believe It must get rid of what it knows, Its bosom does so heave,'" he quoted. "Perhaps it sounds rather dull and Mid-Victorian now."

"Oh, no," said Lady Gwendolen. "Oh, *no!*

"I suppose," she went on after a silence, "we both think of the same thing."

"Each other?" said Mr. Oriel.

"Exactly," said Lady Gwendolen.

"There is only one possible drawback—my dreadful name— Caleb," said Mr. Oriel. "It is a family name. There was a Reverend Caleb Oriel at Greshamsbury when the Greshams still lived there about a hundred years ago. He married one of the Gresham daughters. It is a good Bible name, but no beauty."

"But I shall always like it," said Lady Gwendolen. "I must go home now or mother will worry. I am so happy—Caleb."

"God bless you and keep you," said Mr. Oriel, and she went away.

CHAPTER 6

We think that Lady Gwendolen and Mr. Oriel must have understood one another very well—which is not a bad plan if one is going to get married. It was a gentle attachment of long standing; it was highly improbable that they would be troubled by children, Mr. Oriel was comfortably off and Lady Gwendolen had an income of her own—not very large, but enough to give her a feeling of independence; they had a number of friends in common and both had the same views about the duties of a clergyman and his wife. Everyone was so used to Lady Gwendolen's visits to Harefield that no one thought about them. There was no secret about the engagement and though it had not yet been formally announced and while very few people took a deep interest, quite a number were mildly pleased and surprised.

It must be said to the honour of womanhood that Lady Elaine took the news extremely well. She was delighted that her sister was to be married so suitably, and if the ghost of Dobby Fitzgorman ever rose before her she felt on the whole that she was very comfortably off as she was and when Gwendolen was married she would take her sister's bedroom as a sitting-room for herself. The Dowager, feeling that her position demanded it, summoned Mr. Oriel to visit her early one afternoon and to stay to tea when her daughters would be in. She had made a number of notes—some mental, some written on scraps of paper so illegibly that she could not discover what they were about—of the things a Mother should ask the Suitor for a Daughter's hand, but Mr. Oriel had not been in the room five minutes before she had forgotten all about them in the joy of comparing notes about common friends and acquaintances and Talking Families. By going back some hundred years or so they even managed to establish a very vague connection in that a great uncle of Mr. Oriel's had married someone who was some kind of cousin of the Dowager's late husband—or rather of the Dowager's late husband's grandfather or great-uncle, she could not be sure which.

"But Towers will know," she said. "He keeps the key of the Muniment Room at the big house and has everything arranged and his lawyers have a duplicate key so that if he did die they would be able to get into it."

Mr. Oriel said he had been privileged to see the Muniment Room in Mr. Belton's house at Harefield which, as she doubtless knew, had been a preparatory school for some years now, but Mr. Belton had retained the Muniment Room and had a safe in it for family papers and for various articles of plate which, alas, it was almost impossible to use now because of the cleaning and polishing.

The Dowager said she *did* so understand. There was, she said, quite a large amount of plate up at the Towers and once or twice a year a man came out from Barchester to polish it all professionally if her daughter-in-law had a special dinner—as on the occasion when Princess Louisa Christina invited herself for a weekend and it was impossible not to have her; and what was worse she brought a kind of Lady-in-Waiting with her, called Miss Starter, who could talk about nothing but her own health and her diet.

Mr. Oriel said was that the Princess Louisa Christina who was a daughter of old Prince Louis of Cobalt.

The Dowager said that was so and her mother was a Hatz-Reinigen.

Encouraged by this, Mr. Oriel said was not her lady-in-waiting the Honourable Juliana Starter, whose father was old Lord Mickleham. He remembered seeing a photograph of him by Mrs. Cameron, draped in a rug, heavily bearded and whiskered, and wearing a kind of beef-eater's hat. This was, not unnaturally, Greek to the Duchess, who asked about Lord Mickleham.

"He was a young man about town—I mean a long while ago," said Mr. Oriel. "His son married an heiress—a Miss Dolly Foster. I don't know what happened to the family. That is the worst of London. Here in Barsetshire it is much easier to know who families are. One hears about the cousinships and the inter-marryings. I am more or less connected with half the county, so wherever I go I find cousins—mostly very agreeable people—and we exchange gossip."

The Duchess, though not quite liking the word gossip, was delighted by this news and she and her future son-in-law were soon both up to their eyes in families and between them managed to cover almost the whole of Barsetshire, for Mr. Oriel's people had their root in the Eastern division, though he had seceded to the West.

"And now, Mr. Oriel, when may I come and see the Vicarage?" said the Dowager. "Harefield used to be a charming place."

Mr. Oriel said the little town itself was not much altered, but there were now nasty suburbs and he foresaw a time when a thin red line of Council houses would connect it with Barchester.

"But I shall be dead then," he added, more cheerfully; and then pulled himself up and said that now he was to have so delightful and sympathetic a lady as mistress of his house he would do his best to live, though his years were already approaching the allotted span.

"*Nous avons changé tout cela,*" said the Dowager. "Everyone goes on living. They give one hormones or something. Not that I propose to have them. We all live to eighty at least in my family. Towers's family aren't bad either. His father was over eighty. Of course you know his people came into the dukedom sideways. The man before Towers's father was a poor lot—just as well he died—and he only had one child, a boy, who was peculiar and he died too. That's how we came in."

In spite of his county family knowledge some of this was new to Mr. Oriel and then he and the Dowager plunged back again into what we can only call a blue-blood-bath of connections and friends who were connected with connections, even back to the Mary Thorne who unexpectedly inherited the immense fortune of the rich contractor Scatcherd and married the heir to the Gresham property; and one of her sisters-in-law had married the vicar, the Reverend Caleb Oriel, from whom Lady Gwendolen's betrothed was named. This was some hundred years previously, but when it comes to Families in Barsetshire and many other places a hundred years is not much. Outwardly there have been more changes in the way of living than one realizes. Inside, a good deal of the county carries on its private life, more rooted in the past than the new arrivals—the "off-comes" as they are called in the North.

The Dowager, although not of West Barsetshire, had been well brought up to realize the importance of Families, so she and Mr. Oriel then had a delightful talk about people and titles. Those who had risen from trade—as had the family of Lord Bond over at Staple Park—and were now confirmed by money and marriage as part of the county. Those who had declined from landowners to nobodies most luckily did not know much about their past and cared less.

Mr. Oriel said these last were very well described by Hardy in *Tess of the Durbervilles*. The Dowager said when she was a girl her father had forbidden her to read it, but as she had already read it she had paid no attention. If Hardy, she said, had confined himself to descriptions of the English countryside and country people, he would have done well. But whenever he got out of it, or among the upper classes, he was completely *dépaysé*.

"By the way, Mr. Oriel, do you know our dreadful house, The Towers?" she said.

Mr. Oriel said he had once been there as a small boy when the family still lived there, but couldn't remember anything about it except that one of the housemaids had a wart on her chin with a long hair sticking out of it. The Dowager said that was *exactly* the sort of thing one remembered and her greatest love as a small girl had been the odd-job man at Gatherum, when her parents took her with them on a visit. He used, she said, to run along the kitchen passage and suddenly fall down flat on his back for the amusement of the younger members of the family, who of course adored him.

"His name," said the Dowager meditatively, "was Pendry. I cannot think why one remembers some things and not others. And now, Mr. Oriel, what would you like for your wedding-present? I am of course giving Gwendolen some of my jewellery and other things, apart from what the lawyers will arrange, but is there anything special that you would like—for yourself, or for your church?"

"That is most kind and generous of you, Duchess," said Mr. Oriel. "There is one thing I have always wanted for myself. In my study, which is rather a high room, there are, on two of the walls, bookshelves that go right up to the ceiling. My predecessor had them put in, I believe, and most useful they are, with high shelves at the bottom for very large books and then some shelves for normally large books—if I make myself clear—and so on to the top. Small by degrees and beautifully less—only they aren't beautiful. I am terrified of getting on a ladder, which is the only way to reach the top shelves. If I had a *very* long ladder that was hooked onto a rail running along the top of the bookcase and so could be run along from place to place, it would help me immensely with my library. I hope I am not making a foolish suggestion. I have seen and admired—even envied— libraries with such ladders."

The Dowager, far from thinking it foolish, said it was an

excellent plan and they had a ladder like that in the library at The Towers.

"I shall ask Towers's agent about it," she said, "and if you will allow me I will get him to send the estate carpenter over and see the shelves for himself and then we can get to work."

The combination of her ruthless kindness and the familiar "we" was almost too much for Mr. Oriel, but he mastered himself and said he could not imagine anything more delightful and thanked Her Grace most warmly.

"And now, what about the wedding?" she continued. "Have you thought about it all?"

Mr. Oriel had to admit that he had no very clear ideas. It was curious, he said, to have united so many couples in the bonds of holy matrimony and yet not to see his way to his own wedding.

"That," said the Dowager, "is perfectly normal. Weddings really aren't for men at all. Of course the bridegroom and the best man and various male relations have to be there, but no one ever looks at them. One is told, though I cannot speak from personal experience, that men are much more nervous than women during the ceremony."

Mr. Oriel, a devout admirer of Charles Dickens in whom he found the *mot juste* for every situation, said that his own experience as vicar had been the same and how much he had always sympathized with Mr. Augustus Moddle in his flight from the ceremony. But, he said, in his own case matrimony would be a happiness which he had never expected and felt he hardly deserved, though its blessings were apparent.

The Dowager said briefly, That was nonsense; no one deserved it better. And, she said, how delightful it was to meet a fellow Dickens-lover and when had Mr. Oriel first met his books? Her father, she said, had read some of them aloud to her when she was a very little girl and she had always enjoyed them and when she was a little older she read them all to herself and had never stopped reading them.

"I envy you that very early meeting with him, Duchess," he

said. "I didn't begin him till I was nearly in my teens, so I may not have had quite that unspoilt outlook—that first fine careless rapture. But I have never stopped reading him ever since. It is extraordinary how one goes on finding something fresh in him every time one re-reads one of his books. One might indeed say, in words attributed to the elder Pliny, *semper aliquid novi Africam adferre*—which perhaps I might render as 'Africa always offers something new'—so does Charles Dickens give us something entirely new in every one of his greatest books."

"I am delighted to hear you say so, Mr. Oriel," said the Dowager.

Mr. Oriel said he feared he had been rather prosy. Did she, he said, know that there was a Dickens Fellowship which had its headquarters in a house in London where Dickens himself had once lived and had branches throughout the English-speaking world, all united by love of that extraordinary man.

It was, said the Dowager, quite extraordinary how many things one did *not* know and the older one got the more one knew one didn't know. Perhaps, she said, death was simply knowing that one knew nothing.

"Ah! *sunt aliquid manes*," said Mr. Oriel, and then apologized for being so priggish and pedantic, but there were a few Latin phrases that still summed up, with an economy of words that our language could not emulate, the feelings of the ancient world about death—or life, or love.

"You are just like my dear father," said the Dowager. "He was at Balliol in Jowett's time and knew Latin extremely well, though he only took a second."

Mr. Oriel, anxious to defend the Duchess's presumably deceased father, said that no one need be ashamed of a second in a college where the standard of classical reading was so high. His mother had wanted him to go to Oriel on purely sentimental grounds because it was the same name, but his father had—rightly he thought—sent him to his old college, Balliol. What, might he ask, was her father's name. He knew, he said, that he ought to know, but did not.

The Dowager said Browne—with an "e" at the end.

"Not the Browne who managed to bring a pigling into the college and borrowed a nightgown from the barmaid at the Mitre and dressed the pigling in it and put it in the Master's waste-paper basket?" said Mr. Oriel, greatly excited. "Half a dozen of them were in it and they were all sent down. Luckily it was only a week before the end of term and it was freezing and one couldn't hunt, so it didn't matter."

The Dowager said that was her father but things were very different now, she believed.

Very different, Mr. Oriel said, and not altogether for the better. Women all over the place now. Not that he minded women as such, but when the terms were so short it did waste such a lot of time. At one of the colleges—he would not mention its name—the new buildings actually had bathrooms; one to each two or three sets of rooms—and the women students came in to ask to use them. All very proper of course, but he could not reconcile himself to the waste of time involved. Life, he said, was short, and term extremely short, considering how much one was supposed to pack into one's head.

These delightful praises of Time that Was might have gone on for ever, but the Dowager's daughters came in.

"Caleb!" said his betrothed. "Oh, what a treat!" nor was Lady Elaine backward and kissed her future brother-in-law warmly.

"I must tell you, Gwendolen, what your mother has offered me for a wedding present," said Mr. Oriel and described the library ladder, which both the sisters deeply approved.

"Where have you been, girls?" said the Dowager, not at all suspiciously, but with real interest.

Lady Gwendolen said she and Elaine had been over to the other side of Northbridge to see Mr. Wickham in his bachelor establishment; which, she added, was *far* too comfortable, but then bachelors always were. Her betrothed said they might be comfortable, but he wouldn't be Wickham for anything. A confirmed bachelor who has a good jobbing gardener and can do what he likes in his own house was all very well, but he was missing the best of life.

"If you mean a wife," said Lady Elaine, "she wouldn't stay more than a day in his house. It's all too full of gadgets for being comfortable. I didn't see a pair of lazy tongs, but I'm sure he has one."

Mr. Oriel, alone with three intelligent women, felt that as a pastor he ought to be intelligent too, but all he could feel was a warm comfortable sensation.

"Talking of wives, Duchess," he said, "I was talking to the Dean and he is most anxious for our marriage to be in the cathedral, which is very agreeable to me and I hope to you."

"Listen, Mr. Oriel," said his future mother-in-law, "we must do something about this. Franklin is the real duchess—and an extremely good one. I am the Dowager. You will *have* to call me Dow. They all do. You won't mind, will you? It is so confusing with two of us. Of course if you like you may call me Dorothea, but I don't fancy the name and never did."

Mr. Oriel, who was not without courage and a sense of humour, said Dow would suit him down to the ground and he was sorry he had not anything better than Caleb to offer. Anyway, he said, Dorothea always made him think of that rather stupid young woman in *Middlemarch* who would marry the elderly clergyman and repented it.

Lady Gwendolen, who was very well read, said of all the silly prigs in fiction Dorothea Casaubon was the one, and she herself wasn't in the least like that.

Mr. Oriel said, gratefully, that she certainly wasn't, and taking her hand, raised it ceremoniously to his lips. His betrothed looked proudly round for applause and just at that moment the Duchess came in.

"Well, isn't it just fine to find you here, Mr. Oriel," said Her

Grace. "And Dow and the girls. Well, Mr. Oriel, is it all fixed for the wedding?"

Mr. Oriel looked helplessly at his betrothed.

Lady Gwendolen said in a very unmaidenly way the sooner the better as far as she was concerned.

"Well, the Dean is just crazy to marry you himself," said the Duchess. "He says he likes to do it for anyone who has worked with him. He says in the Cathedral, the week after the Harvest Festival because the offerings will be there—the sheaves of corn and the fruit and flowers and all. Towers says if you don't agree he'll know the reason why."

There was a gentle outburst of thanks from the Dowager and her elder daughter, seconded by Lady Elaine.

"Well, Mr. Oriel, what about it?" said the Duchess.

"I am overwhelmed," said Mr. Oriel.

"Now, Caleb, just relax and pull yourself together," said the Duchess.

Mr. Oriel said he couldn't do both at once.

"Well then, just relax," said his future sister-in-law (or should we say sister-in-law-in-law?). "It's all fixed if you agree. You've only got to name the date."

"I am deeply grateful to Dr. Crawley—" he said.

"Then that's all right," said the Duchess, determined to stop any "buts" that he might be contemplating. "I suppose you know about the banns and everything of that sort," and Mr. Oriel was too overcome to make any protest.

The Dowager said Most suitable and it showed very nice feeling on the Dean's part, and all the ladies talked at once.

"I do think it would be wonderful," said Lady Gwendolen. "How very kind of the Dean."

"Well, it's even better than that," said the Duchess. "Mrs. Joram wants to give the wedding reception for you. The Fieldings would have loved to do it but they may be abroad and Canon Joram's house is much the best for receptions because there are two staircases up to the drawing-room and one can keep people moving. And listen, Dow, Mrs. Joram would love it if you would come to lunch with her one day and just say how you would like things arranged because she wants you to help her with the reception," an invitation which the Dowager was of course delighted to accept.

"Well, All's quiet along the Potomac for the present," said the Duchess. "What about clothes, Gwendolen?"

"Oh!—I hadn't thought about that," said Lady Gwendolen, feeling more and more discouraged by the magnificence ahead of her.

"For the land's sake," said the Duchess, "do *think!* This is going to be a smash hit and it's up to you to do your bit. We won't have bridesmaids, but Elaine can be a sort of Maid of Honour. And I'm going to give you both your dresses, so don't argue. I brought back some lovely materials from home last time and I'll call Lee Sumter and say he must come over and bring some of the newest notions."

The Dowager said What about, and her daughter-in-law said she didn't quite get it.

"Notions about *what,* I mean," said the Dowager.

"Oh, just notions," said the Duchess. "Pretty bits of lace or dressmakers' jewellery. Something real elegant for the girls. And I must get the organist to put a lovely programme on for you. It's all going to be one great big success. And Lee says he has found the cutest little hat for me in New York."

Lady Gwendolen, dizzy but unbowed, thanked her sister-in-law warmly for all the trouble she had taken.

"It's joy to me, honey," said the Duchess. "I arranged most of that big Cutsam van Pork wedding in Baltimore and did it go well? There's not enough to do over here. And just listen. What do you want to do after the wedding?"

But before Lady Gwendolen, who was feeling rather dazed, could answer, the telephone rang.

"See who it is, Elaine dear," said her mother, "and switch on the other telephone," so Lady Elaine switched through to the pantry and went away, while the company went on talking and when she came back no one paid much attention at first.

"Mother!" she said. "Do listen! It's Sally Pomfret. She wants to know if Gwendolen and Mr. Oriel would like to use the villa at Cap Ferrat for their honeymoon. She is going there with the family as usual in August but she says any time after the first week in September."

For a moment all were silent.

"I think I had better talk to her," said the Dowager. "*What* a kind offer. Of course you will like to go?"

Lady Gwendolen said it would be heaven and Mr. Oriel said he was sure he could get a locum and how *very* kind, so the Dowager went to the telephone and settled everything.

"There is only one thing," said Lady Gwendolen when her mother came back. "Will the Bishop want to come? That would spoil the whole thing."

"I don't think you need worry, dear," said the Dowager. "When there was that charming double wedding in the cathedral and Edith was a bridesmaid a few years ago and the Bishop signified his wish to be present—I really can't put it in any other way—one really felt things had gone too far; but most luckily the episcopal throne is extremely uncomfortable—the sort of seat that tilts forward and is always trying to push one off—and a frightful draught from that little window which no one has ever got to shut properly and he had one of his worst colds. So I don't think we are in real danger and in any case His Lordship can't interfere. The Dean wouldn't allow it."

Lady Elaine said she hoped Dr. Crawley would outlive the Bishop, because one never knew what a new dean might do and it would be dreadful if he was one of the Palace lot.

"If the Bishop *were* going to die, he should have done it long ago," said the Duchess. "I wish you could hear our bishop at home. He's just wonderful with so much personality."

"But I thought you didn't have bishops in the United States," said Lady Elaine, and then wished she hadn't spoken, for her sister-in-law insisted on describing to her at considerable length the constitution of the American Protestant Episcopal Church.

Luckily Lady Elaine had the tremendous toughness of the best of the aristocracy and after not listening in the most attentive way said it all sounded very nice; with which the Duchess had to be content and said she really must go home soon because the W.V.S. sewing party were meeting at her house to discuss the plans for their annual outing and as the secretary was away she, as President, would have to be there.

"Dear Franklin, you *do* work for us," said the Dowager, who had considerable respect for her daughter-in-law's masterful way of taking on every kind of local job.

"Well, I did my stenography course and my political science course and my civics course at college," said the Duchess—and if we have not written cah-ledge it is because it would look so silly and would not in the least represent her attractive soft Southern way of speech—"so I might as well do what I can. And I just love the Women's Institutes and the W.V.S. Last time we had a sewing party it was pyjamas for the Barchester General Hospital and the W.V.S. sewed up six pairs of pyjamas all wrong. I mean all the way round each leg, the top as well, because they were talking so much and we had to unrip them all. But they are lovely people."

"Excellent people and very worthy," said the Dowager, "but not exactly good-looking, I should say."

This was, as our reader will already have realized, a moment when the Great Divide between U.K. and U.S.A. suddenly reared its head—at least that was how it appeared to the party. Everyone in the room except the two Duchesses felt the confusion of the word and its two meanings and would have liked to giggle, but nobly stifled the desire.

Then Lady Elaine went to the kitchen, put the kettle on, waited for it to come to the boil, made the tea, put the tea pot on the trolley which was already laden with tea-things and pushed it into the drawing-room. Without a tea-trolley one doubts whether many worthy charitable organisations would exist for more than a few weeks. The foundation of the W.V.S., the W.I., the T.G.—initials which mean a great deal to those who have worked with them—is certainly tea, and during the war years many a housewife skimped herself on the tea ration the better to be able, when it came to her turn, to provide refreshment for her fellow workers. The luckiest were those who had friends in the U.S.A. who—with the great generosity of that great people— sent parcel after parcel filled with the necessities which had over here become luxuries and not always obtainable at that; and among them tea was perhaps the most enthusiastically welcomed. None who were working during these years will forget it and how all the ladies put down their work, their scissors, and their thimbles and settled down to the real business of the day, which as far as we can make out consisted chiefly of talking about all the things they talked about every day.

The Dowager of course wanted the latest news of her grand-children, beginning with the elder family—information which her daughter-in-law was delighted to supply—and going on to Lord and Lady William's baby whom she had not seen for two whole days. She also wished to know if Edith had found a nice Nanny. The Duchess said yes, an extremely nice, competent young woman who knew babies quite well. Her name was Ellen Humble, a niece of Mrs. Belton's old maid Wheeler and of the Mrs. Humble who owned a small stationery shop and lending library at Harefield. The only trouble, she said, was that like all really good nannies she would want more babies as time went on, but she was sure dear Edith would see to that.

The Dowager said it sounded most satisfactory. She had, she said, not seen the Williamses for a few days as she had a cold and didn't want anyone to catch it and was looking forward so much to seeing dear Edith and the darling baby and she was sure Edith would want to have more as time went on. For one baby, she added in a rather Restoration dashing way, might be a mistake, but once you had learnt you would know about the others, which unexpected contribution to genetics made her daughter-in-law nearly have the giggles. She got them well under and said Edith was no fool, thus slightly offending her mother-in-law. But the Dowager had long ago determined never to criticize and had most strictly kept her own law, which was partly why she and her daughter-in-law got on so well. To be fair to both sides the Duchess had also made a private pact with herself always to agree with her mother-in-law. If there arose any matter in which there might be a difference of opinion, she would let her husband do the arguing. After all, the Dowager was his mother—not hers. And in this we think she showed considerable common sense.

As there was no reason for Lady Gwendolen and Mr. Oriel to postpone their marriage, all necessary steps were taken. The banns were to be properly read on three several Sundays after the second lesson and all done in order. The Dean was of course delighted that they wished the ceremony to take place in the cathedral and under his auspices. There were those who said that he gave particular orders that the window which never shut properly above the uncomfortable episcopal throne should not be repaired: but we do not propose to enquire into this. As is almost universal, the bridegroom could not produce so many friends as the bride and Mr. Oriel uttered the dashing words that he almost wished he were a soldier so that he could have the whole regiment on his side of the church. At this moment Lady William, who had come in and joined the discussion, said she would get her brothers, who happened all to be at the London barracks at the time, to come down and help to swell the throng on the *decani* side of the church; though why the right or *decani* should be the less honourable—the bridegroom being after all an important part of the ceremony—we do not know.

"I do wish," she said to her husband, "that Mr. Oriel were in the Brigade, because then they could have the wedding in the Guards' Chapel and the boys would arrange it all," to which

Lord William replied that she was a sentimental goose and in any case there would not be room in it for all the guests; which was perfectly true. It is true that the East end and the chancel at Wellington barracks were now again all glorious within, but the nave was not fully rebuilt since the Germans bombed it and there certainly would not be places for all the guests. For of course when a Duke's daughter (born into the rank of marchioness, let us never forget) is married, it is emphatically an Occasion. Also, Mr. Oriel's large county relationships though scattered were distinguished and if supported by them his side would do very well. And then the party gradually dispersed.

After that there was a great deal of talking and arranging and planning and Lady Gwendolen was so submerged by dressmakers and going up to London to do some shopping and answering letters and thanking for presents, that she saw little of her future husband, as he was almost equally submerged. He was much liked in West Barsetshire and what with that and his wide family ramifications it seemed quite possible that his side would be almost as full as his bride's without having to call in the halt and the blind, or even the Home Guard which still went on in a quiet sort of way, more as a club than anything else, shorter in wind and in memory more unreliable and we may even say deliberately untruthful, remembering more or less Waterloo, Ramillies, and possibly Senlac.

There is a tradition, still followed in many cases, that on the night before his wedding the bridegroom should be given a feast by his bachelor friends there, rather like Jephthah's daughter, to bewail his bachelorhood, a form of mourning which is apt to express itself in drinking healths till the best man says it's time he took Tommy, or Stanley home if he is to come up to scratch next day. Mr. Oriel had been a bachelor for a very long time quite happily and was now extremely happy at the idea of being married, so no such ceremony was needed. But there was a small party for him at the Deanery not exactly on the night before, but a week or so before the ceremony, where some old friends could wish him well. The Dean had suggested the bachelor ritual, but when his wife had pointed out to him that there was not a single bachelor in the Close at the moment, or at least none that one could consider, he had agreed to make it an ordinary party, just of their friends, and to get Mrs. Morland as the extra lady, of which Mrs. Crawley thoroughly approved. There was a short discussion as to the number of guests. The Deanery dining-room table held ten easily and with the extra leaves put in could take up to sixteen if necessary. The Dean was in favour of having the full number, but Mrs. Crawley said certainly not. Ten, or even eight, would be quite enough, she said, and give everyone a chance to talk to everyone else. So the Dean heard and obeyed and we think Mrs. Crawley was right, because her excellent parlourmaid could deal with up to ten, but could not take it upon her to do any more without help. So finally, with themselves, Canon and Mrs. Joram, the Chancellor Sir Robert Fielding and Lady Fielding, the Everard Carters from Northbridge, Mrs. Morland, and Mr. Oriel, it should be a pleasant evening.

Mr. Oriel, with his usual consideration for the feelings of others, was the first to arrive, so that his host would feel there was at least the nucleus of a party and a fellow man to stand at his right hand. Simnet, the Jorams' admirable butler, who also attended—by his employers' permission—the best of the Close parties, received Mr. Oriel almost as if he were royalty. Chiefly, we fear, because he was about to be nearly allied to the aristocracy and if it led to the Duke and Duchess of Towers dining at the Deanery, and better still with his employers the Jorams, he could say his *Nunc dimittis*. As the Towers family and the Deanery had known one another for a long time in a friendly way, but never intimately, we feel that Simnet may have his wish—but one never knows.

"Ha! Oriel," said the Dean when his guest was ushered into the drawing-room, but Mr. Oriel was used to this form of greeting and merely said, "Good-evening, Crawley. I have been looking forward to this evening."

"So have I," said the Dean, and then they both got away upon the burning question of the Palace drains, which had been the main topic of conversation in the Close for some time, but they were checked—much to their annoyance—by Mrs. Crawley coming in with Mrs. Morland, whom she had found struggling with her overshoes in the hall, and had rescued and brought upstairs.

"I hope I'm not too early," said Mrs. Morland. "It was pouring when I left High Rising so I put my goloshes on to get my car out which I will *not* call rubbers—"

"You needn't, Laura; you needn't," said the Dean, unconsciously imitating the "You will, Oscar; you will" of days long past and now rather forgotten.

"—and I had got halfway across the hall here when I found I couldn't walk properly and of course it was because the goloshes stuck to the carpet. So I took them off and then your wife rescued me," she concluded.

Then the Jorams followed with the Fieldings hard upon, and after an interval, though well filled by sherry and not long enough to give the hostess any serious alarm, the Everard Carters, with apologies for being late, but the car wouldn't go properly and they had to stop at the garage and get the mechanic to put it right.

But no bones were broken and the sherry again took its course till Simnet saw fit to announce that dinner was ready. The party then went downstairs.

Of course the one subject on which everyone was burning to talk was the rumour of the Bishop's retirement. Where it had begun no one knew, and as no two people had the same story, it was likely to remain a mystery till Truth made all things plain. But there was a general and we must say gentlemanly feeling that somehow it would not be in good taste to discuss it during dinner. When the ladies retired they could weave their feminine webs of gossip in the drawing-room, while the gentlemen could loosen their cravats, take off their wigs, and pass the punch bowl while blackening all characters of those not present. This of course a poetical way of putting it, but none the less represents the general feeling. The Crawleys had discussed the matter before dinner and agreed that the Bishop should be, as it were, immune while the party were at table, but when the sexes divided, the Palace could be discussed freely.

Luckily the betrothal of Mr. Oriel and the Lady Gwendolen Harcourt was a subject open to discussion; and when we say discussion we mean to be talked about but not criticized, for everyone there was pleased and interested, and we think Mr. Oriel himself was quite ready to join in the conversation, which was chiefly about what alterations he would make at the Vicarage and what delightful dinner parties he and Lady Gwendolen would give. By the time the extremely good saddle of mutton was carved and distributed among the guests, all tongues were loosed. We must say, to the credit of the Deanery, that no direct allusion was made to the Bishop nor to his lordship's draughty episcopal seat, but we think most of the party had it in mind, except perhaps the Carters whose Northbridge life kept them extremely busy, with little time for Close politics.

The Dean, speaking to Mrs. Morland about the widening of Barley Street—much needed, he said, to relieve the congestion of traffic, especially on market day, but also a relic of old Barchester which he would grieve to see destroyed—said the old order had to change, giving place to new.

Mrs. Morland said she thought that was in Tennyson, only *he* said The old order changeth yielding place to new, but she supposed that was because it was poetry. The Dean had a strong inclination to tell his old friend that such cavilling was petty and unnecessary; but he knew that any conversation with her was like trying to catch an eel without putting sand on one's hands and held his tongue.

"Though why One good custom should corrupt anybody I

have never understood," said Mrs. Morland. "Unless of course customs means something *quite* different. I seem to remember something in Shakespeare about custom, but I can't think what. Probably a clown."

"What *do* you mean, Laura?" said Dr. Crawley.

"I don't know," said Mrs. Morland. "I knew *exactly* what I meant a minute ago and then it went. It is extraordinary how you remember something you thought you had forgotten and then suddenly you don't."

The Dean who sometimes found himself like panting Time toiling after his old friend in vain, gave it up, and asked how her next book was getting on. Was it, he said laughingly, her hundredth or her hundred and first.

"You may well ask, Dr. Crawley," said Mrs. Morland. "It is my thirtieth if you wish to know, and they are all exactly like each other and I can never remember which is which."

The Dean said he couldn't either, but he liked them all, which Mrs. Morland appeared to find an agreeable, nay, flattering tribute.

"So do I," she said. "At least I HATE having to write them and I would sooner DIE, but I can't afford not to, so every year I very ANGRILY write another one. I like reading them afterwards, but *really*, I often wish I were a Kept Woman," at which words the party, most of whom by this time were neglecting their own conversation for the pleasure of hearing what she would say next, began to have the giggles, or to stifle them, except Mrs. Joram who obviously felt that novelists are not like other people and smiled enchantingly at Mrs. Morland.

"I don't mean In Sin, of course," said the gifted writer. "I mean to have someone to pay one's bills and take one's railway ticket and take one to good restaurants and know exactly how much to tip."

To the honour of the female sex, all the ladies present freely expressed their agreement, especially on the subject of tips.

"When I was a boy," said the Dean, probably the oldest of the party, "a tip of twopence to a railway porter was considered good. My mother's excellent cook had twelve pounds a year and beer money," which *écho du temps passé* roused nostalgic feelings in the older members of the party.

"When my grandfather first came to London," said Sir Robert Fielding, also wishing to show off, "there were still gin-palaces as they called them, with a notice which ran 'Drunk for twopence. Dead drunk for fourpence,'" and a kind of gentle sigh for those golden days passed through the company.

"It is all very well to talk about central heating," said Lady Fielding. "What was *real* comfort was a fire in one's bedroom and the housemaid coming in to clear the hearth and light it again in the morning. It was *cosy* to be in bed and see her at work."

Kind Kate Carter said wasn't it rather hard on the housemaid.

Lady Fielding said a great many women now, especially with families, worked just as hard as housemaids and were also the cook and the parlourmaid and the nanny and the chauffeur and anything else that needed doing, and then the talk shifted to other subjects, including the vast improvement to Canon Fewling's house by the judicious lopping or pruning of the large acacia in front which had made the drawing-room like an aquarium for a large part of the year. Mrs. Fewling, said Sir Robert, was a most pleasant hostess who really understood food and as Fewling really understood wine, their parties were very agreeable. It was interesting, he said, to see the old houses being re-lived in, rejuvenated as it were, and spoke well for the atmosphere of the Close.

Presently the ladies went upstairs to talk about really sensible and interesting things, while the gentlemen enjoyed the Dean's excellent port. Everard Carter moved nearer to Mr. Oriel and asked how his work on the General Epistle of Jude was getting on.

Slowly, said Mr. Oriel, slowly.

"No harm in that," said Everard. "*Chi va sano va lontano.*"

Mr. Oriel said he could not, from his own experience, agree entirely with that proverb. One could, he said, pursue the noiseless tenor of one's way very happily and yet not make any particular progress.

Everard said he was not well acquainted with the epistle of Jude but he did remember that there was an allusion to some-one called Core and he had never found out who he was.

"But, my dear fellow," said Mr. Oriel, who had never before spoken in so familiar a way to the Headmaster of Southbridge School, "it is quite clear."

Everard said he was sure it was clear if once one knew what it meant. As far as he could remember the gainsaying of Core was mentioned. Suddenly light burst upon him—as it some-times does if one talks aloud to oneself about things—and he said Was it perhaps the same as Korah—only Korah was spelt quite differently and began with a K, but Core in Jude had a C. Perhaps, he said, they were the same in Hebrew.

"Ah, Carter, I have you!" said Mr. Oriel, by which rather affected phrasing Everard was enchanted. "Yes, indeed, Korah and Dathan and Abiram. That is the clue. But why Jude had to spell it differently I don't know. Jude the Obscure would be indeed a fitting name for him," which allusion to an outstand-ingly depressed book by Thomas Hardy amused such of his hearers as had read it.

Everard, among the amused but not wanting to go on with the affair for ever, said perhaps it was spelt one way in Hebrew and another way in whatever language Jude wrote in, and Mr. Oriel thanked him so courteously for his help that he felt rather ashamed. Then there was a slight shifting of places and the Dean came to sit next to Mr. Oriel; first to congratulate him warmly on his engagement and secondly to fix a date for discussing the marriage ceremony with him and Lady Gwen-dolen.

"And the Duchess and the Dowager Duchess probably," said Mr. Oriel. "They are both so kind and take such an interest in our very happy engagement and the wedding." Then they had a delightful talk about how things should be arranged and what enormous pleasure it would give Dr. Crawley to assist at the ceremony; and Mr. Oriel said he hoped that the Dean and Mrs. Crawley would be among the first to dine with Lady Gwendolen and himself as soon as they were established at the Vicarage. Dr. Crawley made searching enquiries about the house and was delighted to hear that it was in good condition and that Lady Gwendolen liked it. And then Mr. Oriel told him about the tall ladder for the library which the Dean approved highly, and advised Mr. Oriel to have a step near the top which could pull out, or unfold, and become a seat, as it was much easier to consult the book one wanted in *situ*, as it were—unless of course one wanted to take it to one's writing-table for more prolonged reference.

This fascinating conversation then had to come to an end as the other men were getting a little restive, longing to discuss the Palace, but feeling it would perhaps be better not to unless the Dean gave the lead. And as they could not exactly ask him to give a lead they all went up to the ladies, who though pleased to see them had been perfectly happy without them; which is a state of things more common, perhaps, than most people would think.

Everard Carter at once went across the room to Mrs. Morland for whom both he and his wife had a great affection. Partly because her sons had been at Southbridge School and partly for the help she had been to them during the first year of the war when all her sons were fighting and she had come to live at the school as a kind of general aide and secretary to the Headmaster's wife and in her own peculiar way had eased everybody's lives considerably.

"Well, Laura," he said. "Tell me all about everything."

"That," said Mrs. Morland, "is an opening gambit—though I don't know what gambit means except that it is something to do with chess which I could *never* understand on account of all the moves being different. Now Halma is much easier. As for draughts I never could remember which way to move anything— I mean straight or slanting. And I used to enjoy Pit because one yelled at the top of one's voice all the time. But I don't suppose anyone plays it now. And I rather liked bézique which my father liked playing and there were those delightful cards for scoring with two hands like a clock and you put them to the right time—I mean to whatever figures you had got to," after which brief and lucid description of a game which we too used to enjoy in the dark backward and abysm of time, she untidied her hair and looked round for the company's views. Her particular company, being Everard Carter, said he was glad to find her in such good form and how was her work getting on.

"If by WORK you mean my writing the same book every year," said Mrs. Morland, "I am free at the moment. I mean I have corrected the page proofs—only of course when I say corrected you know how impossible that is because however much you correct the typescript it gets wrong when it is printed and I simply *cannot* deal properly with those dreadful galley proofs. They are like dead fish—only they are alive—I mean they do *flap* so, and they slither off things. It would be much easier if they didn't cut them up into lengths—I mean if the whole book was on one long bit of paper and you could roll it round something. Only even then you wouldn't know where you were," and she looked quite depressed by the thought.

"I'll tell you what—as Mrs. Samuel Adams still says," said Everard. "But I forgot—have you heard that he is pretty sure of a knighthood?"

"Well, I hadn't heard it and anyway I don't think he would take it," said Mrs. Morland. "What's the use of a knighthood to him? His name is well enough known in the House of Commons and all over the big business world. And I don't think his wife would like it at all. Her people are good Barsetshire landed gently and I think old Mr. Marling would have a fit. You know what happened about whoever it was that wrote a book about the Analects of Procrastinator whoever he was?" at which point Everard felt—as many of Mrs. Morland's friends and admirers had done—that there was a point beyond which her folly was just too much. "Anyway his name somehow got put down for a Lloyd George knighthood, but *most* luckily he got wind of it and made such a row that they gave him an O.M."

Mr. Carter said And rightly too. Dukes were not yet, he said, three a penny; but to offer a man like Adams a knighthood was fantastic. He was, as it were, his own title. Rather like the Rohans, Mrs. Morland said, only she could never remember what it was that Rohans couldn't be and didn't want to be—two quite different things of course—but were just happy to bear their own name.

"I think," said Mr. Carter, with the quiet false modesty of the scholar who knows he is right and looks forward to confounding his audience, "that the words you partly remember are *Dieu ne puis, Roi ne veux, Rohan je suis.* Doubtless the pronunciation of the words would have been slightly different then, but the intention is the same."

"Of course nobody knows how people talked, ever," said Mrs. Morland. "So one just has to think of sayings like *Et tu Brute* being in English."

Mr. Carter, very unfairly we think, said it was a matter of common knowledge that most educated Romans also spoke Greek among themselves and what Caesar undoubtedly said to Brutus was *kai su teknon,* the equivalent of "and thou too, my son"; son being of course only used as a term of affection, not that Brutus was really his son.

Mrs. Morland said that made it more touching in a way and she had always liked Caesar because there was a face of him in her father's study, a plaster cast she meant, and she was sure it was exactly like him.

Mr. Carter said Doubtless it was, but busts and coins were, at all periods, notoriously on the flattering side. Still that was far better than painting people purple and green with their nose like a triangle and cubes for their cheeks, like that dreadful neo-Phallic group of young artists—and not so young as not to know better, he added. But Mrs. Morland, always a passionate stickler for words, said that didn't at all express what he *wanted* to say, and what he *ought* to have said was they were not so young and did had ought to know better; which emendation in English as She is too often Spoke, enchanted Mr. Carter and he asked if he might have it for his own; so she laughed and said Certainly.

By this time he was slightly exhausted by so much talk on a high scholarly level, and seeing Canon Joram approach he got up and offered him his chair. And as Canon Joram was full of the Palace drains scandal all Mrs. Morland had to do was to listen—which she most willingly did, throwing in suitable interjections from time to time.

As one blob of quicksilver attracts another (and what a glad day it always was when the nursery thermometer got broken and we could have the glistening globules in a bit of washleather and squeeze them through in shining rain into a saucer and see the dirt they left behind) so is gossip attracted to gossip and two or three other guests joined them and mild scandal flew from mouth to mouth; or perhaps it would be more correct to say from mouth to ear and so, through caverns measureless to man, into the brain and so down, in a slightly different form, into the mouth again.

Then Mr. Oriel, summoned by a friendly look from Mrs. Crawley went over to her sofa, a small one that held two very comfortably, and they had a long delightful talk about his coming marriage and the changes and renovations he was making in his parsonage.

"Nothing serious, of course," he said. "But I have been there so long that even the place where the plaster came down after that dreadful thunderstorm about three years ago, when the Arundel colour print of St. Ursula and her however many thousand virgins it was fell down behind that heavy oak chest and I had to get the verger to help me to rescue it and re-hang it, hardly shows at all."

He then added that he was afraid he had not made himself quite clear.

"But indeed you have, dear Mr. Oriel," said Mrs. Crawley. "I mean I *quite* follow your meaning. How curiously out-of-date those Arundel prints look now. They were the last word in reproduction for our grandparents; just as the Medici coloured reproductions were to us. What the young fancy now, I don't quite know. But luckily my grandchildren keep me up to date. It is extraordinary how young we have to be—I mean my genera-tion. When my grandmother was my age she dressed like an old lady in black brocade or black wool and always wore some lace on her head. *Most* becoming it was. But as most of the grannies are wheeling prams while the mother is cooking, we can't very well wear lace and satin. Now, you must not have the least anxiety about your wedding, dear Mr. Oriel. Josiah has every-thing well in hand. I know *exactly* what you feel like; as if you were an actor-manager—for after all that is what you are in your own church—and suddenly had to be a super."

Mr. Oriel laughed and said he had always felt sorry for the bridegroom, but in his own case with Lady Gwendolen at his back as it were—

"Now really, Mr. Oriel, you must think more clearly," said Mrs. Crawley. "She will of course be a great support to you and will be by your *side* during the ceremony. Do think of that. Not at your back."

Mr. Oriel said her rebuke—her most kind rebuke—was well timed and he would take it to heart; and if Mrs. Crawley felt his brain would be a better place, she did not say so.

The party began to disperse, for the Close still kept fairly early hours.

"Dear Mr. Oriel," said Mrs. Joram, "I have hardly had a chance to speak to you this evening. My husband and I have a very small present for you and Lady Gwendolen. May I give it to you now? I brought it over on purpose," and from her bag she took a small packet wrapped in tissue paper and tied with golden string.

"May I open it?" said Mr. Oriel, like a child, and he untied the golden string and carefully unfolded the tissue paper. In it was a shagreen case with a golden clasp and on it an O of gold with a delicate gold wreath above it.

"My dear lady!" said Mr. Oriel. "For *me?*"

"Well, of *course!*" said Mrs. Joram. "My grandfather gave it to me when I was quite small—I was Lavinia Oliver you know—and I have never used it because I never found anything I wanted to put in it. It would do for cigarettes, or for visiting cards if you have any. I still have some and I have got the copperplate they engrave them from. So *do* keep it," which Mr. Oriel was enchanted to do, and for a moment quite forgot about Lady Gwendolen; but Mrs. Joram often had this effect on people, without being conscious of it. Then she said good-bye and the party gradually dispersed. Mr. Oriel drove himself home with his parcel, but his chief thought—we are pleased to say—was how much Lady Gwendolen would like it, not only for the gift itself but also for the giver. And we think he was perfectly right.

CHAPTER 7

Let us escape from the overcharged atmosphere of the wed-ding for a time and go over to Northbridge Manor, the seat of Sir Noel Merton, Q.C., and his wife Lydia whom we have known and loved since she was a rather self-assertive schoolgirl in the hideous uniform and hat of the Barchester High School. It had been a marriage of deep and continued affection, only once troubled by Noel thinking he was fond of the charming widow Arbuthnot, who had put him so neatly into his place that even his trained legal mind could not convince him that he hadn't made quite a fool of himself for a few weeks. His wife Lydia had seen it, said nothing, and felt a good deal; but love and loyalty had stood by her and though Noel had the grace never to allude to it he had been none the less conscious of his own silliness, which was for him a subject of true regret and contrition on the rare occasions when it came back to his mind. It is a pleasure to reflect that it was Mrs. Arbuthnot herself who had given him a delicate and well-deserved snub—possibly the only set-back in his successful career as a lawyer, a landowner, and a husband. He had taken her words to heart and his Lydia with all her usual warm-hearted generosity had not only forgiven him though without any uttered word, but had never alluded to the foolish episode again; though what she and her heart may have said to one another at the time we cannot tell.

As all West Barsetshire knows, Northbridge Manor had

belonged to Lydia's parents the Keiths and after their death an
amicable arrangement was made between the Mertons and
Lydia's two brothers—one a Barchester solicitor with a large
practice, the other a very successful London barrister—by which
the Mertons took over the family house and estate. Their children
were getting on; Lavinia the eldest (called after Mrs. Joram—or
rather Mrs. Brandon as she was then) being what is now called a
teenager; but not we hasten to add, with tight trousers of nondescript near-tartan, a pony-tail coiffure and a sham Fair-Isle jersey
which defined far too clearly the uncorseted, un-brassièred female
form divine. Of course Lavinia would be a problem the Mertons
felt. Most daughters now were problems and one didn't know
which one would like least—a daughter who said she must go on
the stage and then dropped it because it's *ridiculous* to expect a
person *always* to be punctual; a daughter who wanted to go to
university because it would be too marvellous; or a daughter who—
like the lovely Rose Birkett, now happily and normally Mrs. John
Fairweather with nice well-brought-up children and a naval husband who had done excellently in his profession—had in her
girlhood been, to put it mildly, a lovely, sluttish, spoilt unmitigated
nuisance.

If Lavinia was going to turn out as kind and charming as Rose
Birkett it would be all right, but one could not have any certainty
in these matters. She was doing well at school and might—so
the headmistress said—be considered almost a certainty for a
University scholarship if her parents wished her to sit for one.
Lydia and Noel had talked more than once about this, coming
to no particular conclusion. Every pro seemed to have a con, and
most cons a pro. Noel had said Lavinia must make up her own
mind when she was a little older and in any case if she wanted
later to go to a university, she must try for a scholarship. If she
didn't get one they could well afford to pay her fees. Anyway
she—like Tennyson's Maud—was not yet seventeen; but far
from being tall and stately she was an ordinary height and took
life easily, apart from the sudden affections for highly undesir-

able friends that the young have to experience. But, which is really important, her parents had brought her up to have excellent manners and though she still occasionally had a temper, or a tantrum, she could be trusted to do the family credit when taken out to dinner—as she had been not so long ago to Pomfret Towers—or to tea with the Deanery.

Mothers always have to worry about something even when there is nothing to worry about and Lydia Merton—though an extremely sensible practical woman—had invented a worry for herself; namely that Lavinia would either get no offers of marriage and remain single, or else would get several very good offers and turn them down—thus again remaining single. Nothing could convince her that if Lavinia didn't marry she would be a bore, like that nice dull Miss Dunsford at Northbridge—only she had defied her octopus mother and now lived very happily in the Pension Ramsden at Mentone where there was a good English chemist and an English chaplain. Then there was a third possibility—that Lavinia might think she was in love with some complete outsider who wouldn't fit into their life or said Pardon if he coughed. If she never married she would be quite comfortably off and might just go on being dull to the end of her life: the nice aunt to whom the young brought their troubles—only she didn't think the young did that now; rather did they yell and blazon them to the world. But that was all imagining, so she gave herself a mental shake. No good worrying about the future and luckily she and Noel were quite well off and Lavinia would have some money whether she married or not and Noel would see that it was all properly settled and tied up.

Then—being a firm Dickens-addict—she suddenly remembered the case of David Copperfield's Dora; the child-wife as Dickens called her and one took it from him—bless him—though one wouldn't have taken it from anyone else, and hoped Lavinia would marry someone rather older than herself, from a nice family. And then, very sensibly, she stopped worrying about all these remote possible contingencies and thought about a party for the young while the weather lasted. Not that it ever does—if by weather we mean fine weather—but one had to gamble on something and if it was wet they could play a kind of free-for-all and any-number-a-side tennis in the big barn, provided the tractor was not at home in it. But Mr. Wickham would arrange all that and she thought for the many-eth time how lucky she and Noel were to have such a nice reliable agent who was also a personal friend and, what was more, pure Barsetshire; able to tackle anyone from Lord Pomfret, the Lord Lieutenant, down to old Bunce the ferryman and Goble the cowman, and more than that could speak the language of West Barsetshire as if he were straight from the soil. Or perhaps even better than the horny-handed sons of toil, for they were corrupted by the movies and the telly, which last was doing its best to destroy the primitive culture of West Barsetshire where, among the old people, an English was spoken probably much as Alfred had spoken it. Another generation or two and civilization—if one could call it that—would probably have killed it. Meanwhile all the older people were bilingual. No one had collected their songs and sayings as the Reverend William Barnes had done for Wessex—and Thomas Hardy too, to a certain extent, though one could never trust him not to come over all educated-like. Beauty vanishes, beauty passes, and perhaps when Mr. Wickham and the old men and women were dead, a generation would arise that knew not Joseph—oh, well.

And while she was sitting at her writing-table, thinking much more than answering her letters, as we are all apt to do, Noel came in to ask if they *must* go to dinner at the Nortons. He could just bear Norton and his wife, he said, but if Norton's dreadful mother Victoria, Lady Norton, was going to be there with her head tied up in a gorgeous toothache like the Queen in Mr. Wopsle's Hamlet, he would have to be very ill, or leave the country.

"Darling, can't you ever stop worrying?" said Lydia. "I know the Carters are free that night. Why not ring them up and ask them to dinner: or they to ask us. Then I can truthfully say we are engaged. Or I can say it just the same whether we are engaged or not."

Noel said he adored her and whichever she did would be perfect, to which her answer was regrettably the words, Coward and Idiot; but both spoken in a way expressing so much love that Noel wondered—as he not infrequently did—what on earth he had done to deserve it. Of course the answer was that he had not done very much, but he had always loved her, even in the summer when for a few weeks he had made himself a motley to the view of all West Barsetshire by thinking that he and the pretty widow Mrs. Arbuthnot were in love; and Mrs. Arbuthnot, who liked him well enough but would never have dreamt of encouraging him and so given Lydia pain, had administered to him a snub that lambs, to use the great words of Mrs. Gamp, could not forgive, nor worms forget. He had admitted his own stupidity and unkindness to himself and had done penance by never speaking of the subject again, in which we think he was wise; while Lydia, in her large generosity, buried the subject deep and continued to give him the love that she had always felt and would carry through all her life.

As a schoolgirl she had of course read a great deal of Victorian poetry, fashionable among her contemporaries at the moment, including Elizabeth Barrett Browning's Sonnets from the Portuguese—a title which implies nothing at all—and had found great solace for the pangs which were afflicting her while she was "gone"—as the schoolgirl language went then—on the chemistry mistress who had very scanty fair hair through which her pink scalp was far too visible—but love laughs at locksmiths. The memory came back to her, and the lines

—and if God will
I shall but love thee better after death.

She did not say them aloud, but she felt them. Probably Noel felt exactly the same, though we doubt whether he knew the sonnet.

"And Wickham says they have swine-fever over Chaldicotes way," said Noel, "but all the proper precautions are being taken and if he comes across any pigs on the loose he will cry Havoc and let loose the dogs of war—by which, I think, he means he will get the proper authorities onto it at once and let them kill and burn to their hearts' content. I suppose if the Great Plague had been treated like swine-fever, they would never have had it. I wonder why pigs are such a nuisance."

Lydia said perhaps it was because of the Gadarene swine, which she always thought was very unfair, because it meant such waste of good food.

"Bless you, my girl, I *do* like you," said Noel. "I always did."

And as he had obviously forgotten, or conveniently buried, the Arbuthnot episode, Lydia was not going to be the one to remind him.

By way of changing the subject Lydia said what about asking the Pomfrets over to lunch with their nice children and all the young people could go on the river or bathe if it was warm enough. Noel said it certainly would not be warm enough and as far as he could see it never would be warm enough again anywhere till they went to the eternal fires, which he felt would on the whole be preferable to a glassy sea; because if people were to cast down their golden crowns upon it, it would *have* to be frozen, or the crowns would sink at once; which re-reading of a nostalgic hymn (though far too long drawn-out both in words and music) made his wife laugh.

"Yes, quite a good idea," Noel said, becoming serious. "If it's proper summer weather, nice and hot, with a thunderstorm in the offing it will be perfect. If it is a normal English summer day there is always the billard-room, or the barn, or a visit to Nanny's cottage," for Mrs. Twicker, the old gardener's widow and ex-nanny to Lydia, was a north country woman with the northern passion for making every kind of bread and cake. "When shall we say?"

So a date was settled and Lydia said she would ring Lady

Pomfret up that evening and why not ask her sister Kate Carter and her husband to come too and bring the children. For the Everard Carters after many years of selfless service at Southbridge School had now retired and taken the Old Rectory at Northbridge, the incumbent Mr. Villars and his delightful wife having gone to Barchester where Mr. Villars had accepted a Canonry.

Accordingly a good deal of telephoning was done, with excellent results and if only the weather would make an effort— like the first Mrs. Dombey—it should be a very pleasant afternoon. The weather obligingly had held up so far, though it was most improbable that this would last.

The Carters were the first to arrive and Lydia at once got her sister to herself to hear all about the Rectory and what improvements they had made since she last saw the house, while Lavinia was put in charge of the younger children. And when we say children, it is because one often thinks of one's friends' children as very young till suddenly one realizes that they are growing up, that they look on one as an amiable frump and will be parents themselves before one can say knife: though why knife—or Jack Robinson either—we do not know.

Kate's three were, as far as we can remember, Bobbie who would be going to Oxford in the autumn, Angela now a teenager of some years' standing, and Philip who was at Southbridge School. We find it difficult to believe that time has so flown, and have had to do a great deal of arithmetic to get their approximate ages. Not that it matters greatly in this Cloud-Cuckoo-Land of Barsetshire; and it is just as perplexing in our own lives; everyone is older or younger than one thinks they are.

All three children were good-looking and intelligent, as might have been expected, and also very well brought up. They were naturally much admired by their younger Merton cousins and the two families got on extremely well; Bobbie, Angela and Philip Carter; Lavinia, Harry and Jessica Merton. So neatly were their ages and sexes matched that their parents amused

themselves by arranging a triple marriage for them, to be celebrated at Northbridge church—but this was only a family joke,
and what was in the future was so far off that no one took it
seriously.

The day chosen for the party was not a particularly pleasant
one—but one couldn't expect much in that rather depressing
summer, attributed variously by "What the Stars Foretell," a very
popular weekly article in the *Barchester Advertiser* to Saturn and
Gemini, by "Pick Your Choice," a very popular article in the
Barchester Chronicle, to the Atom Bomb; and to various other
equally improbable sources by various other astrological and
illogical forecasts. If looked at in an unbiassed way it was simply
a normal English summer in which the peculiar English wear
cotton frocks and flannel suits and do not get pneumonia. Still
Northbridge Manor got all the sun there was on the south side
and things might have been worse. Luckily the younger members were still young enough not to notice the temperature, and
how we should like to have that immunity in our latter years.

When we remember a bedroom with the window never shut
all through the winter, no fire (unless one had a cold, in which
case the most glorious stuffiness was allowed) a flannelette
nightgown it is true, but no hot water bottle, only woollen
bedsocks, and how one slept like a dormouse, we are almost
ashamed of what we wear and use in bed: the luxury of an
electric blanket or pad, a hot bottle down at the foot, the
window only open enough to placate any wraiths of past Nannies, the gas or electric fire kept extravagantly going all night if
it is really cold (though on a low flame or only one bar)—what
would Nannie have said? But Brother Ass works hard, or works
us hard, and surely he is worthy of his hire. In any case on this
chill, damp, foggy November evening as we write, we propose to
have everything as we like it and so get some sleep, and no
nonsense about opening a window when there is not a window
in the rather jerry-built, late mid-Victorian (a poor period

architecturally and in our case structurally) house where we live, whose sashes do not fit their frame or meet closely in the middle. No—shut windows, a hot bottle, an electric pad (despite a superstition that all electric apparatus blows up, burns, and blasts on the slightest pretext or no pretext at all), a nice gas fire, a nice drink of hot milk. All the air we need will seep in through the ill-fitting window frames and so we hope to sleep.

It was not long before the Pomfret party came. Lady Pomfret would have liked to ride over we think, but her husband's wish was more important to her, so she said they would drive over and as for Emily and Giles who had every intention of riding, their cruel parents had said No, and we think they were right. Giles could be trusted to go about on his pony provided his parents knew where he was going, but Emily could not, and goodness knows what foolish trouble they might get into together. Then Lord Mellings, to their great pleasure, had turned up unexpectedly and added himself to the party. In any case he did not truly enjoy riding, though he forced himself to keep it up, and to be with his family was his deepest happiness. Also there is always the question of what to do with the horses in a motor age, unless one lives in a hunting county. And though there was a West Barsetshire Hunt it was entirely out of the Mertons' world— and not much in the Pomfrets' now, though their agent Roddy Wicklow, Lady Pomfret's brother, still kept in touch with it.

The Merton family were hanging about the front of the house to greet the Pomfret family, much to the annoyance of the old parlourmaid Palmer who having known Lydia for much of her life still found it very difficult to treat her as Lady Merton, but would have given the rough side of her tongue to anyone who did not say My Lady; except of course to old Nanny Twicker, once nurse to Lydia and her brothers and sister, who still lived in her little cottage on the estate and found it quite unnecessary to recognize that her ex-charges were rapidly qualifying for grand-motherhood. Her husband had died a few years earlier, and though she mourned him sincerely she had taken on a fresh lease of life as a comfortable widow and intended to live to see Miss Kate's and Miss Lydia's grandchildren. And as no one had ever dared to contradict Nanny Twicker it is quite possible that she will.

There was of course a great noise and confusion to greet the guests and as the Everard Carters with family had already arrived there were three lots of three children all mingling and talking at the top of their nine voices. Lydia had, wisely we think, provided a slap-up lunch in the hope that some at least of the younger members would concentrate on eating and then go on the river and leave their elders in comparative peace.

There were two tables; one for the Merton children and their young cousins and friends, the other for the grown-ups; which we think was a good plan. The young could misbehave—within bounds—if they wished. The elders could talk more or less sensibly as they chose and then the young would go down to the boat house and there would be peace.

"I hope," said Noel Merton aside to his wife, looking across the hall to the dining-room, "that the dear little ones aren't having lunch with us."

"They are, darling," said Lydia, "but quite firmly at a separate table, so that they can go out as soon as they have finished gorging. The only thing that worries me is Ludo."

Noel looked again and saw young Lord Mellings, apparently in excellent spirits, seated between his daughter Lavinia and his niece Angela Carter.

"Ludo looks all right," he said.

"And he *is* all right," said Lydia, "but the thing is, will he *be* all right?"

"If I had my wig and gown and got you into the witness box and bullied you," said her devoted husband, "I might get some sense out of you. What *do* you mean?"

"Only just what I said. He is so old for his age in some ways."

"No harm in that," said Noel. "Lots of us were. Look at Jessica," for Jessica Dean the brilliant theatrical star and wife of

Aubrey Clover who wrote, produced, and acted in all his own plays, came of a good family—almost county by now—but for no reason that anyone could imagine had at a very young age taken to the stage like a duckling to water and was as well known and adored in New York as in London. "But you were always so good with Ludo. Do you remember when he was still a schoolboy and came over to dinner with his parents—in the Coronation summer?"

Lydia said, of course she did. But she did not say that what she did remember was the moment, just as the guests were leaving, when Lord Pomfret had held her hand and she had not withdrawn it. It had not meant much—probably not anything—but somehow it had been a mark in her life; a proof that even at her age one might be—not loved—but somehow gently worshipped. And that had been all. Nor would nor could there have been anything else. Suddenly a silly Victorian song about "She never told her love" came into her mind; words more or less from Shakespeare and a pretty, simple melody. She began to laugh.

With all her true virtues and graces Lydia had not a very profound sense of humour and when she did laugh her husband was always delighted, saying that her cachinnations were to him more musical than Apollo's lute, strung with his hair; and though she did not place the allusion she was pleased. But when was she not pleased with what Noel said or did?

By now the grown-ups had drunk enough sherry and the party went across to the dining-room and took their places at the table, smiling or waving to their little ones who were already well into their food. The phrase "the little ones" was perhaps not quite accurate, as none of the young people present quite came under that heading: but it was enough—it served. The noise from the combined lungs of Mertons, Carters and Fosters— including Lord Mellings—was like the French Revolution, or a game of PIT, if anyone remembers that delightful card game which consisted chiefly of yelling. Lydia's hostess's eye, always on the lookout, noticed Ludo rather tightly packed between her daughter Lavinia and her niece Angela Carter, a very pleasant couple. But he did not stand like the Turk with his doxies around, in the poet Gay's light-hearted words; rather, looking like Saint Anthony when he refused to be tempted by the devil because the allurements offered to him were so boring.

Noel Merton's legal eye, trained, as were also his legal wits, to learn, mark, and inwardly digest anything that came his way, also noticed young Lord Mellings. Vaguely he thought of Garrick, torn between Tragedy and Comedy; but as neither his daughter nor his niece seemed to him cast for the role of Muse, he rejected the comparison and gave his attention to Lady Pomfret.

"I believe this delightful party is to be a water excursion followed by tea," she said.

Noel said the water party sounded to him like hell with the lid off—if Lady Pomfret would forgive the comparison.

"But it is *perfect!*" said Lady Pomfret. "I went to a good many picnics when I was a little girl and it was nearly always cold, or wet; or something really important—like the little oil lamp to boil the water—had been forgotten. My mother used to organize a picnic every summer, up on the downs. There was a deep hollow on the top, why I don't know; the county antiquarians said it was a dew-pond that had dried up. We were taken up in a farm cart—a dozen or more of us and our friends, and my brother Roddy *would* climb all over the cart and get out over the tailboard and climb in again by the shafts and all the nannies—there *were* nannies then and I wish there were now—distributed the cakes and sandwiches and every nanny scolded her own charges and told the other nannies what nice little ladies and gentlemen *theirs* were. And then all the bits of paper and things were burnt and the fire stamped out, and we came home again."

"You *were* lucky," said Noel. "I was a London child and my people usually went to the sea and I was frightened of the waves and loathed being made to try to swim. I still can't swim; but I am told that is just as well, for if you are shipwrecked, or in the Birkenhead, it is much quicker to be drowned at once than to fight and struggle for a raft which then tips up at one end—like that picture that always frightened me so much—in the Victoria and Albert Museum I think—of the wreck of the something-or-other and lots of survivors on a raft in great discomfort and obviously doomed to cannibalism, or to drowning slowly and being eaten by fishes."

"'The judge,'" said Lady Pomfret, "'said he would *not* have the court turned into a circus, nor would he tolerate showing off.'"

Noel said "Touché" and laughed; but to Lady Pomfret it seemed that his laugh had come a little late. Still that was not her business and they went off onto the fascinating rumours about the Bishop.

Lady Pomfret said, speaking of ecclesiastical matters, did Sir Noel know if there were any truth in the rumours of the Bishop's retirement? Noel said that, alas, his life lay between Northbridge and the Law Courts and he missed nearly all the good cathedral gossip.

"A pity," said Lord Pomfret who, finding himself temporarily stranded on the opposite side of the table had heard the end of their talk. "I don't know any place where you get more gossip than the Close. I wish the Lords were like that. We have our own gossip, but it is nearly all political. It must be much more fun to be told that old Canon Somebody roasts cats alive, or that old Mrs. Prebendary Something believes that the eleventh book of Revelations is about to be fulfilled and there will be quantities of dead bodies lying in the streets for three and a half days."

Noel Merton said that, professionally speaking, he did not think the City of Barchester bye-laws would permit such a thing.

Everard Carter said he had been reading the Books of Revelation lately and had easily recognized Victoria, Lady Norton in several of the more unpleasant and reprehensible characters for whom disagreeable ends were foretold. There was a kind of

hum of agreement, as from a Puritan congregation when one of
Cromwell's Ironsides was moved to usurp a pulpit; as whoever it
was did in Woodstock.

"Yes, who *was* it?" said Noel. "I thought I knew my Scott
inside out."

"Who knows what, inside out?" said a voice, and there was
Mr. Wickham. "I came over to see if the men had repaired the
sluices properly up near Parsley Island, and blessed if you aren't
all guzzling still—saving your presence Lady Pomfret—and
yours Mrs. Carter and of course Lady Merton's."

"Well, sit down and have a rere-guzzle, Wickham," said Noel.
"I think you know everyone here—and I think you all know Mr.
Wickham."

A kind of chorus of agreement rose from the company.
Angela Carter we regret to say, crying out "Darling Wicks,"
threw her arms round his neck.

"All right, Angela," said Mr. Wickham, rapidly and skillfully
disentangling himself. "Once is enough. Bless your heart, my
girl, you're as bad as a boa-constrictor."

"What you need then is an un-constrictor," said Noel, pushing a glass towards Mr. Wickham who, remarking "Here's mud
in your eye," tossed it off and then looked round in horror.

"What's the matter, Wicks?" said Lavinia.

"Matter my girl?" said Mr. Wickham. "I thought it was
whisky. I must have lost my senses. It was pure brandy. Mark
One, *premier cru* and whatever those Johnnies say. And I swal-
lowed it whole."

"Like Jonah and the whale," said Giles, "only the whale
sicked—" but a cold look from all his older relations made him
relapse into sulky silence, broken by giggles at his own wit.

"I must be losing my grip," said Mr. Wickham in a resigned
voice. "Listen everyone. The river's all right downstream—so
you and your family can go back to Northbridge like the Lady of
Shalott, Carter—"

Mrs. Carter said certainly not, and the car was much quicker and more comfortable

"—and as for upstream," Mr. Wickham continued, "it's all clear till you get to the sluices. They're opening them tomorrow but it's O.K. today. How is the army going, Ludo?"

Lord Mellings said Very nicely and he got a mount sometimes from people in the neighbourhood.

His parents, who rather naturally still thought of him almost as a schoolboy, suddenly saw him as others might: a young man, passably good-looking, a bit tall perhaps but well built—he would fill out as time went on—and very good manners. Of course he would never sit a horse with the easy grace (we have to say it) of his brother Giles, or the competence of his sister Emily, but nor could thousands of other young men. There was also the question of getting on with one's mount and Lord Mellings had, entirely off his own bat, sought advice and guidance from various friends of every class who knew and loved horses, among whom the old horse-coper Jasper was not the least skilled, and if seriously inclined to crime could probably have stolen, disguised, and re-sold elsewhere, any horse in the country. When the Pomfret children read Grimms' Fairy Tales in their young days, and came to the story of the Clever Thief who stole the horse from beneath its sleeping rider by gently hauling him and his saddle up a few inches with a rope from a beam and moving the horse away from beneath him, they knew quite well that Jasper had done it. They ever praised him to his face for his skill. Jasper of course had not denied anything—though refraining from the downright whopping lies he would have told to outsiders—and so remained a hero to Emily and Giles. As for Lord Mellings, Jasper had come to the conclusion that his young lordship was a dark horse, and so respected him. If Ludo could have heard these words he might almost have felt conceited, nor would the feeling have done him any harm.

After lunch the young people were going down to the river, which was at present fairly full. The elders of both families meant to have nothing to do with the water and we think they were wise. The young went to the boathouse in high spirits and there fell that beautiful silence which celebrates the departure of beloved offspring. Lord Mellings had disappeared, but no one thought he was drowned.

"I don't know what you feel like, Sally," said Lydia Merton to Lady Pomfret, "but I think Indoors. What about you, Kate?"

Both ladies said, with great feeling, that it would be Heaven, so they went to the drawing-room where Palmer had lighted the fire in the large grate. There were plenty of logs off their own ground, but also, we are glad to say, coal in proper coal scuttles of shining brass.

"If I shut the French window and just leave the sash window open about one inch at the top," said Lydia, "I think we shall be safe."

Her hearers could not—to use a hideous phrase—have cared less for fresh air and settled down in the very comfortable chairs to have a comfortable talk.

Noel had taken the men to look at the home farm and was glad to have Mr. Wickham as Master of the Ceremonies. He had managed to learn a fair amount himself in the intervals of his London life, but the advice of someone like Mr. Wickham, born and bred in the shadow of Chaldicote Chase, able to talk with every aged local imposter on his own ground, respected for his justice, rather feared for his sailorly downrightness (for he had served in the Royal Navy towards the end of the First War), popular for his generosity in the matter of spirituous and malt liquors and his capacity for—if necessary—drinking everyone under the table without even a headache; all this was invaluable to the distinguished Q.C. We are glad to say that Noel had more than once been able to help Mr. Wickham with legal questions, or to frighten people who were proposing changes and encroachments which Mr. Wickham did not approve. And we may also say that if Mr. Wickham had settled any matter to do with the county and the old ways—even to infang and outfang and heriot and seizin whatever they are—Noel always found that he had acted correctly; compassionately in cases of need, and in some other cases where there were shady transactions involved, with extreme care and delicacy though the iron hand was under the glove.

It must be said that Mr. Wickham, though conscious of his own use in the county, held otherwise no particular opinion of himself as a person. As one who understood the Barsetshire mind in many small villages and remote places over Chaldicote way, among the cottagers, the clergy, the professional men, the gentry, he moved with equal ease and was equally trusted by all. As far as was known he had never been in love or wished to be married, and was extremely popular with the ladies, married and single. Twice had he, as far as we know, seriously proposed marriage. The second time was some years ago when Margot Phelps—now most happily the wife of Canon Fewling, then the willing drudge of her mother and her retired Admiral father—had been found by him crying in the back yard of her parents' house, worn out by working for them, by her mother's illness, and by an emotion whose cause he did not know.

Genuinely sorry for a fine girl (though no chicken) down on her luck, he had with real chivalry asked her to marry him, with her bedroom to herself if she liked. To his immense surprise she had told him that she had just become engaged to the rich market-gardener Mr. Macfadyen, on hearing which he had nearly sat down on the garden path as Miss Betsy Trotwood once did. But after the shock he was delighted, congratulated himself warmly on his lucky escape and continued his bachelor life, punctuated by visits, and/or gifts of strong waters, from friends naval, military, and civil all over the world. He had, some years earlier, proposed to Miss Arbuthnot, even offering to defer to her views on bird-watching, but luckily for both parties she had refused him.

On this particular afternoon he was very much in his element.

All the guests were interested and what was more important to him, intelligently interested.

"That boy of yours, Lord Pomfret," said Mr. Wickham, "is coming on like anything."

"Do you mean Giles?" said Lord Pomfret, thinking of his younger son's aptitude for the open air life, the estate, his pony.

"Good Lord, no!" said Mr. Wickham. "He's a good chap, Giles. Nothing will ever down him. Run his head into a brick wall as soon as look at you. Probably the wall will fall down and he'll rub his head and go on. I mean Ludo."

"I'm glad you like him," said Lord Pomfret. "It isn't always easy to be the eldest of a family—and with burdens ahead that you can't escape. I wasn't an eldest—I haven't any brothers or sisters—but my father was old Lord Pomfret's heir."

"I remember seeing your father once, at Pomfret Towers," said Mr. Wickham. "A crusty sort of man."

"He had the Pomfret temper," said the Earl. "We didn't get on, I'm afraid. He would have inherited the title if he had lived, but he died before Uncle Giles, so it all came to me."

"Hard lines," said Mr. Wickham, quite seriously. "If you are to carry on a title and have an estate, you have to work till you die."

"I probably would have died," said Lord Pomfret. "I was supposed to be rather delicate—all rubbish I expect—and had to go out to Italy to my father and we didn't get on a bit. But when I met Sally everything was clear. What she has done for all of us, I can't say, and even my crusty cousin, old Lord Pomfret liked her. You see she knows all the country and where you find a fox and what you do when you've found him and who's honest and who isn't—and all about the trouble at Starveacres Hatches. Thank goodness Ludo and I get on quite well, and the others too."

"Your Ludo, my lord," said Mr. Wickham, deliberately making a formal approach, "will make his way."

Lord Pomfret looked at him questioningly.

"I hope so; I hope so," he said. "He is so dreadfully like me at that age—only much better looking. I can only hope that he will do well in his profession. I often wish I'd had a bit of the army myself. And I hope he'll find a wife—later on of course—who can stand by him as Sally has stood by me."

"No need to worry about wives yet," said Mr. Wickham. "And he is lucky to know the Clovers so well. Jessica and Aubrey like him and if he makes any silly friendships—even young gentlemen still at Sandhurst do sometimes, you know—Jessica will tell him exactly where he gets off and—if necessary—how to get out. And Aubrey will point out quite clearly and politely what a fool he has been. Sorry, Lord Pomfret."

"No need to be," said Lord Pomfret. "I know it all. But I don't always know the way out. Sally does. What about that vixen over Chaldicotes way, on your side, Wickham? I am credibly—or at least to my mind incredibly—informed that she has three earths that communicate underground—a kind of London Tube system—and that's why she is never caught."

Mr. Wickham gave it as his opinion, short of tunnelling under the river there was nothing that vixen wouldn't do, and then they joined the others who had followed the young people to the river. Here nine passengers were arguing as to who should go in which boat. There were, as there had been for many years at Northbridge Manor, three kinds; a punt, holding as many as could be comfortably or uncomfortably fitted into it, a light rowing boat which took one or two rowers and one or two (if not too fat) in the steering seat, and one much loved boat known as the coracle, being a kind of very round oval (if we make ourselves clear) of tarred canvas stretched on wood with two very uncomfortable backless seats. Every young Merton and young Carter had fallen out of it repeatedly and it was evident that the young Fosters would be having the same delightful experience; except for Emily who had preferred to wait till someone would take her in something that couldn't tip one out.

Mr. Wickham said give him the Atlantic with a head sea, or

coming round the Cape with a following easterly wind and you saw life; but his life was too valuable to risk on the river.

"You'd better organize then, Wickham," said Lord Pomfret. "I can't. All I can do is to punt a bit, but the water always runs down my arms and right down inside my clothes and I don't like it. I will sit on a cushion on the rear end and paddle if you like. I used to do that quite well on the canal. You know, Wickham, that bit of the canal that still isn't choked up and runs right under the hill and the bargees say they used to lie on their backs and push the barge along with their feet—like walking upside down. And every now and then a shaft right up to the top of the hill to let fresh air in."

"Good Lord! I thought no one knew about that bit now," said Mr. Wickham. "Romantic—that's what it was. But one was young then. Old Jasper's nephew was going over the hill once and he came to the opening of one of those shafts and leant over too far and fell right down into the canal. Luckily there had been a lot of rain or he'd have cracked his head and broken all his arms and legs. But there was enough water for him only to be frightened and a bit bruised. Nothing to the thrashing he got from his father when he got home though."

Of course the result of this delightful moral story was that all the younger members begged to be taken on the canal and to walk over the hill and see the hole. But Mr. Wickham said firmly it was too far and they must amuse themselves on the river as far up as the hatches.

"Oh, lord!" said Philip Carter (who was in that delicate stage when neither the speaker nor anyone else knows what kind of voice is going to come out of him, from the deep thirty-two foot stop to the most high and quivering *vox humana*, or an oboe stop. And if all this is slightly incorrect, we cannot help it, for we know nothing about organs except their glorious noise and the way everything dithers when the thirty-two foot stop is pulled out in the Matthew Passion). "I've not got any bathing things."

But Northbridge Manor was used to guests who suddenly

wanted to swim and kept various swim-suits as we believe they are now called in a cupboard in the boat shed. And as electricity was laid on in the shed, Noel had installed one of those small electric panels that give out warmth but are never so hot as to set anything on fire or, which is almost more dangerous because less perceived, on smoulder.

So Bobbie and Angela Carter with Lavinia and Harry Merton and Ludovic bagged the punt and went up the river. Giles bagged the coracle before anyone else could get it, thus proving himself a true Pomfret of the old blustering predatory breed; while Lady Emily and Jessica, each rather the spoilt daughter though very nice girls, had the rowing boat with Philip Carter as cox. Jessica said she had better row because she knew the river and Emily could row coming back, to which Lady Emily was quite agreeable, all means of transport apart from horses being indifferent to her.

We may say at once that although it was a chilly summer day with a nasty wind from the leaden sky blowing athwart the leaden river, everyone enjoyed each different treat enormously— such is youth—while the grown-ups went thankfully back to the house and a good fire.

Jessica Merton, as hostess, said they had better row down stream because the wind was coming up the river and would help them on the way back. Emily and Philip had no objection so they set off towards Northbridge. The little river was picturesquely bordered with rushes and the yellow water iris or whatever its real name is. On one side was the Mertons' garden, its lawn sloping to the water, and then their farm land. On the far side were a few disreputable cottages inhabited by the Bunce family, probably there in one form or another since King Alfred's time. Old Bunce who used to be the ferryman was now dead, his last words being that he didn't hold with washing seeing as it took the skin off a man—the skin, we think, being a kind of crusted deposit (the product of years of working and sleeping in the same clothes) which formed an effective protection against all forms of weather. His old wife had died some years earlier, her last words being a request for three pennorth of gin and a few unprintable old Wessex words of abuse to her husband and daughters, who were nice girls and had brought up their various children of shame quite beautifully; which children in course of time had done well at school, married, got good jobs and now sent their own lawful children to the grannies of shame for holidays. After the old father's death (which was as peaceful as a prolonged bout of gin-and-water-because-it's-good-for-the-kidneys could allow) his daughters had occasionally gone out to oblige—that is to say they used to work for Miss Pemberton at Punshions in the intervals of having babies and were now in receipt of so many free gifts and allowances from a grateful country that they could often afford to live at home and exercise hospitality of a free and easy kind, being grandmothers in their own right.

"Hullo, Miss Jessica," yelled Effie Bunce.

"Hullo, Mr. Philip," yelled her sister Ruby.

"Hullo, girls," shouted Philip. "How's tricks? This is Lord Pomfret's daughter, Lady Emily Foster. She's a very good rider."

"Pleased meetcher," yelled Effie. "Seed your name, I did, in the *Barchester Advertiser*. You got a silver cup at the Barchester Agricultural last year with your pony, didn't you?"

Lady Emily, who did not know all the people on her father's estate for nothing and how to talk with all sorts and conditions of women, yelled back that she was going to try for the gold one this year.

"Want to know how to win?" yelled Ruby Bunce. "I'll sell it you for sixpence."

Lady Emily, who had not her great-great-uncle's gambling blood in her for nothing, found a sixpence and held it up.

"Chuck it over, ducks," said Ruby, "here's a box." She picked up a stone, put it into an empty match box and lobbed it neatly into the boat. Lady Emily rescued it, put the sixpence into the match box and asked Philip Carter to throw it because he was good at cricket. Philip made a fine overarm throw, nearly capsizing the boat; the Bunces yelled Anglo-Saxon gratitude.

"Now I'll tell you how to win," yelled Ruby. "Back the winner," at which hoary joke she and her sister laughed consumedly, copied by their various delightful grand-offspring. Lady Emily waved, Jessica bent to the oars, or rather sculls, and as it was cold and just beginning to rain they turned and went back to the boat shed.

"You get out," said Jessica to Lady Emily and Philip. "I'll tie her up," so they got out and she tied up and they stretched themselves and went back to the house.

Their various parents, being no longer young, had most sensibly been indoors for most of the afternoon, talking about such eternally interesting subjects as the new Mangold and Wurzel Bill introduced by the member for somewhere outside the county and therefore to be despised, which had just been defeated; and so to that eternally delightful theme—the horribleness of Victoria, Lady Norton and her son and daughter-in-law Lord and Lady Norton against whom, we think, no one had any particular grudge except that they were incredibly dull and undistinguished and did not give good dinner parties.

"We got asked there because of Everard being a Headmaster," said Kate Carter, "and they would talk about some wonderful coeducational school where the boys are *such* gentlemen."

"Kate puts it mildly," said Everard. "The girls remain just like themselves and the boys are young gentlemen of ladylike manners. I don't mean anything *wrong*," he added, at which everyone didn't laugh because they thought if they began they couldn't stop.

"I could say *much* worse than that," said Kate, "but I won't. What do you think we found in our dining-room, Lydia?"

Lydia said she didn't know, but one might find anything at Northbridge Rectory. Mr. Villars had found what looked like part of the piles of a bridge, when strengthening the garden against flood on the river side.

Kate said not exactly that, but the carpenter had to take some boards up because of what looked like dry rot—or was it wet rot—at which point her husband said dry rot was what you found in pulpits according to an old Punch joke; but no one laughed. Kate repeated—though quite kindly—"Either dry rot or wet rot, it turned out to be and no one knew why."

"In fact a story of a cock and a bull," said Everard, but we fear that no one took his allusion.

Lord Pomfret said that when he had to take over Pomfret Towers there was a lot of rot behind the panelling in the hall but he didn't know if it was wet or dry.

"We simply couldn't afford to have anything done about it," he said, "and Wheeler—that was the old chimney sweep from Nutfield who always did the chimneys—said he had once put his brush up the big chimney in the hall, before it was blocked up that was, and what came down you'd hardly credit."

"Was it a bullock and a baby and a whale?" said Lady Pomfret, which completely flabbergasted her audience.

"But that really did happen," said Lady Pomfret. "I don't mean in a chimney. It was at Rottingdean where we used to go in the summer when Roddy and I were small and there was a song about all the interesting things that happen there and one was a very stormy winter when a bullock and a baby and a grand-piano and a whale were all washed up in one week."

"Was that all?" said Everard, rather a doubting Thomas.

"Oh, no," said Lady Pomfret, "there was a cargo of brandy another year and everyone came from miles round and you couldn't get to the sea for people lying drunk in the road."

"That's a fact," said Mr. Wickham, who had come in quietly. "I wasn't there myself because I wasn't born, but my old uncle was and he said another lot of casks came in next year and the whole county turned up, but it was paraffin oil. God help them!" he added piously, though whom he did not specify. "Stomach-pumps forward was the word," which of course made everyone laugh and feel it was just as well their darling children were not there, or nothing else would be talked about for weeks. "I'll go and see if those young people are back. I'm always waiting for someone to be drowned at the Hatches', and off he went.

"Cheerful bloke," said Everard Carter, "but a good bloke," with which Noel Merton agreed, saying he didn't know what the place would do without Wickham, especially as he himself had to be in London for a large part of the year.

"You needn't, Oscar; you needn't," said Everard, but his little parody and *écho du temps passé* was not noticed.

Then tea was announced by Palmer who said she had rung the outside bell ever so long, so if the young ladies and gentlemen didn't come back no one could be blamed; she then retired, leaving everyone with a feeling—quite unnecessary—of guilt. But of course the young ladies and gentlemen were perfectly safe and did come back and there was a sumptuous tea for them at the large round table which could seat ten if needed, and a more refined tea for the grown-ups at another table.

"Sit anywhere, please," said Lydia, adding to the parlourmaid "do we need eight places?"

"Well, madam," said Palmer, who like all good, well-trained servants, had taken offence without waiting for it to be offered, "as you wish of course, but I thought, well, supposing anyone else was to turn up. Of course I can clear one off, madam."

"Oh, no, don't bother, Palmer," said Lydia.

Palmer said, in a voice of ice, Very well madam and left the room.

"What an expressive back that woman has," said Mr. Wickham. "It's as good as Lord Burleigh's nod," at which words most of the party said to itself—if it had noticed it—that Mr. Wickham always had the right word, while the Chosen Few savoured the allusion and despised people who didn't know The Rehearsal.

But the most delightful outings—for one can be very happy even on an English summer day if there is good company—must come to an end. Lord Mellings had left his scarf somewhere and Lavinia said she thought he had taken it off in the boat shed and they had better go and look. So back they went and after a brief search it was found bundled up in a corner.

"Thank you so much," said Ludovic. "I am always stupidly losing things."

Lavinia said, perhaps it was because he was so tall, which is no explanation at all, but he seemed to think it reasonable.

"Father is too," he said, "but he has Mother. She is always saving his life."

"So is my mother," said Lavinia. "She saves father's. I'd like to save people's lives if I knew how. I think Jessica Dean is very good at it too. She made you sing for her at the Coronation Entertainment, didn't she? Can you still sing?"

"Well, I *can*," said Lord Mellings, "and I like it—but only for myself of course, and I'm not much good at accompanying myself either."

"Then let's have a concert," said Lavinia. "You tell me what songs and I'll play them if you've got the music. I'm pretty good at piano. I suppose it's because I'm not so good at lessons. At least I like arithmetic and algebra and geometry."

"But isn't music a kind of divine mathematics?" said Lord Mellings. "Someone said that and I thought it rather good. After all, the sun and the world and everything is a kind of mathematics. Perhaps we are too."

"Then you're addition and I'm subtraction," said Lavinia, which witty and meaningless remark made them both laugh and they came back laughing.

All the good-byes were said and the Pomfrets went away. Lord Pomfret glad, as always, to be going home; his wife hoping the afternoon had done him good—which we think it had; Giles full of future plans for more boating at the Mertons'; Emily wishing loudly that they had a river in their own garden. Lord Mellings hardly spoke at all—but his family were used to his quietness. He had enjoyed the party much more than he thought he would. If he could go again to Northbridge soon. Or if

Lavinia came to Pomfret Towers then they could have a concert in the old schoolroom. No one would bother them and Nurse would give them tea and he would sing and Lavinia would play. If only his father and mother and Emily and Giles could all be out, that would be very nice too, which we think was the first sign of his wish—unrecognized by him—for a private life. The army was a Good Thing. His parents were very nice and he loved Pomfret Towers with all its hideousness, but something was wanting. Probably some music—yes of course, that was what it was.

The party was over, the guests had gone home. Noel and Lydia were peacefully together, the drawing-room fire burned brightly.

"Ah! so the silence is, so is the hush," said Noel.

"What on earth do you mean?" said Lydia.

"Poetry, my love, slightly misquoted," said Noel, "by a gentleman called Matthew Arnold who must have been an infernal bore in many ways. Max Beerbohm made a delightful caricature of him. But every now and then he was a real poet."

"Do read it to me," said Lydia, for they did a good deal of reading aloud when alone.

Noel obediently went to the bookcase where only poetry was kept and took the book back to his chair. He was one of the few readers-aloud who can read without having a Special Voice and do not choke—as we do—when it is too beautiful. Of course he was a lawyer, trained to speak, but there is much more than that. When he had finished Lydia remained silent.

"Do you like it?" said Noel presently.

"'Ah, so the silence was, so was the hush,'" said Lydia softly.

There was silence again and each felt what extraordinary luck it was to live one's life with the other.

CHAPTER 8

There was a slight acquaintance between the Pomfrets and that amiable and prolific writer Mrs. Morland. That is, they had met fairly often at other people's parties; Lady Pomfret had asked Mrs. Morland if she would be kind enough to autograph some of her books which were going to be raffled, which Mrs. Morland had willingly done; Mrs. Morland had deputized for Lady Pomfret at a Women's Institute meeting when her ladyship suddenly went down with influenza. Lady Pomfret had sent a most handsome contribution of dull embroidery by the late Lord Pomfret's mother to the High Rising W.V.S. Bring and Buy Sale. Twenty-three raffle tickets at one shilling each were sold and the winner at once put the embroidery up for raffling again and had the ill-luck to get the winning ticket for the second time, when Mrs. Morland had nobly bought it from her—the money of course going to the W.I. funds—and had given it to the secretary for use again on a later occasion. No one could disentangle the finances of this deal, or coup, but everyone was happy and Lady Pomfret had felt distinctly grateful to Mrs. Morland.

It is, we think, a sign of good blood and deep roots in our aristocracy that a certain number of them are still extremely stupid, obstinate and believers in the Good Old Days. They will kill themselves in doing their duty in the station of life to which it has pleased God to call them, and will be rewarded, we hope, in a better land where there are plenty of servants and they can afford to take over the Hunt and have enormous house parties and lose (and win) huge sums at cards, and have large families who all marry well, a black sheep or two (but asked to remove their names only from the very best clubs), and in general are all for women, painting, rhyming, drinking, besides ten thousand freaks that dy'd in thinking. In fact a delightful wish-fulfilment dream, though whether a celestial fulfilment would really make them happy, we doubt. There are of course a few trifles such as spring mattresses and a good drainage system and electric light and cars and the telephone which one would like to incorporate in that world of all our wish; but it is all a dream. We know—a little—what we are; we know not what we shall be; the readiness is all. And in words that have become almost part of the language now: Carry on Sergeant. Lord Pomfret will carry on. So will his wife. We think that their wish and hope, though they do not talk much about it even to one another, is that their children shall continue in the tradition of service. Lord Mellings was a slow grower, a slow developer, as his father who had been through the same stage himself fully recognized—and so did his mother. What Lord Mellings thought or felt about himself, we do not yet know and possibly never shall. His parents have given him love and a happy home life; his tall and we may say lanky and overgrown body has broadened and strengthened; he has settled down well to prepare for a professional soldier's life. One cannot ask more, or see ahead.

Giles, an indefatigable county gossip, had brought back to Pomfret Towers an account of his day at High Rising and what nice servants Mrs. Knox had and how nice Mrs. Morland was—particularly this last. He was so full of her praise that his parents thought it would be pleasant to ask her to the Towers; that is, if she would like to come, because one never knew with people who wrote books.

"I shall never forget," said Lord Pomfret to his wife, "that winter when you came to stay at the Towers and my aunt had invited that dreadful woman who married poor George Rivers. I wonder what's happened to George. He hardly ever came up to town, because his wife hated the country, so he just stayed down at his place. She gave me a good sickener of people who write books—I mean women that write about 'Middle Aged Woman has Come-back with Young Lover,' at which his wife, who with all her goodness and kindness had not a very great sense of humour, suddenly almost guffawed. Partly at her husband's words, partly at the remembrance of how old Lord Pomfret had stigmatized the Honourable Mrs. George Rivers's works as Hermione's twaddle about old women falling in love with young men. In *his* young days, the Earl had continued with a ribald laugh, it was the old men who fell in love with the pretty young girls.

"But do ask Mrs. Morland, if you like, Sally," said Lord Pomfret. "What about lunch one day next week? I suppose she has a car; it's such a cross-country journey."

His wife said there wasn't a single journey in Barsetshire that wasn't cross-country, and she knew most of the county. Mrs. Morland could easily drive over from High Rising. After all, Giles had ridden over on his pony, and what about next Wednesday. To this her husband was quite agreeable, so she rang up Mrs. Morland who said she would love to come and was it a party, because her only respectable coat and skirt were at the cleaner's and she wasn't sure if they would be ready and with this summer weather one *had* to wear something warm. Lady Pomfret said it could be a party or not, just as Mrs. Morland liked; she rather wanted to ask the Noel Mertons who had been such good friends to Ludo—her elder boy. Mrs. Morland said she had four boys only they were all married men now and she hoped to see Ludo and liked the Mertons. So all was comfortably settled and Lady Pomfret rang up the Mertons and they could come.

"And do bring your Lavinia," said Lady Pomfret. "Ludo says

she promised to do some music with him. He did so enjoy his day at Northbridge."

"And we enjoyed him," said Lady Merton. "I can't help liking boys, because of Colin—my special brother. He was a schoolmaster for a bit and he brought some very nice boys for the Whitsun holidays one year. One of them, Eric Swan, married a sister of Lord Lufton's. I expect you know them. He is a master now at Harefield House School."

It is *not* a snobbishness; but it is a rum thing that if someone you don't know, or only know slightly, happens to turn out to be an old friend of Lupin Pooter whose uncle was a cousin of your brother-in-law, everything suddenly becomes all right. All of which has been set down for us by one William Schwenk Gilbert in his *Bab Ballads* when, as all educated people will remember, Peter Gray a tea-taster and Somers who imported indigo were the sole survivors of a wreck, cast ashore on a desert island, but as they had not been introduced, they could not speak with one another. There were oysters at Peter's side and turtle on Somers's; but neither liked his own allotment. By chance Peter overheard Somers soliloquizing about his old playmates, including Robinson. Gray had been at Charterhouse with Robinson and introduced himself, after which the castaways became friends and each ate the delicacy he desired till the dreadful day when an outward bound convict ship sent a boat off to the island; and who was pulling stroke but Robinson "in an unbecoming convict's frock, Condemned to seven years for misappropriating stock." After this it was of course impossible for them to be on speaking terms again and "Peter has the oysters, which he hates, in layers thick. And Somers has the turtle— turtle always makes him sick."

So Eric Swan became an easy stepping-stone between Northbridge Manor and Pomfret Towers.

Lady Pomfret hesitated about guests for the lunch, wondering whether to have a party or just take Mrs. Morland as one of the family so to speak, having—in common with a good many other quite intelligent people—a conviction that people who wrote books were slightly peculiar and must—in the beautiful words of the butcher when Tom Pinch and his sister Ruth so dashingly brought some beef-steak and Tom tried to cram the package into his pocket—be humoured, not drove. But fate kindly came to her assistance in the person of Lord Stoke who rang up per his butler to ask if he could come to lunch on that day and he would drive over with Mrs. Morland in his dog cart.

On hearing of this expedition Emily and Giles fell into transports of joy. Riding horses they knew and loved, but like the rest of their generation they took road transportation by car for granted. Both had learnt to drive a car within their parents' property when under legal age and it was obvious that they were far better than many license-holders. But to drive a gig, or a phaeton, or a dog-cart, where such still existed, was to them high romance.

The friendship between Mrs. Morland and Lord Stoke was of long standing with a certain amount of criticism on both sides. Never had there been the slightest touch of romance in it. Mrs. Morland had long ago almost forgotten her late husband who was—we believe—quite a good sort but of no great interest. Lord Stoke had, a very long time ago, admired and loved old Lady Pomfret—she who was Edith Thorne. She had married Another and sent back to him the pretty necklace of baroque pearls that he had given her. He had not worn the willow, but he never married and to Edith Graham, now Lady William Harcourt, whose grandmother Lady Emily Leslie was of the Pomfret family, he had given the pearls. It was the joy and pride of West Barsetshire to see him high-seated in his dog-cart, a light rug over his baronial knees, Mrs. Morland at his side and his groom sitting back to back with them. The young Fosters were looking out for him and received him with shouts of joy; though to be accurate it was Emily and Giles who shouted and Ludovic who came to the side of the dog-cart to hand Mrs. Morland down, a gesture which she much appreciated though she would far rather have clambered down unassisted and un-noticed; for do it how you will it is an ungraceful descent for the middle-aged. If only the kind, kind young sometimes realized how the kindly offered shoulder, or arm, or hand can irritate us (though we realize the kind intention) they might spare us. We are not sure whether the kind hand put under the pathetic, frail old Mother's elbow is not the most irritating of all: but *so* well meant—perhaps the most damning faint praise there is.

We need hardly say that Jasper, scenting company—probably not unaccompanied by tips—had lounged onto the gravel as the dog-cart arrived; and even less need we say that Lord Stoke at once singled him out for a really interesting talk. We wish we could have a photograph, or a rough sketch however bad, of those two great characters; Lord Stoke with his grey bowler hat and old Jasper wearing a moleskin cap with flaps which were tied on the top of his head when not needed to protect his ears. Each recognized in the other something he did not himself possess and neither of them would give anything away.

Jasper began the ceremony by going to the horse's head and—to the deep annoyance of the groom—laying one hand on its neck and talking to it in a low voice, though no one could hear what he was saying. What was even more annoying to the groom was that the horse was quite obviously interested in Jasper's remarks and nodded its head two or three times in assent.

Lord Stoke, who knew a good deal about horses and gipsies, went nearer, the better to hear what was going on.

"Here! speak up, pal," said Jasper.

The horse made a whinnying sound and gently pawed the gravel with its off front leg (if this is correct).

"You are Jasper," said Lord Stoke; not accusingly, but as one who states a fundamental and irrefragable (if that is what we mean) fact. "Your people live over Grumper's End way."

"That's right, my lord," said Jasper, skilfully tuning his voice to Lord Stoke's deafness.

"*You* don't mumble," said Lord Stoke. "All the young people mumble now—I daresay what they mumble isn't worth listening to. How's old Pharaoh Lee?"

"He'll be out of Barchester jail next week, my lord," said Jasper.

"Not the first time," said Lord Stoke. "What was it? Chickens?"

"No, my lord," said Jasper. "A broody hen and a nice clutch of eggs, tenth conviction. I warned him, my lord, but he's obstinate. I'll put the horse in the stable, my lord."

"Excuse me, my lord," said the groom with an icy subservience that no actor could have bettered, "but am I wanted?"

"Want? *I* don't want anything," said Lord Stoke. "You go along with Jasper. *He'll* tell you all about greasing a horse's teeth so that he doesn't eat his oats. You needn't be back till about three o'clock. Will that be all right for you?" he added, turning to Mrs. Morland and speaking as a landowner of good birth and breeding.

Mrs. Morland, feeling a slight responsibility for her old friend's peculiarities, said just as it suited him.

"Oh, but not so early, Lord Stoke," said Lady Pomfret. "The Mertons are *so* looking forward to meeting you and I hope you will stay to tea. Can you, Mrs. Morland?"

Mrs. Morland said she would love to, and seeing that Lord Stoke was again deep in talk with Jasper, she said to Lady Pomfret hadn't they better take him indoors because it was *such* a nuisance when the lunch had to be put back; and at that moment the Mertons drove up. Introductions were not needed, there was a Babel of talk and the party went into the house.

When we say the house, it was of course only one wing of the great mansion, most of which had now for a considerable time been occupied by the offices of Mr. Adams the big industrialist and his co-father-in-law Mr. Pilward of Pilward's Entire. The Pomfrets had now for a long time lived in part of one wing of their great unwieldy home where they were contented and, what is more, far more comfortable than they had ever been when the huge house was still lived in by the family. Lady Pomfret had kept enough of the garden to give her pleasure but not be too tiring. A few elderly men about the place were always pleased to dig, or to mow the grass, especially the Green River, a winding path of well-mown grass that led up a gentle slope, overshadowed by beech trees and carpeted in the late spring with bluebells, to the stream and the pool. The housekeeping had been made much easier for Lady Pomfret since Mr. Adams insisted on a small and very modern kitchen on the same level as their dining-room: our reader may have noticed, if she assisted at a dinner party given by the Pomfrets some time ago, that on the whole there was a good deal of real comfort.

Some day an essay might be written on Comfort. It appears to us to have three solid bases; the first good heating; the second good food well cooked, the third really comfortable beds.

The heating had been professionally installed under Mr. Adams's direction and as the whole mansion was now centrally heated he was able to say, with a fair amount of truth, that it added very little to the cost. Both Lord and Lady Pomfret had made an honourable and sincere attempt to pay their share, but Mr. Adams said it would be more trouble to work than it was worth and if necessary he would sting his other commercial tenants for a bit more, as they could well afford it. A piece of casuistry which the Pomfrets gratefully accepted.

As for cleaning and cooking and the beds, they were nominally Lady Pomfret's concern, but the organizing was mostly done by Nurse, who had been with all the children since she took Lord Mellings after the first month and enjoyed being the power behind the throne. She had her reward: partly in feeling that she was the mainstay, the newel post, the prop, the guardian of the house; and also in being the centre to which all the gossip came. The children all turned to her when in any scrape: nearly being drowned by riding his pony across a small tributary of the Rising when in flood (Giles); eating all the strawberries she

could see whether ripe or unripe (Emily); one's *awful* face (Lord
Mellings while going through the most inevitable spotty
stage—but that, we are glad to say, was now past). But though
rather a tyrant in private—which did not hurt the young in the
least—she was truly devoted to the family and looked forward,
we believe, to caring for the grandchildren who would undoubtedly come later. Emily's first of course, as girls usually marry
younger than boys; and then Ludo's and Giles's. And as Nurse is
used to getting her way, we think that all these things will
happen, even if we are not there to see them.

Being only a party of eight at a round table, all knowing one
another, the seating presented no difficulties. Lord Stoke was
between Lady Pomfret and Lavinia Merton of which young
lady he did not take much notice. Not that he despised her, but
he was extremely anxious to find out from Lady Pomfret
whether her brother Roddy Wicklow could spare time to come
over and have a look at a horse he had bought lately and didn't
like the look of. What exactly was wrong he couldn't say. It
looked like a touch of swine-fever but as the horse wasn't a pig
that wouldn't wash. His own impression was that its former
owner had fed it all wrong and not exercised it enough. The
funny thing about a horse, he said meditatively, was that if it
sweated it usually meant it was a bit scared. Now *people*, he said,
sweated because they had played tennis too hard, or any other
game. When he was a young man, he said, he used to play
squash a good deal and always had a shower and a good rub-
down afterwards. Lady Pomfret, who had been a first-class rider
herself, expressed her interest and sympathy about the horse and
said she hadn't played tennis much, because she never really got
the hang of it and one had to be almost professional standard
now for ordinary country-house tennis. Then she turned to
Noel, and Lord Stoke was left to Lavinia who was completely at
her ease and treated his lordship as if he were a nice uncle,
perhaps a little wanting in the intellect. But she met her match,
for his lordship, who liked young people, told her all about

Rising Castle where his forbears had lived for many generations, with its Norman keep and some of the old walls and the cave under its foundations known as the Stokey Hole, and didn't let her get a word in edgeways.

"You know Mrs. Morland," he said to Lavinia, looking across the table at that lady who was talking to Lord Pomfret. "She brought her youngest boy and a friend of his over in the holidays once and they went into the Stokey Hole because someone had told them it went underground all the way to the Tower of London."

"And did it?" said Lavinia. "I'd love to explore it, so long as it isn't too dark."

"Well, you ask your father or your mother to bring you one day," said Lord Stoke. "But you can't go into the Stokey Hole. I had to have an iron gate put across the entrance because trippers used to go in."

"Did you think they'd never find their way out, like Injun Joe?" said Lavinia.

"God bless my soul, do you read Mark Twain?" said Lord Stoke. "I thought it was all Space Ships and Mechanical Men and that stuff now."

"Of *course* I've read Mark Twain," said Lavinia. "But I wish I knew how the Negroes really talked, specially that nice one that went down the Mississippi with Huck Finn. It's all in the book, but one doesn't know what the proper sound of it ought to be."

"You have to be brought up as a child among people if you want to do their talk properly," said his lordship. "There's that writing-feller, Harvey or Hardy or something, that wrote all those books about Dorset. *He* knew how they talked—but if you hear people reading him aloud *they* don't know. Same with Barsetshire. Fellers write books about it but *they* don't know. Women too."

"Don't you like women's books, Lord Stoke?" said Lavinia.

"That's as it happens," said Lord Stoke. "I read all Mrs. Morland's books. Sensible woman she is. She gives me her new book every year. There's that woman that married poor George Rivers—he's a sort of cousin of mine—writes books about old women falling in love with boys. Bah!"

Lavinia had often read of people who said Bah! but had never really heard it said—as indeed very few of us have—and was properly impressed.

"Father reads aloud to us," she said, "but I like reading to myself best. It's quicker. Father always thinks he ought to explain things to us, but I don't want to be explained to if I like the book."

"Quite right, young lady," said Lord Stoke. "Read everything while you are young. My old nurse taught me my letters— started the day after my third birthday. Sensible thing to do. The Cat Sat On The Mat and that sort of thing. Read all you can while you're young. Doesn't matter if you understand it or not. You'll have made friends that you can always come back to, and every time you meet them you'll like them better. Are *you* going to write books?"

"I don't know," said Lavinia. "I shouldn't think so and I wouldn't know what to say. Besides if everyone did nothing but write books, no one would read them" at which Lord Stoke laughed and said she was a sensible young lady and turned to Lady Pomfret.

"Well?" said Ludo, who was on her other side. "I thought you and Lord Stoke would never stop talking. Father told me that old Lord Pomfret used to shout down the table to people when they talked too long and tell them to talk to the person on the other side of them."

Lavinia said Rather like that thing on the B.B.C. when there were square dances and someone called out to them exactly what they must do next.

"I mean," she said, "things like, Lady right, Gentleman left, Now two steps forward. Hold hands, Swing her round and then set to partners,'" which was improvised nonsense and made

Ludo laugh. "Do you like dancing?" she said. "I mean proper dancing."

"I love it," said Ludo. "It makes me feel un-shy; so long as the girl is a good dancer of course."

"But you aren't shy a bit," said Lavinia.

"Oh, don't you think so?" said Ludo. "I try not to be but sometimes it just comes over me. I used to be awfully shy when I was younger and came to dinner with your people. You were too little to come down. I expect you were in bed."

Lavinia said, rather loftily, that was a long time ago now.

"Look here, you've not forgotten we were going to have some songs," said Ludo. "The nursery piano was tuned last week and Nurse said she wouldn't let Giles come and bother us. And Emily hates being indoors. She's like Uncle Roddy, always outdoors. She wants to sleep out of doors in the summer but Nurse says You never know," which made Lavinia laugh.

"That's what Old Nanny Twicker always told us," she said. "She was Mother's nurse and has a cottage at the end of the garden. And she says you mustn't ever sleep out of doors when it's full moon."

Ludo asked why.

"She says your face will be all Drawn," said Lavinia. "I mean all sideways, like this," and she twisted her pretty face to one side and shut one eye which made Ludo laugh.

His mother looked across the table. Ludo was never much of a laugher at the kind of silly family fun that she and Emily and Giles had. His father had a melancholy streak and she sometimes thought Ludo had inherited it. It didn't mean anything—suicide or melancholia or Weltschmerz—but it would be *so* much happier for him if he could—in the nursery phrase—have the giggles sometimes. A vague recollection came back to her of one of George Macdonald's enchanting fairy stories about a princess who couldn't laugh, but she couldn't remember its name or anything about it, so *that* wasn't much help. And if Lavinia could help him to laugh it would be an excellent thing.

All these thoughts of course went through her mind like the wind over a field of corn, including a sudden remembrance that the princess could laugh but had lost her gravity and that was why the story was called The Light Princess—a rush of light and shadow and then lost; but not to be forgotten. Then Lydia Merton claimed Ludo, which set Lord Pomfret free to talk to Mrs. Morland. He did not know her well, but he knew she wrote books that lots of people read and wondered if she would despise him for not reading them himself. To his great relief Mrs. Morland at once plunged into the ever-fruitful theme of Lord Aberfordbury and misdeeds.

"It is quite extraordinary," she said, "what a nuisance he is. He must be a centipede."

Lord Pomfret, while fully sharing Mrs. Morland's low opinion of Lord Aberfordbury, was not up in the latest gossip and begged Mrs. Morland to tell him what his lordship had done.

"It's a long story," said Mrs. Morland.

"But I always enjoy your stories—in your books I mean—and the longer the better," said Lord Pomfret. "I hope you don't mind my saying that," so perjuring his immortal soul.

"Good gracious, no!" said Mrs. Morland. "It is so nice when people like them, because then I think perhaps they are fairly good."

"But don't you *know* if they are good?" said Lord Pomfret. "You must forgive me if I sound ignorant, but I'm not very good at reading. I mean I love Dickens and Scott and Thackeray, but I'm not very understanding about modern novels—I mean by people now. But yours are delightful."

As it was plain that his lordship was getting into a fine muddle from his desire to please and to be truthful at the same time, Mrs. Morland rammed her hat a little more firmly onto her head and took him in hand.

"The great thing," she said, "is to know if you like a book or not. The rest doesn't matter a bit. If you like things like Gibbon, or Gregorovius that go on for ever it is a great help, because they are so long that you can't remember them, so you can always read them again—like Proust."

By this time Lord Pomfret knew that either he, or the gifted novelist, was mad, but tried hard not to show it.

"My books used to be fairly long," said Mrs. Morland, who was far from an egoist, but once launched on any subject always found it difficult to stop, "but that was before the war, so it didn't matter."

As she had apparently finished what she was saying, Lord Pomfret asked why it didn't matter then and did matter now.

"'Thrift, thrift, Horatio'," said Mrs. Morland.

"But your books aren't a *bit* like funeral baked meats," said Lord Pomfret.

"How nice of you," said Mrs. Morland, warmly appreciative of his reference to the Bard. "What I mean is that before the war one could make one's book as long as one liked, and I used to write quite long ones and I still always enjoy reading them. But after the war THEY said books cost so much more to produce that I should have to make them shorter so that they would cost less; only the people who read them have to pay more, so it all seems very peculiar but I never could understand money, except Mr. Micawber's advice, which is just good common-sense."

By this time Lord Pomfret's brain was reeling, but he steadied it manfully and said did she mean not spending more than you have.

"Exactly," said Mrs. Morland, in a satisfied voice, as of a barrister who has got exactly the answer he wanted from a reluctant witness. "And I never have. Annual income twenty pounds, annual expenditure nineteen, nineteen six—but you know the rest."

"I'm afraid I don't," said Lord Pomfret. "Ought I to?"

"Oh, *father*," said Lord Mellings, across Lydia who was between them, "you *must*. It's *Dickens*."

"I don't know how to say it," said Lord Pomfret to Mrs.

Morland, "but I can't read Dickens. I mean I have read some of him, but not to remember."

"Well! the Lord have mercy upon your soul," said Mrs. Morland. "I can only pity your ignorance and despise you."

Lord Pomfret was rather taken aback by this onslaught, but Mrs. Morland was a guest, under his roof, at his table, and had eaten his bread and salt.

"Of course I didn't say that—it was Fanny Squeers I think—but I am not quite sure. I know one ought to verify one's references but if you don't know whereabouts to verify them, you can't," Mrs. Morland went on. "I mean I can't read right through all Dickens to find one quotation."

"I am sorry," said Lord Pomfret, with his tired courtesy. "But I am not much of a Dickensite. I know it is bad taste in me, but I can't help it."

"Now that," said Mrs. Morland, up in arms for seeing things straight, "is just rubbish. There isn't any good or bad taste about what books you read: it's what you like or don't like. I can't read *any* Russian books. Of course not in *Russian*, because nobody can, but not even in translations, though I find Turgenev much less boring in French than in English. Of course all educated Russians—when there were some—used to speak French which perhaps accounts for it."

"But isn't there a Society that knows all about Dickens?" said Lord Pomfret, rather meanly ignoring the Russian question. "They have a branch in Barchester. It's called the Dickens Fellowship, I think. They could tell you."

Mrs. Morland said How stupid of her and of *course* that was what she would do, at which point Noel Merton on her other side claimed her attention, much to Lord Pomfret's relief. Not that he didn't like and respect Mrs. Morland, but her snipe-flights were sometimes—as on the present occasion—quite beyond him.

"I don't know why it is that we meet so seldom," said Noel. "I should like it of all things, but I am so much in London."

"I thought," said Mrs. Morland, not unkindly but—which is perhaps even worse—impartially, "that lawyers *had* to be in London. At least barristers which I suppose is really what you are, only a K.C.—I mean a Q.C. You see, when I was a very little girl there were still Q.C.'s because of Queen Victoria, but as I was only very small when she died I don't remember it and then they turned into K.C.'s and we all settled down comfortably and then it was Q.C.'s again. If we had a President I suppose it would be P.C.'s only that would be confusing because it stands for Police Constable. Or of course it might be Privy Counsellor."

We think that our old friend had really excelled herself in this divagation, and even the eminent Q.C. felt a little addled.

"I should hate to have to cross-examine you," he said.

"Well, I don't suppose you will," said Mrs. Morland. "I have never been up before the beak and I don't suppose I shall. I drive *very* carefully and I got myself re-tested a few years ago and they said I was all right. I believe when you are seventy they retire you or something, but one never really knows and what one hears usually isn't true and so I don't worry."

Sir Noel Merton, Q.C., felt for a moment that he would like to shake Mrs. Morland for her imbecility; but remembering that people who write novels are a race apart (which is a complete fallacy, because—apart from the conceited ones like the Honourable Mrs. George Rivers—they are just ordinary people) he decided to accept her as she was; thus unconsciously repeating that preposterous Margaret Fuller from New England who said that she accepted the universe, on which Carlyle's comment was "By God she'd better." But he subdued his lower self and contented himself with saying that he was not a beak—only a jumped-up barrister. And why beak, he said, he had not the faintest idea.

"Nor have I," said Mrs. Morland. If, she said, the French called a magistrate a bec, that would of course explain it, but she didn't think they did. They had, she said, a bird they called a gros-bec, which meant a hawfinch, but as she hadn't the faintest idea what a hawfinch was, that didn't really help. Or ought one, she said, to pronounce it haffinch—like chaffinch.

In spite of being a very eminent Q.C. and a really educated person, Noel was completely at a loss, and—to his shame and mortification—could not conceal it.

Wasn't it, Mrs. Morland said, a Captain Hawdon who was called Nemo and had been Lady Dedlock's lover, only lover was such a peculiar way of saying someone you had a child by that you weren't married to—she did not mean, she added, that you weren't married to the child, because that would be like Euclid.

Noel, for the first time in his life we think, was absolutely bamboozled. Could she, he said, in the deferential tone with which he addressed any judge whom he thought worthy of it, enlighten him.

"Well: things that are equal to the same thing are equal to one another," she said. "At least they were when I was a girl. It was called axioms, which meant you had to believe them whether they were true or not. But what I *meant* was that Hawdon and Hawfinch have the same beginning though of course the ends are different."

Thankful to have a little solid ground beneath his feet, though he was still giddy, Noel thanked her for her elucidation of a knotty point.

"Though how a point can have a knot, I cannot think," said Mrs. Morland in so judicial a way that Noel wondered if he ought to put his thumbs into his waistcoat arm-holes (which barristers always do in plays or films, but whether in real life we do not know). "*Would* the Gordian Knot have had a point?"

Noel said he didn't know much about it, a comment which his wife recognized as slight boredom—a malady which was apt to overtake him occasionally, for he did not suffer fools with any enthusiasm.

"Sir," said Giles who had been far too busy eating to bother about what people were saying, but was now ready to show off, "the Gordian Knot was a knot that nobody could untie. They must have been pretty wet. I could untie anything. If I'd been Alexander I'd have found one of the ends and then I'd have tracked it."

"You couldn't," said Emily, who had been eating steadily and thought but poorly of this conversation. "It was inside. Both ends were inside."

"They couldn't be," said Giles. "One end would be in the middle and the other end on the outside—just tucked in—and I think they were mugs not to find it."

"All you would have to do," said Mrs. Morland, much interested in this discussion, "would be to poke the end right into the middle of the knot. You could get one of those packing needles—you know, rather curved and flat. When I was a very little girl and we went away for the summer Nanny always took the nursery bath because she could pack everything in it and then she wrapped it in hessian and sewed it up with string. I've still got the packing needle she always used and it comes in most handy. When Stoker—*you* know Stoker, Giles—makes a suet roll with jam in it she wraps it in a cloth and sews it up with that same needle."

"Like a hair-loom," said Giles. No one quite understood what he meant and by the time he had spoken, what he said appeared to him to be meaningless. We have all had that experience.

"That's a different kind of loom," said Emily in a lofty way. "It's something a family goes on having."

"And that is quite enough," said Lord Pomfret. He said it quietly, but both children at once piped down. Lady Pomfret looked at him with a kind of loving pride, for it was largely through her that he had, later than most men, gained an air of authority very becoming to his position. Now she felt that he was no longer in leading strings or—as she suddenly remembered pictures in some old books for children that her parents had kept—in a kind of little pen on wheels which could be pushed about the nursery floor by the child inside it. He could walk alone—and with authority—and it was to her an enormous relief. If only her tall elder son could follow in the same path—and she looked at Ludo with love and hope and trust—if he could work as his father had worked, her heart would be at peace. And someday, she hoped, he would marry the right wife; someone who would be a shield and a fortress and a rock. But there was plenty of time for that. He had begun a profession and was doing well in it. With the right woman—girl—whatever you like; at the proper time. And she began, as mothers will, to sketch a marriage in the lovely chapel of Pomfret Towers—and then she thought of the larger part of the house in the hands of big business and almost sighed. But she quickly pulled herself together and remembered that the wedding would be in the hands of the bride's parents. And who the bride would be she had not the faintest idea; nor we think had Lord Mellings.

But all these thoughts took far less time than it has taken us to set them down on paper—pursuing them as fast as we can and almost outdistanced every time. No one had noticed that Lady Pomfret was years and a thousand leagues away and she picked up the talk exactly where she had left it. Everyone was talking and she noticed Lord Stoke on her right getting on excellently with Lavinia Merton who was carrying on as much of a flirtation as a teen-ager can have with a rather deaf peer of over eighty. But apparently both parties were enjoying it.

"You have a pretty name, young lady," said Lord Stoke. "One doesn't often hear Lavinia now-a-days."

Lavinia said she was called after Mrs. Joram.

"That's Canon Joram's wife in the Close," said Lord Stoke rather accusingly. "Charming woman and she wears well. Now, you take some advice from me, Miss Lavinia. Charming women can always get what they want."

"But how does one *be* a charming woman?" said Lavinia.

That, said Lord Stoke with great presence of mind, was for her mother to tell her.

"I suppose it's partly listening to what people say to you and not interrupting, or saying 'I'll tell you what'," said Lavinia.

"Quite right," said Lord Stoke, pleased by so apt a young pupil. "There aren't so many of those people now. There was Lady Pomfret—"

"Do you mean Lady Pomfret?" said Lavinia in a low voice, looking across the table towards her hostess.

"Dear me, I am talking about long before she was born," said Lord Stoke. "No; she was the wife of Pomfret's—this Pomfret's old cousin whom he succeeded. Their only son was killed—on the North-West frontier I think—and that's how the title came to this man. A good man. Does his duty even if it isn't his choice. And his wife—well, look at her. Good Barsetshire stock and a nice family. Only three but there 'it is. Don't see those big families now—not even with the clergy," and his lordship uttered one of the short barks which showed his own appreciation of his own wit.

Lavinia was naturally enthralled by what he said, her only anxiety being that some of the other guests might have overheard and thought it rather personal, and she longed to hear more.

"You never saw her," said Lord Stoke. "She died a long time ago—before the war. My Lady Pomfret, I mean. Pomfret missed her. So did I. But that's all old history. Edith she was. That nice little Edith Graham who married Lord William Harcourt was called after her. Well—the world goes on. Yes. Edith Thorne she was and the best hands in the county. Do you ride, young lady?"

Lavinia, feeling that she would now forfeit Lord Stoke's good opinion for ever, said she was rather frightened of horses. But Giles rode awfully well, she said. Lord Stoke looked with interest at that young gentleman who was putting away an amount of food calculated to sustain any normal stomach for two or three days.

"Hollow legs, that's what these young people have," said his lordship though not addressing the remark to anyone in particular. "I'll have a word with him afterwards. I've known horses all my life and I'm an old man now."

"What nonsense are you talking, Lord Stoke?" said Lady Pomfret. "You are the youngest of the lot. Years younger than Gillie."

"And I'll tell you why," said Lord Stoke, quite unmoved by this tribute. "I don't worry. Never have. Nearly broke my heart when I was a young man, but heart's don't break. Have you ever *seen* a heart, Lady Pomfret?"

Lady Pomfret said she didn't think she had, except of course that one or two of the Barchester butchers did have hearts, as well as livers and kidneys.

"Well, hearts are hearts," said Lord Stoke, giving a vague impression of an unusual call at bridge. "Damn tough things too, saving your presence. Now livers—that's different. A nice tender bit of liver with some crisp bacon. Always used to have liver and bacon and a fried egg on huntin' days," said Lady Pomfret recognized with admiration the old aristocrat's dropped "g"—almost a mark of his class at one time, and a trait that we believe still lives here and there and long may it flourish. "No wonder people don't break their hearts. They don't go into declines either. My old father had an aunt who went into a decline because she was in love with the curate and he was one of these High Church fellers—confession and simony and all that."

Lady Pomfret, enchanted by his broad outlook on clerical matters, asked what happened to her.

"Her father said he'd horsewhip him if it weren't for his cloth," said Lord Stoke, "and one day in summer, a hot summer it was, he saw the curate bathing in the river. No harm in that—no choir-boys or anything," his lordship added with a fine Victorian leer, "but the old gentleman didn't like it—on his bank it was—so he took the padre's clothes and tied them up—always used to carry a good length of strong cord in his jacket pocket—one of those Norfolk jackets you know—so he tied the curate's clothes in a bundle and threw them into the river above the weir. He didn't know they'd closed the hatches higher up that day, so there was about a foot of water and a lot of stinking mud, but when he did find out he was as pleased as Punch."

Lady Pomfret asked what the end of it was.

"The curate hung about till someone came along and told him what had happened, but the man said it was more than his place was worth to meddle with anything on his lordship's ground and he was sorry he couldn't wait but there was a cow in labour and he must hurry along because he knew the right words to say."

"Do tell me more," said Lady Pomfret, enchanted by this bit of real Barsetshire—the part that still went on underground as it were—the part Jasper knew, and Mr. Wickham the Mertons' agent and a few other favoured people. A part that she and her husband would never know, nor the Mertons. But Giles might, she thought, and he would acquire the knowledge that is hardly spoken but is somehow transmitted. A knowledge that elementary education cannot quite destroy and that will be extremely useful to Giles as he goes on his determined way, so like the old Lord Pomfret whom Giles had never known. And it was nearly twenty years ago that the seventh Earl had quietly died in the lovely full spring of Dunkirk. Twenty years since she and her husband had become the owners of a house too large to live in, of an estate too large to keep and of what had once been wealth but had been whittled down as far as They dared. Oh, well.

So quickly does thought move that all these things had passed through her mind almost in a flash and Lord Stoke placidly continued the story of the unhappy curate without realizing that his neighbour did not hear him. But of course she shook off her thoughts and was at the post just in time to say in a splendidly deceptive voice How *very* interesting that was and Lord Stoke ought to write it down.

"No, no," said his lordship. "'Do right and fear no man,' you know the rest."

The devil then inspired Lady Pomfret to say she thought he was rather unkind. Wasn't the second line, she said, Don't write and fear no woman? Which piece of hoary wit made his lordship laugh in an alarmingly chokey kind of way and drew the attention of the whole table to him and his partner in guilt, and Lord Pomfret first smiled and then really laughed. And to see and hear him thus gave his countess so much pleasure that she would willingly have painted herself with stripes and cavorted on the stage like the Royal Nonesuch in *The Adventures of Huckleberry Finn* to hear him laugh so much again.

What to do with the guests after lunch is always rather a comedown after lunch itself. The young had, luckily, no doubts. Giles and Emily seized Lord Stoke to show him a new calf. The Mertons and Mrs. Morland went with their host and hostess to the estate room where there was a fire, most welcome on a chill summer day. Lord Mellings with a conspirator's glance summoned Lavinia Merton to follow him, which she did, to the schoolroom, or playroom or whatever one liked to call it where the piano lived. There was a wood fire burning, most welcome on a summer day in a room that faced north, some socks airing on the fender and what could only be Nurse—for old Nurse she was not, having come when Lord Mellings was a small boy.

"I say, Nurse," said Ludo, "this is Lavinia Merton. She's awfully good at music and we're going to do some singing."

Lavinia said How do you do to Nurse and shook hands, thus at once winning her approval.

"I say, Nurse," she said. "Do you remember someone called Twicker that used to work over at Northbridge. He was the gardener when mother's people lived there."

"Now, was that the Twicker that married a foreigner, miss?" said Nurse, who in spite of her status was Barsetshire enough to call anyone from any other country an outsider.

"That's it," said Lavinia. "His wife came from Westmoreland

and we all adore her. She makes all her own bread and cakes and we used to be allowed to stay with her for the night sometimes for a great treat" and she nearly added If Nurse didn't object, but wisely didn't. For though nearly every good Nurse or Nanny or Nana is perfect in her own eyes, it does not displease her to think that others are not quite so perfect.

"She asked me to remember her to you," said Lavinia, which was not only a lie, but an example of the peculiar English language and why foreigners cannot always master it.

"Well, I'm sure that's very nice," said Nurse. "And please tell Mrs. Twicker I was glad to have news of her, miss. It's Miss Lavinia, isn't it?"

Lavinia said Yes, and she was called after Mrs. Joram who was an old friend of her father's.

"Now, your father is Sir Noel Merton, the one that's a lawyer," said Nurse. "My cousin's niece was kitchen-maid there for a time and said everything was very nice."

"Oh, which was that?" said Lavinia. "We've had two—I mean that I can remember. Was it Glamora or Jessie?"

Nurse said it was Jessie and she was really Jessica, after the actress because her mother had once been kitchen—maid to Mrs. Dean at Winter Overcotes who was Jessica Dean's mother. And luckily Lavinia remembered her and said she thought she was with Lady Norton now.

"That's right, miss, but she won't be there long," said Nurse. "Downright stingy they are, looking to see if anyone's taken a bit off the joint or a bit of butter. She's going to better herself. She's got a job as usherette at the Barchester Odeon. It's good pay, miss, but to put a girl like her into a kind of hussar's suit in light blue with buttons, it's enough to make a girl go wrong."

"But she hasn't gone wrong, I hope," said Lavinia, who had heard a good deal about Jessie from cook.

"Well, we can only hope for the best and expect the worst," said Nurse, delighted to be able to deliver her soul about her cousin's niece, though we think she would at once have been up

in arms had anyone else presumed to do so. "Now you and Ludo
are going to play the piano, miss, aren't you? It'll be nice for him.
I'll take those socks away and you can make as much noise as you
like," which she accordingly did.

"She does say a mouthful," said Lavinia.

"I'll say she does," said Ludo, in a kind of parody, which made
Lavinia laugh. "Now what, *really*, would you like to do? There's
that book called *Songs of England* that we talked about. Would
you like to try them?"

Lavinia said if he would she would and seated herself at the
piano, which was an upright one by Broadwood, not so old as to
be jangly or have one note which either would or wouldn't play,
according to its whims and the weather; but not new enough to
mind if that time-honoured duet of Chopsticks was played on it.

"It's a lovely tone," said Lavinia. "I say—did you ever play at
Giants and Dwarfs on the piano when you were small?"

Ludo said Nurse didn't hold with strumming.

"Oh, but this wasn't a strum," said Lavinia. "It was what you
might call a Set Piece; like the Battle of Prague, I expect, that
nice young ladies used to play as a duet. And once I did see three
people playing at once. It was at some sort of school kept by
awfully nice nuns near Brighton when a lot of religious people
had to leave France because of trouble—though I don't know
what the troubles were—but anyway they took boarders and
there were three girls in white frocks with their hair all pulled
back from their faces all playing at once. Shall I show you Giants
and Dwarfs?"

Ludo said By all means.

"Well, it's like this," said Lavinia, shifting her chair a little to
the left. "First you play this little grumbly tune as far down in the
bass as you can, and then you play it louder and then you play it
still louder only an octave higher. That's the giants. And then
you play it as high as you can go very soft and tinkly only upside
down. That's the dwarfs. Of course you need two people to play
it, but if I explain, you can be the other one. And the loud giants

and the tinkly dwarfs get nearer and nearer together till they meet and then you have an *awful* scrimmage. And then the giants begin to go back to the bottom again and the dwarfs begin to go up to the top again and they each get gentler and gentler till that's the end. Bring another chair and we'll have a go. You can be the giants because you're the biggest."

So Ludo brought another chair, picked up the tune at once and entered fully into the spirit of the game. The giants came up, the dwarfs came down and their four hands met in the middle in a frightful scrimmage which made Ludo laugh so much that he was only just in time to get his giants safely back to the bottom again.

"That's lovely," he said. "I say, would you *really* like to play some songs? I don't really sing, but I love songs and neither of the others cares a hoot. Emily wants to learn the flute so that she can play in an orchestra, but I do think a woman looks awfully silly with a flute—all affected and lopsided I mean," and we think we know what he meant; and we have memories of a small woman, in a straw boater well tipped forward on her head and a gentlemanly coat and skirt not very well cut, playing the oboe in one of the Three Choir Festivals—we think Hereford—many, many years ago.

So he fetched that very pleasant *Songs of England, with New Symphonies and Accompaniments* by J. L. Hatton, Boosey and Co., 295 Regent Street (alas not dated) and they enjoyed themselves enormously with anything and everything—all the songs we heard from our elders in our youth, from traditional songs like "Barbara Allen" all through Purcell to Arne and Braham and Bishop.

Lord Mellings lost all his nervousness and self-consciousness while Lavinia dealt most manfully with the delightful accompaniments and they laughed and occasionally nearly cried, especially at *The Death of Nelson* and *The Banks of Allen Water*, and came frightfully to grief over a very dull recitative and aria from Purcell's *Indian Queen* and several more. And the more Ludo sang the more he enjoyed himself and let himself go, and the more Lavinia played the more *she* enjoyed herself; but she did not let herself go, for a good accompanist's job is to follow and support. While they were in the middle of "The Woodpecker Tapping" the tea-gong came reverberating through the house and Nurse came in and said they had better wash their hands and go downstairs. Before Nurse even Euterpe must veil her head and flee. So they washed their hands and went downstairs and Lord Pomfret said he hoped they had amused themselves and was glad to know that they had. Lady Pomfret did not ask any questions, but she saw in her first-born's face an eagerness and a pleasure she would gladly have seen more often. It was with great truth that Lavinia said to Lady Pomfret how much they had enjoyed themselves: and it was with equal truth that Lady Pomfret said she had never seen Ludo so happy and she hoped they would all see a lot of one another before he went back to Sandhurst. And so the Mertons took their leave.

Then Mrs. Morland was hoisted into Lord Stoke's dog-cart—his lordship being already seated—the groom got up behind and away they went.

The Pomfrets watched them go down the drive.

"Well, if it prove a girl, the boy
Will have plenty: so let it be."

said Lord Pomfret. His wife asked him what that was. He said Maud, by Alfred Lord Tennyson and was not entirely applicable to this case as there was no kind of feud between the Mertons and themselves. We doubt whether his wife quite understood, but that does not affect deep love at all. And they agreed that though they did not like the "dating" of the young, it would be quite a good thing for Ludo to have a female friend of his own age in whom he could safely confide. For he had, Lord Pomfret said, observed that in affairs of the heart the young not unnaturally would confide in the chimney-sweep sooner than in their own parents who of course knew nothing at all.

CHAPTER 9

Having done its best to wreck the summer and a good many other things as well, the weather decided to be warm and dry for a short time. It was probably only part of the vicious cat and mouse game that it plays with us, but none the less thankfully received. And perhaps received with special thankfulness by Mr. Oriel, for a large wedding with everyone umbrella'd and mackintoshed and many guests coming through the Close on foot would be a damper, to say the least of it.

Lady Gwendolen had said she did not want bridesmaids, which at her age was quite reasonable. Her unmarried sister Lady Elaine would attend her as a kind of Matron of honour and the Dean approved. To all who knew the Towers family it was obvious that the present Duchess would dominate the ceremony—though of course not impinging on Dr. Crawley's part in it—and as she was extremely competent, the Dowager Duchess was delighted to make over all the arranging to dear Franklin and simply concentrate on being the bride's Dowager Duchess Mother and playing the part well. To this end she had visited Madame Tomkins, the French widow of an English soldier and known as quite the best cutter, fitter, and arbiter of taste in the country. When we say widow, no one knew what had really happened to the late Tomkins: he may have died, he may have run away from his masterful French bride, he may even never have existed, but Madame Tomkins's widowhood was an article of faith among her clients. Lady Gwendolen drove her mother to Barchester and dropped her at Madame Tomkins's High Class Dressmaking establishment in Barley Street while she went on to the Deanery. We may add that the Establishment consisted of two rooms in one of the small houses in Barley Street, whose floors were sloping with age. But Madame Tomkins managed to give it, at any rate to her less sophisticated patrons, the effect of being Really Parisian—a place where *haute couture* was Madame Tomkins's washpot, and over the rue de la Paix did she cast out her shoe. The Dowager who had been a good deal in France fell into talk with Madame Tomkins and of course they at once found a common acquaintance, namely a waiter at the very exclusive private hotel where Her Grace used to stay when she went to Paris; a kind of bond which may be much stronger and more useful than knowing the same Duke, or even the same musical-comedy actress.

The Dowager knew exactly what she wanted to look like. Madame Tomkins examined with reverence the length of grey silk, product of a Paris House which would only supply it to customers known to them for at least two generations, and the exquisite black lace, inherited from a much earlier duchess of French blood who had mourned her husband with French thoroughness and at the very best Parisian dressmakers. So good were the materials that Madame Tomkins—a true artist in her way—was deeply moved and almost shed a tear. But remembering how grey shows any stain she suppressed the tear and took the Dowager's directions.

With most of her Barsetshire clients Madame Tomkins was ruthless—and sometimes rude—because of their ignorance; but with One Who Knew she was all zeal and subservience. Also a Duchess is still Someone, we are glad to feel. The better to show her zeal she rapidly sketched one or two possible patterns featuring models about ten feet high with no hips, far too much accent on the divided bosom, and spindle legs on spike shoes. The Dowager approved *en principe*, but criticized every detail mercilessly. Madame Tomkins asked about Lady Elaine's bridesmaid's dress. The Dowager said her daughter-in-law, the Duchess, was arranging that. She had been prepared for disapproval, but Madame Tomkins took it very easily, saying that of course the Duchess, being American, wouldn't *quite* know, but from what she—Madame Tomkins—knew of *ces Américains*, they were very good in the mass.

The Dowager said that was nothing to do with the ceremony, which would be in the Cathedral.

Naturally, said Madame Tomkins, the ceremony would be in the cathedral. For an English miladi to be married by the rites of her own church and not in a registrar's office was correct, and doubtless *le bon Dieu* would give his blessing.

"But not the *Mass*," said the Dowager.

"It is that I do not express myself well," said Madame Tomkins. "I say *ces Américains* are good in the mass—madame thinks I speak of the messe. I express *en masse*."

"If you mean, Madame Tomkins," said the Dowager, "that Americans are on the whole a good lot, I quite agree. *Passons outre*. When can you give me a fitting?"

To most customers Madame Tomkins would have looked doubtful, fetched a large book, and run her finger down the page saying: "Mrs. Aggs, Mrs. Baggs, Mrs. Caggs . . . *and* Mrs. Zaggs. On Thursday week, moddom, if that suits you," and such was her personality that even Victoria, Lady Norton, had to take any date offered to her with an humble, lowly, penitent and obedient manner—though not, we think, heart; for that organ would probably have been registering all the annoyance its owner had suppressed. Short of going to London there was no other choice, so everyone went to Madame Tomkins provided she would take them. And if she could not, or in some cases would not, they had to go to Bostock and Plummer and get a ready-made and have it altered to fit them. Which is all very well for the younger people, and Bostock and Plummer had suited Miss Phelps the Admiral's daughter (now happily Mrs. Fewling) extremely well when Rose Fairweather had determinedly taken her there for a belt (or girdle if you prefer) the better to honour the tweed suit that Rose, with her usual generosity, had ordered on her behalf from Mr. Hamp the bespoke tailor. But the older we get, the more important it is that our clothes should be good—and not too many of them. The young and charming can wear dresses off the hook for two guineas reduced to thirty-seven and sixpence, and any ridiculous dresses which can be worn and thrown away; but that is not for us. As for the peculiar dresses worn in that summer, Madame Tomkins could not conceal her scorn. Nor can we, though scorn is perhaps not the word. Perhaps compassionate contempt is better for people who go about in perfectly straight dresses looking like a depraved sandwich-man, or evening dresses which appear to be made of twenty yards of material billowing from the waist and then turned up at the knees and fastened to the waist again. But youth—if it is pretty—can get away with anything—as we did with hobble skirts and our mothers with a large pad of horsehair worn behind and tied round the waist with tape as a suitable foundation for their dresses and even for their tight-fitting little jackets and voluminous skirts which had to be held up in wet or dusty weather. But all of this is summed up by the late Anatole France in his *Ile des Pingouins*, where the Devil treats the Penguin who is now a woman to a pair of corsets—and they really *were* corsets then—and as he, in the role of waiting-maid, kindly pulls the laces tighter: "*Vous pouvez serrer un peu plus fort, dit la Pingouine.*" We had done it ourself to ourself in our youth without any harm resulting—but we would not do it now.

So Madame Tomkins summoned her assistant of the moment—a nice-looking girl—and rattled off a list of numbers which to us would mean nothing but a computing machine (a thing we do not wish to meet) gone mad, and told her to take down the measurements.

"Thirty-eight, forty-six, twenty-four," Madame Tomkins dictated—though we do not know what these measurements meant and doubtless we have got them all wrong—and then, going down on her knees measured again and gave more figures, and as fast as she measured and spoke so did her assistant take it all down. Not that the assistant had the faintest idea what they meant, nor have we. "*Un point, c'est tout,*" said Madam Tomkins, rising to her feet. "The dress will be ready for the fitting today week. You see, I have a new assistant, *une jeune fille bien élevée, amie de la jeune comtesse du Lufton, mais bête comme tout. Excusez moi, madame, pour un moment.* I 'ear the telephone and *cette Génifère* will moddle something if she answers. I shall be with you almost at once," and went away leaving her assistant with the Dowager.

"Madame Tomkins says you are a friend of young Lady Lufton," said the Dowager to the assistant.

"We were at the Barchester High School together," said the girl, one of those nice English girls that you can't tell from any other nice English girl. "She comes in here sometimes and if Madame Tomkins isn't too busy we have tea at the Kosy Korner Café," and the Dowager noted with approval that she did not say Cafe.

"And what is your name?" said the Dowager.

The girl said Jennifer Gorman; called after her aunt, she said.

"Well, Jennifer, Madame Tomkins is making me a dress for my daughter's marriage at the cathedral," said the Dowager. "If the dress is a success I expect you would like to see it. Would you like a card for the wedding? I am sending one to Madame Tomkins."

"Oh, thank you *awfully*," said Jennifer. "But if Madame Tomkins is going, she mayn't want to leave the shop with no one there."

"I will manage that," said the Dowager and meant it. "I am glad you see Grace Lufton sometimes. I used to know her father-in-law, but he died a long time ago."

Jennifer said she had been to the Luftons and the children

were darlings and Grace usually came to Madame Tomkins when she was too busy to go to London.

"Do you like the work?" said the Dowager—not inquisitorially, but wishing, as she always did, to know how people's machinery worked and whether she could help in any way. There are compensations in being a Dowager Duchess. One is that—if you can live up to the part—people are apt to respect you and indeed to feel flattered if you notice them. And rightly too, for the rank of Duke is a peculiar one, being the only form of aristocracy whose daughters are born into the rank of a marchioness—and Dukes are in the *Almanach de Gotha*, which practically ignores the rest of our Peerage.

Jennifer said she liked it very much. All Madame Tomkins's— and then she hesitated for customers sounded a poor sort of name when one of them was a real Duchess. But having begun it would be silly not to go on. Such very kind people, she said, making a fresh start, came to get dresses and really she was very happy and after all every customer and every dress was different.

The Dowager put up her face-à-main, an action which had often terrified strangers, though it was only because she mostly couldn't find her spectacles and liked something one could safely hang round one's neck and also stick down one's front, and looked at Jennifer.

"That's right, my dear," she said. "Never quarrel with your bread-and-butter. I won't forget the card."

Then Madame Tomkins came back and Jennifer went away.

"A thousand excuses," said Madame Tomkins. "A call from Lady Cora Waring. I make a dress for her for the Palace Garden Party."

The Dowager, in a spirit of mischief we fear, asked whether Madame Tomkins made for the Bishop's wife.

"For 'ER?" said Madame Tomkins. "*Enfin, votre église anglaise où les* clairgymen *se marient! Elle peut bien se contenter chez* Bostock *et* Plummair. *Si elle mattait le pied chez moi*—"

"*Ne soyez pas trop sévère*, Madame Tomkins," said the Dowager. *"Et comme j'ai mon fils cadet,* Lord William, *qui est clergyman et très heureusement marié avec une charmante personne de trés bonne famille—"*

But before she could finish whatever she had meant to say (hoping that her French was fairly correct) Madame Tomkins was practically doing penance in a white sheet. The Dowager, seizing this opportunity, said would Madame Tomkins ring her up as soon as the dress was ready to be fitted and so took her leave. She had arranged to meet Lady Gwendolen at the Deanery and it was only a short way up Barley Street into the High Street and so under the arch into the Close.

We have always felt that to pass from Barley Street under the grey archway into the Close is almost a moment of magic. Barchester had grown outwards—much too far its lovers thought—and now had big manufacturing and residential suburbs of regimented dullness. One thing had saved it from worse encirclement; the river, which curved round the two sides of the Close, with the Palace garden and the other gardens on the Palace side overlooking it and a strong embankment or embanking wall, kept in constant repair by the proper authorities (for we do not know whose business it was). Barley Street was narrow and crowded and jostling, but once through the arch Peace descended. Not that traffic was forbidden and every house had its car, or cars, but there was still a kind of circling charm that made trippers talk less loudly and even occasionally use the wastepaper baskets which had been fixed to the lamp-posts. It was Mrs. Partington and her mop against the tide—but worth doing.

As the Dowager walked up the river side of the Close she thought of the day when—some years ago now—she had been coming away from a party at the Deanery with her daughters and in the cloisters had met her son, Lord William, walking with Edith Graham. She had at once seen that something was up, but very wisely had made no comment. All had gone well. She was very fond of Edith—as indeed were all the Towers family—and Edith was fond of her and indeed of all her new relations and had an extremely good baby, and had expressed her determination to have several more. The Dowager was very fond of her American daughter-in-law too. This relationship can be very difficult, or perfectly delightful. It can also be quite dreadfully dull, as with the Dreadful Dowager and her daughter-in-law the present Lady Norton. We have seen the difficulties of others but we are thankful to say in our own case that we have had the pleasures and the comforts and indeed the joys of daughters-in-law, not to speak of presents for a dozen or so descendants for Christmas and for birthdays. But to Give is one of the Granny-duties, and also delights.

The Dowager had arranged to meet Lady Gwendolen at the Deanery, but by great good luck they met outside Canon Fewling's house, and exchanged news on what each had been doing. Just at that moment Mrs. Fewling came out and was delighted to hear of the Dowager's visit to Madame Tomkins.

"I owe a great deal to her," said Mrs. Fewling. "Mrs. Fairweather—you know her I expect?—" but the Dowager didn't so Mrs. Fewling explained that she was the daughter of that delightful Mr. Birkett, formerly Headmaster of Southbridge School and had married a naval man, and was extremely handsome and very kind. As the word School meant to the Dowager—broadly speaking—Eton, she could not be as much interested as she would have liked to be, but she put as good a face on it as possible, and asked what Mrs. Fairweather had done.

"Well, she simply *made* me think a bit about clothes," said Mrs. Fewling, which at once gave the Dowager a good opinion of Mrs. Fairweather. "I did a lot of work in the war, mostly on the land, and I was always in trousers. I must have looked awful."

"We all do," said the Dowager. "God did *not* create Eve to wear trousers and no one can say that a fig-leaf is the same as a pair of shorts," which was perfectly true, but Mrs. Fewling could not quite follow her Grace's snipe-flight.

"Now that I have been lucky enough to meet you," said Mrs. Fewling, "would you care to see our house? It isn't as handsome as the Fieldings' but it has its own charm."

What woman can resist an invitation to see a house? The Dowager at once accepted for herself and Lady Gwendolen and visited the house from the basement to the attics, approving all she saw and making one very good suggestion about the scullery sink.

"Talking of sinks," said Mrs. Fewling, "have you seen those machines that you can fix to the sink and they mash everything up so that it all goes down the drain and you don't have those awful garbage pails to empty? We are thinking of having one if it isn't too expensive. American, of course, but I think they make them here now."

The Dowager had not heard of them and was very much interested.

"At my age," she said, "one doesn't easily take to new ideas, but it sounds extremely practical. I wonder if Mr. Oriel has one in his kitchen."

Lady Gwendolen said he certainly hadn't. She had been over the kitchen and liked it, she said, and the machine Mrs. Fewling talked about would be extremely useful and there was a very good sink—quite a modern one of stainless steel, so it couldn't chip as one's old sink did if things were banged about in it.

"We must certainly look into that," said the Dowager. "Towers's delightful wife who is American will tell me all about it. I believe she did have one put in her kitchen when she was improving the house. But at my age I find all those things that are invented to help one are really not very helpful. You are always having to clean them, or get a man to come and replace a nut or a spring or something. A saucepan and a sharp knife and a tin opener and a good garbage tin and there you are."

Mrs. Fewling agreed and said the young brides of today cluttered up their small kitchens with so many labour-saving appliances that they needed a servant to themselves to keep them clean.

"With a really sharp knife and a couple of big spoons and a strong fork, you can do most things," she said. "I did all the cooking for my father and mother when I was a girl and till my first marriage; and the fewer gadgets I had the better I worked."

"You must forgive me," said the Dowager, "but I didn't realize that you had been married twice."

"I never meant to be," said Mrs. Fewling, very simply. "My first husband was Donald Macfadyen."

"Not the man who knew all about vegetables!" said the Dowager. "But of *course!* I met him at old Lady Lufton's. The most charming person and a delightful accent."

"Not so much an accent as just the way he talked," said his relict calmly. "It always warms my heart to hear a Scotch voice."

"I am glad to hear you say Scotch," said the Dowager. "People get quite uppish about saying Scots now—but I notice that they don't say Butter Scots, or Scots Broth. On the other hand," her Grace continued, becoming deeply interested in what she was saying, as we all do, "you wouldn't hear anyone say 'Scotch wha hae. . . .' And after all Sir Walter used Scots and Scotch *and* Scottish, if you take the trouble to read him. But I daresay he is all in strip cartoons, or whatever they call them, now."

By this time they had got to the top storey of the house with a view of the river and the water-meadows beyond.

"I should like to do a water-colour drawing of that," said the Dowager. "It wouldn't be very good, but it would remind me."

"But, mamma, you *can't* say it wouldn't be good," said Lady Gwendolen. "You know everyone *loved* your water-colours at the last exhibition of the West Barsetshire Arts and Crafts Society and you sold them nearly all."

"Of course I did," said the Dowager. "A title is still worth something if you know how to use it. Franklin knows that. Anything she makes will always sell at a bazaar for a good cause. One does get rather tired of good causes, especially before

Christmas. I always put everything I don't like on a special shelf in one of my cupboards and then I give them to people who come begging for Bring and Buy Sales."

"And that reminds me," said Mrs. Fewling. "I should like so much to give you a small wedding present, Lady Gwendolen, but one doesn't want to overlap. I was talking to my husband about it and he wondered if you would accept a book from him—I mean one that he wrote. It is about The Church at Sea."

"How *very* kind of you," said Lady Gwendolen. "But—if I may look a gift-horse in the mouth—isn't that a rather sad comment on the state of the Church in so many parts of the world?"

"Oh, but it isn't a bit *religious*," said Mrs. Fewling. "It's about when he was a sailor. He was in the first war and retired when he was a Commander at the end of the war and became a clergy-man. He was very High, but gradually he got through that and became ordinary, only more to the right than the left, if you see what I mean."

Lady Gwendolen said How very interesting and she would love to have the book and was sure Mr. Oriel would love it too, and then they all went downstairs again and good-byes were said.

"I won't forget about the invitation to the wedding, Mrs. Fewling," said the Dowager, who had a Royal memory. "Not that you would need one of course with your husband, but I would like you to have it, and when all this fuss is over, perhaps you would both come to lunch with me one day," which Mrs. Fewling said they would much like to do.

"Very pleasant people," said the Dowager as she and her daughter went away. But they did not get far. The news that they were in the Close had evidently spread and various friends and acquaintances waylaid them, the chief being Lady Fielding who said they simply must come in and have some tea. Tea is always welcome and as the evenings, though chilly, went on practically for ever, there was no particular reason not to go into the Fieldings' house where there was a nice fire in the drawing-room and the windows were all shut. The Fieldings were old acquaintances and had known the late Duke, who had sometimes been able to put in a useful word on cathedral matters in high circles.

It was a matter for admiration among Lady Gwendolen's friends that she took her engagement so calmly and was delighted to tell them all about the Vicarage and listen to their good advice and from time to time to profit by it, but never introduced the subject herself. The Fieldings were too well bred and too considerate to ask all the questions whose answers they longed to know. This the Dowager quickly recognized and approved, so as a reward to them she told them about her visit to Madame Tomkins.

"Extraordinary woman she is," said Lady Fielding. "No one has ever known whether there was a Mr. Tomkins or not, but she does know her job. She made Anne's—my daughter's—wedding dress quite beautifully. Even the Dean noticed it and you know how he never notices anything. And she has been in Barchester for quite twenty years as far as I can remember and always looks exactly the same age. Once a year she goes to France to see her relations and comes back in very good spirits with a bottle of brandy and a long account of how she quarrelled with everyone and then they all had a farewell dinner and a lot of embracing. Strange pleasures some people have."

The Dowager said she wondered why Madame Tomkins hadn't gone back to France when her husband vanished.

"I think," said Lady Fielding, "because she could earn more money here. She must be quite well off. Occasionally she has said something about a commis-voyageur in the silk trade who would like to offer her his heart; but she thinks he wants her to offer him her savings—which must be considerable by now. She has always been a sphinx and always will be."

Sir Robert said A sphinx without a secret and the Dowager said what a delightful description and Sir Robert said he had always known it and didn't know why, or where it came from. It sounded a bit Oscar Wilde-ish, he said, but that was only a guess on his part and then the talk went back to Lady Gwendolen's approaching wedding.

Lady Fielding asked if the date were fixed and the Dowager gave her the day and said invitations would be sent out in the following week.

"What with the Barsetshire Agricultural Show and the Choristers' Outing and the Dean's engagements it was rather a jigsaw," said her Grace. "But Franklin is a splendid organizer and is doing all the work for me. The only thing that makes me a little nervous is that her cousin that she is so fond of, Lee Sumter, is coming over specially for the wedding, because he wants to see how we do it. I am sure he is delightful, but he sounds rather masterful. I feel he might want to have highballs, whatever they are."

Sir Robert, who had not taken much part in the conversation, said if that was the Lee Sumter whose mother was a Beauregard he had met him at a legal celebration when he was over in the United States last year and he was a very good fellow, with an excellent background, and had passed all his law examinations brilliantly and had the most charming manners to his elders.

The Dowager said she was delighted to hear it and felt much more comfortable.

Lady Fielding asked where Gwendolen and Mr. Oriel were going for their honeymoon and was slightly dashed to hear that they proposed to visit several of the cathedral cities where Mr. Oriel had many old college friends, but would not be away for more than three weeks as Mr. Oriel didn't like to leave his flock to a hireling shepherd. Not, he said, that he was really anxious, but he could not help a feeling of responsibility.

Sir Robert said it made him think of that very robustious picture by Holman Hunt called "The Hireling Shepherd" in which an extremely red-faced shepherd in corduroys is holding an equally red-faced blowsy maiden in an embrace which is obviously going to be far from respectful—or respectable either. But he was sure Mr. Oriel could find a locum who would at least leave the girls alone, which made Lady Gwendolen feel quite reassured and the Dowager, to change the subject, asked how the Palace was getting on.

Quite up to standard, said Sir Robert, and perhaps King Log was better than a possible King Stork; but his hearers had not been properly brought up and just thought it was Sir Robert's funny way of putting things. And—while we are on this subject— do any of the young know their *Aesop's Fables* now? We must ask our children (who are rapidly getting middle-aged) if Aesop is still read and if they have one for their own children; and we wish we had our own old Aesop. But life and many years spent out of England are not good for books. They melt and disappear mysteriously, or are left behind in various moves, and we think of them—alone now in strange lands—almost as we would think of a deserted child. One has to cut one's losses in this Piljian's Projess of a Mortal Wale and we have cut a great many in a long life but it is always the books that we miss more than anything and not all of them can be replaced. Perhaps, in some celestial library—but we are not told; and when we get to that library, if we do, we may have forgotten all about our life here. We know nothing and can only, in the words of old Chives the sexton at Southbridge who was also the Vicar's gardener, hope for the best and expect the worst. For we old, while we are here at any rate, so cling to the homely, every-day comforts and wherever we are we shall long, as Catullus did centuries ago, for our *desideratum lectum*—our own comfortable bed at home, among familiar sounds and objects with our books to our hand.

The introduction of the Hireling Shepherd rather naturally led to a discussion of Victorian painting in general when every picture told a story: or if it didn't tell a story it hinted at one, like, said Lady Fielding, that *lovely* picture of the Death of Chatterton in the most *beautiful* clothes on a pallet bed in an attic. But her husband said that was just sentiment and give him *The Last of England* because it made one think.

His wife said Why did it make one think?

Sir Robert said that it was, as it were, the apotheosis of Emigration; and on large scale emigration much of our Empire had been built.

Lady Gwendolen, who sometimes felt that Mamma did really monopolize the conversation too much, said Well, what about Henry Kingsley. He, she said in a rather bellicose way, had described *both* aspects of emigration.

Sir Robert begged to be enlightened, which request from a highly respected gentleman with a trained legal mind made everyone respect Lady Gwendolen.

"Well, Henry Kingsley, who was *so* much nicer than his stuffy brother Charles," said Lady Gwendolen, "went to Australia himself about a hundred years ago, so he knew both sides. I mean one of his books is about people going to Australia and getting very rich and coming home to England and one is about people going to Australia and getting very rich and staying there. And what is more," she added, looking round for possible critics, "someone or other has called his books a Charter of Australia," having said which words she looked round for criticism. But she was the more deceived, for most of her audience did not know that most delightful of writers—so far better than his Water-Babies brother Charles—and the conversation moved on to other subjects.

We need hardly say that what everyone really wanted to know was whether there was any truth in the vague rumours of the Bishop resigning. But no one liked to be the first to attack the subject, so they talked very comfortably about Lady Gwendolen's wedding and everyone agreed that to have Lady Elaine as a kind of Matron of Honour was an excellent idea.

"But I know what we might do—if you agree, Duchess," said Lady Fielding. "When Edith Graham was married Lady Graham said we must have a blue carpet up the aisle instead of the

usual red one, and she arranged for it to be laid down and paid
for it and then most generously gave it to the cathedral. I
feel—though I really don't know why I feel it—that blue would
be *most* suitable for Lady Gwendolen."

"Oh, *do* say just Gwendolen," said that lady.

"Of course I will," said Lady Fielding. "What do you feel,
Duchess?"

The Dowager, very sensibly we think, said that she had no
feelings about the carpet and had thought the blue looked very
well at Edith's wedding and her son William had thought so
too, so if Gwendolen agreed, the blue carpet would be very nice.
We need hardly say that Lady Gwendolen agreed, being by now
pretty well in the stupefied state into which the victims of suttee
(we are told) used to be put before they were burned. But not a
disagreeable state as far as her ladyship was concerned. All she
had to do was to follow her mother's instructions and as she had
now done this for a good many years it did not present any
peculiar difficulty to her. And always at the back of her mind was
the comfortable feeling that Mr. Oriel would be there and with
him she could face *anything*.

It did occur to Lady Fielding that the wedding appeared to be
revolving more round the Dowager than round her daughter,
and she asked Lady Gwendolen about her own wedding dress,
choosing a moment when Sir Robert had taken the Dowager to
the far end of the drawing-room to show her an old print he had
picked up of the landscape as it was before the great Towers
mansion was built, with a small Jacobean house and trees
planted in avenues in all directions, and in the foreground some
small figures playing what might have been played at any time in
history, with some balls and curved sticks. Pêle-mêle, probably,
Sir Robert said. It was curious, he added, how many different
pronunciations that word had. There was, he said, Pell Mell,
there was also The Mall to rhyme with Shall and there were an
Upper and Lower Mall down by the river, above Hammersmith
Bridge, pronounced Maul. Which piece of information natu-

rally led to Cirencester which can be said in three different ways; not one of which we should ever presume to say aloud lest we should expose our triple ignorance.

The Dowager, who had a useful strain of Scotch blood in her, at once countered with Milngavie—celebrated for its football—which is known to its friends as Milguy—with the stress on the guy which is pronounced like Guy Fawkes. After this, of course, there was no holding either of them. Lady Fielding asked what it was all about and for the honour of Barsetshire brought up a reinforcement in the shape of Wumpton Pifford, spelt on the maps as Westhampton Pollingford but only so pronounced by rank outsiders.

Sir Robert said there were a few lines which he couldn't remember by one of the Roman poets but he had forgotten who in which someone called Arrius is uneducated enough to say hinsidias for insidias, and called the Ionian sea Hionian—and probably his equally ignorant friends called him Harrius.

The Dowager said How very interesting and it seemed to bring those old Romans nearer to us.

"Catullus, of course!" said Sir Robert, to whom light had suddenly been vouchsafed. "It is extraordinary how you can forget something you have known nearly all your life, and then it suddenly comes back."

"It is like coming downstairs to fetch something you particularly want," said Lady Gwendolen, "and when you get downstairs you have forgotten what it is and you have to go upstairs again to remember it. I remember when I was quite small forgetting something nurse had sent me to fetch and she told me afterwards that I came back to the nursery in tears, saying, 'I've forgotten my Thing.'"

Lady Fielding, seeing that her husband's patience might give way at any moment and knowing that he might slip downstairs and go to the club, said in the kindest way, that it had been *such* a pleasure to see them and she wished she had not got to go to a meeting of the Barchester Ladies' Club where the Bishop's wife was to speak, with which pious wish the Dowager strongly agreed and said she and Gwendolen must be getting back and could she give Lady Fielding a lift. After one of those very boring unselfish arguments to which The Sex is prone Lady Fielding won, by reminding Lady Gwendolen that the traffic lights and the parking regulations made it almost impossible to get to the Club except between nine and ten in the morning and after seven o'clock in the evening. So good-byes were said and Lady Gwendolen drove her mother home, where they found Mr. Oriel who had been in Barchester and come out by the bus being entertained by Lady Elaine.

Everyone was delighted to see everyone else and Lady Elaine got the sherry and some glasses. The Dowager asked Mr. Oriel what he felt about the blue carpet, as opposed to the conventional red carpet.

"I don't know how many couples I have joined, or helped to join with the Church's blessing," said Mr. Oriel, "but they are all the same in one respect. From the moment they enter the church separately to the moment when they leave it together, the greater number of them hardly know what is happening. Not that they are wanting in reverence, but they have mostly been living under a considerable strain and it is when the strain is removed that they suddenly realize it. I shall probably be much the same."

"I think I know what you mean, Mr. Oriel," said the Dowager, who had never yet used her future son-in-law's Christian name. Not for want of affection, but she had always heard of him and spoken of him as Mr. Oriel and had not yet reconciled herself to Caleb. And we must confess that Caleb is not perhaps the first name one would wish for a son-in-law, but if Lady Gwendolen could like it, her mother did not see any reason to show her own want of enthusiasm except by saying Mr. Oriel, which she did very affectionately. "I know when I was being married I was wondering nearly all the time whether I had a ladder in one of my stockings because when I knelt I distinctly felt something Go."

"I know, mother," said Lady Elaine. "When you suddenly feel something running down your leg and you daren't look. One can stop it with lipstick if one catches it in time, but you must get it before it goes too far or the lipstick looks like blood. But I don't suppose you had any lipstick then."

"Oh yes, we had," said the Dowager, "but we didn't call it lipstick. It was called Roger *et* Gallet's Lipsalve and my mother let me just touch my mouth with it before I went to a ball. But never to put on any more of course. But one must move with the times."

Mr. Oriel said absent-mindedly *Mulier cum non olet, tum bene olet* and then wished he hadn't, for all three ladies wanted to know what it meant.

"Well, roughly, it means that the best advertisement for a perfume is that it should be so delicate that you hardly perceive it," said Mr. Oriel with great presence of mind.

"When I was a girl," said the Dowager (who, her daughters felt, said this a little too often), "of course we were not allowed to use scent, except lavender water. My mother had it made in the still-room from our own lavender. I and my sisters weren't allowed to cut the lavender ourselves because the head gardener said we would make a fine muck of it and it wouldn't do next year's growth no good," which her Grace said with a very good imitation of the older people's way of speaking in Sussex where her childhood had been spent. "We used to have a still-room maid at The Towers when I was first married. Of course all that is gone."

Mr. Oriel said his old uncle over at Greshamsbury used to say much the same and often lamented the death of home-brewing. Times, he said, changed and in course of time we also changed.

The Dowager said How True and a very inspiring thought.

"The annoying part is," said Mr. Oriel, "that it has been said much better in Latin."

"Do tell us it," said the Dowager. "Or shall I say 'tell it us'?"

"It is '*tempora mutantur et nos mutamur in illis*,'" said Mr. Oriel, who had an excellent speaking or reading aloud voice without any affectation, ignoring the Dowager's question.

"That sounded *very* fine," said Lady Gwendolen. "And now please tell us what it means, Caleb."

Mr. Oriel said it meant roughly that times changed and we changed with them.

"But that," said the Dowager, who had enjoyed this little excursion into the classics, "is exactly what my dear grandfather used to say. He was very fond of the classics and used to quote them. Perhaps you know his name, Mr. Oriel—Octavius Manton?"

"Not *the* Manton?" said Mr. Oriel.

"Well, it was a large family and he was only the fourth son," said the Dowager, "and he did very well at Oxford and got a fellowship, but he married and then took orders and got a College living. He knew all about Latin and Greek. He taught me some Latin when I was young and I loved it, but I was never very good at it and I can only read it in those nice editions that have an English translation on the opposite page. My dear husband read with him. That was how we come to know one another. The girls of course never saw him. He died before I was married. One does sometimes miss the people one only knew as a child more than the people one knew later."

Mr. Oriel agreed with her. Those early impressions, he said, were perhaps the strongest in one's whole life. He had seen, he said, the name of some play, or musical play—he couldn't remember—called *Wake Up and Dream* and it seemed to him a very good description of our life, which was a slice of eternity.

The Dowager by this time rather wished she had not got into this metaphysical labyrinth and asked Lady Gwendolen to give Mr. Oriel some more sherry, but he said No thank you, because to go into the open air after even one glass always made him nervous.

"Well, look here, Caleb," said his betrothed. "You have the sherry, I'm driving you back and it's light for ages still."

Mr. Oriel made one of those protests, so maddening to the protestee, saying that it would take up too much of her time and he could *perfectly* well take the bus to Barchester and catch the Harefield bus there.

"Don't be silly, Caleb," said Lady Gwendolen. "It'll take you at least an hour with the changes and probably much more at this time of day. My car's outside. Say good-bye and come along."

Mr. Oriel obediently did as he was told. Lady Gwendolen drove him in her usual rather alarming but very efficient manner back to his parsonage, kissed him affectionately (to the joy of two of the Perry boys who were passing) and drove away. And when we say boys, all three Perrys are now of considerable standing in the different branches of their noble profession, but as we have known them since they were rather rowdy young medical students at Knight's, we find it difficult to think of them as approaching middle age. How very difficult Time is. No one can explain it. Jacques did his best with his seven ages and we think the Perrys were roughly in Form IV and moving up to Form V. But there are no hard and fast rules.

CHAPTER 10

We need hardly say that the Dowager had taken over the roles of mother, secretary, arbiter of taste, and anything else she could think of, ably seconded by her daughter-in-law Franklin, whose ideas about the wedding left the Dowager simply nowhere. But the older lady had traditions of which her daughter-in-law did not have any knowledge. Not for nothing had the Dowager a good background and a long experience of people and how to handle them, and the younger Duchess very charmingly and simply put herself to school as it were, for she had taken very seriously her duties in the station of life to which it had pleased God to call her and while keeping to the tradition of her American upbringing with its noble hospitality, and its wish for comfort, she also threw herself whole-heartedly into making her sister-in-law's wedding a wow; which expression is Her Grace's, not ours. And we think she was right, for a Duke's daughter is decidedly Somebody. And Mr. Oriel, of excellent Barsetshire stock and much loved by his friends and parishioners, was also Somebody.

When first the wedding was discussed, the Duchess had said it was all too difficult. But when pressed for an explanation, it was discovered that she thought the cathedral belonged to the Bishop, for whom and for the Bishopess she had a hearty dislike and scorn, founded entirely upon the prejudices of her English relations by marriage. Which was just as well, for the Palace would have been no use to her at all, and her husband would only consent to meet them on the most formal occasions. However when it was explained to her that the Dean was in command she recovered her usual spirits and went into action.

Some mothers might have slightly resented a daughter-in-law arranging the wedding over their heads as it were, but the Dowager had made a rule for herself to approve everything her children's husband or wife did, which had made for friendliness and peace in the family. And we may also say that the reigning Duchess, with her New England good breeding, always consulted her mother-in-law; or if not exactly consult, she would say exactly what she meant to do, listen sympathetically to any suggestions, and as often as not adopt them.

The only incident which at all ruffled this calm was—and it will not surprise those who know Barsetshire—that Lord Aberfordbury managed to convey to the Duchess that he would like to come to the wedding. This message the Duchess at once relayed to her mother-in-law and both ladies joined in a hymn of hate. The Dowager was, on the whole, for peace at any price and said Why not send him a card and have done. But the blood of her daughter-in-law was up, the American eagle sharpened its beak and talons, and a note in the third person was dispatched to his lordship, informing him in correct and chilly terms that the ceremony was to be confined to the immediate family and friends. This was of course a whopping lie, but there was no alternative.

Everyone else, we think, accepted; from Lord Pomfret (as Lord Lieutenant) and the Duke of Omnium to Madame Tomkins and the hard-working secretary of the Barchester Ladies' Club, whose name we do not know and do not at this late stage propose to invent, as there are already far too many people on and off the stage. Practically the whole of the Close was of course in attendance. Lord Stoke came in his brougham, wearing rather tight black and white check trousers, a cutaway black coat and a grey topper, which piece of period dressing gave intense joy to the small crowd that had assembled outside the cathedral.

Lady Gwendolen behaved beautifully and came up the aisle on her ducal brother's arm, followed by Lady Elaine, almost swimming over the blue carpet, looking neither to the right nor the left until she reached the front pew when she smiled to her mother. Mr. Oriel, ably seconded by one of the Pallisers, was already in waiting and not in the least nervous, though he did say afterwards that it felt rather rum to be standing before the chancel steps instead of taking the service. Only a royal or a ducal wedding could have filled the nave of the beautiful echoing cathedral, unlike many cathedrals in being so full of light and very little stained glass; but the clergy from Close and County had rallied and not a stall was vacant. Mr. Oriel looked towards the Bishop's Throne, which, to his relief, was not occupied. He then blamed himself for not being in charity with all men, but as his bride was by his side charity surged into him again. The service was conducted by the Dean who did everything with dignity and deep feeling and when the bridal pair went up to the Altar both bride and bridegroom were full of quiet happiness.

To Lady Gwendolen's brother, the Reverend Lord William Harcourt, the ceremony was like an echo of the day when there had been the double marriage of two of the Deanery granddaughters and he had seen Edith Graham among the bridesmaids and their eyes had met—only for a moment but in that moment he knew his fate: and now he was her husband and a father.

Then there was the usual surge of relations and friends into the vestry. Lady Gwendolen signed her maiden name for the last time in her usual clear writing. Everyone kissed everyone else, except Lord Stoke who refused the compliment until Lady William Harcourt came up to him. As Edith Graham he had known her, and had taken a liking to her because he had once been deeply in love with Edith Thorne, who had the best hands and seat in the county. Though Lady William had never quite understood the whole story, she was fond of old Lord Stoke. As we get older we do value a sign of affection, or just friendliness, from the children of our old friends; and not till then do we begin to realize why various friends of our parents were so kind to us when we were young, though we may have thought them very old and very dull and probably not knowing anything about life.

As the Cathedral was a good distance from the bride's home, Canon and Mrs. Joram had offered The Vinery, their house in the Close, for the reception. This they had done more than once for friends and the Dowager was grateful when they suggested it. There is something very pleasant—if at the right time of year and with the right people—about a post-wedding party, at which one meets so many old friends or makes some new ones and nothing could be more suitable than the Jorams' house with its handsome wide staircase, its fine double drawing-room filling the whole depth of the house and the back-stairs which were a great help in making people circulate.

In the front room Lady Gwendolen Oriel and her husband were planted, there to receive their friends, who were then gently moved on to the back drawing-room which was also a large room and had windows looking onto the long garden. And to make all easy the Jorams' butler Simnet had a collaborator in Mr. Tozer of Scatcherd and Tozer the big Barchester caterers, famed throughout West Barsetshire for his excellent arrangement of refreshments and his skill with the champagne-nippers, never letting a drop of wine or even a bubble of foam stain the cloth or the carpet. To him, as Past Master in the Art, Simnet resigned the office of bottle-opener: for the rest he was absolute ruler and the inferior assistants—also supplied by Scatcherd and Tozer—trembled before him.

We need hardly say that Lady Gwendolen Oriel was in full possession of herself and greeted almost every guest by his or her own name: a most valuable asset to any hostess and to her husband. For a country clergyman can come under the heading of "More people know Tom Fool than Tom Fool knows" (an extremely witting saying—or so we thought then—of our childhood), and though Mr. Oriel was fairly good at knowing people, the number of faces made him feel as if a kaleidoscope were being whirled before his eyes. His natural courtesy luckily hid a good deal of his confusion, and his wife prompted him valiantly, but there were moments during which he felt like Jean Baptiste Cavaletto when the house-wives of Bleeding Heart Yard, in a sincere wish to help him with the English language, would fly out at their doors crying "Mr. Baptist—tea-pot!" Mr. Baptist—dust-pan!" "Mr. Baptist—flour-dredger!" "Mr. Baptist—coffee-biggin!" (which last we have never met in ordinary kitchen conversation). But Little Dorrit is now one hundred and two years old, so we may be forgiven. And how it can be so old and yet so eternally young is Dickens's genius, for which we give eternal thanks.

One of the first guests to arrive was the Noel Merton's agent, Mr. Wickham, who had dropped in with two bottles of liqueur brandy, the gift (he explained) of old "Sheep" Scrimageour; for most of Mr. Wickham's friends, collected in war and peace, by land and sea, over most of the world, were always giving or sending him similar tributes and no one ever knew who they were and no one enquired. Just the thing, he said, for a party.

"But not for everyone, mind you," he added to Dr. Joram. "Wait till the party has thinned out a bit and then we'll make them look silly. I'll put them in your desk, Joram—unless the drawers are all full."

Dr. Joram said they were pretty full, but not of bottles, to which Mr. Wickham, raising one hand, said "Kamerad" and put them behind the *Encyclopaedia Britannica* which was in a very deep bottom shelf with plenty of room at the back.

"Anything fresh about His Nibs?" said Mr. Wickham, irreverently so alluding to the Bishop. "Here, Harcourt! you must know something. Always about the Close without enough to do and your brother a Duke. And where's your wife?"

Lord William, who had long been familiar with Mr. Wickham and had a high regard for that gentleman, said Edith was somewhere about—probably, he said, with some of her relations. For the ramifications of the Pomfret and Leslie families from which Edith came were infinite, and very few outsiders could grasp them all. Nor could all the insiders. What relation exactly, for instance, was David Leslie, younger son of old Lady Emily Leslie (now long dead) who had been a Pomfret, to the dreadful Mrs. George Rivers whose husband the Honourable George Rivers was some kind of relation of the late Lord Pomfret—the old cousin of the present Earl? As we have known most of them on and off since nineteen hundred and thirty-three, we ought to know; but in spite of frantic research we have given it up. It is much the same in ordinary life, and never shall we remember who is who—or was who. Life is a vain show and as we get older we find it simpler to sit back and look at it—not without pleasure—and let our children do some of the remembering for us.

But we must return from this divagation to The Vinery, where the noise of well-bred people in pleasant converse was now absolutely deafening.

We need hardly say that after a ceremonial drinking of healths and the cutting of the wedding cake, a discussion arose among the younger members of the party as to whether they should all go to the second house at the Barchester Odeon and see Glamora Tudor in *The Cardinal's Mate, A Factual Comment On Life under the Borgias*, with her new co-star Hick Pilldozer. This, after another glass or so of champagne was unanimously adopted and they went away in very good spirits, arrived in time to see the richly-coloured advertisements on the screen and the sixteenth episode of *Foss Crackers the Texan Cowboy* in Glorious Technicolour, and probably enjoyed themselves. And we may say that they were not in the least missed, for their elders were all

longing for a little peace and quiet; by which we think they
meant that if there was any discussing and arguing to be done,
they would like to do it themselves, for there were rumours of
change.

For some time distant rumblings, as of Empedocles under
Etna, had been felt in the Close and were even spreading to less
exclusive regions. No one quite knew where they started, though
there were those who thought they had begun in the Close
Upper Servants' Club, presided over by Simnet, and had been
further disseminated in the lower Cathedral regions by Mr.
Tozer, head of the well-known catering firm of Scatcherd and
Tozer. These rumblings were in discreet reference to the rumour
of the impending retirement of the Bishop, which would of
course include the Bishopess.

"But, Dr. Crawley," said Mrs. Joram, "it is all rather *vague*
isn't it? Wouldn't the Bishop *tell* someone if he was retiring?"

Dr. Crawley said—most untruthfully—that it was not for
him to offer any opinion on the subject, though it was quite
evident to everyone present that he not only could and if he
would, but would also need very little pressing to spill the beans.

"Oh, here is the Chancellor," said Mrs. Joram. "He will know
everything. Sir Robert, *are* we to be delivered?"

Sir Robert said To Whom: or alternatively From Whom, or
even To What.

"Well, you know perfectly well, Sir Robert," said Mrs. Joram,
"*who* we want to be delivered *from*. But does anyone know who
we might be delivered *to*, which is most important, though I
believe it is quite uncanonical, if that is what I mean, to discuss
it here; or at any rate not quite our place."

The Precentor, who had been drawn—or more correctly had
drawn himself—into the circle, said it was doubtful whether
any place would be correct for what—he presumed—those
present wished to discuss.

"Have some more sherry," said Mr. Wickham, approaching
them with a freshly opened bottle. "No, no," he went on as the

Precentor held out his not quite empty glass. "No topping up, my boy. Drink what you've got like a man and then I'll fill up."

With a self-deprecatory air, as of one who yields gracefully to force majeure, the Precentor drank the rest of his sherry.

"Attaboy!" said Mr. Wickham, refilling the glass with great skill high enough for a steady hand; a rather unfair habit of his to those who did not—according to his standards—take their drink like a man. But the Precentor knew exactly what Mr. Wickham meant. He bowed slightly, winked at Mr. Wickham, and drank the contents of the glass in one breath, with quiet dignity.

"And now you can fill it up again," he said, holding out the glass with a still perfectly steady hand.

"Kamerad," said Mr. Wickham, pouring the sherry, and rapidly filling a large glass which happened to be near he drank it at one breath and took himself off to other friends.

"Our friend Wickham," said the Precentor, "is a character; a licensed character, I might say."

The Dean rather dashingly said he hoped Wickham would not get his licence endorsed; which raised a slightly sycophantic laugh.

"But seriously," said Mrs. Joram, "*are* we to have a change in high quarters, Dean? You know how stupid I am about those things. I only want to know *something*, or I wouldn't bother you. And if I am wrong you must tell me."

"I didn't know Mrs. Joram was a Dickens-addict," said Lady Fielding who had joined the group.

"Of *course* I am—I read him again and again," said Mrs. Joram. "But what exactly made you say that?"

"David Copperfield," said Lady Fielding.

There was a moment's silence, as hardly anyone knew exactly what Lady Fielding was alluding to, while having a very distinct impression of what it was though without being able to put a name to it. A state of mind in which we all often find ourselves.

"My wife," said Dr. Joram, who had heard these last remarks,

"is the most illiterate woman I know. But she loves her Dickens
and much will be forgiven to her. You were of course thinking of
Rosa Dartle, Lady Fielding."

"I was," said Lady Fielding, "but not in a horrid way. I mean
Mrs. Joram isn't the least like Rosa Dartle. It's only that Rosa
Dartle always said she wanted to be put right if she was wrong.
Dreadful woman! I wonder if Dickens really knew her."

That, said Sir Robert, was anyone's guess. The words of—he
couldn't at the moment remember the name, or the exact
words—about how one couldn't push great writers into corners
and make them stand and deliver—oh *dear*, what was it he
meant—

"'Others abide our question, Thou art free,' I think," said a
gentle voice from the edge of the little group. "It's Matthew
Arnold; his sonnet on Shakespeare."

Everyone turned to look, and there stood a tall young man,
good-looking with an agreeably romantic tinge of melancholy in
his eyes.

"I always said you were a dark horse, Ludo," said Mr. Wickham. "Come clean—if you will all forgive the revolting expression. How did you know?"

Lord Mellings—for our reader has with great acumen spot-
ted him at once—said he rather liked reading poetry and had
one of those silly memories that things stick in and he never
knew what he was going to remember next—or forget.

We need hardly say that he was at once swamped and over-
borne by almost all those present, each wishing to tell the
nearest hearer exactly how he, or she, forgot or remembered. We
also need hardly say that Mrs. Morland, who had come in rather
late, was able to supply instances of this.

"The worst of it is," she said, taking a glass of sherry from
Simnet who was an old friend and would, she knew, feel
affronted if she did not take it, "that putting it down doesn't help
at all."

The Dean asked Mrs. Morland to enlarge on this subject. His

wife said Not to be so pompous, but everyone was used to her conjugal asides and took no notice.

"Well," said the gifted authoress, putting her hat rather more crooked as was her usual custom before trying to say what she thought she wanted to say, "it is only that if you put a thing down it doesn't help."

"And what you tell me two times is true," said the Dean, slightly misquoting.

"Because," Mrs. Morland went on, "you can put things down— in writing I mean—like *anything*; but if it's just because you wanted to remind yourself about something it doesn't work. I mean, supposing I were asked to dinner at the Palace, of course I wouldn't want to go, so I would forget."

Murmurs of approval rose from her auditors.

"But unless I were really engaged on that date it would be no use writing to say I was sorry I had a previous engagement, because the Bishopess would be bound to find out. I mean, supposing I said I was dining with you," she went on, addressing Lady Fielding, "and she sent his chaplain to find out—"

"I'm sorry to interrupt," said Lady Fielding, "but if a chaplain of his lordship's came to my house—except on business—he wouldn't get further than my excellent parlourmaid who knows *exactly* whom I want to see and whom I don't. She told Lord Aberfordbury, if that is what he calls himself now but I am thankful to say I hardly ever see him as he was quite bad enough when he was Sir Ogilvy Hibberd—and now I have forgotten what I was going to say. Oh, yes. She told him I couldn't see *anyone* at present; which was perfectly true because I had a stye in one eye and was all done up in a pad of cotton wool and Pond's Extract and lying down."

Murmurs of approval, not unmixed with envy, rose from the audience, for not everyone in the Close could get good servants; the old guard being mostly dead or retired and the new-comers only wanting jobs in flats with electric cookers and cleaners and no one in to lunch and the weekend off.

Mrs. Joram who, as a Canon's wife and an inhabitant of the Close of some years standing, had Senior Status as it were, said she had been very lucky with servants, but it was always a help if one hadn't any children. Some people might have thought this was sour grapes with her, but as she was already repeatedly a grandmother by her first marriage when she was still Mrs. Brandon, it was obvious that she was alluding to her later marriage with Canon Joram; a marriage which had been very happy for both parties and no one would have been more surprised than they if they had found themselves elderly parents.

"Of course there was Sara who had a child when she was ninety," said Mrs. Joram, "but I expect they counted differently then. And if she had it on someone else's knees or they on hers, I can't really remember which, it seems unreasonable. But I suppose that is where Faith comes in."

At this point the Vicar of Greshamsbury New Town with his wife were announced. We first met Mr. Parkinson at dinner at the Deanery, several years ago, when he was a new-fledged curate of no particular background, rather conscious of his new uniform and a collar that did up behind. Since then we have with great pleasure noted his gradual steady rise, most ably helped by his wife, to a good living where he had made himself liked and respected. The Dean had stood godfather to their first child, Master Josiah Parkinson, now doing extremely well at the local grammar school to which the Dean had the right to present a boy every other year, alternately with a direct descendant of the Founder. But as the Founder's family had all died out or emigrated, the choice was usually left to the Dean and in this case it had been a very good one.

There was quite a flattering reception for the Parkinsons, whose hard work and shining goodness had raised up friends for them wherever they went. Though if we are to be correct it was partly owing to the Dean and Mrs. Crawley's influence that Mr. Parkinson had been saved—when still a bachelor—from accepting a call to the church in Hallbury New Town which was so

High that whenever it saw the words "Anglo-Catholic" it crossed out the "Anglo," and owing to lack of funds was a Petra-like temple, all front and practically no back. But we presume it was a help to those that liked it; as possibly Petra was, though we prefer a house with good through ventilation.

The Precentor, who had been champing at the bit during the foregoing conversation, now began to say what he had been going to say. But what it was we shall never know, for the Pomfrets came in, shortly followed by Sir Noel and Lady Merton with their daughter Lavinia who was developing a good social sense and hardly ever brought her parents to shame. And—which was even more agreeable—she was getting through the awkward age with skill and celerity; so much so that Lydia almost trembled when she thought of having to arrange a Coming-Out party and perhaps having a dance for her daughter within a very few years—two or three at the most. Luckily she and Noel were very comfortably off now and if Lavinia was to Come Out, it should be done in style, with all the furniture moved and the floor of the large drawing-room polished and the catering done by Scatcherd and Tozer with Mr. Tozer himself presiding, and generous champagne for the older guests and a rationed amount for Lavinia's contemporaries, who in any case did not take much interest in it, still preferring fizzy lemonade or Cup elegantly decorated with floating fruit; but no vintage champagne, which would be a waste.

Sir Noel and Lady Merton were at once engulfed by friends. Lavinia, in spite of the grown-up-ness of being at a real wedding party, was a little out of it, for there were really no people of her own age and she felt rather shy of talking to grown-ups unless they did it first. A voice high above her head said, "I am so glad you have come. Everyone is so grown-up."

"Well, I'm awfully pleased you are here too," said she. "I don't know people and I don't like champagne because it makes me sneeze," which made Lord Mellings laugh, though very kindly, and he stopped one of the waiters and took a glass of fruit cup. Lavinia thanked him and drank it.

"I *was* thirsty," she said.

"I say, Lavinia, shall I come and say good-bye to your people before I go back to Sandhurst?" said Lord Mellings.

"Oh, *do*," said Lavinia, who had no maidenly modesty. "Come one day soon and we'll go on the river and you can stay to tea and then we can go on the river again and you can stay to supper."

"I'd love it," said Lord Mellings. "When shall I come? Quick, because I see Mother making a We-must-go-now face at me."

"I'll ring you up this evening when I've asked mother," said Lavinia, which regard for her parent somehow gave Lord Mellings pleasure. He smiled down at her and melted away through the crowd to join his parents and went away with them

By now the rooms were almost as full as they could hold. Mr. Tozer, who knew inside himself that he was the ultimate judge and ruler of any first class wedding, arranged bride and bridegroom in what he considered a strategic position, with Lady Elaine in attendance. At his nod the photographer from the *Barchester Chronicle* and an inferior photographer from the *Barsetshire News* came forward and made a few quite unnecessary alterations in the position of their victims.

Madame Tomkins, who by the real kindness of the Dowager had been invited to the reception as well as to the wedding, also came forward to arrange the bride's dress and veil properly.

"Excuse me, madam," said the *Barsetshire News*, "but will you get out of the foreground so that we can get everything in focus."

Madame Tomkins, quite correctly we think, looked right through him and paid no attention at all while she arranged the brides' train and her veil.

"*Voilà*," she said, with the artist's pride, "*un groupe bien composé*. Eef I do not arrange miladi's dress and her veil your photographs will be nozzing. And if you are to have your fleshly, tell me first, or I cry. I am highly nervous."

All were silent and held their countenances intently—

fascinated by this clash of art and trade: also by the use of a word which sounded like fleshly—which the bride certainly was not—nor the bridegroom either for that matter.

"I think, madam," said Simnet in a stage aside to Mrs. Joram, "that the lady means she will scream if there is a flashlight. Perhaps there is no French word for it, madam," which last words were fortunately not heard by Madame Tomkins. And as we do not know it either (though doubtless such a word exists in French) we will put the question by. Simnet then looked at the photographers and nodded. The light rushed out and in a moment two photographs were taken. The photographers then departed with their cameras and a promise to bring proofs back almost at once.

Outside the door Simnet was waiting for them.

"The back stair's easier," he said. "It takes you straight down to My Pantry. There's a bottle or two there."

Regardless of the sub-editor's warning to them to waste no time, they had a short talk with Mr. and Mrs. Simnet and before they left they took a photograph of them sitting at their tea-table, which photograph appeared on the following day in the *Barchester News* with the Caption "High Life Below Stairs" and had a great success.

But the photographers were also loyal to their trade and before the party dispersed the proofs were brought back and looked exactly like any other wedding group except that the bride and bridegroom were both at years of considerable discretion. The party began to thin. That is to say the guests who had come from a distance began going home while those who lived in the Close, or the Town, stayed on to gossip and had the pleasure of seeing the bride in her very suitable going away dress. The destination of the happy couple had been kept secret, but no one can keep a secret which includes a Duke's daughter and everyone knew they were going to Brighton because Lady Gwendolen had been there when she was seven and had never forgotten its joys. Also, she greatly wished to see what hotel life was really like, which may sound preposterous at her age; but hotels had never come into the ducal scheme. If you went abroad, or visited any part of England, you always stayed with friends or relations—which in many cases were much the same thing.

So Mr. Oriel, wishing to give his bride all she wished, had dashingly taken a suite at a large hotel on the front, the *juste milieu* as it were between the boarding-house district to the East—once, alas, proud mansions with a great many servants— and the large hotels to the West at some of which people sat outside and took their morning coffee or their apéritif in full view of all the world which was so used to the sight that it mostly didn't bother to look. To both bride and bridegroom this was pure Escape and Romance. We shall not follow them, but we are certain that they will enjoy their honeymoon at their kind, comfortable hotel like children let out of school and then settle down happily in the Vicarage and mingle with the very pleasant society of Harefield. What could be nicer?

The aftermath of a wedding can be rather depressing. There is so much to be tidied—not but what Scatcherd and Tozer's men were past masters at clearing up—and most of the near relations feel they must go out somewhere for a meal. But here the American eagle came into action.

The Duchess of Towers, assuming the ducal mantle, had in a most dashing way ordered a private room at the White Hart and invited her mother-in-law with Lady Elaine, feeling, very sym- pathetically, that they might find the evening at home a little depressing. The Duke would join them there. It was not to be a party, but three ladies to one gentleman seemed a dull way to celebrate. Her Grace then had the brilliant idea of co-opting Mr. Wickham and ran him to earth by the window of the back drawing-room. He was looking out over the garden. When the Duchess touched his shoulder he turned.

"What *is* that noise, Mr. Wickham?" said the Duchess, for by the open window she could hardly hear herself speak.

"Aeroplane," said Mr. Wickham. "I've been watching it. It

will be from the aerodrome over Ullathorne way. There's a
regular service now. Seems rum, doesn't it. It's just taken off,
outward bound."

"Now that noise has gone away I can hear what I am saying,"
said the Duchess, "and so can you. I am giving Dow and Elaine
dinner at the White Hart. Towers is coming. Do join us. One
man to three women isn't fair. Come about seven for a drink
before we have dinner. I told Burden to put us in a private room."

Mr. Wickham said he would like it of all things and he was
only too pleased to be a man if it helped her.

There was a movement in the front room. The Duchess and
Mr. Wickham turned to look. Through the guests came a
pleasant-looking man, apparently looking for someone.

"Why, if it's not Lee!" said the Duchess. "I'm right here, Lee.
It's my cousin Lee Sumter," she added to Mr. Wickham.

The new comer wormed himself through the crowd with
great skill and embraced the Duchess warmly. She then introduced the two men who shook hands.

"You *have* got a fist," said Mr. Sumter admiringly.

"The same to you," said Mr. Wickham, tenderly examining
his own right hand. "I've not met a grip—I don't mean a bag or
a portmanteau—like that since I was a sailor. It was on a
goodwill cruise in the West Indies and we dined on board one of
your ships and there was a young officer who shook hands like a
boa-constrictor."

Mr. Sumter said that would have been Fritz Beverley. He
could practically crack a coconut with his fist and had said that
he met an Englishman called Wickham who drank the whole
upper deck under the table.

Mr. Wickham said to come off it and they must have a drink
to old times.

"Certainly not," said the Duchess firmly. "Once you two get
away talking about Old Bill on the quarter-deck we shan't see
you again. Now Lee, you just stay right here, where I can see
you—and Mr. Wickham, you keep an eye on him, and we'll all

go over to the White Hart together for a drink before dinner. But how did you know I was here, Lee?"

Mr. Sumter said that when his plane came in he telephoned from the airport to the Towers and they put him through to the house and the house had told him the Duchess had gone to a party in the Cathedral, which didn't sound very probable, so he had rung up the *Barchester Chronicle* and they said there was a party at Canon Joram's house because their reporter had gone there. So he had ordered a car to take him to the Close.

The Duchess said wherever he was going, Lee always got there and she would like to introduce Lee to her mother-in-law the Dowager Duchess. Accordingly she took Mr. Sumter in tow, found her mother-in-law, and introduced him to her. Of course his good manners at once won the Dowager's heart and she said it gave her pleasure to meet young men who had been well brought up; which might have sounded a little patronizing though not in the least intended. Nor did Mr. Sumter take it as patronage.

"Well, Duchess," he said, "I come from Virginia where we love horses and good liquor and fair women—and certainly there are two of them here."

The Dowager said calmly that the sherry was not bad, but if he was dining with the family party, as she hoped he was, Burden, the old waiter at the White Hart, really understood wines: or perhaps, she added, she should say liquor. No one knew if Her Grace was speaking seriously, or gently parodying Mr. Sumter; we think a little of both. And she wanted him to know her other daughter Lady Elaine. Mr. Sumter was delighted to have that privilege and within two minutes was telling her all about his Virginian relations and added that she ought to come out and see them. His mother, he said, would love her, and so would everyone. At this moment Lady Elaine did the most dashing deed of her life by saying she would love to and Mr. Sumter said that was fine and he would call his mother that evening and tell her all about it.

The party, having seen Mr. Oriel and Lady Gwendolen Oriel off the premises, now began to melt away. Mrs. Joram, knowing that the Duchess was taking her party on to the White Hart for a meal, begged them not to hurry but they had promised to look in on the Fieldings en route for the White Hart and went away. The Hired Minions had removed all their property, and gone, and only some chairs and sofas with rumpled cushions remained to show that anything had happened.

"Oh, Simnet," said Dr. Joram, "when you have tidied the room, take a couple of bottles down to the kitchen for yourself and Mrs. Simnet. No hurry as Mrs. Joram and I are dining with Sir Robert and Lady Fielding."

"Thank *you* sir," said Simnet. "There's only a dozen bottles left over. We were just about right, sir, but a near thing."

"Well, take four," said Dr. Joram. "I daresay you and Mrs. Simnet will be entertaining some friends. Everything went very well. I hope Tozer's men enjoyed themselves."

"Very much indeed, sir," said Simnet. "But I had taken the precaution, sir, to order in some cheaper sherry which I keep in My Pantry. Tozer's men appreciated it very much sir. No good giving good sherry to *them*, sir. And I let them finish the last of that dozen of beer that you thought was a bit flat. Is there anything else sir?"

Dr. Joram thanked him and said Nothing else, and as he and Mrs. Joram were dining with Sir Robert and Lady Fielding it wouldn't matter if the drawing-room was not tidied that night.

"Excuse *me*, sir," said Simnet, "but tidying the day after is a thing I can't do justice to, and Mrs. Simnet feels just the same. You will find the drawing-room all in order, madam, when you return."

Having thus established Mrs. Joram in her rightful position as mistress of her drawing-room, Simnet made a triumphal exit. And we may say that he was as good as his word and with the assistance of the hired minions who were enjoying life in the servants' quarters with Mrs. Simnet, the whole room was as neat as anyone could wish before the party below stairs broke up.

Dr. and Mrs. Joram had a very pleasant evening with the Fieldings. The Dean and Mrs. Crawley were also there and they had a nice comfortable talk about how well Lady Gwendolen did her part and how well Lady Elaine followed her sister and how beautifully Dr. Crawley had performed the service and what luck the organist was back from his holiday. And so much did they enjoy talking over the ceremony that no one thought about the nine o'clock news so they turned it on a few minutes later and then left it on by mistake. The speakers that evening were in their most characteristic form, especially the gentlemen who gave talks beginning with Ackcherly and so conducted their hearers through despíckable to the era-r-of Iphigēēnia and the contróversy about Uraynus, with a few words on the dangers of pewmonia if your health had deteeriated, whether in Persher or Russher, though this was—they realized—a próvocative subject in which it was difficult to make a dezishion. So it was quite a relief to turn to a musical programme; but they were the more deceived, for they heard about a hundred pipers and ar and ar Who were going to be up and give us a blar a blar. There was, the announcer said, some contróversy on the subject of the dezishions to be made about Irak and now Jack Sprat the well-known pianist was going to play the Moonlight sonata-r-of Beethoven.

Lady Fielding said that was quite enough and turned it off.

"That," Sir Robert said meditatively, "is what is accepted as the norm, as correct speech, by several million people, who are also encouraged to think that fabulous means anything rather large or surprising and hectic means rushing about and being agitated."

"We should have been caned for that, and rightly too," said the Dean.

Lady Fielding said What *did* hectic mean then?

"Permanent," said the Dean. "The consumptive has a permanent flush. Like that delightful Pre-Raphaelite picture—in the Whitechapel Art Gallery, I think—called 'Too Late,' where a gentleman with side whiskers and a boater—if I remember correctly—meets the girl he hadn't been true to, supported by a female friend. Her cheeks are hollow and her face wan, and on each cheek is the fatal flush, and he wishes he had behaved better. Happy days those were."

"*Really*, Dr. Crawley," said Lady Fielding.

"I see what the Dean means," said Sir Robert. "The girl had Feelings. If that happened now she wouldn't go pale with red spots. She would probably make a scene and frighten him out of his wits; or if she were really spiteful she would go for Breach of Promise. And anyway it wouldn't be important."

Meanwhile the younger Duchess and her party were assembling at the White Hart. The old Head Waiter, Burden, was in his element. The private room with the good old-fashioned round table, the spotless napery (except for some iron-mould) though rather too stiff owing to the Barchester Sanitary Laundry which believed in starch; the real silver forks and spoons with the crests of the many owners who had been obliged to sell them at some time; the wine glasses of various shapes and sizes which everyone knew meant variously claret, port, champagne and possibly other drinks as well, though everyone was rather vague as to what was which: all was there. He would have liked the party to be eight, but it was Her Grace's party, not his. So he comforted himself by remembering that Without Him the White Hart would sink into a second-class hotel; in which he was entirely wrong, for the White Hart had so old a reputation that the R.A.C. and the A.A. had—almost on their knees— asked it to become their authorized patrons.

The party arrived punctually. The Dowager greeted Burden as an old friend; a gesture which he fully appreciated, immediately becoming a kind of aged Malvolio, an attitude by which the Dowager was much impressed. The party was easily seated, for as they were only six and all knew each other it did not much matter—especially when dining in a rather dashing and Bohe-mian way—who was next to whom. Mr. Wickham, to his great delight, found himself placed between the two Duchesses for each of whom he had considerable respect as women with no demned nonsense about them. Lady Elaine was between the Duke and Mr. Lee Sumter. She was fond of her brother and looked forward to Mr. Sumter's further acquaintance. And in any case with six people at a round table, conversation is—or should be—more or less universal. By which we mean that it should be almost a free-for-all fight. Mr. Sumter at once adopted Lady Elaine as a kind of aunt by marriage and entertained her vastly with accounts of life in his home town and the ceremonial, still observed, of the different ages of man—or rather of woman—and how he himself had graduated from débutante dances to dances where the older young men and women showed how it really ought to be done.

Lady Elaine said she had never enjoyed dances very much because she wasn't a good dancer and her mother wasn't much good at finding young men.

Mr. Sumter, suddenly filled with chivalrous sympathy for the daughter of a Duke who didn't get enough partners, said that would not have happened in Virginia, where there were plenty of beaux.

"But not for women of my age," said Lady Elaine, quite simply, as one stating a fact.

Mr. Sumter, rather shocked that the daughter of a Duke should think of herself as not so young as she was, said his mother was a recognized beauty and still remained very attrac-tive.

Lady Elaine said she was nearly forty to which Mr. Sumter chivalrously replied that years meant nothing and his mother was fifty and looked like a girl.

"I sometimes think my Mother is much younger than I am," said Lady Elaine, looking across the table to where the Dowager was getting on extremely well with Mr. Wickham. But Mr.

Sumter would not hear of such a thing and said Lady Elaine ought to come over to Virginia where her English ways would be deeply appreciated.

"But my ways—if I have any—aren't English," said Lady Elaine. "I mean, they are just Me. We are all a bit eccentric, you know. The Old Duke who built that ghastly great house which thank goodness is let now to some business people, used to sleep on a camp bed and always fed the hounds in the dining-room on the days when he was hunting."

But, Mr. Sumter said, that was exactly what his great-grandparents and their friends used to do and there wasn't so much difference between East and West.

"Then I suppose people in California are just like people in New York," said Lady Elaine.

Mr. Sumter said he was afraid he hadn't made himself quite clear and then he began to laugh.

Lady Elaine asked him what he was laughing about.

"I'm sorry," said Mr. Sumter. "I was just thinking of some cousins we have in California. They are the nicest people in the world, but they think civilization stops east of the Sierra Nevada."

Lady Elaine said her geography was very bad and she didn't quite know where the Sierra Navada was.

"Nor does my mother," said Mr. Sumter. "She was raised in Virginia and she's never been further west than Little Rock."

Lady Elaine said Wasn't that where the heroine of "Gentlemen Prefer Blondes" started her career, and then they talked about that classic work and laughed very pleasantly.

But the most agreeable conversations must come to an end at a dinner party and the Duke took over his sister Elaine of whom he was very fond. Not that he did not love his sister Gwendolen, but Elaine was not quite so much older than he was as Gwendolen was, and they had always been friends. So Mr. Sumter turned to the Duchess and they had a delightful talk about their friends in the United States and Mr. Sumter brought the Duchess up to date about births and deaths and marriages and told her about all the girls he had thought he was in love with but wasn't and the Duchess asked after various old friends including Woolcot van Dryven who had married one of the Deans' daughters; nothing to do with Dr. Crawley, but a daughter of Mr. Dean the wealthy industrialist (a word we have to use because we have never known exactly what he was except that he had Interests which meant a good deal of traveling) at Winter Overcotes.

Meanwhile Mr. Wickham was well away with the Dowager on such important subjects as whether that vixen had been heard of again over at Staple Park. The Dowager said she wished she could tell him, but Lord Bond didn't like the hunt to draw Hangman's Spinney because he had seen some young foxes at play there.

More likely at school said Mr. Wickham, and he didn't know a prettier sight than a vixen teaching her cubs how to deal with a hen.

"Exactly what my dear husband used to say," said the Dowager. "Not that he ever said much."

"Strong, silent man," said Mr. Wickham.

The Dowager said Not exactly that, but when he did let go, he *did* let go, and everyone agreed that he could swear even better and longer than old Lord de Courcy.

"Of course it's blood that tells," said Mr. Wickham meditatively. "That man's grandfather—or was it great uncle; shocking how one forgets things—was always known as Lord de Curse-ye."

The Dowager who did not know this old story laughed loudly.

"I'm sorry," she said, "but I can't help laughing when I'm amused. My father used to say I had the loudest laugh in this division of the county. We never knew the de Courcys much. I think they have a villa somewhere in the South of France."

"Come off it, Duchess," said Mr. Wickham. "Of course you know she has the Villa Thermogène at Mentone. She did, very kindly, ask me there one year, but I'm a pretty busy man and I do

like a quiet evening. And anyway I don't suppose I could get into
my evening clothes now."

"That," said the Dowager, "is nonsense. I don't think you have
changed at all since I first knew you. When was it?"

"End of the first war," said Mr. Wickham. "I got back with a
bit of metal in me somewhere—I was in the Royal Navy then—
and they put me into Barchester General Hospital for observa-
tion. There was a very pretty nurse there—can't remember her
name—never saw her again."

The Dowager said How sad.

"Sad's not the word," said Mr. Wickham. "I forgot all about
her. But I do remember you visiting there. You used to bring the
library trolley round."

"I wish I could say I remembered you," said the Dowager. "It
was rather fun taking the book trolleys round. There was a man
who said he had learned to read at school but he didn't seem to
fancy it. So he had dropped it altogether."

"Stout fellow," said Mr. Wickham. "Why do something you
don't want to do unless you've got to? There was a fellow in the
bed next to mine who told the girl with the trolley that he was
very well acquainted with literature and had no need of books,"
which made the Dowager give one of her celebrated neighing
laughs.

"It was nice to see the Pomfrets this afternoon," she said. "My
son and Lord Pomfret meet on boards, but I hardly know Lady
Pomfret. Not that I don't want to—just that the families never
knew each other much."

"Fine woman and a nice growing up family. I expect you saw
them at the party this afternoon."

The Dowager said only to smile to; not to talk to. Not, she
said, that there was any unfriendliness, but somehow they had
never got well acquainted. What family had they, she asked.

Mr. Wickham said a boy, a girl and then a boy. The elder son
was a bit of a difficulty. A nice boy, but he had grown too much,

too fast. "He is getting into shape now," he added. "He was at the party this afternoon."

The Dowager asked if he was the young man who suddenly quoted Matthew Arnold.

"That's the one," said Mr. Wickham.

"He is not in the least like his grandfather," said the Dowager. "He was tall and heavily built and had an almost bald head and very bushy eyebrows and a big sandy-coloured moustache and he had very small eyes, but he could frighten people by looking at them."

"I wish *I* could," said Mr. Wickham. "All the girls will be after that boy of Pomfret's till they find he doesn't dance much."

The Dowager asked why he didn't; obviously hoping— though in a kind way—that he had some Deformity, probably hereditary, which made dancing impossible, like Lord Byron.

Mr. Wickham said Some could; some couldn't. He used to dance a bit himself he said and he liked a good waltz, but waltzing wasn't what it was.

"What is it then?" said the Dowager.

"Well, when you and I were young, Duchess," said Mr. Wickham, "you—I mean the man—got a good grip round your partner with your right arm and took her right hand in your left and away you went."

"And how delightful it was," said the Dowager. "I was never good at waltzing and really enjoyed a polka more, but I remember when I was a girl waltzing with old Lord Pomfret and he twirled me round and round in the same direction till I was nearly giddy and when he took me back to Mamma he told her I was a good plucked 'un."

Mr. Wickham asked what her mother said.

"My dear mother didn't like slang,"said the Dowager. "She said she did not quite understand what he meant, but all her girls had good manners and then one of the young Greshams had a row with one of the de Courcys about a badger and they made such a noise that the band leader suddenly stopped playing."

Mr. Wickham said Stout fellow and that was the stuff to give the troops.

"Oh, it wasn't on *purpose*," said the Dowager. "He had drunk a little too much, so they had to take him away and the first violin conducted for the rest of the evening. Nothing like that now, Mr. Wickham," she added, regretfully, after which they had a delightful talk about how nice everything was before all these wars began.

"Do you remember a song, Duchess, about There'll be no Waw-er As long as we've a King like Good King Edward," said Mr. Wickham, but the Dowager didn't, so as there was plenty of talking going on he sang in a rather tuneless voice that fine lyric of one of the Follies' performances. For the benefit of such readers as still nostalgically remember the Follies we subjoin the fine lyric.

> There'll be no waw-er
>   As long as we've a King like Good King Edward;
> There'll be no waw-er
>   For 'e 'ates that kind of thing.
> Mothers needn't worry
>   As long as we've a King like Good King Edward.
> Peace with honour is his motto
>   So God save our King.

The penultimate line requires careful treatment, for honour and motto must be forced into some kind of assonance.

And then they fell into Follies reminiscences, which can go on for ever, but we will not begin to recall them for we should tire the electric light on our table with talking—and though this would not send him down the sky it might make him fuse and we should angrily say, as we groped for the spare bulb "At one stride comes the dark"; and as Mr. S. T. Coleridge has no copyright we can say it or write it as much as we like, or our friends can bear.

Old Burden has deeply enjoyed the scraps of conversation that reached him. Not that he was a curious or wanted to gossip, but owing to his long career as a waiter he was used to every kind of conversation from the Lord Lieutenant and the Duke of Omnium to the Commercials—in whose room he collected an enormous amount of gossip. But we must state in fairness that he had never been known to make use of it in any unkind or doubtful way. This did him great credit, for on such occasions as the defeat of Lord Aberfordbury in the County Council election, and also the matter of the Palace Drains, these affairs had often been discussed in the White Hart private dining-room by those who had to deal with them, or in the larger room which was let for Board Meetings. The *Chronicle* and the *News* would have given as much as five pounds for some information as to what went on and what was, or was not, decided; but Burden was entirely eaten up by his zeal for the tied house and not only turned down any such offer with respectful disdain but also passed the word to the barman to see that Sir Ogilvy's—or rather now Lord Aberfordbury's—efforts to get information should be met with entire want of comprehension or knowledge of the subject, or alternatively, with any incorrect information that presented itself to the barman's fertile mind. As for the Palace Drains, Burden answered all enquiries abut this interesting subject himself and as he knew as little about the drains as everyone else, his *obiter dicta* were accepted everywhere as Bible Truth.

Then the party broke up. Lady Elaine drove her Dowager mother home. They did not speak much, for both were tired and both wondered exactly what the other was thinking but didn't like to ask. When Lady Elaine had put the car into the garage she joined her mother in the drawing-room.

"It all went off very well," said the Dowager. "Gwendolen looked so handsome. I was thinking, Elaine, that you might as well have her bedroom as your sitting-room. Then you could have your own friends whenever you like. It would be quite easy

to put a little sink and an Ascot heater on that landing and then
you would be independent," and most considerately she did not
add that both her daughters' friends had always seemed to her
excessively dull and made it difficult for her to ask her own old
friends.

"Oh, thank you *so* much, mother," said Lady Elaine. "That
would be splendid. And we could easily have a door put at the
bottom of the stairs on the landing and then if my friends did
talk rather loudly you wouldn't be bothered," which the Dowager thought a very good idea.

"Oh, mother," said Lady Elaine, "what did you think of Mr.
Sumter?"

The Dowager said she had only had a few words with him and
he seemed a very pleasant, good-mannered young man and she
hoped to see him again, and how had Elaine got on with him?

"He said I ought to go to America, mother," said Lady Elaine,
"and he would write to his mother about it. It would be splendid."

The Dowager did not sit down flat on the floor like Miss
Betsy Trotwood, but was as astonished as that lady was when
her nephew arrived in rags at her garden gate. She did not
answer at once. This might have been rather terrifying, but her
silence was simply because she was rapidly going through the
pros and cons. Lady Elaine, having shot her bolt, said nothing
and waited. A great many thoughts rushed through the Dowager's mind and to do her justice the first of them were for her
daughter. It certainly would be a little dull for Elaine now
Gwendolen was married. She and Elaine got on very well but
naturally their friends were not always the same. The Dowager
did sometimes think that Elaine, without her sister, might be
getting into an unnecessarily older group of her mother's old
friends. All the family had good manners and also a real *bonté de
coeur*, and perhaps Elaine had been too unselfish; or perhaps she
herself had been a little selfish in keeping Elaine by her. Not that
Elaine had ever seemed unhappy or bored, but—the Dowager

said to herself—to live with one's elderly mother was no inheritance and a visit to America would be good for the girl—for as such she still, naturally, thought of her.

All this thinking was of course so short in that strange thing the human mind that although the Dowager had lived through what felt to her a long period of consideration, her daughter had hardly noticed the pause.

"I must say that sounds extremely pleasant," said the Dowager. "If you went to America I think I should go to Mentone and stay with Lady de Courcy at the Villa Thermogène for a few weeks. She is always asking me and she is an old friend—at least the families have known one another for a long time. The only thing is you are such a bad sailor, Elaine. I shall never forget that time I took you and Gwendolen to Dieppe and she stayed on deck and enjoyed herself and I had to look after you—poor Elaine! I have never seen anyone so sick."

"It wasn't *being* sick, mother," said Lady Elaine. "It was *wanting* to be sick and I couldn't. But when I go to America I can fly, so even if I did feel sick it wouldn't be for long."

So surprised was the Dowager by this sudden irruption of an individuality she had not suspected, that she said nothing. But she had a kind heart and wanted her unmarried daughter to have some life of her own. She herself would not always be there and if Elaine had new friends, a little younger than she was, it wouldn't be a bad plan. So she made up her mind and spoke.

"Quite a good idea," she said. "You had better ask that nice Mr. Sumter to go into it for you. He seems very businesslike. I don't know how long he is to be over here but if it isn't very long perhaps you could fly over with him. I should feel more comfortable if you were travelling with someone you knew. I shall tell Frankie to talk to him about it. And then I shall write to Lady de Courcy. And I shall tell your brother to see about money and to give you some introductions."

As the Millennium appeared to have dawned, Lady Elaine thanked her mother with all her heart. She knew already that between now and the day she left England her mind would go up and down, half of it longing to explore a new world, half thinking of the safety of home. But she was a sensible woman and squashed her lower or worrying self—a self which most of us have but cannot always keep in its place—and set her face towards the New World. At the same time the Dowager's plans for a visit to the Riviera began to take shape and we think it will be an excellent plan for them both. We should very much like to follow Lady Elaine to Virginia, but that is not within our province any more than Mentone is. We do however feel certain that she will meet hospitality and kindness everywhere and make some lasting friendships, and when she is back in England and her American friends come over she will do all she can to return the hospitality and if they come to Barchester she will see that the Deanery opens its doors to them and that her brother and his wife shall give them lunch and show them with fine insular pride the revolting exterior and interior of the Towers. We do not pretend to see deep into the future, but we think Lady Elaine will make a happy life of her own, for one's mother cannot live for ever and when Lady Elaine is alone—and not badly off—she will make another link of friendship between the United States and England and keep open house for her friends when the come over and the friends of her friends. But these things are beyond the scope of this modest chronicle.

Lavinia Merton, pleased at the thought of Ludo's visit to Northbridge Manor, duly rang up Pomfret Towers. Lord Mellings, said the voice that answered the telephone, was out, but her ladyship was in, and in a moment Lady Pomfret's voice said Was it Lavinia.

"Oh yes, thank you very much," said Lavinia. "It's only that Ludo said he would like to say good-bye to my father and mother, so I said if he came one day after lunch we could go on the river, so I told mother and she said of course he must come and I promised him I'd ring up—so I rang up. Is that all right?"

Lady Pomfret, rather touched by this nice girl who considered her parents, said it would be quite all right and Ludo was in the room and she handed him the telephone. A short business-like talk was held and it was arranged that Lord Mellings should drive over if there was a car to spare and if not he would bicycle.

"And give my love to your mother," said Lady Pomfret. "Oh!—shall Ludo bring his bathing things?"

Lavinia said that would be a good thing because then if he fell into the river when he was punting he could wear his bathing things while his clothes were dried.

Lady Pomfret, suppressing the laughter that was bubbling up in her, said if he was going to fall out of the punt he had better put his bathing things on first.

"I expect it will be too cold—it nearly always is now—" said

Lavinia rather sadly. "But there's a little electric heater in the boathouse so it wouldn't take long to dry his things anyway. Oh, and thank you very much for saying he can come."

That was the end of the conversation and as Lady Pomfret put the receiver back in its place she thought what good manners the Mertons' girl had; and what was more—as far as she could judge—a really kind heart and thought of other people's comfort. Then her mind took one of the unaccountable twists it is always taking and went to her beloved husband who was always working for others up to the full limit of his strength; and Ludo too would always push himself to the limit. She had done her best for her husband and though there were many public burdens that she could not share, there were also many small duties and bothers that she could handle without consulting him. And if he did realize that she had walked up the hill Difficulty alone, for his sake, his gratitude was to her the most touching recompense—unsought but cherished. If only—in due course of time—her Ludo could find someone who would share his life in the fullest way. But Ludo was still very young and he was anxious to do well in his profession, and he had certainly improved vastly in health and weighed almost as much as he ought to weigh and, as far as she knew, was liked. And he had a great deal of patience; a most valuable asset for a future soldier and landowner. Well, there came a point at which one's children passed from one's keeping and one could only hope and pray. Not in the lovely cold chapel built of marble and lapis lazuli with gilded carving, all done by the skilled Italian workmen whom old Lady Pomfret had imported, but in one's heart; remembering that the door may be opened to the importunate, that to receive one must ask and that to find one must seek. Oh, dear! she felt. One must just go on and do one's best. And that is the parent's job.

By a gross oversight the weather suddenly took a turn for the better. Perhaps because it knew it had already caused a very satisfactory amount of annoyance and general thwartedness;

perhaps because it just couldn't help it. At any rate it was really a hot day when Ludo came over in his little car to Northbridge Manor. Lavinia was, in a most unmaidenly way, on the look-out for him at the end of the drive and opened the gate.

"That's awfully nice of you," said Lord Mellings, opening the door so that she could get in beside him. "It's such a nuisance to have to get out and open gates and then get in and drive the car through and then get out again to shut them. Father is going to try one of those gates that open of themselves for heavy traffic— I mean cars or farm waggons or lorries—where the back drive runs into Golden Valley. I always hope the horses and cattle have large enough feet."

Lavinia asked whom on earth he meant.

"Well, you know there's a grating you have to go over," said Ludo, "and if you have very small feet like a goat, one of your hoofs could slip through and you might break your leg and never be able to get out till someone came along. Father and Uncle Roddy are trying to invent a gate to beat all gates, but it seems to end in talk. Things do, you know."

"But sometimes they don't, don't they?" said Lavinia. "I say, would you like to bathe or just go out in one of the boats?"

Ludo said she might think him a coward, but he could see how cold the water was without going into it and would far rather go in the punt or the rowing-boat. Lavinia said the punt, because even if you did get water down your sleeves you couldn't tip it over, to which Ludo said But you could stick the punt pole too hard into the mud and then when you tried to pull it out it wouldn't come and the punt slid away from you and that was that.

Lavinia said Then what happened.

"Well," said Ludo, "you hang miserably onto the punt pole and it may keep steady for a moment if it's well down into the mud, but then it begins to tilt and you go very slowly into the water and have to swim ashore and all your friends laugh at you."

"*I* shouldn't laugh," said Lavinia boldly. "I should run to the boat-house and bring the coracle up—you remember the coracle the day you came here before—one can punt frightfully fast in it and I should be back before you had quite gone into the water and rescue you. One of the men could rescue the punt and the pole. There's a heavy kind of boat they use for the weed-cutting in the summer and you can't upset it. But I like the coracle best. Which would you like?"

"Well, as it's a fine day and quite warm, I think the punt," said Ludo.

So they went to the boat-house where the river doors were open and sunlight was flecking the dark green water and Lavinia untied the punt and got in, holding the rope till Ludo was aboard.

"Who is going to punt?" said Lavinia. "Would you like to?"

"I will if *you* like," said Ludo. "I'm not awfully good, but I haven't fallen in yet."

"Mr. Wickham says," said Lavinia, "that you have to fall in three times and then you're all right. And he was a sailor. I mean a real one, Royal Navy, in the first war."

"But sailors don't *punt*," said Ludo, who had now taken off his coat and we must say looked very well in shirt and grey flannel trousers. "I say, does this punt leak? I'm standing in a puddle."

"Not really," said Lavinia, "but sometimes the water does get in. And of course if it's left out in the rain it's bound to get wet."

Ludo, who was manoeuvering the punt through a narrow piece of water, didn't answer. Partly because he was intent on his job, partly because to his orderly mind the thought of a punt being left out in the rain was repellent. Lavinia must have guessed or sensed his thoughts, for she said it was Harry's fault.

"That's my brother," she said, "and there's Jessica, but they are quite young."

"And what are you?" said Ludo, amused by her air of grown-upness.

"I don't know," said Lavinia.

"But you must know your own age," said Ludo.

"Of course I do," said Lavinia. "I'm sixteen. I think it's a dull age—rather fat if you see what I mean. Thirteen is exciting because you are in your teens. And fourteen is dull and fifteen is rather nice. And of course seventeen is marvellous, and then one gets grown up. But sixteen sounds flumpy and you are always growing out of your clothes."

"Nothing to the way I do," said Ludo, from his superior age and height. "It's quite awful. Just now I can wear some of father's things, but if I go on growing he'll have to wear mine," which made Lavinia laugh.

"I say," she said, "do you remember when your father and mother came to dinner here and brought you with them and the Aubrey Clovers were here—ages ago?"

"Indeed I do," said Ludo. "I was wearing my first dinner jacket. At least it was an old one of father's and it fitted me pretty well, but I felt shabby and hoped your people wouldn't notice."

"I'm sure they didn't," said Lavinia earnestly. "And it looked all right."

"But you weren't there," said Ludo. "It was only the grown-ups."

"Of course I wasn't at the dinner party," said Lavinia. "But Nurse was downstairs in the kitchen, so I got out of bed and looked over the banisters and saw you all going in to dinner and Edith Graham was being awfully noisy. I haven't seen her since she married Lord William Harcourt. I think Lady William Harcourt is an awfully good name. I shall marry a duke's younger son too and be Lady man's Christian name Something. What do you think would be a good name?"

"I don't really know," said Ludo. "There aren't many dukes about in Barsetshire. There's the Duke of Omnium of course, but his son is married and anyway much too old for you."

"Well if his son is married, has he got a son I could marry?" said Lavinia.

"He certainly has a son, but as far as I remember he must be about six or seven years old," said Ludo.

"In History," said Lavinia, "people get betrothed when they were quite small. But Lord Silverbridge would turn into a duke later on and then I'd be a Duchess which sounds stuffy. I must think about it."

"What a ridiculous person you are," said Ludo laughing, but very kindly, just because he was amused. "If you really want to be a Lady George or Lady Charles you could try a Marquis's younger son. They sound exactly like Duke's younger sons."

"Have we any Marquises in Barsetshire?" said Lavinia.

Ludo said he was sorry but he didn't know.

"Well, I shall find out," said Lavinia. "And then I'll have a coronet and go to Court," to which Ludo's riposte was—and we think he was justified—"All right, goose."

"I'm *not* a goose," said Lavinia.

"And I'm not a gander," said Ludo, "Look here, shall we go a bit further down?"

"All right, let's just drift," said Lavinia. "Only you'll have to punt to get back," so they drifted slowly down-stream past the Bunces' cottage, tied up for a bit, picked with some difficulty and nearly falling overboard a sheaf of the yellow flags which shone among the reeds, and they turned homewards, for they were still young enough to feel hungry for tea. When they had put the punt away they went up to the house and found Sir Noel and Lady Merton sitting on the terrace, with a view of the river, warmed by the sun and sheltered by the house.

Ludo was welcomed by his host and hostess. The old parlour-maid Palmer announced tea with the air of a captured Trojan princess waiting on Greek warriors among the ashes of Troy. But as this was her general attitude to company no one took any notice.

"Well, what have you two been doing?" said Sir Noel, which is a silly question in that it may sound like (*a*) suspicion that whatever you have been doing is wrong and (*b*) unnecessary and idle curiosity.

Lavinia, who was never backward in coming forward, at once gave an account of their mild boating expedition.

"Do you play tennis, Ludo?" said Sir Noel.

"Which do you mean, sir?" said Ludo. "The tennis court—I mean where we play Royal tennis—isn't in very good condition. What I would like would be to have enough money to have it put into proper order and have a professional player to coach me. I don't suppose I'd ever be really good, but it would be fun. My father says when he was a young man old Uncle Giles—that's old Lord Pomfret that my young brother was called after—used to have a professional living there and all the best amateur players used to come and stay for his tennis weeks."

"I wish I had ever had the chance to learn the game," said Sir Noel. "My profession is full of queer French and Latin expressions, most of them well Anglicized by now. It must be a bit like your tennis jargon.

Far from being offended, or scandalized, by hearing Royal tennis terms so described, Ludo was interested. Sir Noel liked the boy; his good looks, though he needed to fill out a bit, his interest in the King of games, and the feeling he gave one of belonging in a way to an older civilization, yet not afraid of a newer one.

"We must all learn to take our time from the young men," said Sir Noel thoughtfully.

Lavinia said Why and also How.

"Why—you young goose," said her father, "because when you are young you look ahead, but as you get older you will look back—*laudator temporis acti*—and can be rather a bore to the young."

Lavinia said what did that mean, but no one noticed her, for Lord Mellings neatly capped his host's quotation with Horace's comment, or rider, that as you get older you find many good things but when you begin to go downhill many of them gradually disappear. Sir Noel gravely said what pleasure it gave him to find a young man who knew his Flaccus, which made

Lord Mellings blush, though otherwise he showed no sign of confusion. Lavinia suddenly said What about Browning.

What about him, said her father.

"'Grow old along with me, The best is yet to be, The last for which the first was made,'" said Lavinia, adding in an offhand way for the benefit—apparently—of a large and ill-informed audience, "Rabbi ben Ezra."

"Well, he can keep it," said her father. "There may be—and I hope there is—a Better Land—but I can't think of anything better than this life if it weren't for the Income Tax and Lord Aberfordbury and that dreadful man Oliver Harvey of the Board of Tape and Sealing Wax and the river either flooding the tennis court, or very low with stinking mud on each side."

"Et patati et patata," said Lavinia, and we think rather impertinently, but she was Noel's elder daughter and first child and he overlooked a good many things from her that he might have noticed unfavourably in Harry and Jessica; nor was she unaware of the fact.

The Mertons had more than once discussed Lavinia and wondered if boarding school was what she needed. But as she was doing very well at the Barchester High School it would be a pity to swap horses while crossing a stream, so they left well alone. Also, owing to the competent and rather ferocious French mistress Mademoiselle Chiendent, any girl who seemed likely to do well in French was drilled and pushed and praised and scolded according to Mlle C's opinion of her week's work. And very luckily the German mistress, Fräulein Katzenjammer, was just as fierce and strict. She was considered by the girls to be top dog of the two because she often made her pupils cry, while Mlle Chiendent only nagged. But the result was that any girl of any intelligence was fairly fluent and fairly accurate in these languages and also enjoyed reading them.

Ludo, though quite well grounded in these languages at home had felt—with the fine healthy insular view of the English boy—that they were not to be paraded at school. But in the last two years or so he had discovered that they were also a means of communication with foreigners (a term which roughly covered everywhere from China to Peru) and could help one to get on if one's regiment were stationed abroad and also that their litera- ture was not bounded by Lessing and Corneille—though he would come to Corneille as he grew older. Italian conversation was easy to him because he had spent several summer holidays on the Adriatic coast and had learnt the language fluently if not quite conventionally from the various children who thronged the beaches and the servants and anyone else who happened to be about. And he had a quite healthy opinion that if one could speak German well enough to get on with people it would help one if one were sent abroad. Unfortunately the German master at his school, seeing in Ludo a good mind in advance of his age, had let loose upon him the *Wahlverwandtschaften* of Goethe, a work which would sink by its own weight even in the Dead Sea, and almost put Ludo off the Teutonic language for good, till he suddenly found Heine and the many lyric poems of the German language and wallowed in them.

Lydia, interested, asked Ludo what his next plans were.

"Well, with any luck I'll get a commission later on," said Ludo. "You know old Uncle Giles's only son who was Lord Mellings was a soldier, but he was killed years and years ago in India in one of those frontier skirmishes. So there wasn't any direct heir and my grandfather who was some kind of cousin was the next heir. He and old Uncle Giles loathed each other."

Noel asked why.

"I think they just did," said Ludo. "But he died long before any- one thought he would, so my father became the heir. He once did talk to me about it and how miserable he was, because he didn't want a title and lands and responsibilities. I think it was my mother who saved him. You know her brother, my uncle Roddy Wicklow, and mother's awfully like him. I mean she can manage *anything*. I try to learn a lot from Uncle Roddy because you see, sir, someday I shall have to run the house and the estate and go to London and sit in the Lords, and I ought to know more about it. I'm sorry, sir, I'm talking too much."

Noel said of course he wasn't. And what is more he meant it, for young Lord Mellings's confidence and a kind of simplicity had touched him. He would talk to Lydia about it later and see if the boy would come over more often in his holiday time, for evidently messing about with boats was an excellent tonic and one could also be lazy in boats and let one's long back stretch itself on the cushions.

At this moment Harry and Jessica Merton who had been to Northbridge lunching with the Carters at what was now called The Old Rectory came back on their bicycles which they rode round the house onto the terrace and dismounted, leaning their bicycles against the wall.

"Did I, or did I not tell you," said Sir Noel, assuming the air of a hanging judge rather than an eminent parental Q.C., "NOT to ride your bicycles along the terrace. Put them in their proper place and then come and help us to finish the cake."

"Oh, goody, goody!" said Harry, and mounting one bicycle he led the other to the old barn, part of which had been made into a garage, with what we can only call a bicycle rack along one wall. A good many of the younger people who were not old enough for a driving license now used bicycles almost as much as we did before motors were invented; only the bicycles were now lighter in build and had several new brakes and gadgets. But they did not know the full joy of coasting downhill on a fixed wheel with one's feet up on those two little rests that were fixed to the things that hold the wheel up—we do not know their real name. There were those who did it with their legs over the handlebars, but we were strictly forbidden to do it ourselves and in any case would not have had enough courage.

"I say, mother," said Jessica, "we raced Lady Cora part of the way. She's a marvellous driver."

"Young idiots," said Noel to Ludo. "How often have I told them not to race with cars. Not that they could come to any harm with Cora, because she's the best driver in the county, bar none. That's how she saved her husband's life."

Ludo asked what was that.

"County history," said Noel. "Cecil Waring had a bit of shrapnel or something inside him from the war, and it suddenly began to hurt and he went quite green in the face and Lady Cora—they weren't married then—drove him over to the Barchester General Hospital as fast as she possibly could—and she is a very good driver with a very good car and friends with all the county police, so no one stopped her and they got to Barchester in time. And then they got married."

Harry who had come back in time to catch the last words said if he'd been there he'd have taken Sir Cecil in a heliocopter.

"Helicopter, my boy," said Noel. "Do verify your references. The heli part means something that goes round—like a snail-shell. But when words begin with helio it means something to do with the sun."

"Like a heliograph," said Harry. "I read a poem by someone called Kipling—one of the books in your study father—and it was about someone in India and he was sent off on a job somewhere so he showed his wife how to read a heliograph, I mean what the dots and dashes meant, and lots of people saw the flashes and knew what they meant which was to tell his wife not to dance with old General Bangs because he was a flirting person."

There was a short silence, everyone being stunned by Harry's contribution. Harry, who was famous for not being very good at lessons, though a valuable member of the cricket eleven and a good half-back at football, liked boxing and could swim like a fish: Harry knew the poetry of Rudyard Kipling. The grown-ups were considerably impressed and Ludo made a private vow to read the whole of Kipling to himself, wondering at the same time whether his parents had all his books.

"I say, Lady Merton," he said, courteously addressing his hostess though he would have preferred his host, "can one get the book with that poem in it? I don't think father has it, because I've read all his books that we have."

Lydia said there was a very fat book with all Kipling's poetry in it and she had two copies and would like to give him one.

"Oh, I *say*, Lady Merton!" said Ludo, going red in the face with gratitude.

"Come inside and we'll find it," she said, and went with him to her sitting-room and from a bookshelf took the heavy Definitive Edition of all his known poetical work.

"I'll put your name in it," she said. "This is the book I had before I was married and Noel had a copy too, so we can spare one for you. I'd like you to have it," and she wrote his name and hers in the beginning.

"Oh, thanks most *awfully*, Lady Merton," said Ludo. "I'll take frightful care of it. I don't let anyone dust my books—not even Nurse."

"I am glad to do anything I can for your family, because I'm fond of them," said Lydia. "And I know you are fond of books and will be kind to them. Ask my husband to put his name in it too."

So Ludo took the book out and showed his host the inscription and Noel added his name.

"Are you a bit of a poet?" he said.

"Oh no, not a bit, sir," said Ludo. "But I like reading poetry and I like music. When Lavinia came to the Towers we had a lovely singing time together. She plays awfully well, sir."

"And you sing well," said Noel. "At least you did in Aubrey Clover's play. Do you remember—in Coronation summer? That charming lyric that began 'Though I am not twenty, sweet, Here is my heart.'"

"Oh, that was because the Clovers were so kind to me," said Ludo. "I think I'd never have stopped being shy and horrid if they hadn't poked me a bit."

"Well, I think you would," said Lavinia stoutly. "Only don't go and get killed on frontiers when you are a soldier."

Her father said it might be more correct to say when he had got his commission, which made Lavinia say "Brother!" but only to herself inside herself.

"It wouldn't matter much if I got killed or not," said Ludo, "because there's Giles. When old Uncle Giles's son was killed there wasn't a younger brother to carry on. Giles would do it very well. He knows all the cottages and the farms and the poachers and he's an awfully good rider and knows all about the bots and the glanders or whatever horses have. And when he had a pony that used to blow itself out when he saddled it, he got on it barebacked and kicked it round the field and it never misbehaved again. The pony did it once to me and I fell off and cried."

"Oh, Ludo, how dreadful!" said Lavinia. "Were you hurt?"

"Not a bit," said Ludo, "because he stopped near a rick that the men were thatching and I fell off onto a lot of straw," which he said so cheerfully that it made Lavinia laugh, and Sir Noel thought the better of him for it.

Lavinia asked if his father would be a Duke one day.

Ludo said, "Good gracious no! Why?"

"Well he works much harder than lots of other lords," said Lavinia, "so I thought he might get promotion."

"It's high time you had a course of Burke or Debrett," said her unfeeling father. "You will find both of them in my study. Dukes may rank higher, but Earls are much older. It seems quite likely that there won't be any more Dukes—except of course royal ones."

"Not even Mr. Churchill?" said Harry.

"Not even he," said his father, "though he comes of a ducal family. I believe Westminster was the last un-royal dukedom to be created and that's some time ago now. But that's enough rubbish for the present," which words made Lavinia who had started the subject feel rather small, and also determine to learn the Peerage by heart—or at any rate the people's families that she did not know that were peers; and if this is rather muddled, so was she. But we think she had the root of the matter in her.

"The trouble is," said Lydia, "that people *will* die and get born, and one really can't buy a new Burke or a Debrett every time and one always means to put anything one sees in *The Times* about one's own friends into the book but one never does. Or some and not others and then of course it is the others that you want."

Ludo said, most unwillingly, that he ought to go now because he was going to supper with his Uncle Roddy and it had to be early because Uncle Roddy was going to a County Council meeting in Barchester. The Mertons told him to ring up whenever he felt like going on the river and Noel wanted to tip him, but wasn't sure if it would be accepted. The family came to the car to see him off.

"I'll come as far as the cattle-crossing with you," said Lavinia. "Sometimes the gate on the far side is shut after the cows are home and it's such a nuisance to have to stop the car and open the gate and get back into the car and then do it nearly all over again at the shutting end."

So they drove to the crossing and just as Lavinia had said the gate was shut at the other end and she got out and opened it and Ludo drove through.

"Wait a minute," she said and came up to the car. "I say, Ludo, when can we do some more music?"

Ludo of course said Whenever she liked and would she come to Pomfret Towers again, or should he come to her house.

"It would be more fun in your house," she said, "because one is so nicely alone there. Our house isn't so alone—I mean there isn't anywhere where we could make a noise without bothering people."

"Then I'll come and fetch you and I'll run you back," said Ludo. "No one will bother us except Nurse and she likes you."

"Does she *really*?" said Lavinia, for to be approved by the ex-nurse of a new friend that one likes very much is almost like getting the Victoria Cross.

"Of course she does," said Ludo. "Thank you again for having me. My people were awfully pleased because they like your people awfully."

"So do mine. I mean they like yours. I think we all like each other *very* much, Ludo," and as she was standing on the running board she kissed him carelessly, little more than cheek to cheek, just to show good-feeling. Then she jumped down and waved good-bye and went home, pleased with the agreeable visit.

Ludo drove on and so hard was he thinking of her farewell that he only just pulled up outside the gate in time to avoid the onslaught of one of the large S.U.V.P.C. (known officially as Southbridge United Viator Passenger Company) motor coaches full of day trippers who had eaten things out of bags during all the outward journey and were still eating things out of bags on the homeward journey and passing bottles of soft drinks from hand to hand. The passengers, seeing what was obviously a gentleman in a little car, waved and yelled and cat-called and several wits quickly blew up the paper bags their lunch had been in and burst them. Ludo laughed and continued his journey. It is sometimes a little deflating to the spirit to go home after a visit to amusing friends when one is young; for us elders it is often the arrival at the kind house we are visiting that depresses us, against our better judgment, feeling that when we were at home we were in a better place. But Ludo felt a little low. Brightness had fallen from the air. He put his car away, went indoors and allowed his parents to ask him if he had had a nice time, even going so far as to say that he had, and that Sir Noel and Lady Merton had sent all sorts of good wishes, and Lady Merton had given him a book of Kipling's poems.

"A strange genius," said Lord Pomfret. "I think he was most of all a seer. He saw the shape of things to come and knew what was going to happen. There aren't often people like that. How were the Mertons?"

Ludo said they were very nice to him and he had been down the river with Lavinia and he wished they had a river at home, to which his father very sensibly replied that one couldn't have everything and the Mertons hadn't got a fountain fed by a spring higher up the hill and sprouting great sheaves of water.

"*Les grands jets d'eau seltes, parmi les marbres,*" said Ludo in a kind of dream.

"What's that?" said his father.

"Oh, a poem," said Ludo. "But I can't remember who by. I think it was Verlaine. Or perhaps Baudelaire—one of those romantics. It's set to music by someone French—might be Debussy—might be Fauré. One forgets such a lot."

Lord Pomfret said that was quite true, but what he was really thinking about was his elder son and how little one knows one's children. Here was Ludo, finished with school, preparing to be a soldier, and suddenly quoting the French romantics. Well, no harm in that. A knowledge and a love of French literature were all to the good, and the romantics did know how to make verse, and luckily there were musicians who had known how to set it to music. Ludo, though not a musician, liked the piano and could sing without being self-conscious. A Something told his father that when away from home and pressed by his friends—friends that his parents did not know—he might be quite different; a chrysalis becoming for a few hours a butterfly and going back into his shell or cocoon when he came home.

Then Ludo's last words came into his mind. "One forgets such a lot." At Ludo's age one didn't usually forget—nor had one so much to forget as one's elders had. Ludo hardly ever talked of friends outside the Pomfret circle. He hadn't asked to bring friends home from school or from Sandhurst. He had seemed happy in both places and there was never the Day of Misery before going back to school which had racked so many parents' hearts, though they know inside that it has to be and the young must learn that there are disappointments and losses. "*Entbehren sollst du, entbehren*"—the words suddenly came into his mind and he couldn't remember who wrote them—perhaps Goethe. How true they were, One has just *got* to do without things.

To pacify his own mind he went to the estate room, where he saw the men who worked about the place, or visitors on business, and where Eleanor Grantly, daughter of the Rector of Edgewood, now Mrs. Colin Keith, had so competently sorted and tidied the papers—files, letters, forms, memoranda—that he could never manage himself. Now he had an excellent secretary, Miss Cowshay, who from the cashier's office at Pilchard's Store had risen to an important war job in the Regional Commissioner's Office and now most competently filed and when necessary dealt with business papers and, much to his relief, did not have a dog-like devotion for him. And here he had a very special shelf which was sacred to him, dedicated entirely to dictionaries and to books of reference in various literatures. One of the very few occasions on which he lost his temper was if anyone borrowed a reference book without asking, or put it back in its wrong place; and it had come to be understood by his family that if Father was working there he didn't mind your coming in and borrowing a book—but if that book was not back in its proper place within twenty-four hours, unless due notice was given, he could show some of the terrifying Pomfret temper that he had inherited through his own father but had trained and subdued to usefulness. So much so that, if he had occasion to give a necessary talking-to or blowing up to anyone on the estate, the culprit would apologize almost grovellingly and then boast to all his friends that his lordship could curse and swear like a good 'un, by which means Lord Pomfret's prestige rose high. Not that he really used bad language, but he had a way of suddenly hurling tags of Latin or even Greek, remembered from his school days, or very low Italian abuse, picked up when he was with his long-deceased father in Italy, at the heads of the wrong-doers who all liked it immensely and admired his lordship's wealth of vituperation. So much so, indeed, that several of the best words had been picked up and used by offenders and were being rapidly assimilated in the mixture of Ancient British, Scandinavian, Saxon, Norman, Danish and, during the last war,

American tongues that had passed through Barsetshire in the course of time. There was one old labourer, Fred Wamber, who christened his first child Zernebok, a name which Lord Pomfret remembered in Ivanhoe but had never met elsewhere. When questioned the labourer had said his great-grandfather was Zernebok and he had heard tell it was a heathen sort of name but his boy had been christened all proper by the Reverend Thompson and if any man said his—the speaker's—name wasn't Wamber that man was a gormed liar, because his father and grandfather had been Wamber before him. So was history kept alive and the possible lineal descendant of Wamba the Witless was Wamber the cottager.

CHAPTER 12

So Ludo went about his pleasures and his duties, which last included a holiday task; namely an essay to be written on any English historical character except kings. In his excursions among the books and the papers in the library—for his father had given him permission to read and use anything he liked so long as he put the book or the papers carefully back in their proper place when not working on them—he had found some documents of interest about the Pomfrets. Nothing that was new, but facts that were new to him. He knew that the family had lived on the same ground almost since Norman William's time, but had never troubled much about it. Now, thanks to his father's patient reading and arranging old papers—with help from the Barsetshire Archaeological Society and various local enthusiasts like Lord Stoke—he could follow the fortunes of the family from the twelfth century when Giles de Pomfret had built a stout Norman fortress to guard the lands he had been given by King Henry II. This building, probably good for defence but dark, damp, insanitary, and uncomfortable, had been improved as years passed till it was partially destroyed in the Wars of the Roses, rebuild under Henry VII, and battered by Cromwell. In 1689 the Pomfret of the day was created an earl for services rendered to the Prince of Orange and in the same year a younger brother, Eustace, who had rashly adopted the Roman Catholic faith, had found it convenient to go to Italy where he had married a lady of rank and wealth and their children had taken the name of Strelsa and the title Count from the heiress's rank and their lands from her wealth. The family was still represented in Italy, but the two branches had little or no communication, especially now since the name had been made notorious by Count Guido Strelsa who was famous for having been turned out of every gambling hell in Europe.

All this interesting family history had been painfully collected, constructed, and collated by the well-known scholar Professor Milward, with valuable assistance from Professor Marston who knew so much about the Renaissance that his monumental books consisted largely of footnotes. And on the Italian side there had been trustworthy information from Cardinal Boccafiume who boasted the blood of the Borgias, and the Duke of Monte Cristo, that cosmopolitan doyen of the diplomatic world.

But all these delightful facts would not write Ludo's holiday task for him: only he could do it. So he thought and thought and finally decided to write about old Fred Wamber's family, for Fred couldn't read and his wife said she did learn to read at school but she didn't seem to fancy it and what was the good of doing something you didn't fancy and there now! she'd left the pail under the tap and the water must be running over. But Fred was a great talker, so Ludo decided to visit him frequently during the holidays, both in his home and when he was working. He would not ask questions, but he would get Fred talking. If he could then get him to stop talking was a different question, but he could always say his father or his mother wanted him at home now and observe, with his own private feeling of a joke, how Fred would at once turn into the candid friend, only too ready to tell his young lordship where his duty lay. Of course he wouldn't use Fred's name and would sign it "Barcastrian," for it was the fashion for the essay writers to use pseudonyms and hand in, with their essay, a sealed envelope with their own name. In earlier days the boy's handwriting would have been known, but typewriters were now allowed. We believe that Sherlock Holmes could tell from a typescript pretty well who the typer was, but his art must have perished with him at the Reichenbach Falls (for we refuse to believe for a moment that he really came back to life after finishing his inefficient murderer). How that canard got about we do not know; any more than—as it suddenly occurs to us—why a canard should be a joke or take-in, as well as a duck. "Words, words, words": and how fascinating they are. Those of us who know J. M. Barrie's earlier work will remember that when his Sentimental Tommy was sitting for a bursary he handed in his paper unfinished because he could not decide which of several words in the Doric, meaning a number of things or people, would be the most suitable for the sentence he was writing. It seems quite possible.

Ludo went to his own room to tidy himself, and think about the Wamber family and his holiday task. One always said Next day I'll begin, but there were so many next days and nothing to show for them. So he sat down determinedly with a half-used exercise book and wrote A Barsetshire Worthy in large letters, hoping that this might stimulate the Muse. But she had gone to a sherry party on Mount Helicon and did not hear the heart-felt silent appeals from her suppliant. Instead of Clio, Nurse came in with her usual kind and laudable wish to see that her eldest nursling was alive and well after being out all day and, broadly speaking, to tell him what.

"Well Ludo, did you have a nice time with Lavinia? Here are your socks all mended and I've sewn the buttons onto your new shirts properly. The way they sew them on at the place they make them! A stitch and a promise, that's all," said Nurse.

"Oh, thanks awfully, nursie," said Ludo. "We had a lovely time. We went on the river and had a marvellous tea and Lady Merton gave me a book."

Nurse said "She" was the cat's grandmother and so was "We."

"Oh, me and Lavinia," said Ludo, a solecism for which his

father would have pulled him up—though for the grammar, not the *Ego et rex meus* touch.

Nurse said Lavinia was a nice young lady, in a way that made Ludo feel—though we do not think that was her intention— that other girls weren't nice young ladies.

"And Lady Merton gave me a book of poetry by Rudyard Kipling," said Ludo, showing the volume to Nurse.

Nurse said it was a funny name, but those gentlemen that wrote books did have funny names; which she said not critically, but with the infinite toleration that her class have for the eccentricities of the gentry.

Ludo said he was the one that wrote the Absent Minded Beggar in the South African War.

Nurse said that was before her time but she remembered her uncle that was a volunteer went to South Africa and got a medal, and it was a wonder how anyone had time to write a book that size.

This general summing-up of literature made Ludo feel that he had gone too far, so he said there were other funny names. There was Rider Haggard.

Nurse said Mary Corelli had written a lovely book only she couldn't remember its name, but she was never much of a one for reading.

"But you *were*, nursie," said Ludo. "You used to read lots of fairy stories to us when we were small. All those Andrew Lang books that Mother had, with the names of colours like the *Red Fairy Book* and the *Blue Fairy Book* and all the others."

"Now those were *nice* books," said Nurse. "Proper stories with Lived Happily ever after and witches and fairies and ogres. Really, the books some of the children read now. All science and that rubbish and space ships. What about your vest and drawers, Ludo? I thought I told you to put on clean ones yesterday and I didn't find the dirty ones anywhere so I suppose you're still wearing them."

"Well, nursie," said Ludo. "I thought I'd better keep them on today in case I fell in the river and they got all muddy and green, and then you'd only have one pair to wash."

Nurse was evidently impressed by his consideration for her and said All right then and Ludo mustn't forget to leave them out for her when he went to bed, which he faithfully promised to do and asked where Emily and Giles were. Nurse said somewhere with Mr. Wicklow and he might find them in Golden Valley and if he did see them to tell them to come home and get clean for their supper. So Ludo went downstairs. All was quiet. Evidently his parents were out; probably at one of the endless meetings at which one or other took the chair. That was another thing that was waiting for him as he got older and the feeling of happiness that the day had given him was suddenly blotted out. But no good grumbling and looking ahead, so he went on with his long strides and so down into Golden Valley which has changed very little since we first knew it. On the near side of the valley which curved away at each end cows were grazing and beyond them on the far side there was a steep beech-covered slope, and behind it the ground rose again, planted mostly now, alas, with conifers, for money was always needed and Lord Pomfret was doing well with regular planting and selling. Drives for the guns were cut here and there, fern-carpeted, and at the end of the widest was the Obelisk, erected in 1760, a landmark in the neighbourhood. Then more drives cut through the plantations, really to give the commercial wood more air and light, but always looking rather mysterious as if they might lead to a witch's house on chicken's legs or a robbers' cave. Perhaps one of the most romantic views in West Barsetshire especially when, at this early evening hour, you looked down from the hill and saw the old woodman's cottage with blue smoke curling up from its chimney, all very Morland. And if one could have seen inside it probably more Morland than ever with the keeper's wife suckling a fine healthy dirty baby and three or four healthy dirty children playing on the floor or fighting each other on the doorstep, with a pig for company, the whole seasoned with hearty Saxon objurgations. Ludo felt rather romantic—as indeed anyone might with such surroundings and on a warm summer evening with one star shining. He wondered which it was and said to himself he must pay more attention to stars. Perhaps it was Hesperus, the star of evening, shining also over Northbridge Manor.

His romantic musings were cut short by Emily and Giles who came racing down one of the drives accompanied by a large nondescript dog, property of the woodman who was following at his own pace.

From the excited and simultaneous accounts of his sister and brother, Ludo gathered that they had seen a magpie's nest only it was where they couldn't reach it and Tomkins had said he'd send a boy up there because those magpies were thieving birds and the fewer he saw the better pleased he'd be. Up on the top by the monument it was so clear that they could see the spire of the cathedral and that meant bad weather, and they had heard the cathedral bell striking seven o'clock.

"Ah," said Tomkins, "that old bell she kept the right time all through the war. *She* weren't going to ring no gormed silly Summer time, she wasn't. If it was six o'clock, she'd ring six o'clock, not seven o'clock. And now she's just rung seven o'clock. Time I was at home and you my lord and Master Giles and Lady Emily. Your father'll be laying for you if you don't hurry up," which was quite untrue and the speaker and his hearers knew it: but protocol was observed on both sides. All three went down the hill with Tomkins, said good-night to him and his dog and went back to their home where Nurse was waiting for them.

"Now Emily and Giles, you go and wash properly," said Nurse. "Your Uncle Roddy's here, Ludo, and he said hurry up and he'll take you back with him."

Ludo had almost forgotten that he was having supper with the Wicklows and quickly washed his face and hands and went to the sitting-room where Roddy was talking estate shop with his sister and brother-in-law.

"I'm sorry if I'm late, Uncle Roddy," said Ludo. "I was in Golden Valley and then I went up to the Obelisk and Emily and Giles were there with Tomkins and I rather forgot the time, till we heard the cathedral strike seven," but his Uncle Roddy took a liberal view of this and said once you were up on the hill you always wanted to stop a bit longer and now they would go back to Alice. So Ludo got into his uncle's useful little car and in a very few moments they were crossing the river and going up Nutfield High Street.

It is a long time since we first met Alice Wicklow, formerly Alice Barton, when as a young girl she spent a weekend at Pomfret Towers—in 1937 to be exact. She was now what we can only call a Comfortable Matron, with a grown and growing-up family and was an excellent wife and citizen. Nutfield, in her youth little more than one street, running gently downhill to the river with well-built unpretentious Georgian houses on each side, but now grown to a town. But something of its past still lingered in the High Street and she and her husband lived in the pleasant red brick house where his parents had lived. The only noticeable difference in their way of living was that Alice Wicklow though she liked dogs did not want them all over the house, in which her husband agreed with her, which made it much more comfortable for guests, for nothing is more disconcerting than to have a large retriever put loving front paws on your lap just when you are eating a piece of cake or drinking a cocktail. No one guessed then that Sally Wicklow would marry young Mr. Foster who had become Lord Pomfret, and one or two people were annoyed. We may mention particularly the Honourable Mrs. George Rivers. But young Mr. Foster had wooed and won Sally Wicklow before old Lord Pomfret died at the beginning of the war and now they were Lord and Lady Pomfret and Sally's brother was their invaluable agent, and his pretty rather shy wife was a very affectionate aunt to the Pomfrets' children, especially to Ludo. We think this was partly because both she and her husband had felt sorry for the present Lord

Pomfret when he was only the heir-apparent and had done all they could to help him. How deeply Lady Pomfret valued the affection and help of her brother there is no need to say; and her own affection for her brother's wife was deep. Ludo was perhaps as sensitive, a horrid word but Lady Pomfret could not think of a better, as his father, but he had one advantage which his father never had—a safe childhood and boyhood, dwelling among his own people, and now was full of interest in the beginnings of his profession. To his uncle Roddy Wicklow he owed what horsemanship he had and above all a knowledge of the place and the people that would one day be his responsibility. Not a bad foundation. Though she secretly felt that Giles would do it better.

The front door of the Wicklows' house was open in pleasant summer fashion, and the inner door with its upper half glazed was only locked when the family were all out.

"You go in," said Roddy. "You'll find Alice there and I'll be back in a moment" and he went down the path beside the house to see how a couple of young hounds were doing and try to decide whether that bitch would whelp in the night or wait till the next morning; either time would be inconvenient and annoying, but it was part of one's job.

"Hullo, Aunt Alice," said Ludo, looking into the drawing-room. "I'm here."

"Yes, I can see that," said Mrs. Wicklow. "As large as life and twice as natural."

"I don't think I've grown since last time I was here," said Ludo, though without much conviction. "Have you still got the mark on the wall where Uncle Roddy measured me at Christmas?"

His aunt said gravely that they were going to have the mark framed and glazed and bequeath it to the Barchester Museum and Art Gallery, which foolish joke made Ludo laugh, and then he took his shoes off and stood up against the wall while his aunt stood on a chair and laid a book on his head and marked on the wall where the top of his head came.

"All right," she said.

Ludo detached himself from the wall and most impertinently lifted his aunt from her perch and put her down on her feet on the floor, after which they both had the giggles. Roddy, who had come quietly in, stood and looked complacently at them as he might have contemplated a litter of puppies. Ludo, he thought, wouldn't play the fool—or at any rate that particular kind of fool—at the Towers; but when he came to re-think about it, there never was that kind of fun at the Towers and he doubted whether the boy's parents would care for it. He had always loved his sister Sally, younger than himself, and rejoiced in her happiness and admired her ceaseless work for the county, but he would have given a silver sixpence or a singing, soaring lark, for her to have some real good silly fun—the sort she and he used to have when Old Lord Pomfret was alive. Ludo was certainly a Pomfret—but he was a Wicklow too and good yeoman blood would tell. Old Lady Pomfret, she who was Edith Thorne, had that blood in her and the toughness that is concealed behind fine bones and great powers of endurance. Not vitality, for that was something that moved and danced and had brilliant facets; but a quiet solid sense of duty and endurance, never deflected by any urgings from outsiders.

It was to be hoped that the boy would marry someone who could be a support as well as a sympathizer and could laugh with him and at him and share any troubles that might come. At the moment he could not think of the right person, but the boy was young and his future bride—if a bride there was to be— probably a giggling schoolgirl.

Suddenly he remembered the winter when the old Pomfrets had a big house party and Alice Barton had been so shy and self-conscious and miserable and rather like a white mouse in a cage. But Alice, whom he had always been fond of in a brotherly sort of way, had grown through her shyness and he had married

her and their children were healthy and good-tempered and at
the moment were all away at the seaside in charge of a most
competent woman who had been nurse to Mrs. Joram's children
by her first marriage and had a kind of Small Child Hotel, by
means of which she was able not only to lay aside money for the
future but also to indulge in the Nanny lust for power. No
parents were admitted, except to inspect the Hotel before
sending their offspring. And when the parents came to fetch
them after the week or the fortnight—or even longer periods,
especially for what Nanny called "those poor Foreign Office
children"—there were usually yells and shrieks and tears as a
parting tribute to Nanny. The mothers' hearts were always
wrung by this display of sympathy, but the tears never lasted
long and Nanny put the old children out of her mind and con-
centrated on the new-comers—who in their turn would shriek
when they went home. Much as Roddy loved his children it was
heaven to have his wife to himself for a time. Probably she felt
the same and with good reason.

For no particular reason a doggerel rhyme of his own nursery
days, invented by a schoolboy friend who had not quite grasped
the implications which older people might suspect, floated into
Roddy's mind.

> Mother Love, oh Mother Love
> All Earthly Things thou art above,
> You drive us into bed with groans
> And pull the flesh from off our bones.

This fine inspiration of versification—the words again being
from some schoolroom doggerel—still seemed to him to have
merit, though its original begetter, like many other poets, did
not really know what he was saying or writing. But certainly one
would always have the flesh pulled off one's bones—tropically
speaking—and always have anxieties about one's young, however old they became. There would probably come a point at

which one was getting gently senile oneself and then; what then? Roddy Wicklow and his wife had more than once discussed this question with a good deal of laughing and each had cheerfully promised to put the other into the loony bin if he or she showed certain signs of dottiness. But how far must the signs go? Old Lady Emily Leslie had lived in a kind of world of her own in the last years of her life, speaking often of visits to Mamma and Papa—the old Pomfrets long dead now, parents of the autocratic Lord Pomfret who was the present Lord Pomfret's much older cousin by remove. On her grave might well have been the words, slightly changed, graven on her husband's tomb. "He dwelt among his own people." But she also dwelt among her own old servants, which in many ways eases the change. For us there will not be old servants, nor possibly old familiar faces.

Lines from a poem in French floated into Roddy's mind about the happiness of being quiet and peaceful near all one's older friends and relations; laid in well-known ground. Roddy had committed it to memory in his youth and the words came back to him, full of elegant melancholy, till he reached the line about someone who *"dort d'un bon sommeil vermeil, Sous les flots radieux"* and he began to laugh—one might almost say giggle— aloud to himself. Obviously *radieux* was only used because the poet had finished his stanza with the words *"Tous ceux qui l'ont connu, venus, Lui font de longs adieux."* A lovely nostalgic noise but signifying uncommon little. Not that it really mattered; but what the dickens the poet thought he meant, or wished to convey, by a *"sommeil vermeil,"* one could not guess. Symbolists indeed! A symbol was, one imagined, a sign of something or an allusion to something; but if one didn't know what the something was, one had had it.

All these thoughts, extremely interesting to Roddy Wicklow and of no interest at all to anyone else, had gone kaleidoscoping through his mind in a few seconds. It has taken us at least fifteen minutes to put them on paper. Ludo and his Aunt Alice had been talking about his visit to the Mertons and what fun it was to have a river and boats in one's own garden.

"When I was a girl," said his Aunt Alice, "*I* lived in a house with a river, but we didn't use it—I don't know why."

Had her father, the well-known architect Mr. Barton, been there he would have been able to tell them several reasons, the chief being that the reach of the river that flowed past his garden was not like the Mertons' bit. His garden fell away steeply to a swift-flowing water which had once been clear and one could see small fish going about their business and the clean gravel below them. But in later years Big Business had come far too close. A manufacturer had bought a stretch of land about a mile further up and settled down to destroying other people's comfort and amenities. He kept within the letter of the law and did not, as had been feared, get powers to use the river for the works. But a certain amount of refuse was always finding its way into the water and the fish—small fry but pleasant agreeable fry— had moved away upstream and so into tributaries still unspoiled where they could show off their glittering scales and their amusing spots above the clean gravel bottom.

"The Mertons have a splendid river," said Ludo. "Lavinia and I went on it and I punted. It's a bit awkward when you don't get much chance to practise. One of our fellows took a girl on the river in a punt and the punt pole stuck in the mud and he couldn't get it out and he wouldn't let go of it and he went gently over into the water. He couldn't swim and he thought he was going to be drowned and the girl wouldn't speak to him because the punt nearly went over the weir but luckily it got sideways on and got stuck against a post that said Danger and then some men came and got it off and everyone laughed at him," on which his aunt's comment was Silly little idiot; but she had been brought up to handle boats in a lady-like way.

"I don't know the Mertons very well," she said, "but I like what I do know. We must ask Lavinia over. We can't give her a

river, but she could see the puppies. Do you think she'd like
one?"

Ludo said he didn't know.

"Or does she ride?" said his aunt. "Uncle Roddy could always
find something for her."

"I never asked her about riding," said Ludo. "The Mertons
have got a stable but it's a garage. At least it was a barn and then
a bit of it was made into a stable and all the rest is for the cars.
She is very nice."

His aunt, rather unkindly, asked if the She was Lady Merton
or her daughter.

"Oh, Lady Merton, of course," said Ludo. "But Lavinia's
awfully nice too. I say, Aunt Alice, can I tell you something?"

His aunt said she supposed he could if he really wanted to.

"Well, it's rather private," said Ludo.

"Silent as the grave," said his aunt.

"Well, it wasn't my fault," said Ludo.

His aunt said she was sure it wasn't and whose fault was it and
what was the fault?

"Well, you see, Aunt Alice, I was just going away and I'd got
into the car and shut the door and Lavinia came round to my
side to say good-bye and of course I leaned out a bit—"

"And she kissed you good-bye," said his aunt.

"I say, how on *earth* did you guess?" said Ludo.

"Simple, my dear Watson," said his aunt. "These things do
happen. And did you kiss her back?"

"Of *course* not," said Ludo indignantly. "I mean it would have
served her right if I had, but I didn't."

"Didn't you *want* to?" said his aunt.

"I don't know," said Ludo.

"Well! if *that* is all you know!" said his aunt illogically.

"Ought I to have?" said Ludo.

"Oh! bless your heart, where were you born? Where do you
expect to go?" said his aunt.

"I don't know," said Ludo. "I mean I was born at Pomfret

Towers and I expect to go to Germany if my lot are sent out later. If it had been Jessica Clover I'd have known. She kisses everybody."

"Now listen to me, Ludo," said his aunt. "Jessica is The Stage. Kissing is just part of a ritual to her. You've got to work this one out for yourself. Personally I think it's an excellent plan."

Ludo asked What was.

"If you don't know, I can't tell you," said his aunt. "But next time you might kiss her hand and I expect she'll laugh. I think that will settle it. That is if you like her."

"Of course I do," said Ludo indignantly. "I like her awfully."

"I am sure you do, darling," said his aunt, a little confused because half of her was thinking what an excellent marriage it would be and half was wondering if she was behaving like a Procuress, or what that remarkable woman and memoir writer Miss Harriette Wilson described as A Female Ponder. "There is only one thing. What about your father and mother?"

"That's what I wanted to ask *you*, Aunt Alice," said Ludo. "Ought I to say anything? I mean—well not exactly—I mean—"

"Poor Ludo," said his aunt. "I'll tell you what to do. My advice is Don't tell Anyone just yet."

"Not father and mother? You couldn't tell them for me, Aunt Alice?" said Ludo hopefully.

"I could, but I won't," said his aunt. "Tell them just what you've told me, if you feel like it. They'll understand. Did they ever tell you how they got engaged?"

Ludo said they hadn't and he had never thought about it.

"It was a house-party at Pomfret Towers years ago when I was a girl," said Mrs. Roddy Wicklow. "Old Lord Pomfret asked your father to come and stay. He wanted to see what he was like, because he hated your father's father—who certainly seems to have been as selfish and disagreeable as they make them—who was the next heir to the title. Anyway your father, who liked books and pictures and that sort of thing and didn't a bit want to be an earl, came to Pomfret Towers and everyone liked him and he worked awfully hard to learn about being an earl and the place and the property and the people and the cottages and the drains—everything but the hunting, because he had been brought up abroad a good deal and didn't know any more about it than I do. But Roddy's sister Sally did and then he married her and old Lord Pomfret got very fond of them both. That's all."

"I'm awfully glad you told me that," said Ludo. "I mean I think father was awfully—I don't know what. I mean Good."

"He was. He is," said his Aunt Alice. "But whether he could have done all he does alone, I don't know. You have plenty of responsibility coming, Ludo. A good wife will be a great help. But no need to hurry. You might just mention it to your people. And if you felt like speaking to Sir Noel Merton, or Lady Merton, I think they would understand. Only do remember, Ludo darling, that Lavinia is very young still and has got to do a lot of growing up. And you aren't so very old yourself."

There was a silence. Then Ludo said he was most awfully grateful and he would tell his mother and his father exactly what he felt like and perhaps he could say something to Sir Noel and Lady Merton. But he wouldn't say anything to Lavinia.

"You see, she really is rather young," he said. "I might even get into a real war before she is grown up, and be killed. Anyway, don't you bother. You've been awfully decent, Aunt Alice."

His aunt Alice said that was what aunts were for and he could always come to her if he had a difficulty and she would do what she could and so would Uncle Roddy.

"And what would Uncle Roddy do?" said that gentleman, appearing like the Good Fairy, or the Demon King, exactly on his cue.

Anything he was asked to do, as usual, said his wife.

"It's nothing really, Uncle Roddy," said Ludo. "I mean I was just talking to Aunt Alice. I don't mean a secret exactly but something rather private" at which point words failed him. His Aunt Alice gave her husband a wifely look which appeared—

like Lord Burleigh's nod—to mean pretty well anything or everything and had the effect of shutting him up completely.

"Well, I'd better be getting along now," said Ludo. "Thanks awfully, Aunt Alice," and he went back to Pomfret Towers. Here he found his parents—as they so often were—in the Estate Office.

"Well, darling?" said his mother.

"Oh, Uncle Roddy sent you his love," said Ludo, "and said to tell Father not to worry about old Mrs. Skimpton because she's got her Old Age Pension and her son that's in Hogglestock Iron Works is allowing her ten shillings a week."

"That means," said Lord Pomfret, "that she'll get blind drunk on Saturdays and have D.T. on Sundays," which he said with the pleasantly resigned air of the chemist who is called as a juryman in the trial of Bardell v. Pickwick.

"I say, Mother," said Ludo, "I think we ought to ask the Mertons over here. They gave me an awfully good time at Northbridge."

His mother said it was a good idea and what about next Friday when she had a free day for once.

"I was thinking," said Ludo, "that Lavinia might come too. She's never seen the Obelisk."

That also seemed extremely reasonable to his parents and Lady Pomfret began to think of dates and plans. It was all a little complicated—as when is life in the country not complicated—by distances and who had a car or could drive one, or else had a car and a chauffeur; or there were bicycles.

The Pomfrets were doing most of the planning when Ludo, seizing a pause in their talk, said Why shouldn't he take the little car over and fetch Lavinia and he could drive her home afterwards. The little car was more or less his property, though Giles used it within the grounds while waiting to be the right age for a driving license and drove extremely well, having once forced it up to the Obelisk and managed to get it down again without anyone being the wiser. Unfortunately he had boasted about it to

Nurse who had come to see if he had washed behind his ears properly, and Nurse at once threatened to Tell of Him—a phrase which can be very alarming; though as a matter of fact she very rarely did tell, because Giles, with all his faults and his rowdy-towdy ways, was Her Baby.

So a good deal of telephoning was done and finally it was decided that Sir Noel and Lady Merton should come over with Lavinia. It now only remained for the weather to be thoroughly disagreeable, which it whole-heartedly was. As the Pomfrets and Mertons were busy people who could not always call their time their own, the date had to be altered twice, at which the weather took offence and said in its best Blustering Boreas voice that it was damned if it was going to go on being nasty to please *anyone*; which threat it then proceeded to carry out. To all Barsetshire's almost incredulous joy Summer was there. Summer which so many of us have almost forgotten. The kind of weather when you can make plans a week ahead—and even more—in comparative safety. The Mertons were to come over early in the afternoon and go over some of the huge house and see how well Mr. Adams and Mr. Pilward were dealing with it, then perhaps see the view from the Obelisk and go home after tea. A long visit, but in that part of the world time did not always gallop withal. And here we may say that we find ourselves quite unable—having never thought about it before—to parse (if that is the word we mean) withal. We suppose that Shakespeare knew what he meant—though sometimes, and in some of his most beautiful passages, we have our doubts.

The only slight blot upon the Mertons' excursion was that no one—not even Nurse—knew if Jessica was going to have one of her Nasty Colds. Lydia thought perhaps she ought to stay at home in case she infected anyone and perhaps Lavinia ought to stay at home too, but her husband squashed her firmly and said it would seem like Being Rude to do that and she wasn't going to have a cold, nasty or otherwise, nor was Lavinia, and not to fuss. So his Lydia laughed and stopped fussing. Lavinia, after a severe inspection from Nurse, was then passed as being uncontaminated and not likely to be a germ-carrier, so everything was exactly as it had been planned, and almost as punctually as the Count of Monte Cristo the Mertons drove up to the side door of Pomfret Towers, in the wing that used to be the nurseries and servants' quarters.

Lady Pomfret was in her sitting-room said the man who opened the door, wearing a kind of butler's apron, more usual in the pantry than in the gentry quarters, and would they come up.

"I think I remember you," said Lady Merton. "Weren't you with old Sir Harry Waring at Beliers Priory?"

"That's right, mum," said the man. "Beedle's the name. My uncle's Beedle, him as was station-master at Winter Overcotes, and him and Sir Harry always had a bit of a chat and I got took on as you might say, knives and odd jobs. Then when Sir Harry died his nephew had the place and he wasn't married then so there wasn't much to do, and my auntie works here so she said Why not come to the Towers because his lordship needs a man as knows what a gentleman's house is like. So, as you might say, I come. That's what I did. What name is it, mum?"

Lydia said Sir Noel and Lady Merton and Miss Merton.

"Now I *thought* that was the name her ladyship told me," said Beedle. "But thinking's one thing and knowing's another. Will you come up, my lady. Her ladyship is in her sitting-room," and he went upstairs followed by the Mertons, opened the sitting-room door and announced the guests, giving a general impression that he had arranged the party, handpicked those to be invited and was, as usual, the one indispensable person in the establishment.

"Thanks, Beedle. Find his lordship and tell him," said Lady Pomfret. "How *very* nice to see you both—and Lavinia. I won't say you have grown since I last saw you, but you have."

"One always does," said Lavinia. "Except when one is getting very old and then people might say How you have shrunk," which made her hostess laugh. Then Lord Pomfret came in, full of apologies for not having been there to welcome his guests, but one of the cottage children in Golden Valley wasn't well and the parents were at least three hundred years behind the times and were preparing some dreadful kind of witches' concoction for it and he had persuaded them to let him ring up the Barchester General Hospital from the Keeper's cottage and ask for an ambulance, as the child was obviously pretty bad; though whether it was croup or scarlet fever or acute appendicitis he couldn't say.

"So I waited till the ambulance came," he said, "and of course the other children were frantically jealous and wanted to go too."

"I *do* hope the child will be all right," said Lady Pomfret. "I've got to go into Barchester tomorrow and I'll enquire and let the mother know; poor thing."

During this interlude the Mertons had thought their own thoughts. They were kind thoughts, but different. Noel felt, not for the first time, that though he was now a landowner in West Barsetshire with a wife who had the county and the land in her bones, he was still in North-Country parlance an off-come. If such a crisis had arisen at Northbridge he would have offered help at once and in the shape of money and a car if necessary, but never would it have occurred to him to go into Barchester to get first hand news of the patient; news which would—whether good or bad—be of great comfort to the parents who didn't know how one got into a hospital or if anyone would take any notice of them, or if they would be allowed to see their child. And he knew that to some of the older people the word Hospital still meant that you could only see the patient on two days of the week at hours when you could not be free and at a cost you could not afford unless someone would give you a lift. In fact rather like the Reverend Josiah Crawley's excursion to Barchester by favour of Farmer Mangle. Which led him to consider how history—even the short and simple annals of the poor—was always repeating itself. And then he suddenly thought that his Lydia would have done exactly as Lady Pomfret did.

So far did his thoughts lead him, although they were all within the compass of a minute, that he almost started when Lady Pomfret asked how her old friend Mr. Wickham was. But he pulled himself out of his reflections and said Wickham was very well and full of plans for a bit of land the Mertons were thinking of buying which would nicely round off their property along the Barchester road and they could make a drive which would cut off some of the distance.

"I sometimes wonder," said Lord Pomfret, "what will happen when Wickham retires—if he ever does. He is the most re-markable man I know. Is there anything he can't turn his hand to?"

Lydia said there was certainly one thing.

Lady Pomfret asked what it was.

"Getting married," said Lydia. "He is the most determined bachelor. Nearly everyone has tried to marry him—I mean to get him to marry someone—but he just won't. He did want to I think—but it was quite some time ago. He more or less told me about it once."

Of course the Pomfrets begged to hear more, feeling—most reasonably—that Lydia's full stop was full of meaning.

"Oh, it was ages ago now," said Lydia. "It was when old Admiral and Mrs. Phelps were alive. The Admiral wasn't too well nor was his wife and Margot was simply killing herself with parents and the garden and the hens. Then Mr. Macfadyen—you know the big market-gardener—asked Margot to marry him and she said she *must* look after her parents first, but she would like to consider herself engaged. So he went away and she took the pail of that awful stuff hens eat and Mr. Wickham came into the garden and she told him how miserable she was and he said if she would marry him he would gladly look after her parents. But she said she had just got engaged to Mr. Macfadyen down by the hen-run."

"Poor Mr. Wickham," said Lady Pomfret. "I never knew about that."

"Well, you wouldn't," said Lydia. "Mr. Wickham told me about it once and he said he was never so relieved in his life: not even on Armistice Day," at which unexpected ending the Pomfrets couldn't help laughing. And while Lady Pomfret laughed she looked at her husband and thought how grateful she was to anyone who could bring him out of his usual quiet courtesy into what was practically a good vulgar guffaw—or what Nurse called A Fit of the Giggles.

At this moment there was a noise on the stairs and in came Lord Mellings with Lady Emily and the Honourable Giles, who all said How do you do to the guests with an old-fashioned courtesy that made Lavinia feel rather low and common.

"I'm glad you like it," said Ludo to Lavinia. "We have rehearsed it quite a lot and we thought we would try it out on you. I don't mean for a lark," he added, in case Lavinia thought he was rather mocking her parents. "Just to see if it comes off. Do you think it does?"

"I was very much impressed by it," said Lavinia in a rather off-hand way, and then she grinned at Ludo, so he knew she was only laughing at him.

"I say, would you like to come to the nursery?" said Ludo. "We might do some more music. It's a horrid afternoon—dem'd moist unpleasant summer-time," and he paused for a moment to see if Lavinia took the allusion; which we regret to say she did not. "Nurse won't bother us just now," said Ludo, "because someone is having a fit in the kitchen, which is her cup of tea. Come on. Emily and Giles are going to Hamaker's Spinney to see if those earths are properly stopped."

His parents looked at one another, remembering the day when they had been together in the Estate Office: young Mr. Foster who was to inherit the Pomfret earldom and Sally Wicklow the estate agent's sister. Old Lord Pomfret had been delighted, his first words of congratulation being that he supposed they would have those earths in Hamaker's Spinney stopped before a week was out; which was his way of showing that he felt his heir—and his heir's wife—would look after the place properly.

Lavinia obediently followed Ludo and asked about the fit.

"Do you read Dickens?" said Ludo in a rather threatening way.

"Of course I do," said Lavinia. "In fact," she added loftily, "I read him again and again. I expect you mean Guster, in Bleak House."

"Oh, *good* girl!" said Ludo. "You are a person one can talk to."

"Well, so are you," said Lavinia. "Only don't let's talk both at once. It's your turn now. Have you ever seen a person having a fit?"

"Certainly not," said Ludo. "And no more will you."

"Then that's all right," said Lavinia. "I don't think I'm a bit like Florence Nightingale."

"I should think not," said Ludo indignantly. "*Dreadful* woman lying on a sofa and practically killing that poor Sidney Herbert. What a lot of celebrated worthy people these are that one doesn't want to know," to which Lavinia rather impertinently answered that she was glad Ludo wasn't celebrated or worthy. For a moment he wondered if this was kindly meant and then he saw what she meant and began to laugh. And, still laughing, they arrived at Nurse's room.

"Here we observe protocol," said Ludo, knocking gently at the door. The noise of a chair being pushed back was heard and Nurse opened the door.

"I've brought Lavinia Merton to see you, Nursie," said Ludo. "She wants to do some more music."

"Nice to see you again, miss," said Nurse. "Come in and I'll show you a snapshot of me and a pony."

She took from a shelf a large green Album, with some red poppies embossed on the cover and laid it on the table.

"That's my snaps of Ludo and Emily and Giles, miss, ever since I was here," said Nurse. "I came when Ludo was three weeks old. Sister Chiffinch was looking after her ladyship. We got on very well. Her and I had the same kind of ideas. She had some ever so nice nightgowns and a lovely niglige she put on when she brought Ludo in to Her Ladyship for his feeds at night. 'Really nurse' I used to say to her, for she wasn't Sister then, 'really nurse you look quite a dream in your niglige.' There's some that calls it a painwar, but for myself I've always said dressing-gown and always shall. I just said niglige in case."

Lavinia said she always called it dressing-gown and was thankful that she had not forgotten Politeness and said négligé. After a few more words protocol was satisfied and Ludo took Lavinia back to the old schoolroom and the piano.

"Now let's have a concert," he said. "I did enjoy the concert we had last time you came. I found some more good songs in the sitting-room, all tucked away under some old photograph albums," and he showed her the two fat volumes of *Popular Music of the Olden Time*; a quantity of songs, from Summer is icumen (or however one likes to spell it) in, to mid-nineteenth century. At least we think so, but our Chappell is, alas, beyond the long wash of Australasian seas.

With these they had a very happy hour or more and then Ludo said he *knew* that no one ever pulled the piano away from the wall to sweep behind it and he would bet sixpence that the *Songs of England* which had been missing for some time would be there. So between them they pulled the heavy, rather old-fashioned upright piano away from the wall and there sure enough, half smothered in the grey dust and fluff that rooms spontaneously produce, were the Songs of England, their cheerful red binding covered with dust.

"I shall really have to Speak about this," said Ludo and rang the bell, whose wires could be heard jangling into the distance.

"People aren't very good at answering bells now," he said. "Aunt Alice—that's Uncle Roddy's wife—told me that when she was a girl and was invited to the Towers and very shy, she couldn't find her outdoor shoes and didn't like to ring her bell again, but luckily father was about and asked her what the

matter was and when she told him he took a big lump of coal
from the coal-bin that was kept on the landing for the bedroom
fires and dropped it down the well of the stairs into the basement and shouted for Miss Barton's shoes and then someone
came rushing up with them."

As if illustrating his words there was a knock at the door and
in came Finch, once boot and knife man at the Towers, now odd
man for any job that was wanted.

"Look here, Finch, there's no end of dirt and rubbish behind
the piano," said Ludo. "I want you to move the piano right away
from the wall tomorrow and have a good clean-out. Put anything you find there on the table. And see that someone sweeps
behind it regularly. That's all."

"Thank you, my lord," said Finch and went away.

"That was *very* brave," said Lavinia. "Why is one so frightened of other people's servants—if they have any?"

"I've often wondered that myself," said Ludo. "I expect we
and they are just as frightened of each other, only we aren't so
good at claiming our rights as they are at keeping us in our
places. But we have to pretend. Oh! this house, Lavinia!"

"Do you mean too big?" she said.

"Yes. Too big and too small. A few huge rooms and not
enough small ones except just in this bit of it. And even then
father had to cut some of the rooms in half. Luckily they weren't
very high at this end—the servants' wing. In the other part you
really couldn't halve a room when it was about twenty feet high.
Of course Adams and Pilward have managed it—you know that
most of the Towers belongs to them now—and they have
pretence ceilings in a lot of the offices. Some sort of canvas at
least three feet lower down than the real ceilings, and flies and
wasps will get into them and die and have to be sucked out with
the longest Hoover tube on the market. Mr. Adams arranged it
and it works beautifully. It makes me almost wish I had a
chameleon."

Lavinia asked why.

"Because it's such fun to watch them flick their tongues in and out," said Ludo. "I had a tame chameleon at my prep school and the other boys in my dormitory used to collect flies for it. But some idiot didn't fasten the cage properly and the chameleon got out and fell into a jug of water and got drowned. So we had a funeral."

Lavinia said when a mouse got into the water-butt in the garden it had to be fished out because it was blocking the tap one filled watering cans from and all the servants were afraid to touch it and they had to wait for Mr. Wickham.

"Of course Father would have done it at once," she said proudly, "but he was in London."

"Do you like London, Lavinia?" said Ludo.

"Well, sometimes," she said. "I like Christmas pantomimes and shopping with mother and going to one of Aubrey Clover's plays. I say, Ludo, what fun it was when you sang in that play of his in Coronation Summer. At least I didn't see the play actually, but I remember Mr. Clover making you sing it at our house when I was listening over the banisters. The one about 'Though I am not twenty, sweet, Here is my heart.' Can you still sing it?"

"I suppose I could," said Ludo, rather doubtfully. "My voice—if voice it is—has gone down a bit, but we could try."

"Oh, goody, goody," said Lavinia. "Have you got the music?"

Ludo opened a drawer full of sheet music and extracted the song.

"I don't know if I could play the accompaniment at sight," said Lavinia.

"Well, I can't either, but I can play it by heart," said Ludo. "Here, let me have the piano stool."

Lavinia slipped off it and Ludo took her place and began to play.

"But you've got the tune wrong," said Lavina.

"Well, I haven't, so there," said Ludo. "This is just a kind of prelude with a bit of a theme in it, invented by ME," and a very pretty prelude it was—one of which Aubrey Clover himself need not have been ashamed. "Now we begin," and he sang the heartbreaking little song, first heard at the Northbridge Coronation Entertainment, words and music by Aubrey Clover; a song which had since gone all round the world and made even the most hardened ruffians cry. The words were merely an accompaniment to the tune, but were still sung all over England and the United States and elsewhere.

> Though I am not twenty, sweet,
>   Here is my heart.
> You are sweet and twenty, sweet,
>   Where is your heart?
> I'd die for you this very hour,
>   (Quiet, my heart).
> But let me live, just for this hour,
>   Deep in your heart.

"The End," he said softly, and got up. "What on earth is the matter Lavinia?"

"Nothing," said Lavinia in a choked voice and turning her head away.

"Then what on earth are you crying for?" said Ludo, quite kindly.

"It's—it's—it's Aubrey Clover," said Lavinia indistinctly and began to cry again, though in a quiet ladylike way. "Handkerchief please, Ludo," and she stretched out a hand.

Luckily Ludo had provided himself with a clean handkerchief for company and shoved it into Lavinia's hand. She banged at her eyes and blew her nose and rubbed her face and thanked him.

"You see, it is *so* beautiful and sad," she said in a be-blubbered voice. "And it is so *lovely* to cry when one isn't unhappy," in proof of which she went on crying.

Not everyone might have followed this train of thought but Ludo was sensitive enough to sympathize. If he had been less sensitive he might have been happier—perhaps also less happy; never knowing Tears, idle tears and the depth of some divine despair and the once happy autumn fields.

"Yes, it's more comforting," said Ludo, "but perhaps a bit self-indulgent. I mean I don't mind a bit if you cry—I mean I would mind if there was something really to cry about like losing your best gloves or someone running over your dog—but if you are crying with enjoyment, that's all right."

"It's *heavenly!*" said a rather blubbered Lavinia.

"I wish Aubrey Clover were here," said Ludo. "I bet he has never had such a success as I have. He would make a divine song about it. I say, let's make one ourselves. You make one and I'll make one and then we'll see which is best. I've got a sheet of music paper somewhere."

"But I can't make the piano part," said Lavinia, "only a poem part. Oh, and then there's the tune to sing it to. I can't, Ludo."

"Well then, let's have a tune we know and make our own words to it," sais Ludo. "One of those jolly tunes out of *Lilac time.* I saw it when I was abroad only of course it's got a different name there; they call it the *Dreimäderlhaus.*"

Lavinia asked what that meant.

"Oh, the House of the Three Girls," said Ludo. "All bits of Schubert's music. I'll play you a bit—by heart, so if I suddenly stop you'll know I've forgotten what comes next. Do you want it in German or English?"

"Oh, English, please," said Lavinia.

"Well, it's better in German, because it's *German*," said Ludo, "but the English is quite good. You ought to know German because of all the songs," and he plunged into some of the charming lyrics, singing what he remembered, humming when he forgot the words and enjoying himself vastly.

To Lavinia it was almost a new world. Her generation had not been brought up on German music as earlier generations had been. An occasional song recital on the wireless; some symphonies, because symphonies having no words are in a language common to all who wish to hear. Her throat began to choke a little, her eyes felt uncommonly damp and she couldn't help sniffing, while Ludo sang happily on. Presently he looked round, still playing.

"What *is* the matter, Lavinia?" he said.

Lavinia, ashamed of her emotion, did not answer.

"I say, what *is* it?" said Ludo, and the music ceased.

"I don't know," said Lavinia in a voice between a choke and a bellow. "It's so *beautiful!*"

"My *poor* Lamb," said Ludo. "I do appologize. The first time I heard *Lilac Time*—years ago—I cried the whole way through with sheer joy."

"Then you don't think I'm a silly idot," sadi Lavinia, with slightly improved utterance.

"Of *course* not," said Ludo emphatically. "I'll tell you what—as Mrs. Adams always says—have you got a good gramophone at home?"

Lavinia said yes.

"Well then, I'll buy some records of these songs," said Ludo. "When's your birthday?"

"Not till November," said Lavinia.

"Well, I expect I'll have saved a bit of money by then," said Ludo. "Will you promise something?"

Lavinia, who was not a distinguished lawyer's daughter for nothing, said she couldn't promise till she knew what it was.

"Well, if I give you some really good records, can I come over to your house and play them?" said Ludo. "Our gramophone isn't up to much and I don't want to bother father. He has quite enough as it is."

"Of course you can," said Lavinia. "How lovely. And when I grow up and marry a duke I'll give you the most expensive gramophone I can find. He will be a rich duke of course."

"I'm glad he is rich," said Ludo. "I only know two dukes and they are both poor. I mean poor compared with what they ought to be. The Omniums were really frightfully poor, but Silverbridge married that nice Dale girl who came into a lot of money, so it wouldn't be so bad. Except that there will be those wretched Death Duties. I think the Devil invented them. My people can only live in a wing of their own place. The same with the Omniums and the Luftons. And I know the Marlings haven't found things too easy. It's killing the goose that lays the golden eggs. I'm going to ram it into my people that Giles *must* go into business. He is much cleverer than I am and gets on well with everyone and can talk *all* the hind legs off a donkey. Besides, a title always helps if it isn't a very high one. I just might get a job as Lord Mellings, but the Honourable Giles—quite apart from being a much better fellow than I am—will get a job anywhere on his own brains and his charm *and* an Honourable."

"I don't much know about things," said Lavinia, "but I heard father say that Honourables stood a better chance of getting jobs, but they nearly always got their names wrong when people wrote to them. Lots of people think it's rude to put the Hon. Jack Somebody or the Hon. Ethel Somebody. The peerage is full of snags," which view of an ancient institution amused Lord Mellings vastly and he laughed so much that Lavinia laughed too.

"And then there are Right Hons," said Lavinia. "I'm going to learn all about etiquette because people don't like it if you get their names wrong. It doesn't bother us of course, because father is only a Sir. If he turned into a Law Lord I don't know what would happen. I mean I don't know what mother would be. I say Ludo, let's have some etiquette talks when you come over to Northbridge. We've got Burke *and* Debrett. Father gets new copies quite often."

Ludo said her father must be a millionaire to do that and his father's Burke was four years old and his people always made a vow on the first of January to keep their Burke up to date by crossing off the people who died in *The Times*; but they always forgot.

"Well, I'll marry a Duke," said Lavinia, "and then I needn't worry because no one can be higher than a Duchess. I found that bit in a book. I *do* like all those rules. It's all history, I suppose. I feel so sorry for Americans not having titles. I mean it's fun for the family."

"But they have dynasties and we don't," said Ludo. "I mean you come across people called Hovis Kornog Breadbaker the Third," which parody of the hereditary family names, that do keep a kind of spoken record of the past, made Lavinia have the giggles.

This improving conversation was interrupted by Nurse, who said to come to Lady Pomfret's sitting-room and say good-bye, because Lavinia's father and mother had to go home now.

They were good children and obeyed that summons without a murmur. Lavinia shook hands with Nurse and said she had had a lovely time and Ludo was coming over to see them at Northbridge before he went away.

Nurse graciously said that would be very nice and she would see his nails were clean and he was properly washed behind the ears.

"That's quite enough, Nurse," said Ludo. "My ears and my nails are my own property now. But Giles's are awful. If you want a real clean-up, he's your man," and before Nurse could find an answer he had escorted Lavinia to his mother's sitting-room.

Nurse, alone in the room, considered what had just happened. Well, it was like that. You washed them and cut their toe nails and taught them to clean their finger nails and brush their hair and not come stamping into the house with muddy boots: and then suddenly you were a back number. Well, Ludo was a good boy and so was Giles. He and Emily were a bit of a handful, but Nurse could still deal with them. So she tidied the room, putting all the music into the wrong places, and went back to her own room where she was forever darning socks and stockings and letting things down, or out as the case might be. She was a good deal alone, partly by choice, partly because there was not a proper house-keeper's room now; but she knew that her children would always come to Nurse about their manifold sins and wickedness before they would go to their parents. Soon Ludo would not come; but Emily would, and Giles. And in a few years perhaps Ludo would marry a nice young lady with some money and she would be the Grand-Nanny and stand no nonsense from the new babies' nannies. Something to look forward to.

The good-byes and the thanks and the invitation for a return visit were over. Sir Noel and Lady Merton—whom we had forgotten while enjoying the young company—were waiting for Lavinia and they drove away to Northbridge, where Sir Noel went back to his endless papers and Lady Merton to various jobs of local secretary work, while Lavinia went up to the nursery, still so-called, and wrote her diary which, like most of our diaries in our youth, began with a full description of each day's doings and grew small by degrees and beautifully less; so much so that Lavinia had on several occasions made the concise entry 'Forget what did.' But today she had not forgotten and made her entry. 'Lunch Pomfret Towers. Music and conversation with Ludo. Nurse rather bullies Ludo,' which was unfair to Nurse. But to Nurse, Lord Mellings was the little first-born, almost her own child, as her ladyship—though she was only Mrs. Giles Foster then—knew nothing about babies. She, Nurse, had decided when he should go onto bottles and when he should have bits of bread and butter and a little bit of egg pushed into his mouth, and fed with good mutton broth in a spoon, and taught to say a very limited grace which was, we think, intelligible in heaven, though not always in his nursery.

Well, children would grow up and even Giles was out of her hands. She knew her own value and had at present no intention of leaving. She did a good deal for Lady Pomfret now and her room was a gathering-place for the children and their friends and Nurse is always useful. But she would not outstay her usefulness, of that we are certain.

In the library Lord and Lady Pomfret were talking about things in general and how well everyone had behaved.

"I do like that girl of Merton's," said Lord Pomfret. "She has nice manners and a head on her shoulders. And her people are good stock. I hear about Merton in London and I shouldn't be surprised if a peerage came his way. He would do very well as a Law Lord if he wants not to work quite so hard, but that is probably some way ahead still. And he is liked in the county too. A good landowner and a good landlord. His wife is a remarkable woman for whom I have considerable respect even if she does rather lord it over one. But only on subjects she knows, and she knows a lot about West Barsetshire. Much more than I do."

"I like them too," said Lady Pomfret. "Sir Noel always gives me a delightful feeling that he may ask me to elope with him. Of course I wouldn't dream of it with you here, Gillie, bless you. I *do* like you, you know. I always did. Do you remember the day we got engaged in the estate room here and how furious that dreadful Mrs. Rivers was? We must ask the Mertons here again soon."

At Northbridge much the same talk was going on. Lavinia was full of her outing, of how kind the Pomfrets were, of what a lovely time she had been having with Ludo in the old nursery and how they had had some music and talked about lots of things. Her parents said they must ask Ludo over again some time. Then Lavinia went across the garden to see old Nanny Twicker and tell her all about Pomfret Towers and see if the new kittens had opened their eyes yet.

So Lady Merton and Sir Noel were able to sit comfortably and quietly in the drawing-room. The long window was open to the garden, but there was a good fire burning, as there should be on three hundred and sixty-four days in every English year.

"How Lord Pomfret does work," said Lydia. "So do you, darling, but you take it more easily."

"Because I have you to back me up," said Noel.

"Well, he has Sally to back him up," said his wife. "I hope that nice young Mellings will do well. He looks as if his spirit was always a little ahead of his strength. He and Lavinia had a musical afternoon, I gather."

"Calf-love?" said her husband.

"I don't think so," said Lydia calmly. "More like 'Maud.'"

"Maud who?" said Noel. "I can't think of any Mauds we know."

"Tennyson's Maud, of course, you jelly-headed judge," said his devoted wife. "I got it from you. You quoted it once."

Her husband said he might understand Coke on Littleton, but what she said was Hebrew to him.

"'Well, if it prove a girl, my boy/Will have plenty: so let it be'" Lydia quoted, "only one really ought to put it the other way round in this case."

"What *do* you mean, my love?" said the distinguished Q.C.

"I don't mean anything *exactly*," said his wife. "But if she and Ludo do fall in love later, we can give Lavinia a good dowry— thanks largely to you. And I don't think a dowry would be unwelcome at Pomfret Towers. We would tie some of it up for their children of course. And then, when Ludo comes into the place perhaps they will be able to use a little more of the house. Or even to take over one of the good houses on the estate."

"'*Perrine et le pot au lait*'" said her husband. "There's something in what you say. But it is still very far ahead. I'm glad you remembered the Tennyson, though. Lots of people must think of it when their children get named."

"Of course," said Lydia, "this is *quite* different because there aren't any villains. But don't let's bother about it now. Ludo has his army career to think of and Lavinia is very young. Quite probably they will both forget. But if there is a war sometime we shall have to let them get married!"

"As you and I did," said Noel. "I have never got married so fast in my life—nor so happily."

"And then there was Dunkirk and the dreadful day when the

telegram came," said Lydia. "You were in France, no one knew where, and I was looking after mother here and father had been knocked down in Barchester and died in hospital and there was no news. And then Philip Winter who was back from Dunkirk came to see us and a telegram came for me and Philip wanted to open it in case it was bad news, but I said I ought to open my own telegrams and whatever the telegram said, I would love you just the same."

"So you have," said her husband, deeply moved, and he took her hand palm uppermost and put a kiss into it.

"That's what I think of you now and forever," he said.

"There is one good thing," said Lydia. "If you are made a law lord you'll have to have envelopes addressed to you differently, but I'll still be Lady Merton so I shan't have to bother about new visiting cards. And what is so restful is that Harry won't have to be a lord after you."

And to this there really was no answer at all.

COLOPHON

This book is being reissued as part of Moyer
Bell's Angela Thirkell Series. If you are
interested in Angela Thirkell, contact the
Angela Thirkell Society, P.O. Box 7798,
San Diego, CA 92167 or e-mail
JOINATS@aol.com.

The text of this book was set in Caslon, a
typeface designed by William Caslon I
(1692-1766). This face designed in 1725 has
gone through many
incarnations. It was the mainstay of British
printers for over one hundred years and
remains very popular today. The version used
here is Adobe Caslon. The display faces are
Adobe Caslon Outline, Calligraphic 421,
and Adobe Caslon.

Composed by Alabama Book Composition,
Deatsville, Alabama.

Love At All Ages was printed by Edwards
Brothers, Inc. on acid free paper.

Moyer Bell
54 Phillips Street
Wickford, RI 02852